SEEDER
SHADOW WARS

Painted Wings Publishing

Note from the Author

This journey all began with a snippet of a dream. Starting as a scene, now found in the prologue, this concept 'blossomed' into a trilogy, with even more books in the series on the way.

I want to offer a huge thanks to those who are helping make my dream as an indie author a reality. Thank you to those that have encouraged my creative side over the years and have supported me when I doubted. A giant thank you to the beta readers, critique partners, and editors that helped a clueless writer craft a story worth sharing. You saw the shameful lack of detail, the cringe-worthy and rampant use of comma splices, and all the mess in-between. You know who you are and I'm extremely grateful for your help!

Lastly, to you, the reader—thanks for giving the Seeders a chance to share their story. I hope you enjoy and follow their journey to completion!

Consider signing up for my newsletter to get news on upcoming publications, promotions, and bonus content! JHouserWrites.com

SEEDER WARS
TRILOGY

SEEDER
SHADOW WARS

J. HOUSER

Painted Wings Publishing

Prologue

BORDERED BY IMPASSABLE MOUNTAINS, a pocket realm tucked away on Earth was safely shrouded from human knowledge and interference. The hidden paradise was a land of beauty and lush plant growth, filled with an energy that coursed through the very veins of the people who lived there. The inhabitants could sense the cyclical energy shifts associated with the human world, though their own realm lacked any true change in season.

On the western front, people lived simple lives in quaint communities. As simple and quaint as they could be, in the midst of a never-ending war.

***

Murial stared down at her clutch of seedlings, her children. She wore a faint smile, her joy tainted by the vicious aching in her heart. Today would be the hardest day of her life.

Thod walked up behind Murial, wrapping his arms around her. He moved her auburn hair to the side and placed a sweet kiss on her cheek. "Are you going to be okay?"

She swallowed hard, reminding herself that she'd signed up for this. She wanted kids. Murial turned to face her husband, giving him the best smile she could muster. "I'll be great."

She looked around at the new home they'd just moved into. Like others lining their lane, it was much bigger than the tiny cottage they'd moved out of. It was beautifully simplistic with raw, natural wood. Books and potted flowers covered the shelves in the corner. The extra space and larger garden out back would be just enough for this next phase of their lives.

Thod gazed into her eyes. "I couldn't have picked a better woman to raise my boys."

Murial drew a deep breath, her smile warming. "I'll make you proud. And I know you'll take good care of the girls."

He nodded, then patted his pants pocket. "I've got the letter for your dad. Anything else?"

She pursed her lips, thinking of the human dad that had helped raise her. Letters were all they had now. Having reached maturity, which allowed her to have a clutch, she wasn't capable of leaving the Green Lands anymore. She scanned Thod, then glanced back at their seedlings.

"I think we're all set." Murial pulled him in closer. "There's just one last thing."

They shared a smile and she leaned in, giving him a kiss. The kind of kiss only a Seeder woman could give. The kind that imbued him with a portion of her energy, both expressing her love, and bolstering him for the long and difficult journey ahead.

***

It being the first day of spring, Murial and Thod gathered their seedling hopefuls and stepped outside. Walking a few feet from the door, they placed the glistening, round seeds on the dirt in the middle of the lane. A handful of neighbors were proudly doing the same with their own clutches for this year's sprout reveal. Murial breathed deeply, tightly gripping Thod's hand and forcing herself to soak in the wonder and beauty of the moment.

As the sun rose, it peeked over the wooden homes and bathed the eager parents waiting in anticipation. Shortly after the rays reached the seeds, they began to wiggle. Next door, a shout of glee rang out; someone's first seedling had sprouted. Murial and Thod glanced over for just a moment to check it out, then returned to watching their own clutch.

Puff.

"There's one!" Thod rejoiced, squeezing her hand.

Puff. Puff. Puff.

"Come on, girls, show yourselves," Murial cheered in a whispered tone.

Twelve in total sprouted. The other twelve remained unchanged.

The breeze blew, and the palm-sized sprouted balls of fluff began to sway. Murial and Thod knew their time was short. They embraced, and then Thod stood next to the seedlings, like the other men in the street were starting to do. A gust rushed past—this was the one!

The wind swept up the balls of fluff—resembling dandelion seeds floating in the wind, but much more fluffy, like a bichon frise puppy. As soon as they lifted up, Thod sprang into the air, leaping forward into a somersault, transforming into his botanical form. His hair took on a purple hue, spiked like a thistle. A spiny leaf extended from each forearm between his wrist and elbow. His legs were now wrapped in taproots to his ankles.

Thod gathered their twelve sprouted seedlings in his arms and gave a reassuring, loving look to his wife down on the ground. The breeze blew them higher and higher, further from their village.

Murial watched on as he disappeared from sight past the lush hills in the distance. The knots in her stomach took over as she imagined the journey ahead of him and the time and space soon to be between them.

Years. In a completely different realm.

And there was no other choice.

Wiping tears from her face, Murial drew a deep breath and followed the example of the other women, taking her remaining seedlings back inside. She carefully laid them in a basin filled with earth. Sitting down, she gazed lovingly at her little boys, her heart swirling with a mix of emotions. Delighted to see her family grow. Gutted by her mate's departure. And indignant at the other occupants of the Green Lands, the Ivies…

The Ivies considered themselves superior and insisted they'd been cheated out of prime land centuries ago, which was far from the truth. They'd deserted their claim to those lands and devastated the new region they now resided in. Not that truth held much weight in old feuds littered with propaganda.

Murial's eyes glowed green, as she no longer tried to hide the change. This was the only way their species could survive anymore—by tearing their families apart.

Over a century ago, the Ivies had poisoned Seeder territories. Ivy poison, produced by their females, was strong enough to kill a human, but not a Seeder. The Seeder males were barely even affected by the attack. Future generations of females exhibited less power. Most devastating was the effect it had on the young Seeder daughters. Not having their powers yet, they were essentially human, defenseless. Every last one of them perished within a week of the Great Poisoning. After girls in new clutches also failed to survive, the true and lasting effects were realized and drastic measures had to be taken to protect their young.

A knock at the door broke Murial from her trance. She wiped away more tears and centered her energy, her eyes changing back to a deep shade of brown. She opened the door with a smile. "Hey! Come in!"

Sandra, her new neighbor, a short woman with light brown hair who was also in her late twenties, entered, giving Murial a long hug. "Just wanted to see how you're doing."

Murial grinned, pulling back and gesturing for her to sit down. "I expect we're feeling about the same."

Sandra gave her an understanding frown. "They'll be okay."

Murial nodded. "I know." She picked at her fingernails. "It's just different when it's your own."

Sandra crossed her legs, resting her hands on her knees. "How old were you at the time of your bloom?"

"Sixteen."

"Right. I forgot. I was seventeen."

So many years of waiting. Of separation.

Murial glanced down at her remaining seedlings. The boys always took longer to sprout, but by nightfall, they would start to form roots. She vowed to enjoy every moment she had with them before their childhood would be replaced with training. Whether protecting their homeland borders against Ivy attacks, or crossing over into the human world, the boys all shared one thing: they would be soldiers. Looking up with a forced smile, Murial added, "I'll feel so much better once the first one is old enough to go over for protection duty."

Sandra sighed. "We've got this." She gave Murial a calm smile, standing back up. "I just wanted to pop in real quick, but I better get back to my own boys. You know where to find me."

Murial walked Sandra to the door, giving her another hug. "I'm glad we're neighbors."

***

Murial spent the rest of the day preparing a vegetable stew and coconut-almond biscuits. She constantly looked over at her boys. Not that anything had changed about them yet—they were still little glistening seedlings, full of potential. It would be a couple weeks before their roots developed enough to shed their seedling forms, rapidly growing to appear like any regular human.

Sitting down after sunset, Murial grabbed her journal from the shelf. *Day One*. She processed her thoughts and feelings before she began to write.

Human teenagers have it so easy. Then again, when she'd been a teenager, before her bloom, she'd thought she was an average human, too.

It wasn't enough for the Ivies to attempt genocide and lay siege to Seeder borders. Fully-rooted female Seeders were twice as powerful as the males—their energy was used to charge the border walls that kept their lands relatively safe from further Ivy attacks. With these girls being the only thing that kept the Ivies from their goal of Seeder annihilation, their safety was paramount. When the Ivy Kingdom had discovered that Seeders were hiding their daughters away in the human world, it became their new hunting ground.

The Ivies knew their enemies well. They focused on finding the girls during the vulnerable bloom-to-root period when their powers came in. Ivy assassins lay in wait, always watching for a hint of a bloom.

Murial put her pen to paper.

I miss him already. And our girls. I look forward to seeing each one of their faces some day.

She grinned, thinking of her boys.

This is going to be quite the adventure. Things will work out. I know they will. I have to believe it.

Murial tried to imagine the faces of each of her girls—what interests and personalities they would have. Each day without them, without Thod, would be a battle. But she was confident in her husband; he had done so much work ahead of time, planning and preparing, to keep them safe for the coming years.

The fate of the Seeder girls relied on one thing—who was in the know. In the mix of it all were humans, oblivious to the hunt happening around them—the two enemies constantly trying to sniff and snuff each other out.

In their own realm, Seeders had no need to be on the offensive. In the human world, they watched over their daughters and sisters, always observing for signs of the Ivies. Once the girls were old enough, they would show signs of budding, and then bloom, gaining their full powers. Their family just needed to keep them safe and guide them home, without being discovered. And so the game went.

As if high school wasn't already enough of a jungle.

Chapter 1

A CHIMING SOUND ANNOUNCED AN incoming text.

<You ready for this?> Zach asked, sending a silly selfie, a tradition of theirs on the first day of school every year. The selfie showed off his sharp new haircut and friendly hazel eyes.

Mel shook her head and couldn't help but smile. She'd been bugging him all summer about looking like a caveman by letting his hair grow wild. He said it was his 'new aesthetic,' though she figured he just didn't bother, seeing as he went camping every weekend.

She took a deep breath and texted back.

<You know it! The real question is, are they going to be ready for our level of awesomeness? ;) lol>

She took her own selfie, having just finished curling her strawberry blonde hair. Her fuchsia polo shirt made her blue eyes stand out, and she finished her look with a touch of mascara before heading out for the first day of their junior year.

She half-expected another chime to sound, a third picture. But it didn't. The trio was now only a duo. She leaned back against the bathroom counter and frowned while pulling up a picture of the three of them. Mel was in the middle, a shorter Tabatha to her left, a taller Zach to the right. There were so many great memories there. Tabatha hadn't made them a trio until the fifth grade, but after that, they had been inseparable. Now, all Mel was left with was a twinge of abandonment. She knew she wouldn't get another text. Pulling up Tabatha's last known number, she read the final message.

<I know it's crazy, but my mom got a new job and we moved. So sorry I wasn't able to give you more of a heads-up! Love ya!>

No follow-up text ever arrived. She completely ghosted Mel and Zach. Mel wasn't sure if Tabatha had blocked them, or took a permanent social media break, but they lost touch completely. That actually happened a lot in their high school. Not the ghosting necessarily, but the constant shuffling of kids. People were always moving in and out; it was a revolving door of new characters.

Luckily, Mel still had Zach; they'd been friends since the fourth grade when another boy was chasing her relentlessly on the playground and Zach punched him. Not that she needed saving—she could handle herself. But he was a true friend she could always count on. He even offered to stay home and hang out with her, instead of camping with his family, after Tabatha deserted them both. But Mel hadn't taken him up on the offer; it wouldn't have been fair to him. It wasn't right for him to miss out on one of his favorite activities, just to bum around with Mel, playing prisoner to her parents' strict rules.

Mel finished getting ready and headed downstairs. Her mom was already up for the day, in the kitchen, baking.

Mel smiled, the aroma of chocolate cake wafting past her. "If only that had been ready an hour ago, we could call it a muffin and have it for breakfast."

Her mom chuckled as she cleaned the kitchen island. "Sorry. It's only a muffin until it's frosted. Such poor timing on my part, and it'll be frosted before you get home." She rounded the island and gave Mel a hug. "Thought it would be nice to come home to something sweet on the first day of school."

Mel gave her an extra squeeze. "You speak my language. Love you."

Heading down the hall, she snagged her already-packed backpack and closed the front door behind her. Mel surveyed the quiet suburban neighborhood and breathed in the fresh air. Passing that one oddball turquoise house with the half-dead lawn and a thriving patch of dandelions, she turned and made her way to Franklin High, just a few blocks away. Its most notable feature being how old it was, past due for renovation or replacement, it was otherwise a rather unremarkable American high school.

The closer she walked to the aging brick building, the tighter the knots in her stomach twisted. The roar of excited teenage chatter became deafening. Approaching the front door, her first-day jitters melted away once she got a warm hug from Zach.

"You look great. Even better without the cross-eyes in your selfie." He pulled back, smiling.

Mel reached up, rubbing his silky-smooth face. "Oooh. I almost forgot what you looked like under your fur."

Zach rolled his eyes. "Beards are manly."

She cleared her throat and grinned. "Yeah. Sure. I'm just glad you finally took my advice. The ladies won't be able to resist you now." She poked him in the arm.

He tugged on his backpack straps, his cheeks a smidge pink. "Right. So, um … classes?"

Mel pulled out her phone, double-checking the time. "I suppose if I don't have anything else on my to-do list, I could manage some classes today."

He shook his head with a smile.

They approached the busy front door, prepared to tackle the day head-on, happy to have a couple of classes and their lunch break together. As expected, there were some fresh faces Mel didn't recognize, including several new guys—which she was not mad about in the slightest.

Mr. Colburn, the principal, and his vice principal, Mr. Simons, were there as usual, monitoring the halls as students poured in. Mel wasn't sure if it was a tactic to instill fear or show dominance, but it was a tradition on the first day to be stared down like they were interrogating you with their piercing eyes. At least for most students. Mel got a welcoming wink from Mr. Colburn, which would have been absolutely creepy for the average student, but the principal was a close family friend; an unofficial uncle.

She smiled in response to his wink, but her smile faded a tad when she remembered how she'd hurt his feelings once, when she'd told him over a Sunday dinner that she would rather they pretend to not know each other when she entered high school. She didn't want to get teased for knowing the principal. He'd tried to hide his disappointment, but she'd seen an inkling of it in his expression. Despite being hurt by her request, he did a good job of treating her like any other student and keeping his distance at school.

***

Between second and third periods, Mel dropped by her locker to swap out textbooks. Before heading off to American History, she took a moment to touch-up her lipstick in a small mirror. She was lost in thought, planning out her approach for the onslaught of homework, when the slam of a locker behind her made her jump.

"Sorry about that. It kind of jams," a male voice said.

Mel turned around, pleasantly surprised with the owner of the voice. His sandy blond hair was brushed with a wave to the side, very smooth. He wore an open button-up shirt over a plain t-shirt and flashed a confident smile. His dark brown eyes focused on hers.

"I'm Devin. I'm new here. It's Melody, right?"

"Yeah, that's me." She capped her lipstick and tucked it into her pocket. "Well, I go by Mel." She squinted and tilted her head to the side. "How did you know my name?"

"We just had Trigonometry together." He raised an eyebrow. "The teacher called your full name going over the roll."

"Oh, gotcha."

His brow furrowed as he looked past her.

Someone jabbed her in both sides and Mel jumped, letting out a sharp squeal.

"Never fails!" Zach laughed. "Have I told you yet today, how much I love that you're so ticklish?"

"That's not funny!" she protested through clenched teeth.

"That's a matter of perspective." Zach shrugged playfully. "Don't be late for class. I'm not holding a seat for you if a hot new girl wants to sit next to…" He gestured with an open palm along his body like a car salesman showing off his finest exhibit. "All of this."

"Then it's your loss. I'm not arm wrestling over you." She stuck out her tongue and chuckled as he walked away.

Zach and Mel always knew how to push each other's buttons. She loved their playful banter and how drama-free their friendship was. Honestly, he would make an ideal boyfriend for some girl if he would actually try. He just spent most of his time hanging out with Mel (and Tabatha, back in the day…) or enjoying the great outdoors. Dating didn't seem to be at the top of his list.

"You guys together?" Devin asked with quizzical eyebrows.

First day of school and a cute guy wants to know my relationship status? Not bad…

"No. Zach and I are just friends."

"Gotcha." He smiled. "I look forward to seeing you around." He took off in the opposite direction of her next class.

"Hey!" she called after him. "Do you need any help finding your classes?"

He turned around and grinned. "Wouldn't want to make you late. But thanks."

She slowly closed her locker door and smiled. Cute? *Check.* Confident? *Check.*

Maybe, just maybe, she could get her parents to relax on their dating rules this year.

***

Zach and Mel sat across from each other at a long table in the cafeteria.

"So, who's the looker?" Zach raised an eyebrow as Mel eyed Devin from across the room while he paid for his lunch.

"What?" She blinked and met Zach's eyes. "Just a nice guy." Her cheeks warmed as she took a sip of water. "He's my new locker neighbor."

She and Zach never talked about each other's crushes or dating, at least not seriously. Granted, she hadn't ever had a real boyfriend, and Zach's previous two relationships were both short-lived. In the past, if Mel had wanted to talk about a guy, she had Tabatha. It felt weird to put Zach in that position now.

Devin caught her watching him. He waved and made his way across the crowded room.

"This seat taken?" He gave her a friendly grin, gesturing with his chin at the spot next to Mel.

Mel smiled. "It is now."

Devin sat down and peeled a mandarin orange.

Mel glanced at Zach, who was eyeing Devin. "Oh, yeah. Devin, meet Zach. Zach, meet Devin."

The two guys gave each other a 'Hi' and a polite nod.

Zach stabbed at his salad, looking down. "You and me—still on for later, right, Mel?"

She dipped her pizza in a small cup of ranch. "Yeah, of course."

***

13

Mel arrived home after a long day filled with rules and introductions. She grabbed the mail before walking inside. Her mom was watering the houseplants in the living room bay window.

Mel sorted through the mail. "Hmm. Two for Pam Walters. Two for George Walters." She pulled out a postcard with coupons for an oil change. "And one for Resident. Are you and Dad going to fight over it? Who gets to be the lucky resident?"

Her mom chuckled. "I'd like to say we could make a civil decision over that one. But today, maybe we'll generously donate it to the recycle bin."

Mel handed the rest of the envelopes to her mom before heading down the hall to the kitchen. While tossing the postcard in the recycle bin, she spotted the frosted cake her mom had been baking that morning. She sliced a large piece, bringing it and two forks back to the living room on a white saucer. Mel plopped down next to her mom on the settee and dug in while her mom finished looking over the bills.

Her mom shifted her focus after putting the papers on a side table, and picked up the spare fork with a smile. "Tell me about today."

Leaning against her mom, Mel pursed her lips in thought about the entire day. "Oh, ya know… No eating in class. Don't be tardy. Plenty of homework to be had." She took a bite of the cake.

"Any new friends?"

Mel fought a frown, thinking how much better the day would have been if Tabatha had been there. "Um… I don't know." She smiled, remembering her new locker neighbor. "I met a new guy."

Her mom nodded, finishing a bite of cake. "Guy friends are nice. Sounds like a new candidate for movie nights."

Taking a deep breath, Mel set the cake down on the closest side table. "Guy friends are nice. So are *boy*friends. There's this novel concept; it's called dating. It's like movie night. But you *leave* the house. Just two people who share a mutual interest in each other."

Her mom pressed her lips together, narrowing her eyes. "I think I've heard of this concept. I also heard it's not a requirement for high school or a satisfactory youth." She raised an eyebrow. "Believe it or not, your dad and I were young once."

Mel frowned dramatically. "I know. But things change. We have electricity now, and the dinosaurs are gone and everything."

Her mom busted out laughing while Mel picked up the saucer with a good portion of cake still on it. "Can I bribe you?"

"Are you trying to bribe me with my own cake?"

Mel bit her lip. "I can bake you a different one?"

Sighing, her mom stood. "We love you. You know that, sweetheart."

Mel looked down. "Yeah. I love you, too. Anyway, Zach's coming over soon to study."

"Okay. Remember, your dad started his new office hours this week, so dinner will be an hour later."

Mel nodded as her mom left the room. Annoyed, she considered getting changed and going for a jog. Instead, she looked at the remaining cake in her hands and shoved half of it in her mouth.

***

An hour later, Mel and Zach sat in the family room, poring over trees that had been killed in the name of teenage torture and learning. Family pictures covered the walls. There were no windows to allow in natural light, but the lamps lit the area well enough.

"Chemistry is going to kill me." Mel's head slumped to the side, her eyes wide open, lips pouting.

Zach scoffed. "Says the girl that always has one of the highest grades in class."

"Yeah, you know me." She widened her eyes. "Why have lots of friends and go hang out, when you can stay home and do homework all the time?"

He cringed. "Eww, gross. Make more friends? And do things that don't consist of hanging out at your house? *So* overrated."

"You dare mock me in my plight?" She chucked a throw pillow at him.

He ducked and the pillow knocked his water bottle to the floor; luckily the lid had been closed. "Never!" He smiled. "I have sat on *many* a couch in my lifetime, and yours is by *far* my favorite." He winked, then said more sincerely, "I've never minded coming over here and having it be just us."

She sighed; he was always so sweet. "So, *now* I see why you come over all the time. And here I thought people our age valued hygiene, good looks, and a sense of humor. I'll make sure my parents never get rid of this couch, so I don't lose you!"

They both chuckled. "You know..." His face got more serious. "I—"

Mel's mom peeked her head into the room. "Dinner in ten."

"Okay, Mom."

"Mrs. Walters?" Zach called, causing her head to pop back in. "We're having a back-to-school party at my house." He quickly added, "My parents will be there the entire time."

Mrs. Walters wasn't that intimidating physically, reaching a mere five-foot-three with a few extra pounds, but she knew how to wield a mother's stern look and tone. "Sorry, Zach. You know our rules."

Mel had known her mom would say no. She was well aware of the rules, and there were a lot of them. Mel was an only child and her parents were overprotective. Well, *kind of* an only child. They'd fostered a few kids over the years, but half of them were before Mel was born or old enough to even remember. They ended up having Mel when they were older. She always wondered if she was an 'oops' baby, though her parents denied it.

"Please, Mom. Just this once?" Mel pleaded. "Seriously, don't you think I'm old enough?" Their rules were so convoluted. With

Tabatha out of the equation, they had become even more strict. Somehow, Mel and Zach being left alone without her parents as chaperones was some great sin.

"No," her mom repeated while walking back to the kitchen.

Mel hollered down the hallway, "You know, this is why some kids sneak out of the house at night."

Her parents wouldn't budge. And she wouldn't sneak out. That's just the way things worked.

Zach always had to go over to Mel's house to hang out. She was never allowed to go to a boy's house. She couldn't date. Couldn't babysit. It was like they thought she was a fragile porcelain doll. The only time they ever gave in on anything big was this last summer when Mr. Colburn spoke up at a Sunday dinner, saying he thought she could handle a part-time job for the summer, since she wanted it so badly. Her parents respected Mr. Colburn, being a principal and all—his advice carried some weight. Even then, she still wasn't allowed to apply to the jobs her peers could; she went to work as a receptionist at her dad's chiropractic office.

A lot of kids probably would have rebelled a long time ago, being that cooped up. But Mel generally had a good relationship with her parents. She wasn't exactly a homebody, but she was fairly content with her hobbies and small group of friends. Though, lately, the more she saw her peers enjoying activities she couldn't, the more a sliver of resentment began to fester.

Chapter 2

AFTER HER THIRD DAY IN the new school year, Mel was helping set the dinner table. The mouthwatering smell of steak on the grill wafted through the open kitchen window. Her parents, in their old-fashioned style, always insisted on family dinner at the table—and no electronics.

"Set an extra place setting," her mom instructed. "Tom's coming for dinner tonight."

Tom was Mr. Colburn's first name. When not at school, he was fine with everyone addressing him less formally.

Mel stopped and looked at her mom in confusion. "What's so special about today?"

"Does there need to be something special happening, to have friends come over?" Her mom casually brushed away the question.

Not much later, Tom arrived with a smile and side-hug for Mel.

Despite being a weekday night with no special occasion to warrant Tom's presence, the dinner and conversation started out normal.

"So, how are you doing with all the new student interviews?" Mel's dad asked, adjusting his glasses.

Tom let out a long sigh. "We've got a lot of them this year."

After swallowing a mouthful of garlic mashed potatoes, Mel asked, "Why do you guys always drill the newbies so much? I swear they come out of your offices terrified and wanting to transfer."

Tom chuckled. Even sitting down, his broad shoulders helped with the intimidation factor as a high school principal, but unless you were in trouble, his kind face softened his presence. "Gotta keep out the riffraff." He cut into his steak. "We just feel it's important to know who we have in our school, that's all."

Mel's dad cleared his throat. "Speaking of new arrivals, there will be another young man at your school next week."

Mel scrunched her face, perplexed. That was an odd announcement, coming from him of all people.

Her dad continued, "And here." He looked down, focusing on his plate.

Mel glanced over to her mom for more of an explanation.

"It's been a while, but we felt like it was right." The cryptic explanation didn't help. "We're going to be fostering a nice boy." Her mom paused. "He's a senior."

Mel's jaw dropped. "Wait, *what?*" she shrieked. "Are you crazy? Did you just use 'boy' and 'senior' in the same sentence? Living *here?*" Her eyes darted between her parents while Tom awkwardly stabbed at the mashed potatoes on his plate. "I don't get a say in this?"

Her dad scolded her with his eyes. His voice was firm but calm. "Don't be selfish. He needs a place to stay. You could stand to think of others more, kids in need of a good home."

Mel dropped her utensils and pushed her plate forward, excusing herself from the table and heading up to her room. It just didn't make any sense. If they wanted to foster again, couldn't they pick a younger kid, or wait a couple of years until she was in college?

***

"Isn't that ... kind of weird?" Zach said over lunch the next day, cringing. "I'm surprised it's even allowed."

"I don't know. But it's stupid," Mel said while murdering her fries with a fork. She resented her dad calling her selfish. It wasn't like she was some stereotypical only child demanding attention. But bringing a teenage boy into the house just felt ... weird. He could be a creepy perv, for all she knew.

"Maybe it's not such a bad thing?" suggested Devin, who was now eating lunch with them daily.

Mel fought to hide a smirk. Since meeting him, she hadn't heard him say anything negative about another person, or thing, really.

"But, what if he ... hits on you?" Zach asked.

Her eyes shot up from her lunch tray. "Then I'll kick him in the balls."

Both guys flinched at the idea.

***

Saturday rolled around and Mel was forced to wait in the living room with her mom, ready to meet the foster boy when her dad brought him home. They sat on the settee as light flooded the room.

It was painfully quiet. Mel had been warned the night before to be friendly and welcoming. The life of a foster kid was hard enough, and moving in right after the school year started was just another hurdle.

The familiar hum of her dad's car pulling into the driveway announced their arrival, and Mel let out a long sigh, mustering the best smile she could, which wasn't all that convincing.

When the door opened, she was surprised to see a tall, buff, clean-cut guy following her dad. He carried himself with confidence and didn't appear menacing or troubled—no tats, piercings, wild hair, or death metal t-shirts.

"Melody, this is Ben." Her dad took the lead. "Ben, this is our daughter, Melody."

Ben smiled and extended his hand for a handshake. "Nice to meet you, Melody."

She took a deep breath, the scent of a lavender candle in the room calming her. She accepted his outstretched hand. "Call me Mel."

After introducing his wife, Mel's dad offered to show Ben to his new room upstairs.

Shortly after the meet and greet, Mel sat down at the kitchen table with her watercolors. Painting was therapeutic for her. She'd watched every online tutorial she could find, though she favored nature scenes.

"Wow. That's really good." Ben's voice came from behind her.

She glanced over her shoulder, startled to see him towering above her, watching.

She shifted uncomfortably in her seat. "Thanks… All settled in up there?"

"Yeah. I didn't bring much with me."

Mel frowned, humbled by his situation. He sat down at the other end of the table.

She went back to painting, distracted by his awkward gaze, not sure what kind of conversation to start.

He tapped his fingers on the table. "Sorry if this is weird."

She didn't look up right away, considering her response while adding a few more brush-strokes to her tropical scene. At least his room was at the end of the hallway upstairs. Between their rooms was her parents' room and her bathroom. She felt better having a barrier between them, even *if* he was a nice guy.

Swishing the brush in a cup of water, she met his gaze. "I just want to have a normal school year, that's all."

A hint of a grin grew on his face. "You know, they say normal is overrated. But I'll try not to get in your way."

After a little more conversation about school and what there was to do around town, Mel decided Ben wasn't such a bad guy. He wasn't coming across as creepy, or pervy, or weird. He was actually really nice and well-adjusted for a teenager in the foster care system. But maybe that wasn't a fair generalization for foster kids; it wasn't like all of them were troublemakers. Mel figured it would be impolite to ask about his family, and his silence on the topic confirmed she'd made the right choice by not bringing it up. As long as he stayed out of her way, Mel expected they wouldn't have any problems.

Regardless of her truce with the foster boy, Mel couldn't help but wonder why her parents felt like *now* was a good time to rock the boat.

***

It had been five days since Ben moved in. And the last four of those nights involved him leaving the house in the early evening and not coming back for hours. Mel stood at her bedroom window, peering through the blinds at the street below, as if he would materialize and his reappearance would somehow mean something.

Great. Now I'm the creepy stalker. She huffed. But she knew the truth about why he was always gone—her parents were giving him more freedom than they had ever given Mel—and it wasn't fair. She left her room and headed down the hall to her parents' bedroom. Their door was slightly ajar.

"She'll get over the disappointment," her dad said.

Mel stopped and listened. They had to be talking about her.

"I know," her mom replied.

"It's not like they *have* to murder them, to obtain their goal."

Or maybe not about me.

He continued. "Kidnapping or manipulating them into staying for some other reason is just as good."

22

Mel realized it was senseless to eavesdrop on her parents talking about what was probably some true-crime documentary series they'd been watching. She knocked on their door.

Her dad opened it, his brown hair a tousled mess. "Um, hi. What, uh … Come on in, sweetheart."

Mel stepped forward, crossing her arms and leaning against the doorframe. "Is Ben taking driver's ed?"

"No," her mom replied, closing a dresser drawer. "He already has his license."

Mel nodded. "Is he getting tutoring? Or maybe he has a job?"

Her mom cocked her head to the side. "No. What's this about?"

"I'm just curious why he's never around. I guess we didn't talk about *all* the rules. Does he get to go to parties? Or date? Or maybe there's a more reasonable explanation, like he's in a gang."

Her mom scoffed. "A gang? Really? He's a good kid."

Mel stood up straight, placing her hands on her hips. "How do you even know what kind of person he is, if he's hardly here? You didn't answer me. Does he get to go to parties and date? And have, you know, a social life?"

Her dad raised his eyebrows, unamused. "You have *absolutely no* social life? You can invite over anyone you want. Zach's over often enough."

Mel clenched her jaw. "Does Ben get to do things I don't? Yes or no?"

Her mom sighed. "It's not the same."

Mel was astounded at the double standard. "Because I'm a girl? I took those self-defense classes you wanted me to a couple years ago. I have mace."

Her mom clarified, "It's not the same because he's in the foster care system, and almost eighteen, sweetheart."

"Right. He's a foster kid. I get that it might be hard for him. But I'm your own flesh and blood! And you say he's a good kid."

She looked between them, pointing to herself. "I follow the rules. I get good grades. When other kids get in trouble, they have privileges taken from them. I don't even get them to begin with!"

Her dad let out a heavy sigh. "Maybe we should…"

"George." Mel's mom flashed a look of disagreement. "I think," she turned her focus to Mel, "you need to calm down, and we'll discuss this another time."

George pursed his lips and nodded.

Mel scowled and left the room, heading back to her own. Just minutes later, the front door squeaked open. She went downstairs, meeting Ben. "What have you been up to?"

Ben raised his eyebrows. "Didn't realize I answered to you."

She read his face, trying to remain civil. "Are my parents allowing you to date?"

His eyes focused on hers, his lip curling slightly in disgust. "You're not really my type."

Her eyes narrowed with revulsion. "Seriously? Don't flatter yourself." She bounded up the stairs back to her room.

Chapter 3

THE SATURDAY AFTER BEN AND Mel's misunderstanding, her parents hosted a backyard barbeque with neighbors and friends. Like her mom had suggested, Mel had calmed down. Dating wasn't the end-all, be-all. Not that she didn't still want to.

Adding to the annoyance, however, Ben had taken a liking to Stacy, a cheerleader Mel had been friends with in elementary school. As childhood friendships often go, they grew apart and ended up in different crowds. Mel didn't much care for Stacy's constant need for attention. Honestly, she was probably the main influence that had led to Mel mostly hanging out with guys. Too much gossip, drama, and Stacy's chase after popularity, forced a wedge between the two.

Mel's parents were over at the barbeque, flipping burgers and chatting with Tom and a couple of their neighbors—including Mr. Rasmussen, a biology teacher at her school.

"You're wasting your time with that one," Mel warned Ben about Stacy. "She's really stuck up. It's cliché, but she goes for the jocks, the troublemakers, the models. Pretty much every type but yours." She crunched into a carrot stick, her eyebrows lifted in mockery. It wasn't completely true. Ben wasn't ugly, and he definitely worked out. He was just too uptight to be the popular type.

She'd never admit as much, but it drove Mel beyond crazy that he was interested in Stacy. She remembered well how Stacy had teased her, had turned on her, during a particular sleepover a few years back. And it had all happened to Mel at her own house.

Ben gave her a death glare. "I'm not trying to date her. I just want to get to know her better."

"Right, you and every other guy." Mel sang with flippant sarcasm, "Fri-ends. That's how it wo-orks."

Zach plopped down on the empty patio chair between Mel and Ben. "What's this I hear? Girls and guys can't be friends?" He wiggled his eyebrows at Mel as he placed the top of the sesame bun on his burger.

She grinned in response. "You and I don't count. We're outliers."

Zach feigned being hurt, putting a hand to his chest, and turned to Ben. "I'd either say she shot me down with vocabulary from math class, or she's questioning my integrity. You know, out-LIAR?"

Ben stared at Zach, unamused. Despite Zach's attempts to win Ben over, they didn't exactly mesh. And not for a lack of Zach trying—he'd made a valiant attempt earlier in the week when doing homework, and a couple of times already at the barbeque.

Mel's initial assessment of Ben had *definitely* changed. Chasing a girl in the wrong crowd? Stiff and surly? He might not have been a creeper trying to hit on Mel, but he definitely *wasn't* normal.

Mr. Rasmussen wandered over to where the teens were sitting. Mel couldn't help but wonder if the balding man ever dressed casually—he was wearing the same attire at a backyard barbeque as she'd seen him in at school.

"Mel." He nodded. "And this is Ben?"

"Yes, sir." Ben offered a hand to shake.

Mr. Rasmussen shook Ben's hand then turned again to Mel. "I hope you're making your brother feel welcome."

Mel scowled. "He's not my *brother*."

"Sorry," he corrected himself, "your foster brother."

She rolled her eyes. Ben might not have been a *complete* nightmare, but she was far from being sold on the idea of having him around.

Ben shook his head and went inside, clearly annoyed.

"Right..." Mr. Rasmussen pursed his lips awkwardly and walked back to the grill.

"Don't worry about it," Zach said. "You only have to put up with Ben for a year, right?"

A year felt like it was going to be forever. She had to share a bathroom with the guy, and he didn't even clean up his toothpaste in the sink.

***

The next Monday before class, Devin came up to his locker just as Mel was opening hers.

"Hey, favorite locker neighbor," he said.

She chuckled. His locker was on the end—she was his *only* locker neighbor. "How was your weekend?"

Mel found herself dropping by her locker more often than she'd normally have done, just to catch him swinging by to have a quick chat. She hadn't invited him to her house yet, but she'd been considering it, wanting to make him a more official member of the posse. He would add a fun dynamic, and ... she was beginning to see him less and less as just a friend.

He didn't even try to hide his interest—the boy knew how to flirt. After their initial meeting, she'd caught him glancing her way in class. The first time, he'd blushed and looked away. After that, he'd gotten bolder, acknowledging her with a smile. That smile, complete with dimples... She was starting to look forward to seeing it each school day. She didn't specifically save him a seat, but when possible, she picked a desk with an empty one next to her, and he always took that opening.

As they were finishing up their chat to head to class, Devin rummaged through his locker, looking for one last thing. An arm wrapped around Mel's shoulders.

"Hey, Walters, how was your summer? We haven't talked in forever!" Blake was the last person she expected to approach her. They'd been lab partners in science last year and she admired his good looks, as did every girl, but they were hardly friends.

"Hey, yeah. Good. You?" She stumbled to make casual conversation, even blushing at having his arm around her.

"It was great! Got to hang out with the guys a lot. Worked as a camp counselor. But now I'm all geared up for the best year yet." He still had his arm around her shoulder.

Devin closed his locker and stood there in silence as the first bell rang.

Blake aimed his attention at Devin. "Can't build up the tardies this early in the year, right?" He turned back to Mel. "You coming to watch the game on Friday?" He was, of course, a jock—but not a mindless meathead. He was pretty funny in class. And it was sweet, imagining him leading younger kids as a camp counselor over the summer.

"We'll see." Mel smiled as he walked away, knowing it wasn't likely she'd make it to the game.

"What do you see in a guy like that?" Devin scowled.

Mel lifted her eyebrows. "Is that jealousy?"

"What do I have to be jealous of? Jocks have stereotypes for a reason. His muscles try to make up for the air between his ears," Devin mocked.

She furrowed her brow. "That's harsh. How would you like to be treated based on a stereotype?"

"What kind of stereotype is that?" he asked. "Dashing looks, yet still humble?" he kidded with a seductive grin.

His attempt at levity fell flat.

"Would you want people making assumptions about you coming to live here?" She thought of a prior conversation they'd had at one of their locker rendezvous. "Who transfers in the middle of high school to go live with their uncle? That sort of thing could start a rumor. About someone that caused trouble, that maybe got expelled and sent away."

She cocked her head to the side, lips pursed, waiting for a response. He'd deflected most questions about his family and previous high school, which she'd respected, and in some ways almost even liked; it gave him an air of mystery.

It surprised her to see his demeanor change; she'd hit a nerve.

Devin was now looking down at his fidgeting hands, as if choosing his words carefully. "It's not like that." He shook his head. "I'll see you later."

***

Mel's stomach was in knots after watching Devin walk away, guilt weighing her down for bringing up what was clearly a sensitive subject. She thoroughly apologized at lunch and he forgave her, but was still acting a bit put out.

They were at their lockers, sorting out their backpacks at the end of the day, when she decided it was a good time to take the plunge and invite him over.

"Are you doing anything this weekend?"

He perked up, eyebrows raised.

"Zach and I are going to have a movie night. Ben will probably be there, too, I'm not sure if you've met him. And my parents… It's not exactly the hippest joint, but if you're not doing anything?"

"I'll pencil you in," he said with a grin.

"Oh, just a pencil?" she challenged playfully.

He narrowed his eyes while zipping his backpack. "I'll be there."

***

A couple days flew by and Mel was walking back to her locker at the end of the school day when the warmth of an arm linking through her own startled her. She whipped her head to the left to see who had joined her.

"Hey." Blake flashed her a warm smile, towering over her like a bulky skyscraper.

"Hi," she replied awkwardly, utterly confused at having him seek her out twice in one week. She stopped walking, freed her arm, and leaned back against the brick wall. "What's up?"

"I, uh…" He shrugged. "I know this seems like it's coming from left field, but I was wondering if you're busy this weekend?"

Her cheeks warmed. "I don't think I'll be able to make it to your game, sorry."

He grinned. "I didn't mean to come watch the game. I meant like … a date…" He lifted his eyebrows.

"Oh." She swallowed. "I … can't…"

"You can't?" he asked, squinting like a detective. "Like, you're busy? Or seeing someone? Or you just don't know how to tell me I'm not your type?"

She chuckled. "None of the above. My parents just have weird rules." She scrunched her face. "But thanks for asking."

He sighed. "That sucks. I'd go ballistic if I had overprotective parents like that."

"Yeah." She frowned. *This does suck!*

"Well, think about it. Maybe you just need to give them a piece of your mind." He lifted an eyebrow. "We're only young once." He winked. "I've got to get going. Just think about it."

She watched him as he walked away in the direction of her locker. Shaking her head, Mel couldn't help but smile. He wanted to go out? Guys with letterman jackets prowled the popular crowds. They went out with girls like Stacy, not Mel.

Reaching her locker, she dialed the combination.

"Has anyone told you that you have a beautiful smile?" Devin asked as he approached his own locker.

She bit her lip. Feeling his gaze, she looked over at him. "You have a handsome smile, as well."

Her compliment made his grin widen. "We're still on for this movie night?"

"Yes," she confirmed with a firm nod.

"Hey, um…" He closed his locker and leaned against it to face her. "I never really apologized for the whole Blake argument we had the other day. I hope you're not still mad about that?"

She hadn't been dwelling on it, but it was sweet that it still bothered him. "It surprised me. It just kinda came out of nowhere. I know we haven't known each other that long, but at first you came across as a really nice guy."

He frowned. "I *am* a nice guy."

He really *was* usually positive about everything. The weather, the cafeteria food, everything. Not quite to the point that he was *annoyingly* positive, but within a safe distance. She tilted her head to the side. "Then let's start over."

He gave her a half-smile. "Deal." His eyes moved from her face to her open locker door. "So, what does one have to do to get a custom painting done?"

She lifted her eyebrows with intrigue. "Ask nicely?"

"Sweet. I'll think about what I want. I really like your style."

She blushed. Not that she hid her art—she had it on display, hanging in her locker. But she'd never had anyone ask her to paint for them before. Other than her parents, of course, but family didn't count.

He adjusted his backpack strap. "And how would you feel about going over notes for next week's test before movie night?"

"Oh." She thought about it. "Zach is coming over before the movie. Maybe afterward?"

He read her face. "Yeah, sure. You spend a lot of time with him, don't you?"

She shrugged. "We're friends, we have classes together, so … I'd say that's a fair assessment. Why?"

He shook his head. "Just asking. Nothing big." He paused and then pointed at her. "It's not jealousy. I remember last time we had this conversation. It didn't end well."

She chuckled. "Right. Well, I'll see you around tomorrow? I'll text you my address."

He smiled. "Sounds good. I look forward to it."

***

Saturday night rolled around and Zach came an hour early to study. He was his usual friendly self, though he acted a bit off once it got closer to movie time. Mel left the family room to grab them each a drink.

"You get to choose: root beer or orange soda," she offered, returning to the room.

He looked up from his laptop, turning it ever so slightly so she couldn't see the screen. He'd done it subtly, but she noticed.

"I'll take the root beer," he answered with a smile, holding out his hand.

She passed him the can while playfully craning her neck to see what he was hiding. "What's this?"

Clearing his throat, he closed his laptop, setting it to the side. "Nothing."

That piqued her interest even more. "Really?" She grinned.

He raised his eyebrows in protest. "Nothing you need to worry about."

Her eyes grew wide after considering why he'd be keeping a secret from her. "Oh … um … I really shouldn't ask a guy what he's hiding on his laptop, should I?" She couldn't look him in the eyes.

They didn't talk about dating, and they *definitely* never talked about *that!*

He laughed. "Gosh, Mel. Your face is hilarious. No, I'm not into that."

She bit her lip. *This is just getting awkward.* "Right." She cleared her throat and opened her drink, allowing the hiss of the soda can to fill the uncomfortable silence before taking a swig. She desperately wanted to move on to another topic. "So … um…" She couldn't think of anything else now…

Luckily, Ben saved her, entering the family room and dropping into the recliner. Sorting through a stack of DVDs on the coffee table, he stopped for a second to look up. "Sorry, am I interrupting anything?"

Mel choked back a laugh and looked over at Zach, who wore a slight scowl. Apparently, Zach was done trying to make friends with tactless Ben.

Chapter 4

DEVIN WAS THE LAST PERSON THEY were waiting on. He texted he'd be there for movie night any moment. Mel was grateful when Zach started up a more normal discussion after their briefly mortifying conversation.

Shortly after Ben joined them, Mel's mom called for her from the other room. Before leaving to find out what she was being summoned for, Mel pointed to Zach, and then Ben. "I get veto power."

Mel's mom was waiting for her in the kitchen. "Honey, can you give me a hand with cleaning up real quick? I hate for it to be a mess with your friends here."

"Right now?" Mel whined. "Can't I clean it up when they're gone? We're already getting started."

"It won't take more than five minutes. You're waiting for that other boy anyway, right?"

"Yeah. Fine." Mel started to unload the dishwasher.

"So, tell me about this boy." Her mom scrubbed at a large serving platter in the sink full of suds.

Mel placed a couple of coffee mugs in the cupboard. "There's not a lot to say. He's a nice guy. Just like Zach."

"That's all you have to say about him? Does this happen to be the one you mentioned the first day of school?"

"Why are we having this conversation?" Mel stopped and leaned back against the counter, crossing her arms. She thought about what Blake had said, and she agreed. She'd had enough of their overprotective crap. "It doesn't matter if I like him, or any other guy, if I can't date. And it's not like you guys told me about Ben before bringing *him* into our lives. I'm old enough to be trusted. With dating. With information about what goes on in this house." She huffed and went back to putting away dishes. *This is stupid. This year was supposed to be different. In a good way.*

This time it was her mom's turn to stop what she was doing. "What's gotten into you lately? Ben isn't doing you any harm. I didn't think we raised you to be so spoiled."

"It's not just about him!" Mel snapped back. Her face warmed with anger to match her raised voice. "It's everything. When are you going to realize I'm growing up? Every single girl my age can date. But I can't. I can't even go hang out at Zach's house, and you and Dad have known him for *years*! Do I have to wait until I'm eighteen? Does that much really change in two years? I'm somehow going to be mature enough to handle myself and make my own choices?" The chime of the doorbell stopped her tirade.

Her mom pointed at her with the sudsy scrub brush. "Stay! We're going to finish this discussion." She called down the hall, asking Ben to get the door. "Again, it's not about you. It's not that we don't trust you. It's about us asking you to trust our judgment, that we know what's best for you. And yes, two years can make a big difference. Two *seconds* can make a big difference, if the choice is the wrong one."

Mel stood with her mouth agape, flabbergasted. "Really, Mom?! What exactly are you so worried about? It's not like I'm planning on running around and getting knocked up!" Out of the corner of her eye, she noticed Devin standing sheepishly at the entrance to the kitchen.

How long has he been standing there? Of course, he would walk in at this very moment. Tears welled up in her eyes, a mixture of anger and now embarrassment. She shoved the empty top rack of the dishwasher into place and rushed out of the room, avoiding eye contact with Devin as she passed by.

Mel overheard Devin as she made her way to the upstairs bathroom. "I, uh ... brought ice cream for movie night, Mrs. Walters. Just wanted to put it in the freezer."

The argument had probably been loud enough for everyone to hear. Mel was mortified. And just ... pissed. And also really grateful no one came knocking on the bathroom door to console her, or try to get her to come down. She just needed a few minutes to be mad and then clean herself up before heading down and pretending everything was normal.

***

Her mom was no longer in the kitchen when she came down, but the dishes had all been taken care of. Mel returned to the family room and the guys stopped talking, all sporting some expression of pity in her direction.

Oh gosh, not that 'poor little lost lamb' look.

She drew in a deep breath and sighed. "Can we please just watch a movie?"

They took the hint and each presented a movie of their choosing for her to make the final decision.

"You can tell there's a lot of testosterone in the room," she said. "Superheroes and a slasher?" Her eyebrows lifted in disapproval.

"You *do* spend a lot of time around guys," Ben said. "Maybe you should make some girl friends. And then Zach might actually have a chance of finding a girl to go out with him before he graduates." He snickered, and Devin followed suit.

Zach scowled. "I don't see either of you two with girlfriends."

"Meh." Ben brushed him off with a wave of the hand. "Plus, we're both new here. You've had *years* to woo the ladies."

Devin changed the topic, addressing Mel. "I suggested we let you pick whatever movie you wanted."

Ben busted out laughing and threw a package of M&M's from the coffee table candy dish at Devin's head. "Yeah right, you liar!"

"You know what?" Mel spoke up. "I've had a rough night, and you are being idiots. So, we're watching a rom-com, and you will all love it."

Devin grinned.

Mel picked out one of her favorite go-to rom-coms. Ben seemed annoyed at the choice but didn't leave the room. Mel and Zach usually alternated between their favorites, so he was used to being subjected to chick-flicks.

Mel sat on the couch, cross-legged between Zach and Devin, after picking the movie.

Not long into it, Devin adjusted so his right leg was up on the couch, his foot tucked under the other leg. His right leg touched Mel.

And he let it linger there, not adjusting or apologizing for bumping into her. A few minutes later he leaned over and whispered playfully, "You said we had to love this. What happens if we don't?"

She whispered back, "There will be severe consequences."

They both snickered.

His whisper did more than bring a smile to her face. He was now conveniently even closer to her. This boy was smooth. His hand moved over, barely brushing against her leg, just sitting there. She glanced down. *There's no way a guy does that without wanting to hold hands, right?* Her heart beat faster. She glanced over at his face. He met her gaze with a knowing look and then rolled his hand over, subtly offering it up. She desperately wanted to move her hand into his.

Maybe it was nerves or perhaps it was something else, but she wasn't ready.

Of course, her parents always checked in on her constantly when she had Zach over. This would be an opportune time for them to burst in. But after no parental intervention, she stood up and offered to go scoop ice cream for everyone.

Mel leaned against the kitchen counter, face in her hands. Why didn't she want to hold Devin's hand? She did. But she didn't. Why was everything so confusing all of a sudden? Why was everything so weird this year? Zach was acting odd. She still didn't know much about Devin. Ben was a rando addition. And she hadn't admitted to anyone that she'd been texting with Blake the last few days. He'd even invited her to sit with him at lunch, but she'd turned him down, knowing the invite didn't extend to Zach and Devin.

Her mental torture in solitude was interrupted.

"Hey, you alright?" It was Devin's voice.

She moved a finger and peeked out with one eye. Mel drew in a deep breath and forced a cheesy, tight-lipped smile while dropping her hands.

"Yeah." She shook her head. "I'm sorry. I'm being weird. This whole night is weird."

"You don't have to apologize for anything." He gave her a warm smile. "If anything, *I* should be apologizing."

That comforted her. *He really is a good guy.*

"I'm not going anywhere," he said. "I'm not trying to rush anything."

"Thought I'd come help scoop that ice cream," Zach announced as he butted into the conversation, appearing out of nowhere at the kitchen entrance.

Devin threw him a look of obvious frustration for the intrusion. "I don't think it takes more than two people to scoop ice cream. We can handle it."

Zach surveyed the empty counters. "And yet I don't see anything scooped." He rubbed his wrist and smiled disingenuously at Devin. "I wouldn't want you to sprain your wrist with all of that effort."

Mel stood there, perplexed at the exchange. "Oh, gosh!" She rolled her eyes. "Maybe I *do* need to find some girl friends. Then it wouldn't be a pissing match. I'm going to let the two of you work out that ice cream by yourselves." She left them to it, returning to the family room.

Zach called down the hallway, "We'll be right back." And then much quieter, "But not too fast, we don't want to … *rush anything.*"

Escaping the awkward kitchen mini-drama, Mel glanced at the couch. Instead of taking her spot in the middle again, she sat on the floor in front of it. She considered what the guys had said earlier, about not having any girl friends. She frowned, thinking of Tabatha again. Sure, Mel had other friends, but they were really more of acquaintances. With her parents' strict rules, and her extreme aversion to gossip and drama, she didn't have a lot of people in her close circle. And she'd been fine with that for a long time. But then Tabatha ditched her. Not that Mel had really minded it just being her and Zach over the summer, but it still hurt.

Zach… She shook her head. He was the one that just showed up in the kitchen, acting all weird. Had he noticed Devin's flirting? Was that supposed to be him acting protective? This wasn't the fourth grade, and she certainly didn't need Zach, or anyone else, protecting her from Devin.

Devin was being sweet. Mel glanced at Ben. He was oblivious, messing around on his phone while the movie was paused. Why couldn't they have fostered a girl her age, instead of a guy? Then she'd have another girl around to balance things out. She frowned. That was selfish. And it didn't even matter. *Why does it matter if you have more friends of one gender than another?*

Zach and Devin returned, Zach handing her a bowl of cookie dough ice cream as they sat down and resumed the movie. Thankfully, the guys played nice and kept to themselves for the rest of the evening. It only got weird again as they were wrapping up for the night.

Zach gave Mel a goodnight hug in the hallway. "Hey, could we chat for a second?"

She scrunched her nose. "Tomorrow?"

His eyes wandered through the doorway, glancing at Devin, who wasn't getting up to leave yet. "Yeah, sure."

After the room cleared out, Devin helped Mel straighten up the family room.

"Is Zach always like that?" Devin asked, picking up candy wrappers.

"Like what?"

"You're kidding me, right? He's a bit aggressive. Have you guys ever…?"

"Ever what?" she asked while gathering dishes to take to the kitchen.

He followed her down the hallway. "I don't know. Ever dated?"

She gave a half-hearted chuckle. "No. I have no idea what all that was about. I figured you could shed some light on it." She raised her eyebrows in question.

He stood tight-lipped, shrugging his shoulders.

She continued, "As for dating… I guess I haven't done a good job at explaining my parents' Ten Commandments. We haven't dated. I've never dated at all. I'm not *allowed* to date."

"That's a shame, because I was hoping to go out and spend some time together, one-on-one."

Mel looked up, pulling her attention from the ice cream bowls in the dishwasher. She smirked. "I think I figured that out."

He wore a charming, dimpled smile. "Oh, good. I was afraid I was being too subtle." He laughed, running his hand across the countertop. "I don't know, do you think they'd budge if *I* asked their permission? Your mom seemed to like me."

Mel scoffed at the suggestion. "Will you be negotiating how much I'm worth for my dowry, too?"

He seemed confused by the reference.

"If they're not going to budge for me, they're not going to budge for a guy they just met."

He nodded. "Right. Well… Studying?"

"Yes, let's do that."

They went back to the family room, where Devin claimed a spot on the floor, lying down on his stomach and opening his book. "So…" He craned his neck up to look at Mel on the couch. "Trig." He pretended to gag, garnering a chuckle from her.

She joined him on the floor, also lying down on her stomach and spreading out her books. "Okay." She looked up at him, noticing his eyes dart from her direction back to his book with a blush. Looking down, she realized her neckline was … a little low … in that position. She bit her lip and tugged on the back of her shirt to fix things before continuing.

"Right." She cleared her throat.

He cautiously glanced back up. "Yes. So … I kind of hate math."

They quizzed each other for a while. Mel felt bad, realizing he had to be struggling in class.

He let out a loud sigh. "Honestly, this is such a stupid subject." He rolled onto his back, yawning at the ceiling.

She frowned. "Let me show you. Maybe you just need it to be more visual." She picked up her stuff and scooted next to him, lying on the floor in the same direction.

He rolled back over, his arm now touching hers. "Teach me your ways." He nudged her playfully.

She turned to a new page in her notebook and drew some examples. Her heart fluttered each time their hands touched, as they took turns using her pencil to work through the problems.

While she was in the middle of trying to explain an equation to him again, she looked over and caught him staring at her with a smile, instead of looking down at the paper where she was trying to demonstrate her point. "Hey!" She felt her cheeks warming. "Do you want to pass this test?"

He shifted onto his side and reached over to tuck a strand of hair behind her ear. He frowned dramatically. "I guess I don't care that much. But I think it's cool that you're really smart."

She shifted a little to face him more. "I don't know about that. I think with math, you just have to find the right way for it to click with how your individual brain works."

He grinned. "But you get good grades in all of your classes, don't you?"

She looked down at the carpet; they hadn't discussed grades before. It was kind of awkward to do it now, knowing she was almost a straight-A student, and he ... obviously wasn't. At least not with math.

She glanced back at him. "What are your favorite classes?"

He twisted his lips in thought. "Lunch?"

She laughed louder than intended and he gave her a big smile.

He answered more seriously, "Gym is cool, and I like English most of the time. History is pretty interesting."

She smiled.

"Oh," he added, "Trigonometry has its perks."

She arched an eyebrow. "The last half-hour has looked like pure torture for you. Explain to me how it makes the list?"

He wore a soft smile, reading her face. "I get to study with you, don't I?"

Her heart skipped a beat, realizing this whole study session might not have been about him wanting a decent grade at all. He kept his eyes trained on Mel as her breathing became heavier. She knew she needed to say something, but she wasn't sure what.

"You guys wrapping it up?" Her dad peeked in the doorway.

Devin quickly sat up and shuffled around his school supplies. "Yeah. We were just finishing up."

Mel's dad tilted his head and glanced at her as if he disapproved.

She rolled her eyes and also sat up. "We're done." She huffed in frustration as he vacated the doorway. They hadn't been doing anything wrong. She half-expected her parents to come up with a new rule that she had to be a few feet away from the opposite sex at all times, or something equally annoying.

As Devin was leaving for the night, she offered a hug. *Gosh! Why does it feel like his arms were molded perfectly to embrace me?* She melted like butter as he held her close.

"I think you're pretty amazing," he whispered into her ear before letting go and heading home.

Chapter 5

BY THE TIME MEL LOOKED at her phone after Devin left, she already had a few texts, from both Blake and Zach. She stayed up late texting with Zach. He wouldn't say why he and Devin had acted weird in the kitchen, being as vague as Devin had been. She figured the two guys just needed to duke it out or get over themselves.

Luckily, they had some sort of truce when it came to hanging out at school the next week. It mostly involved ignoring each other, but it got the job done.

Blake, however, was continuing his attention toward Mel, even approaching her a couple more times at school, along with his consistent texting. He was waiting for her outside of her last class one day.

"Walters, c'mon. Just give me *one* chance. It'll be a great date. Cross my heart." He leaned against the wall, armed with his letterman jacket and a pouty face.

From their chatting, she was definitely starting to warm up to him. He wouldn't just text randomly, as if she were a backup option when he was bored. She still couldn't date, but if she could, she might consider it with Blake. She wouldn't have pegged him as her type, but there was a certain appeal to considering someone so different from what you'd normally turn to.

"It even comes with a money-back guarantee if you're not satisfied." He smiled.

She raised her eyebrows. "First of all, I told you: I can't. Second, what does that even mean, 'money-back guarantee?'"

He cocked his head to the side. "You know what I mean. It'll be fun."

Both flattered and annoyed, she sighed and walked away. "Bye, Blake."

***

A couple nights later, Mel's parents took her out to her favorite restaurant for a family night. Ben was out with friends, so it was just the three of them. It was nice to get out of the house and have her parents to herself for the night. Things had even been less tense lately.

The waitress delivered their appetizers and Mel happily dug in. She chomped down on a mozzarella stick and then wiped her greasy hands on a napkin.

"We wanted to talk," her dad said.

She finished chewing her mouthful with wide eyes. The last time they had any sort of 'special dinner,' they'd announced Ben was joining them. She dreaded what might come next.

He continued, "The argument you had with your mom a couple weeks ago. About dating?" His eyebrows lifted.

Mel met her mom's eyes before looking down at her plate. She'd apologized to her mom; perhaps it hadn't been a very sincere apology, but she thought they'd gotten over it. "Yeah...?"

"Pumpkin, we just want what's best for you," he said.

Great, another lecture.

Her mom spoke up. "That being said, we've agreed you're old enough to *consider* relaxing some rules."

Mel perked up with a huge smile, looking between them. "Really?!"

Her dad gave a hesitant smile. "Yes. With rules."

"I promise, I won't go anywhere sketchy. I'll take pepper spray. Whatever you want!"

His smile warmed, though his tone was authoritative. "This is what we've agreed on: Dates are to pick you up from home. We have to get to know them. You let us know everywhere you plan to go. Check in with us and be back by curfew. Dates have to be in public places."

"I can do that!" she squealed, wanting to leap over the table and hug them both. "Thank you!"

The rest of dinner was absolutely perfect—the food, the company. Her dad regaled them with stories of amusing mishaps at work from earlier in the week and her mom gave them updates on one of Mel's older cousins that had recently had a baby.

Mel's phone vibrated in her pocket a couple times while they finished eating. On the drive home she opened her messages, smiling at the contents and the thought of her newfound freedom. Zach had sent a funny meme. Devin a random hello. And Blake, another text about going on a date. She was torn; there was definitely more chemistry with Devin, but that might increase the tension between him and Zach. She closed her eyes. Of course, Devin had made it pretty clear he wanted a date. He was sweet and had the best smile. But no … Zach. He still wouldn't talk about why he disliked Devin. And he always had good judgment, facial hair choices excluded.

She shook her head, thinking more about Blake. Here his text was, right in front of her, a direct question. And his encouragement *was* what had given her the opportunity in the first place, helping her to stand up to her mom. And … Blake could be a 'starter' date… She could see if maybe he really was her type, how she felt about him once they were in a different setting. And if it didn't go well, she would at least know and be able to get him out of her hair.

She shot off a text and got a quick response.

<Saturday?>

<It's a date!>

***

It took Mel quite a while to get ready for her afternoon date. They were only going to grab a bite and go mini-golfing, but she wanted to look nice. Her makeup was usually pretty basic, and she didn't fuss over her hair much on the daily. She ran down the stairs as soon as the doorbell rang.

Blake looked sharper than usual. Wearing dark jeans and a plaid button-up shirt with the sleeves rolled up, he gave her a huge smile. "Walters!"

"Hey, come inside. I'm almost ready." She beckoned him in.

He stepped inside and from around the corner they could hear Ben.

"Heyyyyyyy…" Ben's voice trailed off, going from casually welcoming to awkward confusion once he saw who was at the door. "Blake, what are you doing here?"

"Ben, right?"

Reading the room, Mel threw a glare at Ben and ushered Blake to the family room before she went upstairs to finish getting ready. Ben followed right after her and blocked the bathroom doorway while she spritzed some perfume.

"What was that about?" she asked.

"Why are you going out with *him*?" He paused a moment. "I thought your parents said you had to go out with someone they knew."

Her jaw dropped. "How is that any of your business?" She thought of their encounter shortly after he moved in. "What was it *you* said? 'I didn't know I answered to you?'"

He didn't respond; instead, he just crossed his arms.

"My dad said he'd have to pick me up and they would get to know him before we head out. That's exactly what's happening right now." She huffed. "Plus, you're the one chasing after Stacy. They're in the same crowd. A bit hypocritical of you, don't you think?"

He narrowed his eyes. "He has a reputation, you know."

She pursed her lips and avoided eye contact. She might have heard rumors that Blake dated a lot. But she didn't like judging people based on rumors. She wouldn't be alone with him anywhere, and he hadn't been aggressive about anything. "You know, when you first came here, you didn't seem all that bad. But you're getting on my nerves."

He frowned. "I'm sorry. I just … don't want you getting hurt."

"I appreciate the gesture, okay? I can take care of myself. Can you get out of my way now?"

Ben stepped aside and Mel grabbed her purse from her room before going downstairs. By the time she reached the family room, her parents were already in there, grilling Blake.

"Cool, you've met, you know the particulars. Can we go now?"

Her dad looked at his watch. "We'll see you in three hours, not a minute later."

***

Mel teased Blake as he drove his pickup. "So, you want to risk me beating you and hurting your pride, eh?"

"Dinner and a movie is how you make out, with bad breath." He laughed. "Lunch and mini-golf is how you actually get to know someone."

Okay, that earned some points. Who talks like that?

They dropped by a local Mexican mom-and-pop restaurant first. The air carried the scent of chilis and refried beans. Latin music drifted down from overhead speakers, not quite loud enough to muffle the sizzle of fajitas.

"So, what's your thing, Blake?" she asked, scooping some fiery salsa with a chip. "I thought for a while that you and Stacy were an item. And you've never shown any interest in me before now."

"No, no. Stacy and I aren't exclusive or anything like that. We just spend a lot of time in the same crowd." He took a sip of his horchata. "As for you, Walters, I think it's good to branch out sometimes. Meet new people." He smirked. "Is it corny to say you blossomed over the summer?"

She grinned. *Yes, that was corny.* Mel didn't have a false sense of modesty. She knew she wasn't ugly, but she wasn't exactly used to guys lining up to date her. Stacy was more the type to let her curves do the talking for her. Then again, Mel reasoned, maybe she *had* matured a little herself over the summer break—why else would two guys be so interested in her this early in the school year?

When she didn't answer, he carried on. "I saw that new painting of the field of sunflowers hanging inside your locker door. Did you make that?"

She smiled. "Yeah. I love to paint. That one's a mix of acrylic and watercolor."

He took another sip of his drink. "I've noticed people's locker decorations almost always say something about them."

"Oh really? And what does mine say about me?"

He gazed into her eyes. "Like the artist, the painting is beautiful."

Her cheeks flushed red hot.

The rest of their lunch was filled with good conversation. He was genuinely interested in her and her family, asking lots of questions about how her summer went.

"And that foster—Ben, right?" he asked.

"Yeah. That's his name."

"I didn't know your parents fostered. Is that a new thing?"

She shook her head, setting her plate to the side. "Not really. They've fostered a little over the years. But he's definitely the weirdest I can remember."

"Hmm." Blake nodded. "What's so weird about him?"

She was getting annoyed. Why were they talking about Ben on a date? "I don't know. I'm sure it's just how close we are in age. The last fosters were a brother and sister, seven and nine." She squinted while trying to remember. "I think I was eleven or twelve at the time?"

"Gotcha. Before my time." Blake had moved there a couple years earlier. She'd first met him as a freshman. "It's cool they help out like that."

While waiting for their check, Mel excused herself to use the restroom. As she stood up, she recognized someone staring at her from across the room.

You've got to be kidding me. "I'll be right back, you stay here."

Before she even got to the bathroom, she sent off a text.

<WHAT RU DOING HERE?! GO HOME!>

By the time she came back out, the spy was gone. But Mel was still livid.

She was so flustered, she knew she wouldn't be able to enjoy the rest of the date. "I hope you don't hate me; I'm not feeling so great. Could we take a rain check for golf?"

"Yeah, sure." Blake raised his eyebrows. "Everything alright?"

Coming out from the bathroom and telling your date you weren't feeling well? Yeah … that wasn't embarrassing at all. But at that point, she really didn't care. She was too angry to care. "I'll be fine. I just want to go home."

He seemed a bit put out. She didn't think he'd seen that Ben had followed them to the restaurant. But he *did* shift his questions to Ben again, and Ben's friends, on the ride home; so maybe he had, after all.

"Why do you think they put someone so close to your age as a foster?" he asked.

If Ben wasn't ruining the date, Blake was.

"I don't know." She stared out the window, wishing there was a redo button for her first-ever real date.

Once they got back to her house, Blake walked Mel to the front door and offered a hug. "Let me know if you need anything, okay?" He sounded really sweet, until his arms slithered down her back and to her hips. "Kinda sucks we didn't get to finish. But that doesn't mean it can't end on a good note."

He pulled her closer while leaning in for a kiss. Her heart was beating fast as her eyes grew wide, taken completely by surprise.

"Um…" She turned her head last minute, cringing. "I, uh…"

Luckily, her mom opened the door and saved her from having to finish the conversation.

"Melody. You're back early." Her mom stared them both down.

Blake was quick to take the cue. "Hey, I'll text you." He gave her one last grin before turning and heading back to his truck.

Mel followed her mom through the door, shutting it with a sigh of relief.

"That's a first date?" her mom chided.

Mel's mouth hung open. She'd just been grateful for the rescue, but was now being scolded for having someone try to kiss her? "I didn't ask for that!"

Her mom sighed and shook her head. "Well, that's not what it looked like." She paused while Mel grappled for words. "Do you plan to see that boy again?"

"No!" Mel's brow furrowed.

"Good," her mom replied curtly. "Why are you back so early, anyway?"

Mel narrowed her eyes. "Do you know who followed me on my date?"

"What do you mean?"

"Ben. Ben was at the restaurant. That creep followed me!"

Her mom frowned skeptically. "That doesn't seem right."

"No. It doesn't." Mel glared, half-accusing. "That was humiliating, like I needed a chaperone."

Her mom shrugged innocently. "He just wants what's best for you. It's probably a coincidence, anyway, honey. I'm sure he meant nothing by it."

Right. An astounding coincidence. By sheer happenstance, he showed up at the same place, at the same time, during my first date with a guy he seemed annoyed about, when my parents were the only ones I gave the location to. Coincidence.

"A 'coincidence,' Mom? 'That's not what it looked like,'" Mel shot back before heading to her room, fuming.

Before shutting her door, she made out her mom's voice from down the stairs. "I'll talk to him."

Ben hadn't returned to their house yet, so Mel couldn't confront him in person like she wanted to. And he conveniently remained missing the rest of the day, returning home after Mel went to bed.

He either stayed in his room or snuck out before she woke up on Sunday. She stared at his closed door, wanting to knock on it and give him a piece of her mind, but she knew she'd lose it. In the end, she didn't have any concrete proof, but … she knew something was off. And she couldn't figure out why her mom would protect him.

For the rest of the weekend, Mel barely spoke two words to her mom and dad. From what she'd gathered from other friends growing up, she had pretty amazing parents—ones that would actually apologize when they realized they were in the wrong. But they didn't this time; maybe they hadn't realized they'd stepped over the line, or maybe they genuinely hadn't been involved and Ben had acted alone. Along with relative silence between herself and her parents over the weekend, Mel ignored Blake's texts, and even Devin's. The only person she replied to was Zach. He came over Sunday night to go for a walk.

Mel's parents were out of the house, off visiting a friend in the hospital. She forgot to tell Zach not to knock, and she regretted it when Ben got to the door before she did.

"We're just going for a walk," she barked. "And if you ever stalk me again, I'm going to murder you in your sleep."

She slammed the door behind her and turned around. Zach's eyes were wide in shock.

"Let's go," she ordered.

They walked half a block without saying anything.

"So ... haven't ever heard you threaten to kill anyone before." He nodded thoughtfully. "Does that mean I should invest in a shovel?"

She took a deep breath. "I feel like I'm going crazy. It's not just me, right?"

He didn't answer.

"Everyone's being so weird, right?"

"Well, I was going to say something after our last movie night." He cleared his throat. "But Romeo wanted to steal more of your time." He glanced over at her.

She met his gaze, but said nothing.

"When you and your mom were in the kitchen, Ben was acting weird. He was grilling me the whole time."

"About me?"

"Not directly. Some about your friends in general. All sorts of personal questions about me and my family. He only asked about you when he asked about our friendship." Zach laughed awkwardly. "I felt like it was the talk I never had with your dad. 'What are your intentions with my little girl?'" he said in a deep voice, trying to imitate her dad.

She smiled at his impression. "I don't get why my mom comes to his defense, or why they would put him up to spying on me. I feel like he's brainwashed them or something. I think I'm going to talk to Tom—er, Mr. Colburn—about it."

"That's probably a good idea. But until then, you sleep with your door locked, right?" He looked at her, both eyebrows raised. "I'm serious."

She acknowledged the crazy of the situation with a nervous chuckle. "Yeah. And I'll have my mace closer to me, too."

They walked a bit further as the sun set in the sky.

"Got a rash or something?" Zach asked.

"What?"

"Just, you've been scratching your arms this whole time."

She looked down and stopped scratching. It was the weirdest thing; she hadn't even realized she was doing it again. She'd woken up that day with both arms itching, the exact same spot on each forearm, between her wrist and elbow. She crossed her arms. "I'm fine."

"And what about your choice of a first date?" he casually asked.

Mel rolled her eyes. "Such a creep. I can't believe he thought I'd want to kiss him after half of a date. And when I said I wasn't feeling well!" She wanted to reassure her best friend. "I'm not going out with him again. You have my word on that."

He looked relieved. "Why go out with some bozo like that when you've got me?"

She managed a faint smile. She knew Zach always had her back.

They turned around and started walking back to her house. Her mind replayed the botched date as a breeze stirred the wind chimes on a neighbor's front porch.

"I blame this all on Tabatha, you know," Zach joked. "She left us and these creeps all came to fill her place."

Mel laughed. "Such a jerk, I can't believe her!" She got a little more serious. "I mean, it *does* suck that she dropped us like a sack of potatoes. But we can hardly blame her for Blake, I'm sure he's been the same since he moved here. And Ben, I think he's just a freak of nature."

Zach shoved his hands in his pockets. "Don't forget Mr. Ice Cream trying to put the moves on you."

She tilted her head to the side. "That's not fair. He's never done anything to you." She looked at Zach, waiting for a response. "Why don't you like him?"

He stared down at the sidewalk. "Well … I … maybe I'm just not a fan." He looked back at her, squinting. "Do you like him?"

She paused a moment. Why the sudden interest? They never talked about crushes. Why did he care so much? And why did Blake or Ben care about *anything* she did?

Mel shrugged, continuing to walk. "He's nice."

"Right. But there are a lot of nice guys out there that might be better for you. I mean, the fact that you're able to date now … I think that's great."

Mel huffed. She'd been forced to wait to date, and *this* was what all of that hopeful anticipation had led to. "I don't know how much I care about dating right now, if this is how it's going to go. Calling what just happened a date, is like calling a dumpster a five-star hotel." She kicked a pebble off of the sidewalk, into her neighbor's yard.

Zach pressed his lips together and nodded, not saying another word on the topic.

Reaching her house, they ended their stroll with a longer and tighter hug than usual.

Chapter 6

DEVIN WAS WAITING FOR MEL at their lockers first thing the next morning.

"Blake?" he asked in shock. "You tell me you can't date, and then you go out with *Blake*?"

"Can we please not start the week this way?" She moaned. "I get it. Everyone realizes he's a creep. I was stupid. I vote we move on." It was a bad memory she wanted to wash away. Blake had even texted her a couple times already to ask her when they were going to go out again. He said she 'owed' him a date because they ended their first one early. She resented that. No one ever 'owed' anyone else a date. She couldn't for the life of her figure out why she'd gone out with him in the first place. Any charm he'd held was now long gone.

"Okay, no more talk about Blake. But ... I kind of thought we had a thing, that maybe..." He rocked his head back and forth.

She blushed. "Devin, I like you. But can we just dial things back for now? Have a movie night without a soap opera? You, me, Zach." Rolling her eyes, she added, "We'll make sure Ben is out of the house."

Devin raised an eyebrow.

"I didn't mention that part? He's practically a stalker. I'll tell you more at lunch." The bell rang. "Are we cool?"

He forced a smile. "We're cool."

Before she turned to go to class, she thought to ask, "How did you hear about Blake, anyway?"

He gave a delayed response, first scanning her face, then shrugging. "People talk."

"Greaaat..." She let the word drip with sarcasm while walking away, only imagining the kinds of rumors she might be part of if Blake hadn't taken kindly to her rejection.

***

Tom could always be found in his office after school. Mel headed down there to chat about the Ben situation. She could have talked to a guidance counselor, but Tom was like family. He understood what her parents were like and usually gave solid advice.

She made her way through the busy office and tapped on his partially open door.

He grinned and stacked some papers when he spotted her. "Come on in! Not in trouble, are we?"

"No. Nothing like that." She smiled, sitting down across from him at his desk.

Mel went on to explain how Ben was acting, and how her parents weren't taking her seriously regarding him. "Parents are supposed to trust their own kids more than a stranger off the streets, right?"

He assured Mel that her parents had her best interests at heart and, while it wasn't technically legal for him to disclose anything about Ben, he divulged that everything on Ben's school record was squeaky clean from his past. "I'll talk to your parents, okay? We'll get it sorted out."

She hoped it wasn't just a platitude. It wasn't like her parents, or Tom, to be so dismissive. But he seemed sincere, and he had never steered her wrong before.

Mel picked up her backpack and was heading out when she heard a familiar voice coming from another room in the school office. She snooped and peeked in the half-opened door.

"I'm telling you; he *has* to be one of them!" Devin hissed.

"Miss Walters, how can I help you?" Vice Principal Simons spoke up as soon as he saw her, calmly sitting up straight in his chair.

She fidgeted with her hands guiltily. "Nothing. I was just chatting with Principal Colburn for a second."

"Great. Was there anything else I can help you with, Devin?" Mr. Simons smiled.

"No, sir, thanks." Devin picked his backpack up off the floor and exited with Mel.

Devin looked at a text that chimed in right after they left the office. "Fancy walking home?"

Mel often walked to school, while Devin usually had a car he borrowed from his uncle.

"You sure you want to walk? Is your place far from mine?" she asked as they left the building.

"Your place is actually along the way," he said.

"It's kind of stupid I didn't know that, right? But I guess it doesn't come up much when everyone always has to come to me." She gave him a faint smile. "You could live with a family of killer clowns and I wouldn't know it."

"We try to keep the killer clown part quiet, so we'd appreciate you respecting our privacy." He tried to keep a straight face and successfully earned a giggle.

"What was that about back there?" she asked. "Did you get in trouble for something?"

"Okay, if we're being serious about secrets…" He looked at her with a raised eyebrow. "Mr. Simons is my uncle."

"No way!" Her jaw dropped. "Why didn't you tell us? That's who you came here to live with?"

"I've got a reputation to uphold." He brushed off his shoulder coolly. "Okay, I don't know that I actually *have* a reputation." He sniggered. "But it's like you and Mr. C. I know you guys are chummy, but you don't act like it at school. No one wants to be friends with someone that has an authority figure breathing down their neck."

"Touché. I fully understand that." She playfully nudged his arm. "But look at us. We have friends in high places." She tapped her fingertips together and let out a villainous laugh.

It garnered the handsome smile and laugh she was looking for.

"I told you we make a nice duo." He returned the nudge.

***

Whatever Tom did, it seemed to work. The next few weeks were peacefully mundane. And somehow, no rumors about Mel and Blake circulated, at least not that she'd heard about.

Her parents didn't nag her about anything, and Mel barely even saw Ben around the house. She would have continued to be frustrated at the hypocrisy of how few rules they seemed to have with him, if she wasn't happy to not have to be around him. She was even a little worried about him being out at all hours, possibly getting into trouble. Then she noticed he was sitting next to Stacy every lunch at school. Of course, a girl like that might cause her own problems. Mel was both impressed and annoyed that he'd actually caught Stacy's attention.

That is, until one random day at lunch. Stacy literally bumped into Mel in the lunch line, almost spilling her tray.

"Gosh! Sorry, Melody!"

Mel struggled to not show her annoyance while straightening the food on her tray. "I've gone by Mel for a long time."

"Right." Stacy frowned. "Mel. I should have known that. I, uh... I just wanted to say I'm sorry for the way I treated you, for the way things ended between us."

Mel stood there, stewing in the awkwardness of the situation, as they had to wait for their turns to pay for their food. "No problem. Life happens."

Stacy handed the lunch lady some cash and turned around again. "I'm glad we could talk." She gave a weak smile.

Ben was impatiently waiting for her at the end of the line. "Come on, Stacy."

She followed him and they sat at Stacy's usual table, but at the far end. Away from Blake and some of his closer buddies. Maybe Ben was a good influence on her? She had hardly spoken to Mel in years, and when she had, it was never anything kind or ... like whatever that just was. Mel couldn't help but wonder if she'd been wrong about them. Perhaps they really did make a good couple. And Ben didn't even have his hands all over her like some guys were happy to.

Mel still couldn't help but roll her eyes, noting that Ben and Blake were now in the same crowd, even if they sat at opposite ends of the group.

"Your account number?" the lunch lady drawled with impatience.

Mel snapped back from her musings. "Yeah, sorry."

***

The next movie night, Devin asked if he could bring a new friend. He brought a girl named Heather. She was a super-friendly, cute little blonde thing with a slightly nasal voice.

"Thanks so much for having me over!" She pulled Mel in for a hug.

"Sure thing." Mel smiled.

Heather was a little spunky compared to Mel's normal crowd, but she seemed like a sweet girl. And frankly, it was nice to balance out the hormones of the group. Mel grinned as they watched the movie. Heather and Zach seemed to get along well enough, and things hadn't been too awkward between Zach and Devin lately. She noticed some scrutinizing glances, perhaps, between them, but no open animosity. It was nice to consider more options than just staying at home, now that their group was expanding more, and included a girl her parents could feel better about.

Halfway through the movie, Mel accidentally spilled soda and cleaned it up. She returned the soiled rag to the kitchen, Devin following her.

"Hey, flashbacks to our first hang-out. Hiding away in the kitchen." He smiled as he leaned against the island between them.

She shook her head with a smirk, turning on the water to rinse out the rag. "Heather seems really nice. It took me a while to recognize her, but I think we've had some classes together. I guess she's pretty quiet in class, but a chatterbox in smaller groups, huh?"

Devin chuckled. "Yeah, that's a good way of describing her."

Mel wrung out the cloth and faced him. "She's really pretty."

He looked over his shoulder to the doorway that led to the main hall. "Yeah. I guess you could say that. She's a new friend. Not really my type."

Mel smiled. She'd felt a hint of jealousy at first, when she saw Heather and Devin arrive together. He hadn't told Mel he was bringing a girl. She pressed her lips together, not sure if she should ask... "So, what is your type?"

He glanced over his shoulder again, then went back to looking at Mel. He grinned and raised an eyebrow. "The kind who secretly thinks the best of everyone, even when she's wrong. And loves her family, even when she's frustrated."

She looked down at the floor, biting the insides of her cheeks.

"It also doesn't hurt when she's beautiful and smart. Oh, and the creative type—I like that."

She glanced at his face, matching his grin.

He looked over his shoulder again.

"Why do you keep doing that?"

He chuckled. "Waiting for someone to burst into the room and ruin our chat like last time."

She smiled. She'd put Blake behind her and wanted to give it some time before dating again. But if Devin had asked her out, right then and there, she knew she wouldn't turn him down.

"C'mon." He gestured with his head. "Let's get back to the movie."

Chapter 7

AS CHRISTMAS APPROACHED, THE TOPIC of Winter Formal came up. They decided to go together as a group—Mel, Devin, Zach, and Heather—no formal dates.

Mel pulled her new dress out of the closet, talking on speakerphone with Zach.

"You really went all out? Cummerbund and all?" she asked.

"Yeah. Figured, why not?"

Mel searched her closet, trying to remember where she'd placed her dress shoes.

"So, if four of us are going stag, but together, does that make us a herd?" he asked.

She chuckled. "These are the reasons I keep you around."

"I really look forward to seeing you tonight."

Mel put her shoes next to the dress on the bed. She looked in the full-size mirror in her room, deciding which makeup she'd pull out. She squinted, taken aback at the color of her eyes. They'd taken on an almost greenish hue. She blinked a couple times. No—blue—

like they always were. Shaking her head, she grabbed her water bottle and sipped.

"I guess maybe I should let you go to finish getting ready," Zach said.

"Yeah, sorry. A little distracted. Just lining everything up. I'm sure tonight will be one to remember. See you there."

After ending the call, Mel curled her hair, then slid into the teal satin dress she'd bought on a special shopping trip with her mom. She then turned to applying makeup. After getting dolled up, she stood for a moment, admiring the girl looking back in the mirror. She smirked and traced the neckline, a deeper V than she'd ever worn before. This was her first formal, and she had Devin on her mind. Unlike Blake after being turned down, Devin was patient, continually building their friendship. She figured she'd see how the night panned out. Maybe *she* would be the one to ask *him* out.

Mel and Ben drove to the dance together, being relatively civil with each other these days. She wondered if Stacy's influence was equally good for him, helping calm him down. Unfortunately, Stacy was sick and had missed a few days of school. She wouldn't be at the dance so Ben was also going stag, meeting up with friends.

Despite the dance being held in the main school gym, it was decently decked out for the occasion. Snowflakes sparkled, hanging from the ceiling on fishing line. A winter village backdrop was set up for couples and groups to get pictures. The music was fairly good and their group was all smiles. Ben even dropped by and asked Heather to dance a couple times.

Devin was the first to ask Mel for a turn on the floor. He was an amazing dancer—able to do all the spins, dips, and everything in between. He was a great leader as well, which was good because Mel had one-and-a-half left feet.

"I dare say, you do look rather dapper tonight." She smiled while dancing. "And how did you learn to dance like this?"

He spun her and pulled her in close. "Lots of practice," he whispered in her ear. After another spin, he brought her in again and whispered in the other ear, "Or maybe it's all natural." He held her out at arm's length and bit his lip seductively; she giggled. At the end of the song, he planted a sweet peck on her cheek and winked.

Before joining the others, his eyes wandered over her face and dress. "Do you realize how breathtaking you are?"

She'd already been feeling warm—now her cheeks were positively on fire. She locked eyes with him, feeling a new connection. Something had changed. It wasn't just his compliment. She couldn't put her finger on it, but she could get lost in his eyes. Her heart racing, she decided that sometime that night, she'd talk to him about going on a date. But she didn't have it in her quite yet. She averted her eyes, wringing her hands. "Thanks."

They rejoined the group to chat during a fast song.

"Gosh, it's hot in here," Mel complained, not ten minutes later. Truth be told, she'd been feeling a little off all day. She hadn't said anything, not wanting to miss out.

"Maybe it's time we brave the punch and see if it's been spiked." Zach laughed and gestured for Devin to come with him.

Mel and Heather stood in the corner, fanning themselves with their hands and talking about upcoming Christmas plans. Across the room, Mel noticed Devin leave Zach's side, following a guy she vaguely recognized as a sophomore out of the room.

She continued to people-watch. Vice Principal Simons was one of the chaperones. When their eyes met, he twitched slightly before glancing back at the door she'd seen Devin leave from. She realized she really didn't know much about Mr. Simons at all, especially for being Devin's uncle.

Her focus shifted back to Zach, and then Heather. Mel wondered if they might make a cute couple. She mentally shelved that one, not too sure of the pairing, and even less sure of her ability as a matchmaker. She'd tried suggesting some girls to Zach before, but they never worked out.

Zach awkwardly carried three cups of punch back to the girls.

"What's that about?" Mel shouted over the music, motioning with her head to the door Devin went out of.

Zach shrugged. "I dunno, he just said he needed to talk to someone."

They drank their punch and chatted at a table to the side of the dance floor. Mel looked past the crowd of people, eyes fixed on the door, waiting for Devin to return. Another slow song came on.

"Hey, Mel." Zach turned, offering his hand to her.

A trained dancer, he was not. But she enjoyed the slower pace, simply swaying and talking about the dance décor and music. It was like hugging him, except with romantic lyrics in the background. And not *quite* like hugging him. She was acutely aware of his hands placed on her hips.

"I must say, madam, you look very magical tonight." He wiggled his eyebrows.

"I do, do I?" Her face got a little warmer. She teased back in an English accent, "Are you saying I require magic to make me look presentable, good fellow?"

He squinted. "You're not the kind of girl that needs to fish for a compliment." He smiled and brought her in a little closer. "To be honest, I've been lucky all of these years to have you to myself. I got in under the radar at a young age, before your parents realized they wanted you to be a nun."

Mel couldn't help but laugh at that.

His playful face and tone changed to a sincere one. "I'm just saying—it doesn't take much for my best friend to go from stunning to hot." And then he tried to backpedal, breaking eye contact. "Well, hot isn't very, um … just…"

She couldn't help but smirk at him struggling. And the fact that he'd just called her 'hot.' That was definitely a first.

"…just, you look great."

The song was ending as he added, "I've seen you that way for a long time … I always thought we might … become something more." He searched her eyes as though he were hoping for a response.

She was speechless, standing there with his arms around her, her heart beating fast as her breathing intensified. It's not like she'd never considered it. He was great. But she'd always thought he was joking … not genuinely flirting.

Their magical moment melted away as Heather interrupted them, followed by Devin not much later.

Mel sat out the next couple of songs. Partially to take in what Zach had just said, and partially because she was starting to feel worse. Her throat was dry and her stomach ached. She noticed Blake looking in her direction. He had been cold in the hallways at school since her rejection, but he seemed to be getting over it, as he gave her a casual wave across the dance floor. Zach was chatting with Heather and Devin, but looked over at Mel longingly a couple times, as though he wanted to go sit with her, but wasn't sure if he should give her some space.

Devin came to join her with a cup of water. "You okay?"

"Yeah, I'm sure it's just how hot it is in here. Is it hot to you?"

"It's warm, but not that bad." He felt her forehead and held her hands; they were clammy.

She loved the feeling of their hands touching, but felt guilty after Zach's declaration.

"Let's go outside for a bit, get some fresh air and see if that helps," Devin said.

She happily obliged.

It definitely did some good, feeling the cool air on her burning cheeks. A light coating of fresh snow crunched under their feet, a rare occurrence in these parts.

They walked a few yards down the sidewalk and approached a bench. Devin cleared the snow off of it and laid his suit jacket down for them to sit on. After sitting, Mel bent over, burying her face in her hands. He gently scratched her back.

"Thanks, this feels nice," she said. She'd meant that about his suggestion to take a walk outside, but she didn't at all hate the feeling of him scratching her back. Her mind wandered to Zach.

This doesn't actually happen to people. At least not girls like me. It wasn't like she hadn't ever seen Zach as potentially more than just a friend. Friends make the best partners. But it was high school, and she hadn't been able to date, and didn't want to risk changing their dynamic.

And then there was Devin. He always said the right thing, and was on a different level altogether. And the chemistry—that could power a steam engine. Devin had respected her request to not talk about dating after the Blake disaster, but his interest was still obvious, his charm as alluring as ever.

After a minute of trying to gather her thoughts and strength, Mel raised her head and leaned back. Devin moved from scratching her back to draping his arm around her shoulder. She looked over at him.

"And then … Zach…"

He furrowed his brow.

"He just… He told me he likes me. You know…?"

His face relaxed into a dimpled grin.

"You knew? Of course, you would know. I'm apparently daft at this sort of thing."

He chuckled softly. "Daft, no." He pressed his lips together as though he were picking his words thoughtfully. "Fantastic at reading romantic cues? Also, no." He offered his free hand like he had on their first movie night.

She didn't feel the same hesitation this time. She put her right hand in his and Devin pulled her in tighter, his lips gently caressing her cheek for the second time.

Mel grinned. "I don't know. I did a good job at picking up *your* romantic cues." She glanced at him out of the corner of her eye. "Then again, you're not exactly subtle."

He bit his lip. "Maybe not."

She leaned against him, melting in his arms for a few minutes.

Only feeling mildly better after a while in the cold, she took in a deep breath and shook her head a little, closing her eyes.

"Are you still feeling sick?" he asked. "How long have you been feeling like this?"

"Yeah, I'm still so hot, despite the cold. And just getting kind of dizzy. Um... I've been feeling kinda weird all day, to be honest."

He felt her forehead again. "You're burning up, maybe I should take you home."

"I don't know." She rubbed her forearms. "It's so crazy. It's like the same exact spot."

Devin looked at Mel's arms. "Are they hurting?"

She leaned away, nodding. "Yeah. Right here and here." She drew a line across each arm between her wrist and elbow. "I didn't even realize it before Zach pointed it out, but it was super itchy one day, in the same exact spots." She narrowed her eyes, examining her arms. She'd only noticed the aching at the beginning of the dance.

Devin squinted. "Zach knows your arms were itching? Does anyone else?"

She looked at him with a grin. "That I had dry skin for a day? No. I don't think I announced that one on social media."

He chuckled. "Let me take you home."

"I'm sure I'll be fine." She grimaced. "Maybe just a few more songs."

"*I'm* sure you'll feel better away from a huge crowd and blaring music," he countered. "You're not going to have any fun in there if you're feeling this way. Let me take you home."

He was right. She was getting increasingly nauseous and lightheaded, which became much more evident the moment she stood up again.

Devin steadied her with a hand on her back and escorted her to his car, pulling out his phone before heading out. "I'm letting the guys know I'm taking you home so they don't think I kidnapped you." He sent off the text and started the car, then held her hand on the ride back to her place.

She leaned her burning face against the cool glass of the car window. Halfway to her house she asked, "Do you think someone really did something to the punch?"

He quickly replied, "No, I doubt it."

"Did you have any?"

He glanced over at her and squeezed her hand. "No, but I'm sure more people would be sick if that was the problem."

She closed her eyes to keep everything from spinning, taking slow breaths. "That's right, you left to go talk to that kid. What did he want?"

"What? Oh, that's nothing. I've been doing a little tutoring."

"Really? What subject?"

"You like that, don't you? All this time and I'm still a man of mystery."

Mel managed a small smile. She knew, for sure, that he *definitely* wasn't tutoring Trigonometry.

Chapter 8

MEL FELT A LITTLE BETTER away from the crowds and noise, but her symptoms persisted the next day. Her mom doted on her while she napped most of the afternoon on the couch. Mel assured Zach she was fine, after waking up to texts from him, worried out of his mind that she'd left without telling him. Apparently, he hadn't gotten Devin's text. She felt crummy for not talking to Zach even once after his confession, and before going to bed.

"You're sure you'll be fine, honey?" her mom asked with a frown.

Mel moaned. "I'm pretty sure the only thing I'm in danger of is this couch swallowing me whole."

"Your dad and I will only be gone a couple of hours. Ben knows you're home alone. You can text him if you need something."

Mel internally scoffed at the thought of ever asking Ben to come to her rescue. Zach and Devin lived close enough. Either of them would be her go-to, even if she and Ben had been getting along lately.

***

A half hour later, Mel woke to the sound of the doorbell and stumbled over to answer it. It was Devin, with a small vase of daisies and a dimpled smile.

"Checking to see how my favorite girl is doing. Can I come in?"

She thought about it for a second, her head cocking to the side. "If my parents catch you here, you might not live to see tomorrow."

He cracked a mischievous grin. "I like to live on the edge."

She let him inside and he followed her to the family room, where she flopped back on the couch, sprawling out and claiming every inch of it.

Devin crouched in front of her, setting the vase on the floor. He gingerly moved a few wisps of hair from her face, frowning. "You don't look much better."

She lifted a hand and flapped it at him. "Stop it, you're making me blush."

He grabbed her hand, kissing it. "Where should I put these flowers?"

She looked around the room for a good spot. But what would she say if her parents asked how flowers mysteriously appeared out of thin air while they were gone? She gestured with her hand again. "Upstairs, first door on the left. You can leave them on my dresser."

He wore a cat-that-ate-the-canary grin. "You're inviting me into your bedroom? You move quick. I'm not sure I'm that kind of guy." He batted his lashes.

She squinted, acknowledging his playful banter. "You're killing me."

He kissed her hand again. "No killing today." Standing up, he took the vase up to her room and returned with two glasses of water from the kitchen. "Hydration is important, drink up."

She sat up and accepted a glass as he took a seat next to her.

Mel downed three-fourths of the water and pointed to the TV. "If you stay, you have to watch a chick-flick with me."

He motioned his head to have her move closer to him. She set her glass down on the coffee table and obliged, being wrapped in his arms, laying her head on his shoulder. They'd barely even started anything between them, but it felt natural to be with him.

Ten minutes into watching the movie, he whispered in her ear, "You don't think it's anything contagious, right?"

She moved her head to look at him. "I don't know…"

He studied her eyes. "I'm going to assume it's not. I'd hate to catch something if you decided you wanted to kiss."

Her cheeks flushed red. "Is that your way of asking?"

"It depends, is that your way of saying yes?"

She glanced at his lips. Just lying there in his arms, for those few minutes, had helped calm her. She appreciated that he wasn't too shy to ask, and not so bold as to launch at her face without invitation. She gazed into his eyes, sharing a look of wanting.

Mel leaned in and closed her eyes. His soft lips caressed hers with a couple of sweet, slow kisses. He then nibbled her lower lip, drawing it in. She returned the nibble, following his example.

Her heart picked up the pace and his breathing quickened. He moved his hands to hold the back of her head, leaning in for something more than just a simple kiss. He felt like the sun on a warm spring day, like every part of him was designed just for her.

He slowed down and pulled back, leaving her with the soft caresses that he had started with. Mel caught her breath and studied his face; Devin was beaming and gazing into her eyes.

"They're beautiful. Your eyes."

She smiled. He glanced up at her hair. The absolute maximum Mel could muster that day was to put on a bra and brush her teeth, both of which she was now immensely grateful for. Though she was in cute pajamas, they were still pajamas. And her hair had to be an embarrassing, disheveled mess. She moved her hand up to smooth out her hair, but Devin grabbed her hand.

"I brought more than the flowers to cheer you up." He reached into his pocket with his other hand.

She smirked. "I think you've already done a good job of that."

He pulled out what looked like a piece of jade stone carved into a triangle, hanging from a long chain. "Can I put it on you?"

"It's beautiful."

He went around to the back of the couch and fastened the chain around her neck, leaving a kiss there before sitting down again.

She held the pendant in her hands for a moment. "I'll have to get a shorter chain." It was far too long; it would hide under her shirt at its current length.

"No, it's meant to be that way." He smiled. "Then it's our secret. Turn it around."

The pendant had a sun carved into it. "It's supposed to be worn that way, too, with the sun facing you. It's like a permanent hug from me." He winked. "Will you wear it for me? All the time?"

She marveled at the workmanship. "Yes, definitely."

"That's exactly what I wanted to hear."

He gave her a peck on the lips and they went back to watching the movie. With his arms wrapped around her again, she felt comfortable, calmer, better.

She couldn't focus on the movie much, distracted by the moment they'd just shared. She smiled at the warmth of his body, at his assertiveness, at how natural it felt to be there in his arms.

An hour later the credits were rolling. Mel was nervous about what was going to happen next. She'd never kissed anyone, and that had been quite a doozy.

"Can I ask a favor?" She shifted from his embrace, turning to face him. "Can we keep this, what's between us, well … between us?"

"Is this about the 'your parents would probably murder me' thing?"

"Well, yeah. But not just them." She wrinkled her nose. "It's not fair to Zach. I don't want to parade it around him now that I know how he feels. I just want us to be discreet."

Devin looked disappointed. "I get it. I would be ashamed of me, too."

"No, I swear, it's not..." She noticed he couldn't keep a straight face and lightly punched him in the shoulder. "Don't be a jerk."

"Sorry." He laughed, rubbing his shoulder. "I'm just kidding. I totally get it." He stood up and reached down to her, helping her up. He drew her in close, his hands on her lower back. "I'm good with secrets, they make things more fun."

Mel looked up at the ceiling, shaking her head and taking in a deep breath. She couldn't have wiped the smile off of her face if she had tried.

"Do I get to ask a favor, too?" he asked.

She looked back at him. "What?"

"One more kiss before I go?"

She put her arms around his neck and slowly, gently caressed his lips with hers.

The sound of the garage door opening startled them.

"Crap!" she yelled. "Take the kitchen door to the patio, then go around to the gate."

He stole one more kiss, like his life depended on it, before dashing down the hall and out the kitchen door. Mel lay back down on the couch, pretending to be asleep, making sure the necklace was tucked under her shirt.

"Hey, sweetie, we're home," her mom called. "How are you doing?"

Mel gave the best performance she could muster of opening her eyes and stretching. "Home already? I'm starting to feel better."

***

Mel was grateful Zach didn't bring up his feelings for her again. It seemed more natural for them to pretend he hadn't professed romantic feelings, to allow their friendship to continue as it had been. While things were unspoken and calm with Zach, and her parents had technically given her permission to date, she didn't want to do anything to jeopardize what she was starting with Devin. Under the radar, they didn't have to deal with Ben's date-stalking, or her parents' rigid dating rules.

She and Devin tried to be as discreet as possible around others. Pretending was harder than she thought it would be—her stomach fluttered at the very sight of him. But they did their best, holding hands under a blanket at movie night, resting hands on thighs under the cafeteria table. Her focus would flee every time he would slowly draw on the palms of her hands with his fingertips; the lighter his touch, the more distracted she became.

Once winter break started, they resorted to talking on the phone more. Her parents wanted to have family night more often than usual, so they weren't having group get-togethers at their place during the break. Still wanting to see each other, Devin and Mel knew they'd have to be sneaky. Right before Christmas, they planned to rendezvous at the mall to have a date, under the guise of Mel needing to do last-minute Christmas shopping.

"I just need to pick up a couple more things," she told her parents after dinner. "But is it okay if I'm back late? Heather and I talked about watching a movie." She swallowed the lump in her throat. She wasn't accustomed to lying, least of all to her parents. They'd given their permission to date, but after how the Blake disaster ended, with a near-kiss ... she knew they wouldn't approve of her relationship with Devin.

"That should be fine as long as it's not too late. You're sure you don't need the car?" her mom asked.

"No. She's picking me up." Starting to sweat, Mel looked down at her phone. "I better get going. Love you."

"Make good choices," her dad called out as she left through the front door.

She closed her eyes and breathed in the cool air. A text came in from Zach.

<What are you up to tonight?>

Mel sighed while trying to think of a lie. She didn't want to risk him showing up at the mall. Since she'd already used Heather as a cover with her parents, she figured she might as well double-down on it. <Girls' night at Heather's.>

Devin's text came in. <On my way.>

She walked to the end of the block and waited for his car to pull up. The lies were exhausting, but seeing his bright smile melted away some of the stress. She hopped in the car and he leaned over for a kiss.

"I've missed you!"

Her heart fluttered. "I missed you, too. Let's get out of here."

As they walked the mall hand-in-hand, Mel reminded Devin, "I really do need to do some shopping."

He was helping her pick out a gift for her dad when she decided to bring up the elephant in the room.

"Is this... Are we ... exclusive?" she asked. "Like I said, this is all new to me and I don't want to assume the wrong thing."

He raised an eyebrow. "Unless you're running around with some guy I don't know about, I thought that's what this was."

She chuckled. "Definitely not. Just making sure." She bit her lip. "I've been thinking about a present for you ... but ... wasn't sure, and don't know what you want."

His warm smile matched the cheery mood of the holiday music playing in the store. "I already have the perfect present. I get to spend time with you."

She arched an eyebrow. "You know that's pretty much the cheesiest thing I've ever heard, right?"

He let out a breathy chuckle. "Maybe. I'm not sure what to get you, either."

She shrugged. "Let's not worry about it. I really don't need anything."

Minutes later, Mel was sorting through ties, trying to pick out one for her dad. She hated shopping for him; he was the hardest to shop for, of anyone she knew.

Devin stood behind her and wrapped his arms around her midriff. He rested his chin on her shoulder. "I like the yellow one."

She agreed. Though she feigned indecision for a couple more minutes, savoring the warmth of his embrace.

With some proper shopping under their belts and a couple bags at their feet, they sat on a bench near the food court, sharing a large smoothie. Mel sat sideways, her legs bent over Devin's lap, her feet on the bench at his side.

"Guess what?" she said.

He smiled. "Mmm … I got nothin'."

She leaned over and whispered in his ear, "I bought us some time to watch a movie if you want. I told my parents I was going to go watch one with Heather."

He laughed. "That's awesome. You know, you were such a good girl when I first met you."

The giddiness drained from her face. But he wasn't completely wrong… She had changed. She was now the kind of girl that lied to her parents, and snuck around, stealing kisses and even making out with a secret boyfriend. "Thanks." Mel twisted to set her feet on the floor, now facing the same direction as him. Fidgeting with her hands, she whispered, "That makes me feel like a two-dollar hooker."

He huffed in frustration. "I didn't mean it like that. C'mon. You're still a good girl, an amazing girl. I love…" He paused, before adding, "…spending time with you."

She looked over at him with a somber face. "I don't know. Every time we do something like this, I'm happy. But then I go home or see Zach, and I'm tired of lying. Maybe we should just tell people."

He rocked his head side to side. "I know we've kept this a secret because *you* wanted to, but I'll admit, I kind of like not having us under a microscope." He clasped his hands together, putting them under his chin. "But … I get it. It sucks having to lie to people you care about. How about … let's talk about it after school starts back up again?" He grinned. "I would rather your dad not kill me at Christmas time."

Her smile returned. "Deal." She slung her legs back up on the bench.

"Are you still wearing the necklace I gave you?" he asked.

"Every day, with the sun-side to my heart," she proudly reported.

"Mmm, that makes me happy." He reached over and kissed her, one hand holding her neck and hair, the other on her waist. He moved down to nuzzle her on the neck and she let out a giggle.

She looked up and realized they now had an audience. Her eyes grew wide. "Oh crap!" she whispered.

Devin immediately stopped. "What?" He turned to see what she was looking at.

Ben was standing a few yards away, staring at them. And rather livid by the looks of it.

"What if he tells my parents?" she panicked under her breath.

"I'll handle it." Devin cleared his throat as he got up, shoving his hands in his pockets. He approached Ben, who had been walking by with Heather.

Mel doubted Ben cared what Devin had to say. And it wasn't really his concern who, or if, she dated. They'd been over that before. Heather awkwardly backed up, allowing the guys to chat more privately. Mel wondered if Heather's presence there would help or hurt her alibi with her parents, assuming Devin could convince Ben not to blab.

They weren't that far away, but Mel still couldn't hear what they were saying. Whatever it was, it looked like a heated discussion.

Out of nowhere, Ben shoved Devin.

"Ben!" she yelled.

Ben looked over at Mel, still seething mad. He turned back to Devin, aggressively pointing at him, whispering what she could only assume by their behavior were threats.

Devin looked in Heather's direction, then back to Ben, and had the last word. He turned, stomping back to Mel and picking up their shopping bags. "Let's get you home."

Making their way to the parking garage, Mel grappled to understand why Ben was the way he was. Maybe she *should* have asked more about his biological family. Maybe they had violent tendencies. Why was he so mercurial, so spastic? Maybe he'd been separated from siblings in the system and was taking this foster 'brother' thing a bit too seriously?

Devin and Mel hopped in his car and drove in silence for the first five minutes.

"He's a moron," she said. "He should be medicated."

"He's not going to cause problems with your parents. Just don't say anything to him." He kept his eyes on the road, puckering his lips in anger. "It'll just make things worse."

"You're sure?" She cocked her head. "Maybe I *should* say something to my parents, if he's going to be mental like this."

"No." He threw her a glance as they went over a speed bump. "I promise, he won't say anything."

She gnawed on her bottom lip. Ben didn't like Devin. He hadn't liked Blake, either. He'd always been moody with Zach. She shook her head. Ben hated all the guys that showed any interest in her. But he'd made it clear he didn't want to date her. And he was with Stacy, anyway.

"What did he say to you?"

Devin huffed. "I don't want to talk about it, okay? Let's just pretend this never happened."

They parked a few houses down from her place so her parents wouldn't see who she'd actually gone with.

He ruffled his hair. "I'm sorry, okay? I'm being stupid."

"What do you mean? You have nothing to apologize for." He wasn't making any sense.

"No, I'm not being smart. I just … really like you. And … this is just making things complicated."

She frowned and tried to say something, but it was hard with her heart being ripped out. She felt tears coming to her eyes. This was her first boyfriend, so she didn't know what it felt like to be dumped, but it sounded like he was thinking about it. "Are you… Do you want to break up?"

His head jerked over to look at her, frowning. "Do you?"

"No. But I get it. I wouldn't want to go out with me right now, either."

"Come here," he said, sliding to the edge of his seat. She moved to the center, and he put his hand up to her face, wiping away a tear as it tried to run away. "You are … amazing. I'd be willing to risk a hell of a lot to keep you."

She gave him a hesitant smile.

"I'm placing my bet on you, okay?"

"Yeah," she whispered.

"But maybe let's just take a step back. I probably shouldn't see you until after winter break," he said, moving his hand away from her face.

"Yeah. Fine," she answered dejectedly. "You're sure he won't say anything?"

Devin gave her a soft smile. "Yes."

"I, uh, I'm still wondering if *we* should say something." She rubbed the back of her neck. "What if he tries something … tries to hurt me?" He obviously had violent tendencies…

Devin raised his eyebrows. "Has he ever tried anything with you before?"

She shook her head.

He shrugged. "He won't hurt you. He's all bark, no bite." He must have sensed her continued hesitance, reaching out and holding her hand. "Let me handle this one, okay? I'll take care of Ben." He gave her hand a double squeeze. "And I'll take care of you."

"Okay." Mel forced a smile and grabbed her shopping bags, getting out of the car.

While lying in bed that night, she heard the door open downstairs—Ben had come home for the night. She resisted the urge to confront him, instead remaining in bed, not sure whether to be angry or sad about the way the night had ended. If she told her parents about Ben's crazy behavior, she'd have to fess up to lying to them and sneaking behind their backs. She double-checked her door lock and gave Devin the benefit of the doubt. Shortly before falling asleep, a text came in.

<Things will work out. <3 >

And then another.

<I'm not going anywhere.>

Chapter 9

DEVIN WAS RIGHT; THINGS WOULD work out. At least on paper. The next morning while Mel was eating cereal at the kitchen table, Ben joined her, sitting across from her, just looking at her.

Staring at her cereal bowl, uncomfortable about his gaze, she wondered what Devin would say about this. Mel looked up. "Do you have something you'd like to say?"

Ben looked intently into her eyes. "I would *never* hurt you."

She bit her lip, studying his face. Devin must have told him off, sharing that concern.

"That doesn't mean I have to like all of your friends. Or *secret* boyfriends."

She glared.

"Hey, sweetie," her mom's voice came from the hallway.

Ben stood up, putting a hand on the table. "I've said what I needed to say."

Mel's mom's cheery voice drew closer, and she appeared from the hallway. "Oh, hi, Ben. Good morning." She turned back to Mel as Ben took a couple steps back. "I only have these two wrapping papers left. Which one do you want?"

Mel watched Ben, who was now standing behind her mom, out of her view. He shoved his hands in his pockets, ever so slightly raising his eyebrows. Was it a stand-off? Or a truce? He wasn't tattling on Mel.

She focused back on her mom. "I'll take either."

Pam looked the rolls of wrapping paper over once more. "Use up the rest of this red one. I'll take the blue."

"Sounds good." Mel glanced back up at Ben. *We'll call it a truce.* "No problem here." She smiled at her mom. "Red is much more festive and I think that'll be more than enough for what I need."

Out of the corner of her eye, she thought she saw Ben nod before he left the room. She hated this kind of drama, especially around Christmas. As Mel finished her cereal, she sported a small grin. Devin must've been pretty persuasive.

She and Ben never said a single word about the incident after that. Her parents never brought anything up. Devin kept a steady stream of texts and calls coming her way. Christmas was awesome— her mom and dad shocked her by gifting her a family trip to Costa Rica. They mentioned going for spring break, or at the start of summer; the reservations were flexible.

Ben was uncharacteristically happy on Christmas Day, which was only that much more humbling to Mel, reminding her that although he probably didn't want to be stuck at her house any more than she wanted him there, he didn't have any choice in the matter, and this was a safe, happy home and family. They even exchanged a smile as she hugged the gift he'd bought her—a new watercolor set. She'd only gotten him a basket of sweets and other junk food because that was what her mom had recommended, but he seemed to enjoy it.

New Year's Eve was also a quiet family event this year. Mel was bummed her parents insisted on not having friends over; she'd secretly hoped to rally the posse and sneak away at midnight for a smooch with Devin. But … it was probably good to take time and work on her relationship with her parents after all the lies, even if they weren't aware of them.

***

On New Year's Day, Mel invited Zach over to hang out. She could hardly look him in the eye when she opened the door. Even their hug had some obvious hesitance from both sides.

"Come on in." She smiled and turned to the family room.

"Yeah. I'm glad we finally get to hang out." He followed her and they sat down on the couch.

She had tried to figure out what to say to him. About not responding to his declaration of feelings, about dating Devin. The only thing that came to her mind was 'Sorry, but I chose Devin instead.' And that just didn't feel right. She was at a loss for words.

"So, how's the new puppy?" she asked. He'd been texting her pictures of the new golden retriever they'd gotten for Christmas.

He smiled. "Good. He's super cute."

She nodded. This was painful. At times in their friendship, she'd thought about him that way, in a more-than-friends kind of way. But she hadn't said anything, worried about ruining things between them. And now that *he* had brought it up, and things hadn't progressed, she was terrified things might be ruined between them anyway. She couldn't win.

"Costa Rica? Are you excited?" he asked.

"Yeah. Of course, it'll be awesome."

She noticed his hands fidgeting. His face was a bit whiskery. Was he not shaving because it was the holidays, or because she'd hurt him by not saying anything and he was having a hard time, or because he was trying to send a message—that he used to care about her opinion and didn't anymore? Then again, he could have just needed to buy a new razor, too.

The small talk was hard, the tension thick.

"So, uh, just you and me today?" he asked.

"Yeah." It wasn't like they hadn't talked, or been in each other's presence since the dance, but this was their first solo face-to-face hang-out since then. She read his face. "Just us. 'Cause I want to spend time with my best friend." She pursed her lips, hoping that's what they still were.

He smiled and nodded. "I like spending time with my best friend, too. Works for me."

Relief washed over her, but she didn't know if she could handle more of the small talk. "Movie?"

"Sounds good."

"Great. You get to pick this time. I'll go make some popcorn."

A few minutes later, Mel returned with a bag of microwave popcorn. "Sorry, we only had the low-salt stuff."

Zach quickly turned off his phone, tucking it away in his pocket. "Okay, sure."

She did her best to ignore it, but it wasn't like him to be secretive like that. Then again, she could hardly judge, after keeping him in the dark about her relationship with Devin. For all she knew, Zach had moved on and there was a girl he wasn't ready to tell her about.

"Cool." She set the popcorn on the coffee table and settled down on the couch. And shifted a little further away from Zach. And then back to be closer again. *When did our proximity matter?* If he still had feelings for her, would sitting too close give him the wrong idea? If she sat too far away, would it be insulting? *How close did we used to sit?* She tried to settle on a place. An inch closer might be too close, an inch further felt like it might as well be a mile.

"Mel?"

She looked over to meet his gaze.

Zach tilted his head to the right, looked down at the cushion between them, and then met her eyes again. "Don't be weird. I don't bite." And then he grinned and pelted her with a fistful of popcorn.

She laughed, scooching a bit closer while pulling kernels out of her hair.

Zach chose a scary movie. One of those that has you screaming 'No! Don't go into the basement alone!' It wasn't really to Mel's taste, but since he had let her choose the last time and it had been a Jane Austen, she was happy to go with anything that wasn't focused on romance.

By the end of his visit, what had been said—or what didn't need to be said, at least for the time being—was enough. Their goodbye hug was much more natural.

***

Once school started back up, Mel and Devin agreed to go much slower, but she was still beyond excited to see him. They gave each other a simple hug at their lockers and didn't even touch each other the rest of the day.

There was usually a buzz of excitement the first few days after coming back from winter break, but the school's mood was downcast on account of the news that Stacy had been diagnosed with leukemia and had to leave the state for treatment.

Mel felt a twinge of guilt that she hadn't made more of an effort to reconcile with her. She wondered if maybe Stacy's sudden humble apology in the lunch line stemmed from her already knowing something was wrong. And Mel felt sorry for Ben, who had obviously gotten pretty close to Stacy. Maybe that was part of why he'd been acting like such a jerk before—he probably knew about it a while ago and didn't know how to process it.

On the third morning back, between first and second period, Mel opened her locker to unload some books, only to cock her head in confusion at the item before her. She moved a hand up to her neck. *Huh ... I could've sworn I...* No. Obviously, she hadn't. She hadn't put on Devin's necklace that morning. She couldn't have. Because it was sitting right there. She didn't recall taking it off and leaving it in her locker. She vaguely remembered she'd taken it off the night before and put it on her nightstand. She shook off the weird feeling like the bad case of deja vu it was, then slipped on the necklace, smiling as the sun symbol touched her skin, sliding down her shirt.

Not more than a minute later, Devin strolled up to his locker. "Fancy meeting you here."

She grinned. "Coincidence? Or destiny that we're locker neighbors?"

Devin dialed the combination. "Whatever you call it, I know I'm not mad about it." He winked.

Mel unzipped her backpack and pulled out a thin, wrapped gift. She handed it to Devin.

"What's this?" He carefully opened it, smiling at the painting she'd made for him.

"I guess I should have asked for a request, but I also wanted it to be a surprise." It was a new watercolor of a seaside landscape.

"I love it." He beamed. "But I thought we agreed on no presents."

She shrugged. "You told me a while ago you wanted a painting. We're well into the new year, anyway." She moved a thumb up, underneath the chain of her necklace. "We can call this an *early* Christmas present if we call mine a *late* Christmas present."

He carefully put the painting on the top shelf of his locker. "I can accept that." He glanced over at her neck. "Still calm on the home front? Ben didn't cause any more drama, right?"

She closed her locker, leaning up against it. "Nope. All good there. I still don't know how you did it."

"Isn't the answer obvious?" He put a book in his locker. "It's the power of that necklace. It's our good-luck charm." He closed his locker with a smile.

She opened her arms and they shared a hug.

"Mmm, you smell good. New perfume?" he asked.

Mel pulled back. "We girls call that 'shampoo.'"

He chuckled as the bell rang. "I'll see you later."

***

Mel had gym as her last class for the new semester. It was nice to take a long shower and not have to rush to get to the next class or be sweaty for the rest of the day. A week after returning from break, she was taking her time brushing her hair, straightening out her necklace, and even applying some mascara. She was in better spirits now that Devin was holding her hand again. Only under the table at lunch, but she'd take it. The locker room had cleared out. She swung her backpack over her shoulder and opened the door to the hallway.

"Walters." Blake was leaning against the painted brick wall, all alone.

She rolled her eyes at the thought of him waiting for her. "What do you want, Blake?"

"I just want to talk." He grinned. "You look different."

"Okaaay?"

He walked up to her. "I think you should give me another chance." He had his usual arrogant smile, the one she'd convinced herself was genuine, before realizing he was a handsy creep.

"Sorry, I'm seeing someone." She started to walk away.

"Really? Who's that?"

Everything about this exchange was rubbing her the wrong way. "That's none of your business." She scowled.

"I know your type." He stepped in front of her, blocking her path.

She lifted her eyebrows. "What type is that?"

He moved closer. "You think you're better than everyone else. You think there's something special about you."

"You're crazy." She shook her head, trying to fathom why she had ever given him a chance. And why she'd stood up for him in the first place. Turning to walk around him, he surprised Mel by grabbing her wrist and whipping her around.

"Maybe I'm just impatient." He furrowed his brow, twisting her arm painfully.

"What's wrong with you? Leave me alone!" She tried to yank her arm free, but he had a tight grip.

He twisted harder and she cried out in pain. He pushed her against the wall. "I bet your boyfriend thinks you're a great kisser. I can give a second opinion."

"You're sick, Blake. Let me go!" Her heart was racing, but her body just … froze.

He was peering into her eyes and leaning in.

"Leave her alone!"

It was like fourth grade all over again. Zach was at the end of the hallway, fists clenched at his sides, there to fight for her. He wasn't scrawny, but there was no way he could win in a fight against Blake.

Blake loosened his grip but didn't let go completely.

A deep shout roared down from the other end of the hallway. "BLAKE HUNTERS! MY OFFICE. NOW!" It was Tom.

Blake quickly let go and backed away, putting his hands up like it was all some kind of misunderstanding. He scowled at Zach and Mel, before walking down the hall as ordered.

Zach offered her a hug, and she started to cry in his arms.

"It's okay," he whispered. After a couple minutes, he stepped back, wiping up her fresh mascara streaks. "Do you want me to call your parents for you? Or, um…" He cleared his throat. "Devin? Where is he?"

"I don't know, he's usually tutoring after school." She looked down.

"I know about you two," he confessed.

She looked up and frowned sheepishly.

He let out a small chuckle. "You suck at hiding how you feel about a guy as much as you suck at knowing how a guy feels about you."

Her heart was heavy with guilt, having kept it a secret from him. He was more understanding than she'd given him credit for. "I'm sorry. I should have said something. I was a jerk to leave you hanging."

He shrugged, though his eyes still showed disappointment.

"It's not like I've never thought about you like that before. Or that you're not attractive. It's just ... timing."

He rubbed his hands together uncomfortably at her confession. "That doesn't really make me feel better, but thanks." He tried to force a smile. "We don't really need to talk about that right now. Let me walk you home."

***

Once they got to her house, Zach led Mel into the family room.

"What are *you* doing here?" She was surprised to see Devin sitting on her couch.

"I'll ... leave you guys to it." Zach sounded just as confused. "Text me later?" He gave her another hug before leaving.

Devin got up and offered his arms. She buried herself in them as he set his chin on her head. "I should've been there for you."

After a minute, he invited Mel to sit together. He held her hands. "Is your arm okay?"

She wiggled it and furrowed her brow in confusion. "Yeah, actually. In all the chaos of everything, I kind of forgot about that."

He gave her a weak smile, something still clearly weighing heavily on him. "Blake," he paused, "is a problem. I can't really explain it, but I don't think he's going to just leave you alone. He's probably trying to provoke you." He paused again. "Or me."

She was understandably confused by his cryptic warning. Especially since Blake didn't seem to even know *who* she was dating.

He buried his face in his hands. "Why does this have to be so complicated?" He took a deep breath. "Just, try not to react. Ignore him. Find a way to keep your distance. I'm sure he'll be suspended for at least a few days, so that should help."

"It's not like I went looking for trouble," she said, defeated.

"No, I know. Cause you're a good girl, right?" He winked, gently lifting her chin with his hand.

He always knew how to make her grin.

"I see you're still wearing the necklace?" He glanced at the chain visible around her neck. "Well, it wasn't a very good luck charm today." He frowned dramatically. "I think it must be getting low on batteries."

"And how does one replace the batteries on a stone?" she asked, playing along.

He jerked his head back, dropping his jaw, as if she had insulted him. "No, no, no. One does not *replace* the batteries. One must *recharge* the batteries."

"Oh, so sorry." She smiled more sincerely, biting her lip. "How does one *recharge* the batteries?"

"Let me show you how." He pulled her in for a kiss. It was as sweet and wonderful as the first. Not as passionate, but…

"Wait a second," she whispered, pushing him away. "I saw my mom's car out there."

He grimaced. "Yeah. I, uh … talked to your parents?" He squeaked like he was asking a question rather than making a statement. "I dropped by to see you, and then I decided to come clean about wanting to date you. And," he shrugged, "I lived to tell the tale."

She threw her arms around him, giving him a quick peck, and then a tight squeeze. For a split second she was annoyed that he'd gone behind her back to talk to them, but she was too happy to hold a grudge. Zach knew, her parents knew—there didn't have to be any more secrets.

She stepped back to look at him. "I don't know what spell you had to put on them, to make *that* miracle happen. But I'm sure they didn't give you carte blanche to make out in the family room. You should head out."

She saw him to the door, and he gave her one last tight squeeze before leaving.

"Love ya," he whispered in her ear.

She didn't know what to say to that, and luckily, he didn't linger awkwardly, expecting a response. Perhaps it was just a knee-jerk reaction, like when you accidentally tell a customer service stranger 'okay, love ya, bye' over the phone.

She slowly made her way to the stairs. When she looked up, Ben was sitting at the top, within hearing range. Her trigger response was to be annoyed at his eavesdropping, but he surprised her. He shifted to one side, leaving enough room for her, then patted the carpeted stair for her to come sit down.

"You alright?" He frowned.

"I'll be fine. How did everyone hear about it so quickly?" She plopped down next to him.

"The school called your mom."

She nodded, realizing she and Zach probably should have stopped by the office before leaving. "I'm sorry about Stacy. I know you guys are close."

He smiled. "It's fine. I'll see her soon enough." He looked down at his hands, speaking softly. "I know I sometimes act … irrationally. You think I'm a jerk, and that I don't care. But I do, okay?"

"Thanks." She had to give him some credit—he'd spotted Blake as a perv from the start. *But … he still doesn't like Zach or Devin.*

They sat for a second, each waiting to see if the other had anything else to add to the conversation.

"So," he broke the silence, "you really like Devin?"

Mel laughed. "We're not having this conversation, Ben." She stood to continue walking up the stairs, briefly looking down at him. "But I mean it, thanks for caring."

Mel went upstairs and washed her face, then headed to her room to grab her painting supplies. Her mom appeared in the doorway, frowning.

"I wasn't sure if you would want to talk about what happened, or if you needed some time to yourself."

Mel put her things down and gave her mom a big hug. She closed her eyes, processing what Blake had done. "I... I don't know."

"That's okay, sweetie. If you want to talk, you know your dad and I are always willing to listen."

"Thanks, Mom. You guys are the best." She was beyond grateful to not have another scolding about her poor judgment for her first date, and ... they were cool with Devin and her dating.

Her mom left the room as Mel picked her things back up and went downstairs to paint. With each brush stroke, she replayed her stupid mistake of a date with Blake. And then the events of that afternoon. He was so hot and cold; she couldn't make out what had prompted him to lash out, out of nowhere like that. In the end, his motivations didn't matter. She was mostly disappointed in herself. What was the purpose of her parents paying for self-defense classes, if she was just going to freeze up? It had been a couple years since she'd taken them, but still...

By the time she sorted through her train of thought, a beautiful, thorned rose had emerged on the page.

***

Devin was right that Blake would be suspended for a few days. Tom called Mel into his office the next day to talk about the incident.

"How are you doing? I talked to your dad, he said you're alright, physically?"

"Yeah, he didn't hurt me that bad."

"It doesn't matter how much he hurt you, that behavior is unacceptable. I wanted you to know we're taking it seriously. If he approaches you again, or threatens you, in any way, let me know. Don't even waste your time talking to a teacher. I'm not too busy, alright?"

She nodded, wishing she could give him a hug. She was lucky to have someone like him watching out for her. But this wasn't her family friend after Sunday dinner; right now, he was the principal, in his office. "Thanks, I'll let you know if there are any more problems."

"Can you tell me what was said? What the discussion was about, from your side of things?"

She went over what had happened.

He squinted. "Do you know what would have caused him to react like that out of nowhere? He didn't say anything odd? You didn't do or say anything that he reacted to?"

She furrowed her brow in confusion; she'd just explained the whole situation, not leaving anything out. "No… I'm not sure what you're getting at… Are you trying to say this is somehow *my* fault?"

He straightened up in his chair and shook his head with a frown. "No. Never. I would never blame the victim. I'm just trying to do a thorough review for our records."

He dismissed her back to class. Mel slowly meandered through the hallways and couldn't help but wonder why it felt like more than a simple interview about an incident. Tom's probing felt insulting. It was a pretty open-and-shut case. Blake was an egotistical, perverted jerk. She'd frozen up. That was … it. She knew she was probably just overthinking it, but why would Tom doubt her, question her behavior and motives? She never did anything to deserve Blake's assault, or Tom's scrutiny.

Chapter 10

WHEN BLAKE CAME BACK FROM suspension, he kept his distance, though his eyes threw daggers every time they met Mel's.

She did her best to move on, which wasn't too difficult with how over the moon she was about finally being able to be more public about her relationship with Devin. It was out in the open. Their hand-holding was 'above the table' now, but they tried to keep PDA to a minimum around Zach so things wouldn't be too awkward. And she was seriously grateful her parents didn't sit her down for another sex talk. They only stressed that their dating rules still applied. Curfews, expecting to know where she was going, etc.

While they could now date openly, Mel still tried to keep things fairly normal, under her parents' rules. Some days after school, Zach would come over and they'd study, hang out. Her parents allowed him to bring his new puppy over once it was better potty-trained.

More of her after-school time was spent with Devin, again, at her place. Aside from studying, he tried teaching her how to dance. She taught him to play several board and card games. She was astounded that he hadn't played most of the standard games everyone knows.

"This isn't my favorite, but it's still a well-known one. We each get armies, and basically take over the world," she explained while setting it up on the kitchen table.

"Risk, huh?" He shrugged. "Let's give it a go."

He was doing really well for a first-time player, but didn't seem to actually enjoy it much. He was distracted, distant.

"Imagine if it were this simple," Devin mused. "To win or lose an actual war this way."

She glanced at him, perplexed. "I guess I've never really thought much about it."

She took her turn. When she finished and looked up, she caught him staring at her, grinning.

"What's on your mind?" she asked.

"I'm just happy." He picked up his dice and rolled them from his palm to his fingers, and back. "Where would you go, if you had no limitations?"

"Like on a trip?"

"Yeah."

She thought for a moment. "I actually have a whole list of places I want to go. My parents have always said I should take some time off before deciding what college I want to attend. They say people waste too much money getting degrees they don't use. So, I'm hoping to save up and travel a little while I figure it out. Somewhere warm would be nice. Honestly, I'd considered Costa Rica on my short list of fun places to visit. But I guess my parents beat me to that."

"You don't think it would be too weird to live in a different culture?"

"It's not like I'm planning on moving there permanently, it would just be a visit. I don't want to move anywhere too far away from my parents."

He nodded thoughtfully and started his turn.

"What about you, have you traveled much?" she asked.

"Not really, not compared to a lot of people."

He still never talked about his family. He'd get awkward every time she asked, so she'd stopped asking a while ago, figuring he'd get there when he was ready. But his uncharacteristically downcast mood prompted her to give it another go.

"So, if your family never plays board games, or goes on vacations, what did you guys do growing up?"

He rested his chin on his hand. "My parents—"

Ben walked into the kitchen to grab something from the fridge. Devin stopped talking, instead following Ben with his eyes. Only after he left, Devin continued, "My mom is a nurse and my dad is in the military. I came here to live with my uncle because they're gone so much."

She frowned. "I'm sorry. That sucks. But that's cool your dad is in the service. Tell him thank you next time you talk to him."

He smiled. "I'm sure he'll appreciate that."

She figured she wouldn't push things any further. He still seemed like he wasn't ready to open up more. "You know you can talk to me, right? I'd like to think I'm a good listener."

He gave her another half-hearted smile. "I know, and you are."

It killed her that he was struggling with something. But she promised herself she wouldn't be a clingy, or jealous, or needy, girlfriend.

***

Mel won the game, though she was certain Devin let her win.

"You changed your strategy, I'm sure you should have won." She put her hands on her hips in accusation.

"I don't know what you're talking about." He smirked.

She walked him out the front door, standing on the porch. She squinted playfully. "No letting me win. You only do that to little kids, and I'm pretty sure I haven't been one of those for a while."

He wrapped his thumbs through her belt loops and pulled her close. "No. You are *definitely* not a little kid. I'd say you're an amazing woman." He leaned in and gave her a sweet kiss.

She couldn't help but smile. "You're pretty amazing yourself."

He gazed lovingly into her eyes. "And I *didn't* just let you win. Sometimes, you have to change your strategy, to get the results you want. I'd say a slow death in the game gave me more time with you tonight."

She shook her head. Wrapping her arms around him, she gave him an appreciative kiss. And she *really* appreciated his sweetness.

His phone rang in his pocket, ruining their moment. She pulled back, and he looked at his phone, smiling. He pushed the ignore button and shoved it in his pocket. He picked up where they'd left off. His phone rang again. He pulled it out and turned it off.

"You're sure you don't need to answer that?"

"Yep." He grinned before meeting her lips once more.

Mel groaned when the front door opened behind her a couple minutes later.

"Mel, I need to do some laundry. Will you move yours?" Ben asked, squinting at Devin.

She glared. "Seriously? I'm kind of busy right now."

Devin rubbed the back of his neck, looking at Ben with a menacing grin. "It's funny, isn't it? It's almost like he actually *is* your brother. They're meant to be annoying, aren't they?"

Ben scowled. "Maybe you should go home."

"I probably should." Devin gave her one last peck on the lips before taking off.

Mel followed Ben into the house. "What's your problem? We've gone over this."

"I just don't think you should be getting so serious with him."

"Why?" she challenged. "What do you know that I don't?"

He shrugged. "I'm just saying, you shouldn't."

"Wow. That's a pretty valid reason. I'll make sure to file that away." She grabbed her laundry from the dryer and went up to her room for the remainder of the night.

She couldn't help but wonder, though—who had been calling Devin? Was there something Ben knew that she didn't? Or was he only being his usual meddling, annoying, self? Her stomach knotted, thinking of how Ben had called it on Blake. Could he be right about Devin, too? No. The only thing Blake and Devin ever shared were their interest in her. Devin was a thousand times better.

She looked up to her ceiling, staring at the glow-in-the-dark stars. Devin had disliked Blake, too. She snorted out loud. *Devin probably doesn't object to himself, and I care about his opinion just a smidge more than Ben's.*

***

After a couple months in a secret relationship, and then bumming around the house openly as a couple, they were finally going to go on a legitimate date. Valentine's was coming up and Mel insisted she didn't need any sort of elaborate plans, she just wanted to spend time with Devin away from the constant supervision at her house. Keeping her parents' rules, they decided on a basic dinner and movie.

After a nice Italian meal, avoiding anything too garlicky, they went to the theater for a new release they'd compromised on. Devin was more interested in it than Mel was, but she was plenty happy just to be with him.

The credits were starting, and he didn't waste any time pushing up the armrest separating them. She snuggled next to him as he put an arm around her. She kissed his cheek and smiled. He sweetly tickled her neck with his fingers and she guided his lips down to hers with a hand under his chin.

Their kiss didn't last long as he pulled back, brow furrowed. "You're not wearing your necklace?"

"Oh." She frowned. It was just a little piece of jewelry, but it was something special from him. She regretted not taking the time to put it on. And, of course, it would be on a romantic date that he'd notice. "The chain got a little tangled. After my run and shower this afternoon, I didn't get around to putting it back on."

"It's been a few hours?" he asked, reading her face.

"Yeah. Just a couple." He was overreacting … showing a possessive side she hadn't seen before. She cleared her throat, feeling uneasy. "It's just a necklace."

He moved his arm down, no longer holding her. "It just means a lot to me. It's … a family thing."

"Oh, you didn't tell me that." The guilt piled up, knowing he missed his parents. "I'll put it on as soon as I get home. You're not … mad at me, are you?"

"No. Of course not." He shifted away from her. "I feel like snacks, after all. Any requests?"

She shook her head, watching him walk away to get concessions. After a couple minutes of him being gone, Blake walked into the theater and her stomach knotted. He was holding a girl's hand and glared at Mel once he realized she was in the theater. He slid his hand into the girl's back jeans pocket as he guided her to a seat just a few rows in front of Mel, then promptly started to make out.

Mel rolled her eyes, determined to not let him spoil her night.

Devin came back with a huge soda and popcorn, bringing the armrest down between them to put the drink in the holder. "There we go. Lots to share," he whispered.

She shook her head again. This was her first Valentine's with a boyfriend, and he was acting weird. She picked up the soda and moved it to the armrest on her side, putting the shared one back up. "You can let me know when you want a drink." She smirked, trying to bring back their romantic moment.

He shifted in his seat and munched on a handful of popcorn.

She frowned again. "Seriously, what's wrong? If it means that much to you, I need more of an explanation. I want to enjoy some time alone with you, and right now, this is as close as we get."

He sighed. "It's nothing. Honestly. I just want to watch the movie."

"Fine." She moved the armrest down and transferred the drink back, crossing her arms.

"Is that … Blake?" he whispered.

"Yeah. Wonder if she knows what a winner she's with." Mel scowled.

He set the popcorn down in the empty seat next to him. "Let's go back to your place."

She furrowed her brow. "Why? I'm not leaving just because that jerk is here."

Someone in a nearby row shushed her.

"Please?" he pleaded. "For me?" He stood up and extended his hands.

Mel reluctantly got up.

He drove her home, parking his car and looking over at her. "I'm sorry. I'm just off today… Family stuff."

She frowned. "Fine."

Devin grabbed her hand and gave her a smile. "I promise, I'll make it up to you another time. As for tonight, we can head inside and play a game or something?"

"No. I'd rather just call it a night at this point."

He matched her frown, nodding. After walking her to the door, he left her with a tiny peck on the lips.

She went straight to her room and plopped down on her bed. Staring at the knotted chain on her nightstand, she scowled at the stupid thing. She was starting to feel pretty tired anyway, but this wasn't how she'd wanted this night to go.

Mel remembered how sweet he had been, taking care of her, when he first gave her the necklace. And how hard it was for him to be separated from his family. She sighed and unknotted it, putting it on and lying down. Even if he made it up to her, her first Valentine's with a boyfriend, like her first-ever date, would not be the kind of story worth telling her kids someday.

Luckily, he did make it up to her. The next day, he was right back to being his normal self—with a bounce in his step, a sincere apology, and plenty of affection when they could sneak it. They rescheduled their date, and he planned a fun surprise, taking her to a painting class.

Chapter 11

BEFORE MEL KNEW IT, IT was mid-March. The drama seemed to calm down on all fronts. Mel tried to talk her parents into letting her go camping with Zach's family over spring break, but they weren't having it. Instead, she'd be staying home, and talked with Heather about possibly having a girls' night at some point. While Mel's parents originally had aimed for spring break in Costa Rica, her dad had a chiropractic convention, so they decided they'd move it to right after school ended.

The Friday before the break, Mel woke up feeling off. She'd started to feel pretty worn down the night before, and hoped to sleep it off. She wasn't any better in the morning, but hated missing school and having to play catch-up.

Before heading out for the day, Mel stopped by the kitchen for her usual morning hug with her mom or dad. Instead, she found them scrambling around the room with towels, sopping up the carnage of a burst pipe or leak of some sort.

"Do you guys need help?"

Her mom waved her off. "It's okay, sweetie. We'll be fine. Have a good day at school."

Devin was late to school, so she didn't get to see him before starting classes. After missing all of her morning hugs, and feeling cruddy, she sulked a little until she saw Zach, armed with a warm hug.

But she still felt off. By the last period, she *knew* she should have taken a sick day. Nauseous and overheating, she showed up at the gym and didn't even have to ask to sit it out.

"Are you alright?" Mr. Cress, her P.E. teacher, asked. Mel didn't know him that well, though P.E. teachers weren't all that chatty about their personal lives like classroom teachers could sometimes be. He looked down at her with concern in his brown eyes. "You're pretty pale. How long have you felt this way?"

She shook her head. "I'll be fine. Last time this happened, I got better the next day."

He furrowed his brow. "Sit today out."

She watched the class from the old gym's run-down bleachers, drinking some water. She was embarrassed every time Mr. Cress would glance over or check in on her. But she got to meet a nice girl, Emily, who also had to sit out, having recently broken her ankle.

After class was dismissed, Mel returned to the locker room, getting dressed and folding up her practically unused gym clothes. Lightheaded, she realized she'd left her favorite water bottle in the gym—sipping during class had helped. She exited the locker room and crossed the hall to go grab it. The gym was empty, the doors open. She bent over into the bleachers and grabbed the bottle, right where she had forgotten it. A sudden dizzy spell forced her to sit down.

She started panicking, wondering if this was what it felt like to be drugged, or have a heart attack. She was sweating, her heart racing and breathing labored. Sure, she'd been a little off earlier in the day, but whatever was happening was coming on rather suddenly. The room spun as she felt an unsettling energy build up—like when a person is restless and can't sit still. The energy magnified by a thousand. She bent over, falling to her knees on the gym floor in pure agony. She wanted to call for help, but her voice betrayed her; her clarity of mind waned.

Mel wanted to curl into a ball until it all went away, but her body had other plans. Her muscles twisted, forcing her to hold her head up. Her face and arms were itching, as if dozens of spiders were crawling all over her.

The next thing Mel knew, her throat was closing—something had wrapped around it, strangling her. Gasping for air, she tore at the cords, fighting with every molecule of energy she could muster to free herself. She felt it tugging, pulling tighter, even stinging a little as if she were being cut.

Then a deep voice cut through the darkening haze. "I've got a weed, one of your girlfriends. Get to the gym. Let's take care of her."

As Mel was teetering on the edge of consciousness, a familiar voice lunged into the gathering darkness. "GET OFF HER, YOU LEECH!"

She heard footsteps running up behind her and a *slash*.

The cords around her neck slackened, and she finally ripped them from her throat.

Mel slumped onto her side, heaving and gasping for air. The excruciating pain from whatever was happening to her still coursed through every inch of her body.

Struggling to focus through blurred vision, Mel thought she saw Ben, of all people, and her assailant, brawling just a few feet away. They weren't just swinging punches, either. But Ben … looked different. They both did.

Ben had some sort of growths on his arms. Were they green wings? No… And when did he dye his hair? He had also never given any indication that he knew how to fight at this caliber, but he was landing punches, agile on his feet—he even kicked the other guy in the head at one point.

The other guy was mostly attacking with … dark rope? No, vines! They sprouted from his wrists and he seemed to be able to control them. If she wasn't completely incapacitated, she may have begun to question her sanity.

"Nice! Two weeds for the price of one," the backup called out as he arrived. The newest voice belonged to none other than Blake. His wrists also shot out those dark green vines, covered in small leaves. His odd ability matched his fighting partner, whom she now recognized as a kid from her English class.

"Nuren might want the female," Blake said.

Blake went after Mel with a set of vines. Ben lunged forward, using the green blades on his arms to slice them off before they reached her. Using the distraction, the other attacker wrapped a vine around Ben's leg and pulled it out from underneath him. Ben landed with a heavy *thud*.

Blake turned his attention to Ben; Mel still wasn't in any position to fight for herself. Blake wrapped vines around one of Ben's wrists. Ben grunted and kept slashing at their cords, time after time. But it was a numbers game, and they had four weapons to his two.

"I NEED YOU TO GET UP, MEL!" Ben yelled in her direction.

Did he know what he was asking?! She closed her eyes to summon every ounce of strength she could to stand up. She pushed herself to her hands and knees. A vine wrapped around her ankle and she reached back, grabbing it. She instinctually used the energy she had been fighting against to bend and crush it.

Blake swore.

"MEL! I NEED YOU TO GET UP!" Ben yelled again.

She lifted a knee and forced herself to stand, barely balancing. Ben reached back. "Give me your hand!"

She stretched toward him and he managed to grasp her hand. A light transferred from her skin through to Ben's. With his free hand, he flicked his wrist at Blake, and something like stakes, or maybe spikes, impaled Blake in the throat. Blake fell back and didn't move.

Still holding her hand, Ben did the same maneuver against the other fighter and she saw at least one stake each find a place in his chest and shoulder, with one grazing his neck. He fell back and Ben let go of Mel.

On the verge of passing out, she closed her eyes and heard Ben slash off the remaining vines that had wrapped around him.

"We need to go," he barked, taking off his jacket and wrapping it around her.

She tried to walk, but he hastily swept her off of her feet, out of the building and to a car. Ben opened the passenger door and shoved her in.

"Buckle up!" He slammed the door and got in to drive. Jamming the keys in the ignition, he started the car and sped out of the school parking lot.

He pounded on the steering wheel. "Damn it!" Whipping out his phone, he made a call. "I've got Saffrona. Two Ivies in the gym. Tell Pam to be ready in five."

Through her haze, she made out her mom's name. Pam. It also registered that Ben was bleeding.

He started yelling at Mel. "You're such a pain in the ass! You know that? Everyone else was just fine! Tabatha was a breeze. Even Stacy made it out undiscovered. And she was a cheerleader, a flipping cheerleader with tons of eyes on her." He took a breath in the middle of his rant. "Where's your boyfriend's necklace?"

Her eyes widened as she recognized what he was saying, and asking. *He never even met Tabatha before she moved. And what about the necklace?* She moved a hand up to her neck. It wasn't there. When she returned her hand to her lap, her fingertips were coated in blood. Her own blood. And her hand was literally glowing.

He didn't stop for a moment to let her try to formulate a sentence. Even if she could have, he probably didn't care to hear what she had to say. "Why weren't you wearing it?! Never mind. It doesn't even matter now."

Mel closed her eyes and leaned against the passenger window, wincing and fighting back tears. Not just from the pain, but from the whirling confusion, and from … whatever had just happened.

She heard the familiar sound of a garage door opening. They pulled in and it closed behind them. Ben got out of the car and slammed the door shut, going inside the house and leaving her behind. The door to the kitchen opened again and her mom came running out.

Ben opened the door. "We don't have time, Pam!"

She looked back at Mel, her face and voice full of concern. "Do you think you can make it inside, sweetie?"

Pam went back inside at Ben's insistence while Mel forced herself to move through the discomfort, opening the door and hanging onto the car to help her keep balance. As soon as she made it in the house, she saw her mom feverishly packing her clothes in a duffle bag.

"Help her to a chair!" Pam ordered Ben. "You could be a little nicer," she scolded. "There's only so much she can do about it."

Ben helped Mel to a chair at the kitchen table.

"Where's the charm?" Pam asked. "Sweetheart, where's your green necklace?"

Mel searched her foggy thoughts. She didn't know.

"Look at her," Ben said, pointing to Mel. "She's gone too far."

Pam frowned. "We could still try." She looked to Mel. "Do you know where it is?"

Beyond rattled, still in agony and the throes of confusion, trying to remember when she'd last seen or worn it wasn't Mel's top priority.

Ben's phone chimed and he walked down the hallway to the front door. Pam resumed packing Mel's things when the front door opened and Mel heard Ben talking to someone. She heard Blake's name and the name of the other kid, Ken.

Ben returned to the kitchen, Devin close behind him.

Devin pulled a chair to her side, sitting down and grabbing her hands. "Gosh, Mel." He looked panicked. "What happened?"

Ben was still clearly frustrated. "What do you think happened? She lost it."

Devin ran his finger under her collar, where the necklace would normally sit. He looked up at Ben. "Can Thod help?"

Ben shook his head. "No, we've got one more, she'll be out any time now. We can't risk it."

Devin pursed his lips. "I'll take her. That means you have two of mine."

Ben rubbed his forehead. "Fine."

Devin looked back at Mel and smiled reassuringly. "It'll be okay. We're going on a road trip." He grinned. "I know, you're so excited, you're practically glowing."

She raised her eyebrows and glanced down again at her glowing skin. The joke wasn't lost on her, but she didn't have any energy to respond.

"Did you kill the leeches?" Devin asked.

"I don't know." Ben ran his fingers through his hair while pacing.

"I texted my dad and," Devin paused, "someone else. They'll stop by the gym."

Pam zipped up the duffle bag and handed it to Ben. He left to take it out to Devin's car, returning with a blanket from the family room to wrap Mel in.

"You'll be fine, sweetie." Her mom's look of concern was less reassuring than her words. "You can trust Devin."

Devin picked Mel up, barely exerting himself. He carried her out to the car and buckled her in. Hopping in the driver's seat, he buckled up and rolled the window down.

"Take good care of her," Pam pleaded.

"Try to keep your hands off my sister," Ben threatened.

"I absolutely will, Mrs. Walters." Devin assured her, putting the car in gear.

"Devin..." Ben was giving him a death glare.

"Stay focused, Ben, we've got people counting on you," was all Devin said to Ben's challenge. Even in her current state, Mel could tell Devin's tone was playfully antagonizing.

Devin reached over to squeeze her hand and backed out of the driveway.

Soon after leaving the city limits, he pulled the car off to the side of the road and parked. He looked at Mel, whose eyes had been fixed on him since getting in the car; at least during the times she had her eyes open.

He wore a sympathetic frown. "It's pretty rough, isn't it?"

"What's going on?" A tear rolled down her face.

"What's going on, is you're going to be one-hundred-and-ten percent okay. I need you to trust me. Can you do that?"

She nodded.

He reached back and grabbed a bottle of water from the backseat. "You need to stay hydrated. It's a forty-five-minute drive and then we can get you more comfy. There will be plenty of time for questions."

She cracked the bottle open and drank. It helped a little.

***

They pulled into a long gravel driveway and Devin turned off the car. He carried Mel into a small, dark house. All the curtains were pulled, blackout style; the walls were white and the carpet brown. He sat her down on a stiff couch and turned on the lights, taking in a deep breath of the stale air. "Mmm. Home sweet … not home."

The house was simply furnished; no care had been taken for décor. The walls were mostly bare, and everything looked plain and practical.

Devin disappeared into a room down the hallway only to emerge a couple minutes later, scooping her up. He took her to the same room, a bedroom with two beds. After laying her down on one, she curled up in a ball. Devin went down the hall and came back with a first aid kit, breaking out rubbing alcohol and sterile pads.

He shook his head. "They did a number on you, didn't they?" The alcohol stung as he tended to her neck and ankle. "The great thing is, you are going to heal like a champ now." He smiled. "No scars for you. This is just an added precaution."

She still had no idea what the heck was going on. And somehow, she didn't even care. Whatever her body was going through was brutal, and she was barely keeping it together.

He took the bloodied supplies to the bathroom and washed up, returning with another bottle of water. "Let's have you drink some more. Can you sit up?"

She guzzled the water down after Devin helped her sit up. He took the empty bottle from her as she slipped back down into the fetal position. He crouched and gingerly brushed the hair from her face, smiling lovingly.

"This reminds me of the first time we kissed. Do you remember how sick you were that day? It's going to kind of fade back to that before you feel better. Unfortunately, there's not a lot we can do about how you're feeling right now, but you should be loads better in the morning." He gently rubbed the back of her hand. "I think the best thing we can have you do is try to sleep it off."

She whimpered in pain.

He winced. "I'm going to go hit the lights. I'll let you choose: I can sleep on that bed over there, or if you'd prefer, I can cuddle up next to you—maybe it'll help." He put his hands in the air. "Total gentleman, I promise."

She nodded ever so slightly.

"The second?" He kissed her forehead. "Okay."

After turning off the lights, he crawled into bed and wrapped his arms around her. It was a long night of agonizing pain, surging and draining energy, nausea—the whole package. She was grateful to have him there with her through it all.

Chapter 12

MEL WOKE THE NEXT MORNING to the sound of running tap water from down the hallway. Footsteps drew close and she pried her eyes open to see Devin standing at the other side of the room, brushing his teeth in nothing but boxers. He noticed her gaze and held up his pointer finger, mumbling with his mouth full of foam. He finished in the bathroom and came back to the bedroom.

He crouched next to Mel with a sympathetic smile. "Hey, gorgeous, you're awake. How are you feeling?"

She considered how to respond for a moment, looking him over. Even if it felt like she had a nasty hangover, his attractiveness registered. Mel looked down to see she was still in the clothes she'd worn to school the day before. He must have noticed her eyes wandering—he popped up to his feet.

"Oh, yeah." He started rifling through the closet and holding clothes up to himself to see if they would fit. "I, uh … I promise nothing happened. You were just really hot last night."

She managed a small grin.

He stopped and turned back to her. "That didn't come out right." Pulling a t-shirt off of a hanger, he tugged it over his head. "While I'm sure you are *very* hot in bed, what I mean is, you were *literally* very hot, like … emanating heat from your body during the change."

She lay still. Everything from the day before was rattling around in her head. She didn't even know where to start, what to ask.

He zipped up a pair of clean jeans and grabbed a fresh bottle of water, returning to her side. "Can I help you sit up?"

She shook her head, opting to force herself to slowly scoot up against the wall at the head of the bed.

He felt her forehead and looked her over. "It'll probably be a few more hours, but the worst is past. I've never actually heard of it happening like that; you had me pretty worried there."

She finished off the bottle of water. While feeling ten times better than the night before, she was still worn out.

"Absolutely no rush, but when you're ready to get cleaned up, there's plenty of hot water." He winced. "I, uh … probably should have waited for you to wake up, but I looked at the bag Pam packed for you. She forgot to pack you a toothbrush, but that's not a problem. We keep extras around here. I set one out for you on the counter."

He eased down on the edge of the other bed. "What can I do to help?"

The idea of a shower felt fantastic—she was drenched in sweat, not to mention the blood from the cuts on her neck, which had soaked into her shirt. But she didn't think she could stand yet. And she desperately needed some answers, anything, to help ground her.

"Where are we?" Her voice was froggy.

"We're at a safe house. Only a few people know where this place is. No close neighbors. We'll be okay here."

"Why do we need to be at a safe house?"

"I've never actually done this part of it, so I may not explain everything the best. Let's start with what you remember about yesterday."

She stared at the wall as if reading invisible ink, trying to make sense of what she could remember. "Why did they attack me?" Tears welled up from the blur of trauma.

He frowned. "Mel, there's a lot you don't know about yourself. So, it'll take some time to get through all of it. You were being protected, and," he swallowed, "we let you down. I had to take care of something, and Ben got held up, and it was just bad timing." He whispered, "I'm really so sorry."

Nothing made sense. "Why would I need to be protected? I never did anything to them."

"No, love, it's not like that. Do you remember who attacked you? I'm not sure what all you were able to see or hear while your body was going through … what it went through."

She adjusted herself to sit up a little straighter. "It was Blake, wasn't it? And another kid from our school? But there was something … not natural about them."

His lips twisted into an ironic grin. "Natural. Yeah… Yes, it was Blake, and you're right, the other leech was from our school."

"You guys said that a couple of times, 'leeches.' They were like some kind of monster."

He winced at that. "I don't know that there's an easy way to tiptoe down this road. Let me just lay it all out there and you can ask questions as we go."

"Okay."

He squinted at her and rocked his head back and forth, as if formulating the best angle to start from. "They weren't human, Mel. And neither are you, and neither am I. We're not from here."

She pressed her lips together and furrowed her brow, but said nothing.

"I can only imagine it sounds crazy. *I've* known my whole life, but you haven't—that was to keep you safe, and to give you a normal life."

He kept pausing, reading her face.

"We call the jerks that tried to hurt you 'Ivies,' or more appropriately 'leeches,' because that's what they are. They cheat and steal and do anything to get an advantage. Including killing people like you."

She spoke up, the reality of what she'd seen and heard the day before still swirling in her head. "You said we're not people."

"No, no, no. We're people, we're just not *human* people. You saw them transform; you saw their vines?"

She nodded.

"That's where their name comes from. You and I, we're more like them than we are like humans. We're botanical beings. We have abilities that humans don't have and can't understand. Did you see how Ben looked when he was fighting? Did you get a look at yourself?"

She remembered that Ben had changed, and obviously *something* was happening to her.

"You and I, and Ben, and … several more people in town, we're called 'Seeders.' Our form is more floral. You really should see yourself when you change—you're breathtaking." He beamed. "Anyway, long story short, Seeders and Ivies are from the Green Lands. We live different lives, have large families, and unfortunately, fight a lot. The only reason you grew up in the human world and I didn't, is because we hide our daughters and sisters in the human world until they're old enough to fully mature, to bloom. That's what you just went through." He paused. "What questions do you have for me?"

Only about a million. "Did Ben kill Blake?"

He huffed. "I don't know for sure. By the time our guys got back, there weren't any bodies. So, either they got up from the fight,

117

or one of their cronies or generals was nearby and picked up the bodies before we could get there." He quickly added, "But you won't see them again. Even if they survived, they've been made and know we would hunt them down."

"He… Did you guys know that's what he was?"

Devin frowned. "We suspected, obviously, after he first attacked you. But sometimes humans are just jerks like that. We couldn't be sure. We can't just go around taking out suspects or interrogating them and giving ourselves away. I just wish…" He closed his eyes and shook his head. "I wish one of us had been there. I feel horrible."

"I don't blame you."

"Thanks, Mel." His eyes frowned as though there was turmoil still hiding behind them.

So many questions ricocheted in her mind, and she knew some were more important than others. But she decided to go with an intriguing one, one that offered physical proof and validation. "So, you can look like Ben? Can I see?"

He beamed at the request and transformed before her. His arms each sprouted a long, sharp green leaf, flaring out at the wrist and ending at the elbow. The serrated edges were menacing, and perfect for cutting Ivy vines, as Ben had done. The tips of his hair turned purple. He lifted his pant legs to show almost flesh-colored roots wrapping around his ankles. "These are mostly good for armor."

As freaky as it was to see, it was also really impressive that Devin could change himself so drastically, with so little effort.

He reverted back to his human appearance. "Honestly, if I'm not fighting, I like this form—it's not as bulky. Even back home, this is how everyone walks around."

"So, you're saying I can look like you?" She was genuinely wondering if this all had to be some kind of hallucination.

"No. You look even better." He winked. "Your leaf blades are wider, softer, more rounded. Honestly, you're kinda sexy any form you take." He cleared his throat. "Anyway, um … your eyes and hair change differently—if you want to see in a mirror, you still kinda look like that as you finish blooming."

Mel definitely wanted to see. She considered whether she trusted her body enough to stand yet. "I think I'm ready to get cleaned up."

"Your wish is my command. Let me draw you a bath. I don't want you getting dizzy and falling in the shower, alright?"

He left the room and popped back in as the water ran. "I, uh … put your stuff back in your bag and left it in there, so you can," he swallowed hard, blushing, "pick what you want to change into."

She managed a smirk at his discomfort. Served him right for rummaging through her things like that. Then she started to blush herself, wondering what her mom had hastily packed from her underwear drawer. He mentioned only the forgotten toothbrush, so she assumed at least the clothing basics were covered.

Devin offered a hand and helped steady her as she got up and walked to the bathroom. "Let me know if you need anything."

She sat down on the edge of the tub as he stood in the doorway.

"Um…" He broke eye contact. "There's one thing I need you to check."

She raised her eyebrows. "What?"

"Well, the roots that I showed you, you have them, too. But yours are still developing, and they'll continue to for a while, even after you feel better."

She nodded.

"Well, um…" He seemed even less comfortable with this topic than rummaging through her clothes. "Just, they start at your hips, and work their way down to your ankles. But we need to know how far down they are when you're done in here. So just," he cleared his throat again, "take a look and let me know?"

She nodded again, acknowledging the awkward in this whole situation.

After Devin closed the door, Mel soaked in the tub until it barely had any warmth left. The scene from the day before played through her mind. She considered everything she had just experienced and what Devin had told her; it reframed her entire life. It took less than a day for her world to come crashing down around her. She wasn't human ... she was a *creature*.

And people wanted her dead.

She drained the water and then crawled on her knees, turning the showerhead on. She stayed kneeling, letting the water run over her, muffling the sounds of her sobbing. Her life had been ripped from her without warning; the circumstances hazy, the consequences exhausting. And the dust hadn't even started to settle.

After there were no more tears to cry, she pulled herself to a standing position and finished cleaning up with the toiletries in the room. She dressed in clean clothes and brushed her teeth, gazing at the glowing green eyes staring back at her, slowly fading. Staring at herself in a near catatonic state, she picked up a brush and ran it through the hair that was fading from yellow back to her natural strawberry blonde. Curious, she plucked a hair out; it instantly faded to her regular, human coloring.

She was running her fingers over her neck when Devin's knock at the door pulled her from the abyss of her thoughts. "The door's unlocked."

Devin slowly cracked the door, then fully opened it, seeing she was decent. He walked up behind her and wrapped his arms around Mel's body, holding her close and standing cheek-to-cheek while looking in the mirror. "Are you okay?"

She didn't respond, fixated on her neck where the vines had dug into her. There were barely any signs of injury by now.

He grabbed her hand and pulled it down, replacing it with his lips. "All better."

Mel continued to stare blankly into the mirror. "I never asked for any of this."

He frowned. "No one asks to be what they are. It just … is what it is. We are who we are."

"My life is a lie," she whispered.

He pressed his lips together, remaining silent.

After a moment, he kissed her on the cheek and whispered in her ear, "Your life is full of so much love, more than any human could ever have." He gave her hand a squeeze. "Let's go sit down."

He had her sit at the small round table in the kitchen area. "Do you feel up to more than water? Let's see if that'll help." He poured some apple juice, and she drank it while he rifled around in the fridge and pantry. "We're never really sure when we'll need this place, so we don't keep much around that's perishable. I could make you some oatmeal, or frozen waffles?"

She shook her head.

"Granola bar?" He raised an eyebrow.

She shook her head again.

"I need you to eat something. You need to get your strength back." He grabbed a bag of sliced bread from the freezer, toasting a couple slices and smothering them in peanut butter and honey. "My specialty."

Chapter 13

MEL SLOWLY RISKED EATING THE breakfast Devin had prepared for her, one small bite at a time while he watched. She polished off one piece of toast, ready to start the second. "I want to hear my story. Start at the beginning."

Devin explained how Seeder seedlings sprouted, how the girls were escorted by their fathers to the human world and placed with host families.

"You're saying my parents aren't really my parents, right?"

"Pam and George are just as much your parents as your biological parents are, if you ask me. Everything they've ever done was to protect you, from the moment they got you."

She furrowed her brow. "They lied to me my entire life."

He frowned, then continued by explaining the complex family dynamics they had to work with—Seeder mothers raising their sons in the Green Lands, preparing them for protection duty with their fathers in the human world. Seeder girls couldn't survive back home, not with their poisoned lands, not when they were trapped within their own borders by the enemy. He offered to let her call home, but she was too conflicted to broach the topic with her parents at the moment.

"So, Ben is legit my brother?" His annoyances instantly became more endearing. She'd always imagined what it was like to not be an only child. Foster-children excluded, of course.

"Yep, he is. And he's actually a great guy if you give him a chance." Devin shrugged. "He's one of my best friends back home. He's just hyper-focused on the work, so he comes off a little less than friendly sometimes."

Devin's explanation about Seeder families sending brothers to protect their sisters clicked, and she went wide-eyed. "Wait, you're not one of my brothers, right?!"

He grimaced in disgust. "No, Mel. No. Gross, no! We're not human but we're also not perverts! Your dad strategized with mine to join forces with their girls. We help each other out, watch each other's backs."

She let out a sigh of relief. "You said you're friends with Ben, but you two never hung out."

"Part of the plan is carefully controlling who's seen together. If one person's discovered, it could spread out like a web and jeopardize us all."

She narrowed her eyes. "What about at the mall? And that time at my house? Not friendly and not exactly neutral."

He laughed. "Really?" A mischievous grin was plastered on his face. "I was there to help keep his sister safe. Not fall for her. Our relationship hasn't exactly been G-rated." He laughed again. "He wasn't super excited to see us that close. I get it."

Blushing, she stood up from the table, her plate now empty. She remembered their first movie night, when Ben seemed … uncharacteristically friendly, laughing and teasing, even teaming up with Devin against Zach... Devin and Ben *were* actually friends. "Keep going." She shoved her hands in her pockets, pacing the room.

"Well … I trained up on the human world, took the place of one of my brothers that escorted a sister home, and Ben came in to take the place of the one that helped Tabatha get home."

She cut him off. "I still can't believe that. She completely ghosted me. She was one of my best friends."

"We don't have reliable communication between our worlds. No internet or phone lines. And she needed to move on with the next part of her life."

"Wait." Mel furrowed her brow, sifting through her questions. "These Green Lands. Where are they? And what do you mean by 'next part of her life?'"

He slowly tipped his head to the side. "It's here. Like, on Earth … I'm pretty sure. But you have to be one of us, green folk, someone from the Green Lands, to be able to open a rift to go between the realms. We're going to teach you how to do that."

Her eyes widened at the thought. Things were sinking in. She wasn't just some freak of nature, she could now magically go to some mysterious place no one had ever heard of. "When you say Tabatha moved on, is that what you mean? She's over there now? If she can't text, why couldn't she visit?"

He rubbed the back of his neck. "Yeah. She went home. So did Stacy. And … there's just a lot to cover."

"Keep going."

"So, I was assigned to watch you, as well as others. Everything was planned out. Your mom and dad knew who I was, we played by their rules." He bobbed his head awkwardly, shoving his hands into his pockets. "I was actually the one that talked your parents into relaxing their dating rule in the first place."

She blushed again.

He elaborated. "I … liked you. And after your fight with your mom, I figured I might be able to convince them. You were miserable. I wanted to date you. I figured it was a win-win. Of course, I didn't expect you to choose Blake over me…"

"Yeah, thanks for reminding me." She rolled her eyes. "I dated a guy that wants me dead. And there's nothing quite like having a guy walk in when you're shouting at your mom that you won't get knocked up."

He tried to stifle a laugh. "I mean … on the topic … well, this is kind of the birds and bees, but … now that you've bloomed, you're considered an adult in our culture, and physically, you've changed. But you won't actually be able to have your own clutch for several years."

"Clutch meaning kids?"

He nodded.

"How absolutely refreshing." She feigned excitement. "I really *don't* have to worry about getting knocked up as a teen!" She stopped pacing and pointed down the hall. "There are *two* beds in there."

He put up his hands. "Trust me, I was *not* expecting anything." He grabbed her dishes and started to wash them. "Once I realized you were budding at the dance, we prepared the charm—the necklace, to help temper your changes. It helps to stretch out the process, so it's not as noticeable or excruciating. If you don't wear a charm, the process can be done in a few days, but it's so hard on you that you can slip into a pretty serious coma. It's rough."

He cringed. "There's so much raw power surging through you, the human body can't handle it." He started to dry the dishes. "If you hadn't forgotten to wear it, we might have been able to stretch it out until near the end of the school year. You could have stayed undetected."

She thought back to when she last remembered wearing it. It was probably a full day that she'd forgotten it. "Why didn't we get it from my gym locker before coming out here?"

"Once you reach a certain point, it's useless to put it back on; the process has to take its natural course."

Thinking about it, she remembered what were supposedly inconsequential conversations when her mom would hug her in the morning before school and ask where 'that pretty necklace' was, when Mel would forget to put it back on after a shower. And now their ruined Valentine's date made sense. Blake's presence ... not having the protection of the charm.

And then there was... She crossed her arms. "I'm guessing that necklace doesn't magically put itself into my locker?"

Devin pursed his lips, shaking his head.

She raised an eyebrow. "And who would have had access to my locker to put it there?"

He wore a soft smile. "Someone that cares about you?"

She still couldn't believe it. It had been around three months that she'd been going through this change and she hadn't known it.

He tilted his head to the side. "You must've been feeling pretty miserable, for a while, to go full-bloom. If you'd complained more to me or your parents, that would have given us a hint."

She let out a heavy sigh. She'd forgotten the necklace, she'd sucked it up when she felt sick, and it backfired. "So, all of this is my fault. That's awesome. Ben got hurt; I got hurt. We're out in the middle of nowhere." She continued her pacing. "But in my defense, it's not like anyone was honest with me about it. It's not my fault I didn't know a silly piece of jewelry was what stood between me and being murdered."

"No one's blaming you," he replied softly. "I'm just explaining how it works."

"Yeah, well, it's stupid." She scowled. "That no one told me. That this all could have been prevented ... by a stupid necklace."

He frowned. "The system's not perfect. I get that. We could have done a ring, or bracelet, something else. But the stone has to touch your skin to work. And honestly, everyone tried their best to make sure you were wearing it at all times. We just ... slipped." He looked into her eyes. "They wanted you to live a normal life. For the sake of the family network. For your own happiness." He huffed. "And I have to trust Ben's judgment about how things went down back at the school. I'm just … we're just … doing our jobs the best we can."

That stung. That's what she was to him, a job.

Devin shook his head. "Your parents were overwhelmed yesterday morning, and I slept in, so I didn't double-check that you were wearing it first thing." He looked down. "Not our finest work."

He paused.

She didn't know what to say, other than, "Go on."

"I suggested you'd be more likely to wear the charm faithfully if it came from me instead of your parents, with the way you had been arguing with them about dating and Ben's arrival. And," a slight grin formed on his face, "we were pretty darn sure you were blooming, but I kinda wanted to see what your eyes would look like. And … I hoped you felt the same about me, as I did you." He mused on the event. "Gosh, you are seriously an amazing kisser. And the way your eyes light up, the green is mesmerizing."

She scoffed at his fond memory. "The irony of my parents keeping me under lock and key just to set me up to have a fake boyfriend seduce me. Every girl's dream."

"It's not like that!" He startled Mel—Devin had never raised his voice at her before.

"It's not like what?" she yelled back. "You were *assigned* to me. Every aspect of our relationship was planned. You manipulated me and lied to me, every single day!"

He threw the dish towel on the ground. "No!"

She'd never seen him so angry. Her eyes grew wide in shock as he stomped over to her. Surprised, she stepped back against the wall. Her breathing was heavy.

He immediately stopped, just a couple feet in front of her. He frowned, reading her face. "I'd never hurt you," he whispered. He looked down, shaking his head.

She steadied her breathing as he stood there, silent.

Devin balled his fists and held them up to his forehead. He finally said something, dropping his fists. "But I did what I had to do, to keep you and a *whole lot* of other people safe." His voice was firm. "Things went as far as they did, because I love you. I didn't *fake* that. I regret nothing. I'm not apologizing." He stayed in place, but his breathing calmed, his eyes softened. He glanced down at her lips, then back to her eyes with a frown. Barely above a whisper, he added, "I came here for my sisters. To meet and help my dad. I came for my family." He shook his head and walked away. "You need to realize it's not all about you."

Back in the kitchen, he picked up the towel and finished cleaning up. "By the way, go look in the mirror."

She headed to the bathroom and turned on the light. Her eyes were glistening green again, even more than they were before her shower. Her hands were glowing, like they had when Ben grabbed her hand during the fight. She'd been just about to ask if she could leave the house to go for a stroll, to clear her mind, but that was obviously out of the question now.

She walked back out, sitting next to him at the table. "What's this supposed to mean?"

He met her gaze. "This is exactly what Blake was trying to make happen. They know that as soon as you start the process, you have your powers, but you don't know how to control them. One moment of passion, one moment of rage, and they discover you. He tried to kiss you, hurt you. He was trying to get you to react, tip your hand.

"First, he'll fish around, dating lots of girls, asking questions, saying certain things to see if he can get a reaction. And then he'll try to get closer if he suspects you. It's just one of their tactics. Not all of them are jerks like him. Some are more suave, friendly, convincing."

She furrowed her brow. Yeah, he had a reputation... And apparently, he wasn't just a flirt because he was a jock.

"I still don't get it. He obviously knew. Why did they wait? And if we knew, that he knew, why didn't we stop them?"

Devin sighed. "He obviously *didn't* know. Otherwise, they would have come for you earlier. And they would never normally be stupid enough to take one of us on in the middle of a public place in broad daylight like that. If you were going through the change without the charm, you were an easy target, and a lucky find." He shook his head. "Anyway, it's pretty clear they suspected. But ... I think it just shows that they don't understand exactly how our changes work, and the jade. They don't go through that whole thing. It would take a lot more than what Blake did, for you to show with the charm on. If he had tried that on you a week from now, it would be a different story. And we *did* follow him. Though the other guy, Ken ... he wasn't even on our radar."

"But why would he be so stupid, to do something that would get him suspended? Just to fish for a reaction?"

"Well..." Devin smirked. "Honestly, I don't think he's too used to rejection, so he may have genuinely been pissed about that. Other than that, it's just speculation. You said something about him saying he was tired of waiting?"

She nodded. "Yeah, something like that."

He shrugged. "I don't know. We have different motives. Ours is preservation. Theirs is ... pride—personal and as a people. He might have gotten in trouble with their general about not doing a good enough job on his mission. Showing his cards like that, I'm sure he had his backside handed to him with a reprimand for being a pathetic soldier."

"You and Ben won't get in trouble, will you? For this?"

He smiled. "You're sweet. We'll be fine. Our guilt is enough punishment." He drew a deep breath. "Will we hear about it? Yes. But honestly, I was about ten times more terrified when I had to talk to Thod—your biological dad—after Ben spotted us at the mall."

She tried to suppress a grin. At least he had to do some suffering for his part in all the deceit. And the thought of this mystery dad coming down on him, it was kind of cute.

Though, it became less cute when she thought of all of their sneaking around, just to have her parents actually know about it and pretend they didn't. "They seriously knew we were dating the whole time? I, uh … I'm not sure how I feel about this, us, and being set up that way."

He furrowed his brow. "No." He pointed at her. "I see what you're thinking. You got *permission* to date because I asked for it. But none of our parents knew we were actually together until the run-in at the mall. They knew we were friends, and that you'd be safe as long as you were with me." He frowned. "I didn't lie about enjoying not being under a microscope with you. It felt kinda nice, to just be us."

She raised her eyebrows, still skeptical. "You didn't plan things with my parents at all? They didn't 'coincidentally' leave the house for you to come over to kiss me and give me the necklace?"

His face turned pink. "I was supposed to come over to hang out and check on you when they were home, but I knew they'd be gone, so, I … well…" He cleared his throat. "They were a bit annoyed that I did that, and that you let me in. But it got the job done." His deep brown eyes focused on hers. "I'd happily get in trouble, and risk anything, to be with you. And to keep you safe."

Mel looked down at her hands, processing everything. It was still shocking to see a slight glow to her skin. Her thoughts drifted back to the talk of concealment. "How do I control it?"

He managed a weak smile. "That's what we're here for. Despite the unfortunate timing of your bloom, at least it happened right before spring break. I'm going to teach you."

Everything about this change, this reveal, was an undeniable suck-fest. But at least there was something she could do about it; she was up to the challenge. "Alright."

He placed a hand on hers. "Mel … I'm … sorry, for getting so angry earlier. That was uncalled for. But I stand by what I said. I only lied to you because I had to, and because I care about you."

"It's okay," she whispered. "I know you care." The question bubbled up in her; she had to know. "When did you actually start to like me? When was anything between us real?"

He grinned. "Before we even met. When one of the girls whose profile I'd studied raised her hand more than once in Trigonometry. Great questions, right answers. And beautiful."

She looked down, drawing a pattern on the table with her finger.

"I know I've had to lie to you. And I meant it, too, when we were at the mall and I said I knew how much it sucks to lie to someone you care about." He raised his eyebrows. "But I've never had to fake an attraction to you. We're encouraged to keep you away from guys that aren't in the network, so you don't get too attached to a human or Ivy, but it's not like I was tasked with dating you."

He took his hand back and slumped down in his chair. "I'd understand if…" He whispered, "I was only supposed to be your friend. I promise. But I really…"

She sat up straighter, looking over at him, her heart aching.

"It's one more thing they take from us." He shook his head. "Everything got so convoluted. I had orders. I just…"

She watched him pick at his fingernails, frowning. That was almost exactly the same look he'd had when they were playing board games one night. That distant, regret-filled, hurting gaze. She remembered him asking how she'd feel, living in a different culture. How he'd reluctantly talked about his mom and dad … which, his mom being a nurse could be true, if she had healing powers like Mel had just witnessed with her own injuries, and his dad *was* a military man … just not the kind she'd thought.

Amidst Devin's passion, and confidence, and humor, he had his own heartache. Just like her parents' lies, she knew it was going to be hard sorting things out with Devin. But despite all of his flaws, all of what he'd had to do, she knew this side of him.

She gave him an encouraging smile. "We'll figure it out."

He wiped at the corners of his eyes. "Thanks. I promise, no more lies." He frowned. "I mean, I still have to follow orders. What our parents want … stuff like that. But from now on, I'm one hundred percent me, you don't have to doubt any of that."

"Okay," she whispered with a nod.

They sat in silence for a moment. She didn't know how to feel about any of this. Everything was so big; so many questions remained unanswered. Mel plucked another from her mind. "You said no more lies. Can you tell me what you've already lied to me about? Like the charm. You once said you were recharging the batteries on the necklace you gave me. That's not a thing, right? I thought you were just flirting, but now I guess I don't really know."

He laughed, then stifled it with a hand over his mouth. "Sorry. I promise I'm not laughing at you. It's just cute. No, nothing either of us did or could do, affects the way it works." He cocked his head to the side. "As for other lies, I'll give you what I can…"

He didn't actually give her that much, explaining that he was hesitant and unsure as to whether or not he'd have permission to do so, if it might compromise the cover of a different family member. But he promised he'd share more with her as he could.

He sighed, sitting up straighter. "Want to see something neat with that light in your hands?" He reached out with one hand and she obliged. He grinned and waved his free hand in the air. A misty shower of lights rained down.

Her jaw dropped in amazement.

He smirked at her awe. "You have *so* much power in you."

"Ben grabbed my hand in the fight and then did something, that's how we got away."

"Yeah?"

She described the spikes that shot from Ben's hands, impaling the attackers.

"Gotcha, yeah. We call those darts. They're pretty handy. We can do those on our own, but they're a lot more impressive with your kind of power." He now held both of her hands, rubbing them tenderly with his thumbs. "Our people are so much stronger together, than we are alone. We're better when we fight side by side. I don't want to fight with you. I want you by my side."

She surveyed his face, knowing that, despite everything going on, she had fallen for him. "I want that, too."

Chapter 14

"HOW ABOUT I TELL YOU MORE about your family?" Devin suggested at the kitchen table.

Mel raised her eyebrows high. "Not an only child anymore, right?"

He laughed. "I suppose that would be a bit of a shock. You have twenty-three brothers and sisters. Actually, I guess it's kind of like you're twenty-four-uplets? One more thing we have in common." He winked. "I can't tell you too much, because even if they've gone to live in the Green Lands already, we rely so heavily on anonymity. But Ben said he only let a couple of names slip?"

"Tabatha and Stacy? Sisters?"

He nodded.

"It's actually kind of cool, now that I realize Tabatha didn't just forget about me. And Stacy? That's a little hard to wrap my head around. How did she do when she learned all of this?"

"I'm not sure." Devin shrugged. "Ben did most of her detail and training." He lifted an eyebrow. "After school, when you thought he was off having a social life."

She nodded, another piece of the puzzle fitting into place.

"Him moving in with you guys was a last-minute change. That's probably why it didn't go as smoothly as it could have." Devin chuckled. "It was hard to keep a straight face when you all thought he was trying to date Stacy."

"Oh, gosh, yeah." She shuddered. "That's seriously weird. Like … I may have had a crush on one of my brothers and not known it…"

"Yeah, it's complicated. But you have to remember that while all of your sisters came to this world, not nearly as many of your brothers have. And it doesn't mean you've even met all of them— they don't all necessarily go to the same school."

He had told her as much, that maybe only half of her brothers would come to the human world, over the years, for protection detail. The others continued their education back in the Green Lands, helped protect their borders against the Ivies, and contributed to society in other ways.

"Tabatha, Stacy, Ben, and I really don't look much alike … I would never guess we were related," she said.

"In botanical appearance, all females take the same basic form—the yellow hair, green eyes. Same for the men, we look like our fathers with the purple hair tips. But in our more human forms, there's a lot of diversity in our genome. It's actually kind of weird to be over here and see families look so much like each other."

That was actually pretty cool. It made her more curious about how her people came to be.

More than once, in the blur of the reveals, a name and face had crossed her mind. "What about Zach?" She had been too afraid to ask where her closest friendship now stood in the mix of things.

He hesitated. "I can't give you an answer on everyone you want to know about right now. But I know he means a lot to you. He's not one of us. We don't know if he's Ivy or human. Our best guess is that he's just an ignorant human, but we have no way of knowing right now."

That answer didn't give her any sort of comfort. At least Zach wasn't trying to Luke and Leia it … but to imagine that he could be an Ivy was impossible. She was sure Zach had to be human. He was so sweet and thoughtful.

She moved back to siblings. "So, I only get to know about Stacy, Tabatha, and Ben?"

He frowned. "Sorry, yeah. For now. But you'll get to meet them all when you come back to the Green Lands. The ones I've met are all really cool. I'm sure you'll recognize a few from your high school. But some attended private schools or homeschooled in the area."

Mel nodded, musing to herself. Her parents had tried to do that when she'd first started school, and had suggested it again later on, as she got older. But Mel thrived in public education, with the structure, opportunities, and social life. She realized how much more of a shut-in she could have been, if they'd not only denied her social outings and dating, but regular school, as well.

"Your mom back home is really awesome, too, Mel. You guys are going to be so excited to meet each other. Her name's Murial. She's an *amazing* cook. Our moms hang out a lot."

Mel fought a smile. She didn't even know these people. But she was somehow drawn to them… They were real, legitimate people. People like her. "Our families are really that close?"

He grinned. "You're *literally* the girl next door. We're neighbors." He chuckled. "Honestly, if I'd known who you were, I probably would have gotten to know Tabatha better before coming over." He rubbed his hands together, wiggling his eyebrows. "Gotten some good dirt on you."

She smiled. "Then I'll consider myself lucky."

He laughed. "Anyway. I've known your mom my whole life, but obviously your dad just since I got here. They're both pretty cool.

Gosh, your dad…" He paused and took a breath in obvious admiration. "He took out two Ivies single-handedly last year, completely undiscovered."

That made her more than a little uneasy. "Did someone else in my family get attacked?"

He shook his head. "No. But they let it slip that they were Ivies. And they would have killed any of us, if it had been the other way around."

She scrunched her nose. "That's kinda weird … hearing my biological dad is a murderer. Doesn't exactly bring warm, fuzzy feelings. It kind of … creeps me out."

He furrowed his brow. "No, it's not like that. You still don't get it. He deserves a lot more respect than that."

She was taken aback by how adamant he was, defending her Seeder dad's character.

"Try to imagine leaving your mate, the love of your life, for sixteen, seventeen, eighteen years. Years without contact, other than a rare letter brought by a new son. And to spend all of those years focused on watching your daughters from afar. Every scraped knee, every breakup—you can't hug them. You can't let them know who you are. Worrying for their lives. Training and coordinating night and day to make sure your sons do what they need to. Falsifying documents. Even having to start from scratch to position yourself in a good place in the community, balancing a job with all of that. You need to give him a little more credit. Yeah, he can be deadly, he'll get the job done. But he's a family man."

She frowned and slumped in her seat. The pressure and guilt were growing. So many people were literally giving so much, risking so much, just for her. And she never knew it. Even if she hadn't been an only child, she conceded her existence had been pretty self-serving to that point. Memories flashed through her mind of yelling at her mom about being so strict, about hating Ben for his actions.

"Now the Ivies, on the other hand… Those bastards are one hundred percent assassins. They *literally* have no reason to come to the human world other than to hunt us down and kill us. Well, I mean you girls; taking out one of us guys is just icing on the cake. They don't come here to vacation or settle down."

Mel realized she needed deeper answers if she was in the middle of a war. "Why do they hate us so much? Why can't we just work things out?"

He sniggered and shook his head as though he were amused at the thought of ever being on good terms with the Ivies. "It's a core difference in who we are. Seeders, we spread out, we nourish, we focus on our families. They hate us for our diversity, consider themselves better than us. They blame us for things we never did. All they do is destroy. Ivies live in a wasteland, a place they decimated long ago, and now they try to take over our homes and resources. They even punch into the human world instead of respecting it the way we do." His mouth puckered with rage. "They don't have a single redeeming quality."

Devin was so passionate, goal-oriented, and clearly smart. Strong and tender at the same time. He had already expressed his love for Mel. She hadn't reached that point yet—she still needed to figure out who she was as a person, before she could figure out what they were as a couple. But she was starting to wonder if it was love. She looked down at her hands; the glowing had subsided.

"Do you think we could go for a walk?" she asked.

He decided they could risk a short stroll as long as they kept close to the house. They walked hand in hand down a dirt path on the safe house property, obscured from any neighbors or roads by trees. Mel soaked in the sunshine and savored the breeze. It was calming, it was cleansing, it was a much-needed breather from the crazy.

At her request, Devin told her what he could about his family. He shared fun childhood memories he had with his brothers and mom, Sandra.

"You know, all of you girls were given a name by our dads after sprouting. They're different from what your human host families gave you." He twirled a strand of her hair around his finger. "Yours is Saffrona. I'd love to call you that in private, if you're okay with it."

"That's pretty." She smiled. "I remember hearing Ben say that when we were leaving the gym. We could try it out, or maybe Saff for short?"

He matched her smile. "Could I kiss you, Saff?"

She bit her lip. It was cute for him to ask, and fun having a secret name he could call her. "Yeah."

He leaned in, holding the nape of her neck. Her heart pounded like it always did when they kissed. His kiss took her away to another world altogether. His lips were soft and supple. And warm. Really warm.

"Oh crap." He backed away and held her at arm's length. "We can't do this out in the open, not until you learn to control yourself."

She was actually starting to recognize the cues, like a warmth in her eyes. They must have started to change again.

"We can't get distracted, we're not just here to hide. There's a lot of work to do." His smile faded. "A lot."

She nodded and took his hand as they turned to head back to the house.

"So, what's next? You said we have all spring break together, just you and me?" she asked.

He grinned. "Do you know how much I love that we get to spend an entire week alone? And how much it sucks that it's not just for fun?"

"Yeah, yeah, yeah. Says every guy after telling a girl he can only kiss her inside an empty, secluded house, but not out in the open." She winked and nudged him.

He pursed his lips, shaking his head. "You're not going to make this easy for me, are you?"

She laughed. "I feel like you enjoy a challenge."

***

After returning to the house, Devin offered to make some lunch. Only the slightest aching lingered from Mel's change and she had developed a healthy appetite. She sorted through her packed bag and made up her bed with fresh sheets from the linen closet while Devin took care of the cooking.

She came into the kitchen, leaning against the counter while he stirred a pot on the stove.

"So, I have a secret name. Do you have one, too?"

"Afraid not. Just boring Devin here."

"I'd say you're anything but boring. Though…" She reached out her hand for a handshake.

He looked at her hand in confusion.

She grinned. "Hi, my name is Saff, humans call me Mel. Nice to meet you."

He narrowed his eyes at her, not sure what she was getting at.

She shrugged. "I just figured, I'm not sure how much of the real you I know. I'm assuming some of your hobbies and responsibilities were covers. I'd like to get to know what you're really like."

He smiled and shook her hand, pulling it up for a kiss before letting it go. "Nice to meet you. My name is Devin. One of the top in my acting class." He put a hand over his heart and lifted his chin comically in pride. "As evidenced by my *amazingness* at blending in here. Pretty great marks in sparring, thus my *deployment* here." He flexed a bicep and threw her a seductive look.

She giggled at his silliness.

"And someone that appreciates beauty, as evidenced by my stolen heart." He gazed into her eyes. That look—it got her every time. His eyes, his dimples, just everything about him drew Saff in.

She bit her lip. "How about I help with cooking?"

"Are you trying to throw me out of the kitchen? I thought I made a pretty mean peanut butter toast this morning."

"Maybe I just want to cook with you." She raised her eyebrows in challenge.

"It's almost done, but please, be my guest." He stepped back, hands gesturing to the pots on the stove.

She moved over and began to stir. "I really don't cook much. Does it matter if it's clockwise or counter clockwise?" She looked over her shoulder with a grin.

"Oh, there's *definitely* a technique. Let me show you." He moved up behind her, wrapping his left hand around her waist and putting his right hand over hers to stir. "See, just like that. I know it's *immensely* difficult, but you might just learn."

She chuckled. "You're such a great teacher. I think I'll keep you."

He took the wooden spoon from her hand and set it down, then spun her around, starting to dance. "I wouldn't have it any other way."

She'd almost forgotten how skilled he was at dancing; it didn't matter that there wasn't any music playing. "You know, you still only told me how you did in school, with acting and sparring. What did you do in your free time back home?"

He cocked his head while thinking about it, not losing his rhythm while dancing. "Our lives are pretty simple, Saff. We don't get much choice in the schooling we do. You're trained to fight, no matter who you are. You take a lot of classes that would prepare you for life in this world."

"Like dancing?"

He chuckled. "That one's not exactly compulsory. Actually, it's quite hard to get into a dancing class. Imagine what it's like, not having a single girl your age or younger in the entire village until you turn fifteen. Absolutely every girl is older than you until those from your year start to trickle in."

"Wow … yeah. That's crazy to imagine. And sad." Her contemplative look turned into a jovial one. "No wonder you fell for the first girl you saw when you came here."

He stopped dancing and gave her a frustrated look.

She frowned. "I'm kidding."

He shook his head and went back to stirring the food. "I don't think it's very funny. It's a pretty messed-up life compared to how Ivies and humans get to live. Remember that, when you get mad about everyone keeping it a secret. *You* got to live a normal life." He paused. "And I don't exactly appreciate you discounting my feelings like that, even if you don't feel the same way about me."

She touched his arm. "I'm sorry, I really didn't mean anything by it. And you know I feel the same way."

He turned to face her. "Do you?"

He had outright said he loved her, but that was a huge step for Saff. "I don't know if I'm ready to say what you want to hear. But that doesn't mean I don't care about you. I'm the one that never had to pretend, remember?"

He sighed, his shoulders dropping. "I'm not trying to rush you, I never have. Maybe it's just the Seeder culture in me, but I don't take relationships that casually." He still carried a tone of frustration in his voice. "And I want you to remember, just because I wasn't forced to live away from my homeland growing up, doesn't mean my childhood was all fun and games. And I didn't come here to vacation or date."

Shame stung her eyes as she looked at the ground. "I'm sorry," she whispered. "I'll go set the table."

She sat at the table while Devin finished up, watching as he stirred and added extra seasoning. They had lived vastly different lives. And, while she got the short end of the stick in some ways, maybe it wasn't such a raw deal after all, compared to the men of their kind.

He set out a hot pad and a pot of rice and beans, then started to dish them up. "I accept your apology. I know you're going through a lot. You have lots to take in."

She fidgeted with her fork. "Thank you."

He continued with a straight face, "I'm good in the garden. Love going on nature walks. I like reading, and swimming, and you'd be a fool to try and win a poker game against me." He cleared his throat. "And, uh, I never got into those dancing classes. My mom and aunt taught me."

She smiled and he grinned back.

"It's nice to meet you, Devin. I look forward to getting to know you better."

He gave her a nod and they dug in. It wasn't on his list, but he was not at all a bad cook, either.

Saff picked up a forkful of food, gazing upon the beans. "Is this cannibalism?" She glanced back at him.

Devin stared at her. "That's morbid."

She busted out laughing. "Come on. We're part plant!"

He cocked his head to the side. "We're more human than hydrangea. We're part mammal, too. I don't know about you, but I'll take bacon or a salad any day over dirt and sunshine."

She grinned. They were weird, but at least not *that* weird...

After eating, they sat together in the living room. It was still natural to be close to Devin. He put his arm around her and she leaned against him.

"So, let's recap here," she said, grabbing his free hand. "Not human. Being hunted by assassins. I have powers and family I never knew about. And I'm from a place called the Green Lands?"

He nodded. "Good summary."

"You haven't talked much about the Green Lands." Her anxiety was building, her mind having rehashed some of the things he'd been saying. "All of my sisters are back there now?"

He nodded. "Unless they're back here secretly for a visit. But you still have one sister here."

Saff pursed her lips. "They all moved to some other world, or realm, or whatever you call it. And you've said things about me going there." She turned to face him. "That's the expectation of me, right? I'm expected to move?"

He nodded with a slight frown. "Yeah, Saff. This isn't our world. You never would have grown up here if it wasn't necessary."

It was a strange notion, and a sad one. That the parents she loved might not have been the ones to raise her, if things were different. And only Seeders and Ivies—'green folk,' as Devin had previously referred to the residents of the Green Lands—could travel between the worlds. She wasn't just leaving behind normalcy and safety, she was leaving behind her family.

"No one would force you to go," he added. "But... Well, that's the way it's supposed to be."

Saff gnawed on her lip, scanning his face. She still wasn't sold on the idea, and there was so much left to learn. She barely knew anything about this alternate home. But she tackled it one question at a time. "You said, what was it? We open a doorway?"

He nodded. "A rift."

"How much work does that take to learn? Could we go take a look now? That could help me feel better about all this."

His mouth hung open for a moment. "Not that easy, unfortunately. And forming a rift isn't the hard part. We'll be teaching you to catch a breeze to get to the nearest rifting location."

She raised an eyebrow. "Catch a breeze?"

He grinned. "Sorry, like I said, I've never explained it all before. Seeders can't just rift from the ground. 'Catch a breeze' is how we say 'fly.'"

Her eyes grew wide. "Wait, what? I can fly?"

He chuckled. "Yeah. But as you can imagine, that's not the easiest thing to master. And we won't have time to focus on it this week. Right now, we need to use our time to make sure you'll be safe when we go back into town, when spring break's over."

She nodded, eager to learn more about her new abilities.

He pulled one of her hands up to his lips. "So, let's get started on powers?"

She smiled. "Yes."

"The priorities for this week are to learn how to conceal your energy, defend yourself, and transform. Let's start off with concealing, masking. You don't see me change every time I have emotions, because I've learned to center my energy. It's even more important for you, because your energy is stronger." He handed her a small mirror. "Close your eyes for this exercise. I want you to think of Blake."

Her eyes snapped open. "I never want to think about that jerk again."

"Do it, Saff. Trust me."

She sighed and closed her eyes again.

"Think back to when he pissed you off the most. Can you envision it?"

"Oh yeah."

"Good. Think about what you'd have liked to do to him."

"If he hadn't pinned me by twisting my arm, I would have kicked him in the groin and punched him in the face!"

"That's my girl. Picture yourself doing that."

She had a smile on her face.

"Now open your eyes and look in the mirror."

The transformation was glaringly obvious. "Yeah, that's a problem."

"Close your eyes again. Visualize all of your energy coming from your heart. And when you feel emotion, it starts to spread to the other parts of your body. Imagine coaxing that energy back into your heart, extracting it from your mind, neck, arms; drain it all back and then seal it there."

She took a few deep breaths, envisioning it the way he'd explained.

"Good. Now open your eyes."

She looked in the mirror. "It worked!"

"The trick is learning to harness it before it gets away from you. It's better to prevent the physical changes in the first place."

She frowned. "That sounds like I have to walk around emotionless … avoiding people… That's depressing."

"I don't know. I feel a heck of a lot of emotions whenever I'm with you." He grinned. "It's not too depressing when you've got it down."

She blushed. "Yeah, well, you've also had years of practice."

"Touché. But it's not like you can't have emotions. It's more like separating your emotions from your energy. Seeing the energy as an internal layer, so the emotions can reside by themselves in the outer layers, on the surface. Let's practice a little more."

Devin ran her through several visualizations—times in her life where she'd been excited, happy, sad, angry, afraid. She practiced trying to keep the energy contained and then bringing it back quickly whenever she let any spread.

"You're actually doing amazing for your first day! And I'm not just saying that." He was beaming at her progress. "Let's try this one. Close your eyes, take a deep breath, clear your mind…"

She expected to hear more instruction but instead felt his lips on hers, his hands moving to hold her head. He gently pulled her to standing and wrapped his thumbs through her belt loops. She enjoyed every moment of it.

He stopped and studied her face as she opened her eyes. He grinned. "Nope, going to need a lot more practice."

She looked at her hands. "That's not fair, you ambushed me!"

He chuckled and walked away. "That's the point, Saff. They're not going to wait for you to be mentally and emotionally prepared before they attack."

Returning from the bedroom with a book, he invited her to sit next to him on the couch again. She gave him the stink eye for his sneaky demonstration.

Devin shrugged. "Hey, there's a reason I'm good at poker, and probably the *only* reason Ben even let me bring you here—I'm a master at controlling my energy and emotions. I focused on it in my studies so I could better teach it."

She raised an eyebrow. "Is that a challenge? To see if I can spot green eyes? I'm willing to try kissing you until it happens. I can take one for the team."

He laughed. "As much as I love your willingness to sacrifice, there are two problems with that plan. One: My eyes can't glow green like yours, at least not yet." He leaned over and gave her a peck. "And two: we have a lot we need to get done. Let's go over some basic fighting and protection forms."

Chapter 15

DEVIN SPENT THE NEXT COUPLE of hours showing Saff a book about the abilities of their people. One of the most notable differences between the genders amongst Seeders, was that the females of their race could heal others. Similar to the female Ivies, Seeder females' leaves were softer, less sharp than their male counterparts. That was part of why the Ivies rarely sent women to the human world—they weren't as lethal of assassins. But female Seeders weren't left without the ability to fight. Their blades could still cut Ivy vines, and they had a natural agility and lightness that aided them in various hand-to-hand fighting styles like humans had.

"Learning to fully transform, to catch a breeze back to the Green Lands, that's the end goal, and not easy. Part of that is mastering how to extend your blades properly," he explained.

She was still reeling from that reveal. 'Catch a breeze.' She could *literally* fly. Saff flipped the page back and forth. "Wait, it doesn't say anything about the dart things Ben did in here."

"Those are in the male chapters, they're not inherently a female ability."

She wrinkled her nose at the unfairness of it. "That sucks. Those seem like they would be really helpful…"

He shifted uncomfortably in his seat. "Well, there's a way for our girls to be able to do the darts, but it's not something you're going to be worrying about right now. We're focusing on basics."

Saff flipped through more of the book. It explained how the female form possessed more energy, and it could be shared, transferred to males if needed. "Like what Ben did. Can my energy be … taken from me, or do I have to give it?"

"You have to give it, no one can take that from you without your willingness," he answered.

She sighed in relief. "Good. That would be so … violating…"

"You're no damsel in distress." He nudged her arm.

Past the different chapters covering male and female abilities, there was a section titled 'Mixed Forms.' He took the book from her hands, closing it and setting it down. "That's something you'll learn about later. It's definitely beyond the basics. Right now, we keep you hidden, alive, and prepare you to go home."

He said it so casually. 'Go home.' Devin really didn't realize that *this* was her home. The only home she'd ever known.

He stood, holding out his hands. She obliged, joining him.

"Our abilities are all basically physical, transformative. They're not like magic tricks or silly potions. They come from your essence and relationship with nature; they're actually pretty intuitive once you understand and practice a little. Cup your hands together like you're holding something you don't want to get out."

She lifted her arms and followed his directions. It reminded her of when she would catch grasshoppers as a little girl and they would hop around between her palms without being harmed.

"Close your eyes again. Now you're going to do the opposite of what we've been practicing. I want you to envision the light, the energy in your heart and let it spread, but only to your hands. Like you're using a squeegee to guide it there."

She opened her eyes and her hands; her hands were glowing.

"That's not enough. You got it to reach your hands, but you need to *contain* it there. Right now, it's like you're forming a channel from your heart to your hands. You need to clear out your arms and push it all into the gap between your palms. Try again: Open the channel from the heart. Reach to the hands. Concentrate it there."

She closed her eyes and tried once more.

A couple of deep breaths and a minute later, she looked again. She had successfully filled the space between her hands with a ball of light. She held it there like it was a handful of water. "Oh my gosh! What do I do with this?"

"Let me show you how you can help in a fight." He made a fist and flicked it open, spraying a handful of small darts into a corkboard on the wall that had seen some damage over the years. "If you'll allow me, I'm going to access that energy—is that alright?"

She nodded in consent.

He put one hand over hers, cradling the light between them. It surged through his hand as he tossed more darts into the cork. They were ejected with more speed and were three times as wide, and twice as long, as his original darts. Even he looked a little shocked and impressed. "That's a heck of a boost, right? The only reason Ben could use your energy earlier without you understanding it is because it was flowing from you unchecked during your bloom."

He squinted, calculating something. "Remind me to teach you another way to do this … another time."

She made a mental note to remind him.

He walked over to the wall of darts. "There's not really a way around this. You need hands-on experience." Pulling one of the larger darts from the cork, he cringed while slicing a gash in his own arm.

Saff gasped. "Are you crazy?!"

"It hurts a lot." He sucked air in through clenched teeth. "What do you think you can do about it?"

She looked from his bleeding arm to her hands. She'd read about healing in the book, but not in depth. Closing her eyes, she envisioned more light forming as it had before. Successful, she cupped her hands on his wound. "This is it, right? How do I know when it's done?"

His squinting eyes relaxed. "Exactly. There are different techniques, but this is a pretty basic one. It takes practice to know when it's done the job." He looked down. "Honestly, I think you've already fixed it. Go ahead and take your hands off."

Removing her hands, the light dissipated; the wound had closed up. Though there was still residual blood on his arm and now on her hand. They went to the bathroom to wash up.

While drying her hands, Saff became lightheaded and almost took a spill before he caught her.

"Sorry, should have had you sit for a little while first. Shouldn't have had you do that right after a round of darts. Healing can take a lot out of you, especially when you're new at it, so it's not something you want to expend energy on for every bruise and scrape." He helped her back to the kitchen table.

"Noted." She sat down, laying her head on the table until she recovered. "Can we please not stab or maim you anymore? I'm not a fan."

He poured her some water to drink. They practiced more with controlling her energy and wrapped up for the afternoon when her energy was spent. Devin dug through the cabinets and freezer to find something to make for dinner. "It really zaps you when you're first learning, because you have to put so much into making your body do what you want. But after a while, it's as easy as breathing."

They sat down for a dinner of frozen pizza and canned peaches.

"When can I meet my birth mom and other family in the Green Lands?" She assumed it must be pretty amazing, if ten of her sisters had already chosen to leave this world behind. She was still conflicted, but more excited after learning more about her powers. "It sounds like I might be making changes to my summer plans!" She thought of her parents' gift—the trip to Costa Rica. To say things were now a little complicated would have been a serious understatement. "Or maybe some of them could find time to come here?"

She envisioned how fun it might be to get everyone together. "I mean, obviously it would have to be in secret, but I can just imagine what my mom and dad would do, having a barbeque with twenty-three of my siblings, together with my biological parents someday!"

Devin swallowed a couple times and looked down at the table. "There's a lot that has to be taken care of, in a short amount of time. And your choices will have permanent consequences." He looked back up at her. "Saff, you have to choose."

Her eyes narrowed. "What do you mean, choose? Between my families?!"

He rubbed his hands together nervously. "That's part of it. Let me just explain how it works, okay?"

He had her full attention. She wondered how there could possibly be more to this big revelation.

"Your physiology is so unique. That's why you were raised in the human world, right? You couldn't survive the poison back there without your powers. But … what's different about you doesn't stop there. There's a reason your mom isn't here like your dad is. Once you bloom, like you just did, you only have a short amount of time before you take root. That means you're *permanently* selecting a home, which world you'll live in. Our energy is stronger in the Green Lands.

"It's like…" He rocked his head back and forth. "So, the cool thing is, Seeder females are the most powerful beings in the Green Lands. You have a strong tie to the energy there. But with that … comes the downsides." He bit his lower lip. "It's like a two-step tethering. When you go back, like Tabatha, you 'root'—you're connected to the realm. You can't just come back and visit whenever you want. Once you're mature enough, like our moms were when they had us, the final phase sets in, and you … can't leave."

He paused, scanning her face. The chaos of the new restrictions in her life overwhelming her, she struggled to form a question.

He continued in his explanation. "After you take root over there, you have enough of a boost to get back here for a short visit, but that's all. Once a year, for maybe a week in the spring. That is, until you mature to the age where you can have a clutch of seedlings yourself, usually ten years down the road. Like I said, at that point, you're never able to return to the human world. Pam can't go to our world, and Murial can't make it back here. They'll never meet."

Her heart dropped. She stared at the table, running her fingernails across it. Asking her to move to another realm was bad enough. But it wasn't a simple road trip or flight away to come back and visit.

His voice carried guilt. It was obvious he disliked being the bearer of bad news as much as she disliked being the recipient of it. "Our roots aren't as deep, us guys. But we can still only go back and forth maybe, at most, a handful of times a year."

She looked down at her hands, trying to process. "That means if I go, I could only see my parents once a year? My friends. Zach. I… I wouldn't… College… I mean, I don't know what it's like over there … what you guys do for education, careers." Her breath quickened, her heart thumping in her chest. Her vision blurred with a coating of tears. "That's horrible. What if I don't want to choose?"

He tilted his head with a sympathetic frown. "Not choosing between worlds means you choose the human world, and all that comes with it. If you don't learn what you need to, to catch a breeze by the time you root, you'll never see your homeland. You'll never meet your mom, or most of your family. Your energy is cut off from the Green Lands and dies out. You revert to human form for the rest of your life. Well … mostly human. Technically, you can't have kids with a human, and if you root here, you couldn't have Seeder kids, either. In case that matters to you." He pursed his lips. "And, not to be selfish, Saff, but you and I couldn't be together."

Her chest ached as though she'd just had the wind knocked out of her. Rubbing her forehead, she looked at the table, trying to understand all that her choices meant. "You said I have a short amount of time to learn this and decide if I want to go back. How long is that?"

He frowned. "I asked you to check what your roots look like, in the shower. How, uh, far down do they reach?"

She moved a hand to her hip, then showed him with her thumb and pointer finger. It was probably two to three inches of these weird growths.

He nodded, biting his lip. "About what we expected." He took a deep breath. "I'm not saying this to make you feel bad."

Her heart sank further.

"If your change had been completed with the charm on, you'd have three, maybe four months. But … your timeframe was accelerated. You only have maybe a month."

"A month? A month!" She covered her mouth with her hand and stared into Devin's eyes. Her eyes warmed—they were glowing bright green again, forming more tears.

She stood up from the table. "I need to go lie down."

Shock overwhelming her, she didn't even try to not cry. She wished he'd led with all the downsides first. She had powers—that was great! A new family she hadn't known about—exciting. Assassins lurking in the human world—less than ideal. Leaving her entire life behind, permanently, and only having a month to learn everything and decide—impossible.

She never came back out that night. As she sniffled into her pillow, she heard Devin cleaning up in the other room. Eventually, he joined her in the bedroom, lying down on the other bed.

"I'm sorry," he whispered once the lights were out. "Goodnight."

***

Saff woke in the morning to the smell of coffee wafting into the bedroom. The shower was running down the hall as she made her way to the kitchen and poured herself a cup of hot brew. She cringed at the bitterness, but needed the pick-me-up. Seeder energy and human energy were related, but not one and the same. She felt at 'full charge' in the Seeder department. Not so much in her human mind and body.

After plopping down onto a dining room chair, she laid her head down on the table. Shortly after the shower turned off, the bathroom door opened. Devin strode out with a towel wrapped around his waist.

"Hey beautiful." He smiled. "I'm seeing a pattern here. You keep catching me in compromising situations in the morning." He pointed at her. "You, ma'am, are scandalous."

She managed a weak smile, taking a sip of her drink.

After getting dressed, he joined her at the table. "I'll have you know that you are adorable when you're sleeping."

She certainly didn't feel adorable. Her eyes were puffy, her head ached, and she surmised being run over by an eighteen-wheeler might feel a bit like this.

He gently placed a hand on the table. "Before you say anything, I want to make a proposal. I know I threw a lot at you last night. And I'm not going to pretend like these are inconsequential decisions you need to make. But I think what we should focus on is your training. No matter what you choose, you're going to need to be able to protect yourself until you take root or return home—to our home, that is. You need to learn to harness your energy before we start back up at school. We're going to be back at Pam and George's house a week from tonight."

"They're my parents," she snapped. "They deserve to be called my parents, not just 'Pam and George.'"

Devin fixed his eyes on hers, speaking softly. "You're right, I'm sorry. We'll be going back to your *parents'* house a week from tonight. And I know they'll be excited to see you, and you'll have tons of catching up to do." He raised his eyebrows and smiled. "I'd even put money on grumpy ol' Ben being happy to see you."

She nodded ever so slightly.

"Do we have a deal? Focus on the short-term needs, sort out the other stuff as it comes up?"

"Is there anything else you haven't told me that I should know about? Anything you're keeping from me?"

He frowned. "I'm sorry. I told you I haven't done this part before. But, no. Nothing else big, I don't think. Not intentionally, anyway."

She studied his face. "Okay. We'll focus on training." She knew she had a heck of a lot to figure out and not nearly enough time to do so. But trying to appear normal and keeping herself safe seemed like the logical place to start.

He gave her a half-smile. "And, you know, we can still enjoy our time together. I really love just being with you."

Her cheeks warmed as she looked down at her hands, thinking of him coming out in a towel, knowing how livid her parents would be. "Ditto."

He grabbed a granola bar for each of them and sat back down. A couple questions nagged at her from the previous night.

"Why am I even going back to school? It's not like I'm going to graduate, or even finish up the rest of the school year, if I go to the Green Lands. And if the Ivies might know what I am, aren't I just making myself more of a target by going back?"

He raised an eyebrow. "Have you decided you're going home?"

She shook her head, opening the granola wrapper.

"Then you'll continue school. And even if you were going home, we don't know for sure that Blake or Ken survived. Whether or not they did, it's true, they still might have tipped off the others. If that's the case, they also know we'll be extra vigilant."

He motioned for her to join him in the living room to start practice for the day. "If we're lucky and the other Ivies don't know who you are, then we don't want to give them any reason to suspect you by changing your behavior. You might just be one of many names on their list of suspected Seeders. If we do something to confirm their suspicions, that implicates all of us. They'll wonder if your brother is a plant, if you're dating a Seeder; all eyes will be on us."

She stifled a laugh.

He wrinkled his forehead. "What?"

"Sorry, you said my brother is a plant. That's, you know … true."

He pursed his lips to suppress a smile and shook his head. "You are a dork."

She wore a huge grin. "But you love me anyway."

He bit his lip. "I do." He took a deep breath. "Anyway … you'll have plenty of eyes on you at school. I can't go into the details, but you'll be in good hands. Your dad texted to let me know they expect your last sister to leave in the next week or two, so you'll have even more of our focus."

She realized that most of the time he mentioned 'mom' and 'dad' he meant the Seeder ones. "When do I get to meet him?"

"Probably not until you're ready to leave, assuming he goes back with you. I'm not sure what he's worked out with my dad on who will stay, since I've got sisters that will be here longer."

She crossed her arms, still somewhat frustrated at being in the dark. "Why can't I know more about who's on our side? That would make me feel a heck of a lot safer at school. I would obviously keep it a secret."

He shook his head. "It's out of the question. It's not about whether or not we can trust you. You may give it away without knowing."

She scowled. "I'm not a gossip! What, only men are capable of keeping secrets? The fathers and sons of the Seeder networks?"

He rolled his eyes. "One of us in this room spent *years* preparing for this situation. And that person is not you. Think back to when you were oblivious to Ben, Tabatha, and Stacy being your siblings. Can you honestly tell me you wouldn't throw in an extra smile in the hallway if you knew? You wouldn't accidentally look over at Stacy and wonder how she was progressing with her training? You wouldn't have reacted differently at all to Ben getting caught spying on you?"

She thought it over and cocked her head to the side. A memory flashed through her mind. Stacy, being nice in the lunchroom. She wasn't making amends because she was sick; she was doing it because she knew she was leaving... If it was true that Stacy didn't even know she had this in common with Saff ... she still gave away that something was off. "Fine. I see your point."

He smiled and pointed a finger at her. "Bingo."

Saff scrunched her nose. "Why is it that I love and hate everything that comes out of your mouth?"

Devin showed off a huge, toothy smile.

"That wasn't a compliment."

"You said you love me."

"I said I love *what you say*, but I also said I hate what you say."

He sat beside her on the couch, sliding an arm around her shoulders. "But you'll forgive me. I like to focus on the positive. You said something about love, and my mouth." He raised his eyebrows in challenge.

She pursed her lips and shook her head. "You think you're such a charmer."

He feigned taking offense. "How dare you! I *know* I'm charming."

She giggled. "Let me see if I remember how much I love those lips."

She drew him in, running her hands through his hair. His hands trailed along her legs, eventually resting on her hips.

Saff moved her lips to his neck, trailing the kisses higher until she reached his ear, whispering, "You said I'd be in good hands, and I guess you were right. I like being in your hands."

He let out a loud laugh. "So, this is how it's going to be all week? Flirting with the teacher?"

She didn't answer; instead, she focused on giving him a hickey.

Devin chuckled, leaning away and grabbing the small mirror. "Saff?"

She finished her handiwork with a smirk. "What?"

He held up the mirror. "If we're going to get distracted, we should at least work on your training so you don't look like *this* every time we kiss."

She frowned, spotting her green eyes. She took the mirror from his hands and set it down. "I'm insulted by that! I'm not distracted. I just needed something to heal." She flashed a mischievous grin, then put her hand up to his neck, pushing energy to it. The hickey faded. She planted a peck where the hickey had been. "A kiss to make it better, for added measure."

He smiled. "You're good."

Chapter 16

GETTING MORE ON TASK, SAFF and Devin spent the rest of the morning and afternoon practicing what she'd learned the day before. It was grueling work, but they needed to push hard—time wasn't on their side.

While taking a much-needed break, Devin pulled out his phone. In the chaos of her discovery, Saff's had been left behind, though they agreed it was probably for the best.

"We need you to send a message to Zach and post on social media about our fun spring break getaway. Everyone needs to know you're alive and living a normal life." He handed her the phone. "Here, apologize to Zach and explain that I surprised you with a road trip to meet my parents. You dropped your phone and it didn't make it; that's why you've been out of touch."

She started to type a message. "You're going to have to teach me to be a convincing liar and how to come up with stories like this on the spot." She looked up and noticed he was visibly offended. "Sorry, I didn't mean it like that. I just mean … I'm not used to this kind of stuff. Living in secrets and shadows is your thing." She finished typing up the message. "Here, come check it before I send it."

While he was reading it over, she smiled. "You know, you say you're amazing at poker and acting, but now that I look back, you gave yourself away a few times."

He looked up, raising his eyebrows. "Really? Give me an example."

"Mmm. When we had that argument about Blake and stereotypes. I said you could be judged as a troublemaker because you moved here in the middle of high school. I could tell for the rest of the day that I'd hurt your feelings."

He smirked. "Maybe I didn't expect the same girl who was stealing my heart, to hurt it. Plus, I'm only human, I'm not perfect."

She lifted an eyebrow. "But you're not human."

He threw his hands in the air with a hint of a smile. "It's a saying. The kind *you* learned growing up!"

She smiled wide. If everyone in the Green Lands either grew up over here, or trained to blend in … it might not be so foreign after all.

He went back to reading her message to Zach, mumbling under his breath with a smile. Approving of the message, they sent it off. Devin returned his cell to his jeans pocket, then opened the living room coat closet. "Next on the list," he said, starting to pull out equipment. After grabbing a few things, he closed the door and began to set it up. He extended poles and popped open two lights with white umbrellas, like photographers use, then hung a green sheet on the wall. "Gotta make it look convincing. Let's get some pictures for social media. We've got a guy that edits us anywhere we want to be."

"Wow, you guys seriously think of everything." She joined him in front of the green screen.

"I know this is going to be tough," he said with a straight face. "But you'll have to pretend you enjoy spending time with me."

She frowned. "Dang it. This may be the hardest thing I've had to do in the last week!"

He poked and tickled her until she giggled and begged for mercy.

They took some standard cutesy couple pictures, changing shirts a few times, and then texted them to his contact. Later that night they'd get them back to post.

"So, handsome, we're visiting your parents? How long is the car ride? Do they like me? What kinds of things are we doing?"

He collected the photo shoot equipment, putting it back in its place. "It's a four-hour drive to get there. Of course, my parents love you, why wouldn't they? And we're spending our week hiking and playing board games."

"What if I don't want to go hiking?"

He raised his eyebrows. "We're hiking. Everyone that needs to know back home has the same story down."

"Fine. I hope I remember to wear sunscreen." She stuck out her tongue playfully. "What are our favorite road-trip snacks?"

He looked confused.

"You really didn't grow up in the human world, did you?" She grinned. "Finally, I get to be the teacher! This is a quintessential fact. You know what junk food is, but you really ought to know its place in road-trip culture. I think we should argue over Red Vines versus Twizzlers and both agree that *no* chocolate should have raisins in it."

He raised his hands. "I'll go with whatever you say. You're the expert on this one."

"Seriously though, I would never guess that you and Ben weren't from this world. It has to be pretty different from ours over there. You really blend in."

He nodded. "One appreciates when someone admires their hard work. Thank you. I mean, we learn really early how to talk like we're from here, what kinds of references to make, even if we've never been to a place or done the activity."

Her smile faded to a frown. "I would love to show you around, give you a real human experience. But I'm guessing we're not going to have time for that, are we?"

He squinted at the ceiling. "How about this… Promise me you'll try your hardest, and I promise I'll let you take me on an adventure before you leave."

Her smile returned.

"But I mean it. As much as I love getting lost in your glowing green gaze, I want to see a normal human looking back at me when we make out."

"Deal!" she said. "Should we practice that now?"

He laughed and shook his head. "This girl … one-track mind. What am I supposed to do with you?"

She replied in a playfully sexy voice, "What do you want to do with me?"

He shook his head. "You're killing me, Saff."

"Okay, okay, okay."

"Anyway…" He cleared his throat. "To finish answering your question, we also tutor new arrivals once they get here. Teach them things on the spot, like how to drive a car. How to use electronics. I wasn't completely lying about tutoring after school."

She put her hands on his waist, finding herself continually enamored with his dedication. "You guys are underrated. It's like you never have a free second to just enjoy life. You're always on the job. How do you even manage it? And go to school?"

He raised both eyebrows. "One of the secrets … our 'parents' don't care that much if we skip class on occasion, and they don't give a crap about our Trigonometry grades. We don't use that nonsense in the Green Lands."

She sighed pensively. "You know what, I don't think we use Trigonometry here either." They both laughed.

After hours of more strenuous practice, they'd earned a solid night's sleep. They lay down, facing each other from their separate beds.

"Will you tell me more about the Green Lands? What's it like?"

She couldn't see his face in the dark, but she could hear his smile in the softness of his reply.

"You'll love it, Saff. In a lot of ways, it's not all that different from the human world. We have roads and houses. But life is simpler. Excuse the pun, but it's more 'down to earth.' We have gravel or dirt streets. No cars or pollution. Actually, no electricity at all, as you know it. But we have our own equivalent for a lot of things—lamps, solar showers, all that. More basic diets—we're generally vegetarians. Everyone, and I literally mean everyone, has a garden; we grow a lot of our own food. We don't have the same technology, but we do have entertainment."

She smiled. It sounded so primitive. But also idyllic and peaceful.

"Our society is more cooperative, family-centered. Couples live in fairly small cottages, until they have kids—then there are, I guess you'd consider them like apartments or dorms? Housing lots are shared amongst neighbors to accommodate a variety of needs. Property lines and ownership aren't like they are here. A family quickly goes from two to thirteen—then builds up to twenty-six—then shrinks as the kids grow up, move away, pair off. Our schools are tailored to the needs of war on the home front; how to be prepared for the human world, and also basics like history, art, literacy.

"Of course, this is all the Seeder side of things. I've never been to the Ivy side, but from what I understand, it's like Detroit. It's the armpit of the Green Lands."

She chuckled at his last description and then yawned. "It sounds so beautiful. Well, not the Detroit part, but the rest of it."

"It is, Saff. I wish I could be there to see your face when you first arrive."

She was exhausted, but stayed awake long enough to give it more thought. Devin assumed she would go back to the Green Lands, giving up her life here. She envisioned herself walking through the simple streets lined with cottages. Unique people, just like her, in family-centered communities.

She frowned. Family. Her parents. And kids ... the Seeder way of life was so wholly unhuman. And Zach. She was over the moon about getting to see Tabatha again, and sharing this exciting adventure they were both on. But Zach had already been hurt by losing one of his best friends.

A thousand other thoughts swirled in her mind, until she drifted, not-so-peacefully, off to sleep.

***

After some vigorous drilling of concealment exercises the next morning, Saff sat down at one end of the couch to take a break. Devin joined her. He grabbed a throw pillow, tossing it on her lap, and lay down.

He closed his eyes. "Mmm. Hard work. Nap time."

She chuckled. "Yes. It must be so tiring for *you*. The one whose job is mostly to talk."

He opened his eyes and smiled. "Hey, now." He laid a hand on his chest. "It's exhausting, seeing you so exhausted."

She rolled her eyes with a smile. Reaching a hand down, she held his and took a deep breath. She was ready to ask some harder questions.

"You expect me to go back."

He kissed her hand. "I hope you go back."

"I'm still trying to figure all that out. Why I should move to the Green Lands. Why me, or any of the other girls of our kind, would choose to go there. It's such a big change. And you have to admit that it doesn't come without a huge sacrifice."

He squeezed her hand. "The energy, the abilities. How do you feel, now that you have them?"

She shrugged. "They're obviously amazing. But it feels superficial to give up my way of life for them."

He frowned. "No. It's more than that—it's a unique feeling. I immediately sensed the change when I first came here. The air here is … thinner, more draining. Back home there's a warmth, a richness. And I don't just mean a warm temperature. It's … different. You really don't feel a pull to go there? Something in your heart?"

She pondered his description. "It's hard to say. I don't have any way to compare like you do." She ran her fingers tenderly through his hair. "And my heart…" She smiled. "My heart is telling me a lot of different things."

He broke eye contact. "I hope you come home." He added with a small smirk, "Did I mention we live about ten years longer than humans?"

She nodded at the nice bonus, but her heart was still heavy. "If you were in my shoes, and lived a happy life, blissfully unaware of this war … can you honestly say you'd choose to leave this behind and surround yourself with that? Just walk into a world at war?"

He looked her in the eyes, furrowing his brow. "No, love, it's not like that. If you can make it through this month, you'll be perfectly safe over there."

She was a bit skeptical about that. He grew up there; he was bound to have a different perspective. "I'm in danger here, because of Ivy assassins. But half of my brothers stayed there, too, to protect Seeder territory? That sounds like a no-win situation."

He sighed. "Around the time of the poisoning, we erected *huge* border walls to protect our villages, powered by the excess energy of our women. With the wall and our regular patrols, the Ivies haven't actually gotten through to harm our communities in decades.

"It's a stale war. I don't even know if there's been a significant attempt at breaching our borders in our lifetime. They still keep us on our toes, though, every time we've tried to expand to unharmed neutral areas, to be able to keep our families together. But the shadow wars here, in the human world—that's the most dangerous part for you. If we lose our women … by Ivy hands…" He looked at her knowingly. "Or by choice … that weakens the safety of our borders."

She felt the weight of the decision on her shoulders. He wasn't trying to give her a guilt trip, but it still led down that alley.

"One person doesn't make that big of a difference, though, right?" she asked.

Devin took a deep breath. "Maybe not. Though, if everyone thought that way and stayed here…" He pursed his lips. "Our women used to be stronger. The poison doesn't kill our girls once their powers come in, but they're not able to store as much energy as they used to. The contributions required now are still comfortable, not too demanding, with our current population."

Saff mulled it over. "So, the powers make me able to survive, but I'll actually be able to do less than I can now?"

His look of confusion made it evident she'd misunderstood. "No. You actually get a boost once you root, and then when you reach full maturity."

"You just said we can't store as much energy because of the poison."

"Oh, that. What I mean is that the generations after the poisoning aren't as strong as they used to be. But what you have now won't go any lower." He raised his eyebrows. "And you're actually really powerful for your age. Not lying."

She blushed. "I have to ask. They poisoned our lands, breaking up our families … and they obviously don't have qualms about killing us … but we really don't do *anything* to provoke it?"

He scowled. "No! They used to live just like us, *with* us, even. They're the ones that moved away and set up a corrupt kingdom, and attacked us without provocation."

"Alright. I just … needed to make sure."

His expression softened. "If anything, our people are pacifists to a fault. The Ivy Kingdom barely has a proper border, from what I've heard. We've boxed ourselves in with our walls, and never take the offensive. That's why this has gone on so long. We'd lose a lot of lives if we took them on, if we attacked, so the councils never do anything." He sighed. "It's like a hundred-year siege. Kinda…"

"Would you do things differently?" she asked, sensing his frustration.

He huffed. "I don't know what I'd do. I don't like any of it, but … it's the life we were given. For now, I'm just happy that I'm with you." He gave her a smile. "Meeting you makes it all worth it for me."

She bit her lip as her face warmed again.

He cleared his throat. "I mean, I'm glad I volunteered to come help my sisters and meet my dad. But…" He gazed lovingly into her eyes.

She grinned and shook her head. He was smitten, as was she. But she needed logistics, not just feelings. "What if we all stayed here? Just relocated?"

He lifted his eyebrows. "Aside from abandoning our homes, and giving up our culture and what makes us special?"

She wrinkled her nose, embarrassed for having oversimplified the situation. "I get it."

"Remember, too. Our moms literally can't come back. And … when I said you were picking a permanent home, I meant it. Once you've rooted over there, you can't survive over here for more than a week."

She frowned. "Right. That was a stupid question."

He gave her a reassuring smile. "Not stupid. Maybe someday we can figure it out. We can end this crap and put those leeches in their place."

She smiled back, though it didn't reach her eyes. "I'd love to see that, end this craziness." She paused for a moment. "You and Ben, and Ken and Blake, you've used words like that, 'leeches.' Is that just a nickname?"

He squinted. "Well … we're Seeders, but they sometimes call us 'weeds.' It's an extremely offensive term. And instead of Ivies, you could say our equivalent version for them is 'leeches.'"

She nodded. "Gotcha. I was pretty out of it, but I heard another one. 'Nuren,' I think? Is that a derogatory term for humans?"

He furrowed his brow and his mouth dropped open. "Wait, what? No … all of us just call humans … humans. What about Nuren?"

His drastic change in demeanor was startling.

"Well … I… I don't know. Like I said, I was pretty out of it. Is that a bad word? I don't remember anything else. I just remember that word because it stood out at the time. I think it was Blake that said it."

He sat up and pulled out his phone, typing. "Bad word … no. Bad news … possibly."

He looked genuinely spooked.

"What's that supposed to mean?" she asked, growing more worried.

He put up a finger. "Just a second." His phone chimed and he groaned. "I was right."

"What?"

He turned to face her. "Nuren isn't just a nickname. Nuren is a person. That's a known identity of Ivy royalty."

He was clearly concerned. Her heart beat faster to match his mood. "Right, but what's that supposed to mean for me?"

His expression was calculating. After a moment, he bit his lip and shook his head. "Honestly, I don't know. It might mean nothing. But ... a connection like that to their palace... Nuren's *not* a lackey. It just kind of freaks me out to hear one of their names mentioned here."

He took a deep breath, forcing a smile. "I'm sure I'm overreacting. We'll look into it. If you remember anything else, let me know. For now—I think it just means we better get back to work."

Chapter 17

THEY WORKED HARD ALL WEEK. Saff could even form her blades, though not for long, and not nearly as rigid as they would need to be for catching a breeze or extended fighting. One of the hardest tasks for Saff was separating her emotions from her energy. But she had it down enough that they felt fairly comfortable she could get through a school day and be safe. They would, of course, avoid extreme emotions and circumstances as much as they could, just as a precaution.

"I'm really proud of you. I mean it," Devin praised her the night before they were to drive home. "Now, I told you a while ago that there was something else I could teach you, about energy transfer." He sat down on the sofa. "It goes against everything I've taught you so far. Want to spice things up?"

Still standing on the other side of the living room, she rubbed her chin. "With that introduction, how could I resist?"

"So," he said, blushing, "it's a tradition when sending off a male you love." He quickly added, "Nothing too scandalous. And no pressure, if you're not ready."

"Okay…" Her interest was sufficiently piqued.

He fidgeted awkwardly with his hands. "So, instead of channeling the energy to your hands to share, and instead of suppressing the energy when you kiss, you can actually imbue him with energy *while* you kiss."

"Oooh, that sounds like a challenge I'm willing to take on." She smirked, then dragged over a kitchen chair and sat directly in front of him. "Just like a regular kiss, right? But focus on where the energy is going?"

He nodded with a shy smile. "It's supposed to be pretty … amazing."

She took a deep breath. "You don't say. I think what we've got already is pretty amazing."

His face turned a couple different shades of pink.

Devin was Saff's first boyfriend, and while they hadn't talked about him possibly having a previous relationship, she realized it wasn't likely. Given the slim pickings back home… She felt a little more nervous.

"So you haven't, um…" she started to ask.

"Your first kiss was my first kiss."

She loved that. He could be confident and borderline cocky, and she wondered how much of that was his training. But at the heart of it, they were sharing this journey, these special moments together.

"I, uh," he paused, clearing his throat "well, you know, planned on kissing you to confirm that your eyes would glow, when I suspected your change." He looked her dead in the eyes. "I got carried away, I … really… Gosh, Saff."

She remembered it well, licking her lips. She'd never envisioned her first kiss being a full make-out session, French kiss and all. But she had zero regrets.

"Anyway." He let out a short breathy chuckle. "We kissed enough to make your hair change—that's indicative of more emotion than the simpler stuff that does just the eyes." He sat up straighter. "But … if you're not ready, we can try this another time."

She smiled at his sweetness. "It's a kiss. I can handle a kiss. Let's give it a try."

Saff placed her hands on Devin's shoulders, pressing her lips against his. She kissed him softly as she tried to visualize her energy moving. The tingling warmth traveled up her chest, through her neck, and into her lips and tongue.

The moment her energy started to transfer to him, it ignited them both into a frenzied passion. She climbed into his lap, closing the gap between them. His hands caressed her back, moving up under her shirt. Saff's hands roamed to his belt buckle.

She said what she'd finally realized was in her heart. "Devin, I love you, too."

He slid his hands off her back and pushed her off of his lap. He covered his face with his hands. Even *he* had partially transformed this time, his hair tips now purple. "No, no, no. We can't do this."

Her eyes still glowing, her heart beating a mile a minute, she sat with her mouth open, confused. "I thought … I just…" She swallowed. "Did I do something wrong, say something wrong?"

He stood up and started pacing the room. "No, Saff, of course not." He clenched his fists, then ran his hands through his hair. "You are … gosh… Why do you have to make this so difficult?"

She bit her lip, devastated and embarrassed. "I just thought, we're going home, and then if I'm leaving, I might not see you for a year or two, and…"

"It's not that simple." He pleaded with his eyes. "You know I love you. You seriously have *no idea* what you do to me. I want you in every way possible." He closed his eyes and drew a deep breath. "This is not something we guys have to teach our sisters when we come over." He stood for a moment, pinching the bridge of his nose.

"It's just… Okay, let's first put aside the fact that every single member of your family would want to murder me. It's actually one of our highest laws." He shoved his hands into his pockets. "You've bloomed. You're an adult. Your physiology has changed. Our kind... Saff," he sighed, "we mate for life. That's a huge commitment I can't let you make, especially without understanding it." He looked down. "I guess ... I'm assuming that's what was about to happen. I just..."

Her eyes drifted down as she wrung her hands.

He sat back down in front of her and lifted her chin. "It's not a 'no,' it's a 'not right now.'"

She pressed her lips together, looking at the ceiling, trying to hold back tears. "No, I get it. Not a big deal."

"Hey, look at me."

She lowered her gaze to meet his and wiped away a tear.

"I'm sorry everything's so complicated. It sucks. There's so much you still need to learn about yourself. Remember when I said there's a way for our women to throw darts?"

She nodded.

"Well ... that's part of that beautiful, but complicated process. Once you mate, some of your abilities transfer. I told you once that we're stronger together, and that's one of the many ways. Your darts would fall somewhere between the plain ones I can throw on my own, and the kind I can do with your help. The green eyes, that's also a thing we only get from you."

She faintly smiled. "Humans worry about STIs and STDs, we get to have STPs—Sexually Transmitted Powers."

He gave her a small grin and chuckle. "I guess that's one way to put it."

She nodded again with a sniffle. "I should go to bed, anyway."

He looked down and pursed his lips. "Yeah. Okay."

She got ready for bed and turned in for the night. Devin chose to sleep on the couch in the living room. She was grateful, at first, that he stayed out of the bedroom. She was ashamed that she had allowed herself—allowed that kiss—to take her so close to such a serious step. But then she missed his presence, their nightly conversations in the dark. A familiar feeling ached in her gut. If he were a room closer, it might be too close. If he were a room further away, it would have been as if he were an entire realm away.

***

Devin came into the bedroom in the morning. "What's going on?" he asked groggily, squinting at Saff.

She barely spared him a glance before continuing to pack her bag. "I just don't want to wait to head home. I want to get on the road earlier so I can spend time with my family before going back to school tomorrow. Is that alright with you?"

"Yeah, if that's what you want."

"It is."

They tidied up everything to leave the house ready for the next time it would be needed. Saff was ice-cold and quiet all morning. After getting in the car, Devin tried to hold her hand, but she pulled back.

They rode in silence for several minutes.

"Saff, you're not being fair to me. It's not that I didn't want to be with you last night."

"You should go back to calling me Mel. That way you don't slip when we're around other people."

"Right," he said, his voice petering off to a whisper, "of course."

A couple minutes passed before she spoke again. "If I don't have much time left here, I'm going to spend any time not in school or training how I want. I'm going to spend a lot of time with Zach—that's nonnegotiable."

His reply was far calmer than her mood. "I wouldn't stop you from seeing him. I know he means a lot to you. You just have to remember that he can't know anything."

"I'm not stupid, Devin!"

"Dammit, Saff! Mel ... don't take this out on me. I don't make the rules." He kept his eyes on the road, his jaw clenched.

She leaned her head against the car window, crossing her arms.

He continued, "And I know you're not exactly sunshine and rainbows about me right now, but you're going to need to remember the story, and pretend everything is normal. If you don't want to see me anymore," he paused, "then we'll have to make the breakup believable."

She glanced over at him and then went back to looking out the window with a frown. "I never said that's what I wanted." She took a deep breath. "I'm not as good of an actor as you are, but I'll do my best to be excited about returning from a fun vacation."

The rest of the forty-five-minute drive went by in complete silence.

They pulled up to the Walters residence and Mel hopped out. Her mom ran out to give her a big hug. "Sweetie, I'm so happy you're back! Come on in. I want to hear how everything went."

They entered the front door and were met by Ben, actually smiling, clearly excited to see her. "Hey, Mel, how did training go?"

She glared, put up one hand, lit up a ball of energy, and absorbed it back. "Send me a report card."

She turned to her mom. "Where's Dad? I want to give him a hug."

Pam stood with her mouth wide open. "Um ... he's in the garage."

Devin came in, carrying Mel's bag. Mel wouldn't even look at him, promptly heading down the hall to the garage.

"What did you do to my sister?" Ben demanded.

Mel lingered at the door to the garage, needing to know what Devin would share. Where he'd draw the line between his duties and their relationship.

"You know what, Ben? This one's not on me. I didn't do anything. If you want to know more, you can ask Mel."

He continued, "Mrs. Walters, you should be very proud of her—she's an amazing woman. I'll message everyone an update with where she is in training, and we can sort out the rest of it. I'm going to head home."

***

Devin didn't waste any time dawdling. By the time Mel emerged from the garage, he had already left.

"Do you want to talk?" her mom asked with a hesitant frown.

"I'll be fine. I just want to lie down for a while and get unpacked." Mel grabbed her bag from the hallway and headed upstairs.

She threw her bag on her bedroom floor and shut the door behind her. Her cell phone sat on the nightstand; her mom must have unpacked her things that they'd retrieved from the gym. She flopped on the bed and picked her phone up to scroll through all of her missed texts and messages. As expected, there were several from Zach before she'd messaged him from Devin's phone. She returned the phone to her nightstand and lay on her back, looking up at the glow-in-the-dark stars on the ceiling. They weren't very noticeable in the daylight, but they gave her a focal point. She visualized moving her energy around within her body. Back and forth. Filling her entirely and shrinking down, concealed in her heart. Like the anger and sorrow and frustration also in her heart.

Someone knocked on her door.

"I don't want to talk," she hollered.

"I'm coming in either way, so you better be decent," Ben replied.

He opened the door and stood in the doorway. She glanced in his direction, then went back to focusing on her energy exercises.

"Devin was right, you're a natural," he said.

She found no comfort in his compliment. "I guess I better be, since I screwed everything up, right?"

He frowned. "Hey, I'm sorry I got so mad. It caught me off guard, that's all. No one blames you. That was actually a pretty brazen attack from them, right there at school."

"Doesn't change the facts though, right?"

He sighed. "What can I do to help you?"

She quietly scoffed. "I wish I knew. I just need to sort things out for myself."

"Let me know when you figure it out, okay? I'm guessing you don't want to talk about what's going on between you and Devin?"

She practiced flaring out her arm blades, looking them over. 'Blades'—like a wide blade of grass, and like a knife blade, when sharpened. "That's a hard pass."

"Right... Well, if you need me to pummel him, I'll do it." He leaned in, trying to make eye contact.

She smiled. "That kind of talk is a lot less creepy, now that I know you're my real brother."

He smiled back. "Would it be helpful if I took over the bulk of your training? It's good to have more than one teacher, anyway."

"Sure. Let's try that."

"Okay, I'll get the details sorted out. Sure there's nothing else I can do for you right now?"

She thought for a moment. "Can I have a hug?"

He came over and settled down on the end of her bed with his arms wide open. She sat up, leaning over, and he squeezed her tight.

It was sad, realizing this was actually her first hug with Ben, her real brother. "Sorry I almost got you killed," she mumbled into his shoulder. After pulling back, she looked down at his wrists—the bruises and cuts from the fight were still healing. She ran a finger over them to finish the job.

He gave her an appreciative smile. "Ditto. I'm sorry I wasn't there when you needed me. That won't happen again."

After another long, solid hug, he let her go. "You've been through a lot, and I'm sure you want to get caught up with Pam and

George. But we're working within a pretty tight timeframe, and we really need to make sure you're okay with going back to school tomorrow. We'll need to practice today."

She nodded hesitantly. "Yeah, I know."

"Let's say an hour? I'll clear space in the garage."

"Sure." A faint smile formed on her face. A brother. Her real brother. He wasn't so bad. And she had a heck of a lot more of them waiting for her. If she gave up her life as she knew it…

The floorboards creaked as he stepped from the room, bringing her back to the present.

"Ben?"

He popped back in, leaning against the doorway. "What's up?"

"You're really close to Devin?"

He looked down, pursing his lips. "Have been for years." He raised his head. "If we stay friends, I guess that depends a lot on how he treats you."

Knowing Ben was actually her brother made her want *even less* to share anything about her dating life, but she needed more information. "Pretend he's dating someone else's sister. You think he can be trusted?"

Ben let out a sigh. "I trust him with my life. And I trust him with yours." He shrugged. "It's just, you know… You spend your whole life not only hearing about sisters, but preparing to meet them all, and protect them. And then you two are … well…"

"I know you saved my life, and I'm grateful for that." She raised her eyebrows. "I'm all ears for anything you have to say about him, if you think there's something you should warn me about. But if you'd be equally protective of me with any other guy, then you're going to have to accept that I get to choose on this. I'm done being micromanaged."

He looked up, shaking his head. "I'd like to think I'm not friends with a complete jerk."

She grinned. "Such high praise."

He rolled his eyes.

She remembered a couple of remarks Devin had once made. "I understand you all think everyone needs to be super careful about our identities. But why would the Ivies suspect Devin of being a Seeder and protector, if it's normally just brothers taking care of sisters?"

Ben crossed his arms. "Just because it's not normal, doesn't mean it's never been done before. Each family chooses how they approach the protection of their own clutch. And tactics change, on both sides of the war."

She nodded in understanding.

Ben frowned. "I guess I was too distracted with the fighting. You really heard one of them mention Nuren?"

She matched his frown. Human life was definitely less complicated. "I think so. Why does it feel like things are even worse than they seem, when you and Devin ask about that?"

He shook his head dismissively. "It's okay. We've got you covered. It's just one of those things to take note of. Their network could be more complicated than we were expecting in this town. It means their tactics might be different than we've seen before."

"But in a hundred years of living like this, surely a member of their royal family has been seen or talked about in the human world."

He tilted his head to the side. "Communication between our villages may be limited and slow, but something that big ... I feel like we'd know." He gave a forced smile. "But I'm sure we'll be fine, alright? I'm going to get the garage ready. We can talk more later."

"Okay." Her heart was heavy as he left.

Because a *regular* network of assassins after her wasn't complicated enough...

Chapter 18

THERE OBVIOUSLY WEREN'T ANY ROMANTIC distractions with Ben's training. But even putting that aside, he was a more militant teacher than Devin. They drilled over and over on what Mel had learned during her spring break, and he even introduced more direct fighting techniques.

Ben pushed her hard on forming her blades as they practiced in the garage. "If you can't get that down, then you can't protect yourself, or catch a breeze."

She shook her head, frustrated at the concentration it required. "Why don't we just call it flying? 'Catch a breeze' sounds pretentious."

He scowled. "That sounds stupid. Human airplanes fly. We catch breezes."

She chuckled. "Fine. Whatever."

Finding it too hard to practice defense techniques with both arms sporting blades, they focused on having her do just one, and working with that for now. Ben pulled out spools of rubbery cord and standard rope, each about as thick as one of her fingers.

"It's hard to find something that compares, but these do a decent enough job." He strung them up taut and she practiced cutting the cords with one of her blades.

"Come on, Mel," he drawled. "If you don't focus, your blades won't stay rigid. The leeches aren't going to stay still for you to slowly *saw* away at them."

She threw a scowl in his direction. Taking a deep breath, she attempted to deliver a swift slash to the rubbery cord. Not quite enough—her arm bounced off. It was such a weird sensation. She could feel her blades, but they weren't nearly as sensitive as her regular skin. She prepared for another round and sliced clean through, beaming.

Ben gave her a nod of approval as she moved over to the more traditional rope. Right as she went to try on it, her phone chimed with a text. Distracted, she lost control of her blade and instead gave herself a rope burn.

She sucked in air through clenched teeth.

"Focus!"

Mel had to keep reminding herself why she was putting up with this. She had to protect herself. And … one month. No … one of those four weeks had already been used at the safe house. Three weeks, and maybe some change, if she was lucky. She gritted her teeth, focused her frustration, and took another shot at the rope, easily slicing through it.

"Alright. Let's do that a few more times." He started to restring the ropes.

They practiced a couple new techniques until after dark and every ounce of her energy had been used up. Ben explained more about what to expect in any possible future attacks. She was plenty familiar with the damage Ivy vines could do, though he explained she'd actually gotten off pretty easy.

"If they hook their leaves in right, if they get deep enough and then give it a good yank…" Ben winced. "They can do some serious damage." He ran a finger along his wrist. "This is where the vines come out. Their vines can regenerate, so don't let your guard down if you hack some off." He moved his finger up a little further on his wrist. "If you can manage a deep cut here, it severs the vine. They might be able to recuperate, but definitely not before you can take care of them." He looked into her eyes. "It's a narrow target. If you're fighting for your life, go for the obvious lethal moves when you can."

Mel swallowed hard, her mind replaying memories of the attack. In the school gym. The school she'd be back at the next day.

Going back to school while she sorted things out was less than appealing. But removing herself from society altogether wasn't an idea they could entertain, either. She'd have to break one of their covers, pulling them away from other duties. And she'd lose what little time she had left with her parents and friends. That is, assuming she planned to go back to the Green Lands.

She sat down for a minute on the cool garage floor, resting and thinking things over.

"I don't really get a choice in this, do I?"

Ben took a deep breath and sighed. "It's not really my place to say. But you *do* get to choose."

She took a swig of water, wondering how true that was. Questioning how much she owed him for saving her life. "You could have died, trying to keep me safe. I know everyone expects me to go. And maybe, if I had more time ... it wouldn't be such a hard decision."

He nodded thoughtfully. "Everyone back home *does* want you to come back. I won't sugarcoat it. Mom ... would take it hard. And your energy is the strongest I've seen from an unrooted girl—and we're not even in the Green Lands. Don't underestimate your potential."

She frowned, thinking about what Devin had said. That the female energy was what kept Seeder borders safe. So, her potential was ... what? It was like telling someone that has O-negative blood,

Congratulations, you're a universal blood donor. You're so useful! She didn't want to just be 'useful' in that way. She wanted to do something with her life, she just wasn't sure what that was yet. All her life she'd been restricted. By her parents' rules. By school rules. Waiting to be old enough to figure out what she really wanted. The gut-wrenching thing now was that she *had* a choice. Too big of a choice. A permanent choice. And both options held pain and sacrifice.

In the absence of her reply, Ben added, "Don't worry about me. Any of us that come here, volunteer to do so. I signed up for this."

That comforted her a smidge. Her mind jumped back in the conversation. Her mom, the Seeder one. She would take it hard if Mel didn't return. But what about her human mom? It wasn't like it was going to be easy on her, either. "Tell me a little about our mom."

He smiled. "You don't look all that much like her, but I agree with Dad that you two have a lot of similarities. She loves to paint." His smile grew to a smirk. "And she can be stubborn."

Mel chuckled. "Sounds pretty awesome, if you ask me."

"She grew up here. In this town."

Mel cocked her head to the side. "Really?"

He nodded. "And our parents fell in love here."

"Wait. Devin said this isn't normal, for families to team up."

Ben straightened up the spools of cords and other training supplies. "No, they were in their twenties. He came back to … work on a project. She was visiting her host dad for spring break. I shouldn't say too much. I just figured you'd think it was cool."

There was that feeling again—half-truths, edited stories. Now she was curious about her mom, and their story, and her mom's human host dad that might still be in this town. But the secrecy was souring the wonder.

"Do you have any human friends?" she asked, furrowing her brow.

He sat down next to her with a chastising expression. "I'm not a bigot. I've made human friends."

"Oh." She hadn't meant to imply that. "No. I was just wondering, 'cause … you know… Everyone we hang out with, other than Zach of course, and … maybe Heather?"

He lifted an eyebrow. "You know I won't give you names, right?"

Her cheeks warmed. She could really stand to have a girls' night. "Well … I guess I just wanted to know if I'm safe to hang out with Heather, and, I don't know. This is all messed up, Ben."

"Hey." He frowned. "I'm sorry. Stacy's parents weren't as strict, right? But Pam and George did what they thought was best. And I know it seems like you're surrounded by us … and you're not completely wrong. Seeders don't usually have two families team up this closely. But we *do* still maintain human relationships. Partially because we want to, and partially because it's smart to."

He cracked his knuckles. "As for Heather … the reason your parents never restricted you from hanging out with girls is because it's pretty rare for them to send female assassins. They've got the poison thing, but like you and the other Seeder girls, their leaves aren't as sharp, and they're not as strong. I mean, I'm assuming that's why they don't send them. They're matriarchal like we are, but I don't really know their social dynamics other than that. I'm not saying it's impossible, but it's unlikely there are any here." He threw her a glance, eyebrows raised. "No matter who it is, just be careful, alright?"

She nodded thoughtfully. "Will do."

Thinking back to his mention of Stacy, she asked, "What was it like to train Stacy?"

He shrugged. "After she got over the shock, she was pretty dedicated. She was really excited about it all and getting to go home."

Mel scoffed. "I find that hard to believe."

He tilted his head. "Her process went smoothly, so she wasn't under the same stress you are. But even then, everyone has their reasons."

Mel shook her head. "She was popular. All the guys wanted to date her." Mel wanted to make sure Ben didn't think she was jealous. She never had been, at least not the way she remembered it. "Not that everyone wants that, but *she* sure did."

"People change, Mel."

She definitely knew that—that's why they'd stopped being friends. "I guess so. But I guess I really didn't know her anymore."

He wore a faint smile. "Funny, 'cause that's what she said about herself. That she barely knew herself anymore." He took a deep breath. "There's lots of reasons to return home. The powers, culture, family. Some people don't get along with their host families as well as you do, or don't fit in at school. And some girls like the idea of a fresh start." He met Mel's gaze. "I, for one, hope she's able to have one. That people give her that chance."

Mel looked down, nodding. "Yeah. Me, too."

***

Mel showered and headed to her bedroom to pass out for the night. Her mom came in and sat on the end of her bed while Mel brushed out her wet hair.

"You may not be our biological daughter, but your dad and I want you to know that we've always considered you our own. We love you so much, honey. And it kills us you had to find out this way."

Her mom paused, frowning. "The reveal and change are usually a celebration. It's exciting to learn about this whole new side of you, about all the people that love you, about a future you never could have dreamed of. But you didn't get to have that experience."

She stood up and hugged her daughter. "We are so proud of you, and so happy for you. We've always known you weren't ours to keep forever. I hope you can forgive us."

"Of course, Mom. I love you." Mel squeezed tighter, aching at the thought of having to leave her parents, her home. When she pulled back, she scanned her mom's face. "Can I trust that you guys will actually be honest with me now? About everything?"

Her mom wore a deep frown. "Yes. Dad's already asleep for the night, but we want to sit down with you and talk more tomorrow about any questions you have."

Mel nodded, but didn't think she could wait on some things. "Devin—did you guys plan for us to date?"

Her mom's jaw dropped. "No. Why would you think that?"

Mel shrugged. "Because Seeders want girls to return to keep their lands safe."

Her mom raised an eyebrow. "We didn't let you date because we wanted to keep *you* safe." Her face softened. "But also because we were selfish about wanting you to ourselves. We would have been happy to let you live to your last day without dating anyone." She grinned. "But it's natural for most teenagers to want to date. And you were a smidge persistent."

Mel smiled.

"He asked if he could date you and he seemed like a nice enough guy. He was already one of your protectors." Mel's mom pursed her lips. "Didn't think my daughter would sneak behind my back to date a guy, especially when she already had permission to date."

Mel frowned. "I think we can call that a draw. Because there are a lot more lies in this family than I ever imagined, too."

Her mom pressed her lips together, nodding. "You really like him, don't you?"

Mel fought back tears, and her energy. "Yeah, well, it's not like I'm deciding to go back there just to chase a guy."

"I know." Her mom pulled her into another hug. "You'll make the right choice for the right reasons. We believe in you."

"Thanks," Mel whispered.

Her mom stopped at the doorway before leaving for the night. "I understand you have some big choices to make. We want you to do what you think is best for *you*. Your dad and I want you to know that we don't want you making any decisions based on concern for us. We'll always be proud of you."

"Thanks, Mom." Mel sighed. "You have no idea how hard this is."

Her mom gave her a sympathetic frown. "Get some good sleep. Love you."

"Love you, too."

The door clicked closed. Mel sat back down on her bed. Her mental pros and cons list was so skewed, so scattered. She thought back to what Ben had said, about different reasons for returning to the Green Lands. The problem was, she couldn't relate to some of those reasons. She didn't need a new start, or have a horrible family. Despite that, she had started to feel a pull there. And that scared her.

Mel struggled to find sleep, her mind forming a list of every family event she would give up by following everyone's expectation of moving to the Green Lands. She'd never have another Thanksgiving or Christmas with her parents. Had she done enough to savor last year's? No more opportunities to make her parents a special breakfast on Mother's or Father's Day. She imagined trying to feel happy celebrating those days with faceless strangers in a foreign place.

The word that plagued her the most, was 'enough.' What was *enough* of a reason to stay, or to go?

***

Mel lingered in her room the next morning, staring out her bedroom window before heading out for the day. This was it. She was going to put all of her concealment practice to the test. She was walking into a den of wolves. At least that's how it felt. *Maybe it's more of a nasty compost bin than a den of wolves, since we're part plant, and this definitely stinks...*

Devin, and now Ben, had reassured her daily that there hadn't been any chatter in their network about new Ivy activity after the attack. It looked good for them. Ken and Blake probably hadn't been able to share her identity before they died. But it was clear, by the missing bodies, that at least one Ivy remained in the area. And the likelihood that she was near the top of their list, after Blake's obvious suspicions ... made her stomach churn.

Forcing herself to leave the house, she walked through the neighborhood with a frown. Getting a root canal without numbing sounded like a more pleasant alternative to school.

The high school within her line of sight, Mel rolled her sore shoulders. Every muscle screamed at her. Ben walked several paces in front of her as her 'foster brother' and secret personal bodyguard. He had a spring in his step that Mel scowled at with jealousy. He was used to this kind of vigorous training.

And the elephant in the classroom? Just the earth-shattering revelation of her true nature; needing to conceal her identity and control her body; getting over the trauma of being attacked and knowing that she was walking into a place where assassins were after her. Don't forget having to remember an elaborate lie, and pretend she *wasn't* fighting with her boyfriend. No big deal.

Oh yeah, and Mr. Rasmussen's unrealistic expectation that they would have studied for his class during spring break.

Today is going to be a winner.

Chapter 19

WALKING THROUGH THE HALLS AT school, it was surreal to think that so many people around her had no idea what was going on right under their noses. Locker doors squeaked and slammed. Teens chatted and laughed. Pen caps and papers littered the floors. It was like strolling through a museum of teenage normalcy, something from her past. Even if Mel chose to stay and be human, she wondered if she could ever really go back to who she had been, or planned to be.

Mel ached to be normal enough to only have to grapple with the simple decisions her human peers had to make. Everything that seemed regular, or even important, just a month ago, melted from the scope of her attention. Lost in her thoughts, she roamed listlessly to her locker with just enough time to sort out her books and get to class on time. Devin was waiting for her when she arrived. She gave him a hug and kiss before heading off. There was no spark. It was clinical, all for appearances. They hadn't so much as exchanged a text since he'd dropped her off the day before.

Zach hunted Mel down after first period and gave her a giant hug. She had a genuine smile plastered on her face. They hadn't ever had a wild, flashy romance like she'd had with Devin, but Zach felt like home—she knew he was always there for her.

"Gosh, Mel, I thought you were dead!"

His words gave her a traumatic flashback; she could almost even feel the vines still choking the life out of her. *If only he knew how close to the truth that was.*

"You could have messaged me sooner to let me know what was up."

She shook off her daze. "Sorry, I just got caught up in the fun of the trip. I promise it won't happen again."

She tried to hide it, but her heart sank as she realized that if she chose to return to the Green Lands, her promise would become a lie. She would go missing without warning. Like Tabatha, she would have to ghost him.

"You okay? Something looks different about you."

Wait, that's the kind of line Blake would use. Great. Now the paranoia is setting in. How was she expected to live a double life, pretend things were normal when the weight of the world was smothering her?

"Yeah, I slept like crap last night. Thanks for noticing." She laughed. "How did your camping trip go?"

The warning bell rang. "It was awesome. It involved a friendly muskrat and less-than-friendly mosquitos. I'll tell you more about it at lunch."

***

Her mind wandered all day, unable to focus on a single thing her teachers were saying or the homework they assigned. At lunch, Zach sat across from Mel at their usual table.

Devin was all smiles and wrapped his arm around Mel after sliding onto the bench. He kissed her on the cheek and whispered in her ear, "I hope you're doing alright."

She smiled and elbowed him as if he had said something flirty.

A couple members of Blake's jock posse walked by. "Way to go, Devin! How was the honeymoon?"

The rage on Devin's face spelled out the horrible things he wanted to do to them, and Mel knew the actual extent of what that could be. Devin met their challenge. "Grow up, morons! Unless you want to end up like Blake."

Mel flashed a look of shock at Devin. What was he doing? He couldn't talk like that!

"Do you think it's true what they're saying? He got locked up in juvie?" Zach said.

She could relax. *The cover story must be out.* "He deserves worse than that if you ask me."

They took turns discussing the happenings of spring break. Mel let Devin do most of the talking, and he was pretty convincing. But Mel knew Zach recognized something was off. When Devin wrapped his arm around her again, Mel flinched. It was a split second, but she caught Zach's concerned glance the moment it happened.

Hoping to deflect any suspicion, she shook her head and shivered. "Gosh, I really need some caffeine. I'm so jumpy today." She hoped it would be enough.

"Hey, Mel, do you want to go over notes for history after school?" Zach offered.

Maybe it wasn't a good enough performance. Either way, she definitely needed some Zach time. "Let me check with my parents."

After texting with Ben about her training schedule, he agreed that she could have Zach over for a couple hours after school the next day. He wanted to reserve that whole evening for training.

"How about tomorrow? My mom has about a thousand chores for me to do tonight." She rolled her eyes to lean into the lie. "A nice 'welcome home' gift for going on vacation, I guess."

Zach's eyes darted from her to Devin, then back. "Sure. If that's what you want."

***

Mel was dreading the last period of the day. Just walking down the hallway where Blake had pinned her against the wall made her feel dead inside. Her eyes were drawn to the gym door, her heartbeat racing, her palms getting sweaty. She considered excusing herself from class to go to the nurse's office, but decided against it last minute. Luckily, today they were holding P.E. on the outside track. Having had some time to recover from the exertion of the previous night's training gave her enough energy that she thought running laps might actually help her clear her mind and work out some aggression. She was right; it did her some good.

After showering, she grabbed for a hair tie from the bottom of her gym locker. Her hand brushed against Devin's necklace. Picking up the charm on its long chain, Mel cradled it in her hand, rubbing the little sun symbol. This tiny thing had made all the difference in her life. If only she had known. In a way, it had brought her and Devin together, and also symbolized what was tearing them apart. She stared at it for a couple minutes, lost in her thoughts, before tucking it into the pocket of her jeans and closing the locker door.

Walking into the hallway, she couldn't resist the call of the gym. She found herself standing in the doorway, envisioning how it all must have played out, according to her limited point of view and hazy recollection. She imagined Ben running up, how she lay pathetically slumped over in agony. There were invisible footprints on the floor where her assailants stood. It was like she was there all over again. She looked at the path Ben had taken to get her out, and remembered where the bodies had fallen. Mel imagined them getting up and walking away to lick their wounds, or being dragged away by another Ivy. A faceless brother would have passed where she was currently standing, to collect her backpack and water bottle.

"Melody."

She gasped and jumped, turning to see Tom walking down the hall toward her. She realized her emotions were not in check and quickly turned back to the gym, closed her eyes, and reined her energy back in. She could only hope Tom hadn't seen any physical changes.

"Sorry, didn't mean to startle you," he said.

"Hi, Tom. I mean … sorry, Principal Colburn."

"We'll let it slide this once." He winked. "I heard you had a fun adventure for spring break? You were missed at Sunday dinner."

"Yeah, my boyfriend took me to meet his parents. It was great."

"Devin's his name, right? He seems like a nice fellow."

"Yeah, he's … he is."

"And that foster boy isn't giving you any more trouble, is he?"

"No, we've sorted it out." She didn't feel like another interview, already exhausted from a day filled with lies. "Anyway, I'd better run. Lots of homework and chores." She forced a smile. "The work of a teenager is never done."

"No problem, I was just passing by. Take care of yourself and tell your parents hi for me."

"Will do." Mel watched as he walked away. She liked Tom. He always gave great advice. What would *he* have to say about this doozy?

Her chest tightened. He could be Ivy, he could be Seeder, or he could just be a standard-grade human. He could be anyone. She wouldn't be stopping by his office for advice on this one.

Instead, she glanced one last time at the gym, taking a deep breath.

***

Mel took her time walking home—delaying the inevitable pain of training, taking a breather, and sorting through her thoughts without the constant noise of public school assaulting her. Not that she was alone—Ben was with her, although almost a full block ahead.

Before starting on training, Mel's mom reminded her that she and her dad wanted to have a chat. Mel had been trying to sort through all of her feelings on her situation, but really wasn't sure where she stood, or what they were expecting.

"We love you, sweetie," her mom started, as they sat down together in the family room. "First, do you have any questions for us?"

Mel blinked a couple times, not even sure where to start. "You don't think I could have handled knowing who I really was?"

Her parents frowned and held hands. "Some decisions were up to us, while others had to be agreed upon with your ... other ... dad," George said. "Even if we had permission to tell you when you were little, we wouldn't have." His eyes pleaded lovingly. "We didn't want you to have to worry about this your whole life. We knew they wouldn't come after you until your bloom, but who wants to live all their life with that hanging over their heads?"

Mel stared at her lap. "You could have at least told me when Devin found out about the change..." She would have taken the necklace more seriously.

"I'm sorry," her mom said. "You're right. We weren't ready to let you go. We ... just wanted more time with you before everything changed for good."

Mel looked up at her. "Like more game nights and Costa Rica?" She'd put that together the night before... An elaborate experience she'd never have (if she returned to the Green Lands), and their increased persistence in wanting to spend more time together. And now ... with three weeks or less left, they'd never go to Costa Rica together, unless she stayed here to be human.

They didn't respond, just nodding in confirmation of her suspicions.

She scanned their faces. Despite their explanation, she was still angry, hurt, confused.

Her dad's eyes welled up with tears. "We should have had *several* more months with you. Normal months. Happy months. But we failed you. And now…"

Mel swallowed hard, remembering how Devin had said she was allowed to live a 'normal life.' Her parents were good parents—she loved them. In a lot of ways, they had a healthy relationship. They would often be the ones to apologize after a disagreement, and confess that they weren't perfect, that even they, as the adults, were always learning. *What's done is done.* Dwelling on something they couldn't change wouldn't help.

"So … family secrets… My biological dad?"

Her mom sighed. "That's one thing we can't budge on. He has dozens of Seeders and humans he coordinates. And it's not like he always lives within the confines of human laws, you know?"

"It's not like he's some outlaw, though," her dad added. "But creating and maintaining fake identities is just *one* aspect of his job. And everything is compartmentalized. I'm sorry. But his wish is to remain anonymous right now. And…" He looked down, rubbing his knee. "And I know it's selfish … but this is still *our* time to enjoy with you while you're here. He'll, um, well, if you return like you're supposed to…" His voice faded. "You'll have time to get to know him and ask all the questions you want down the road."

Mel took a deep breath. "Fine. Fosters, other kids. Not all Seeders, right?"

"No." Her dad shook his head, wiping at his eyes. "A mix, over the years."

"How did you guys even get into this? With them being so secretive?"

"Well…" Her mom chimed in. "I knew some Seeders when I was younger. And we've kept in touch in one way or another."

Mel raised her eyebrows in surprise. Seeders obviously used to be more open. "How did that happen? That Seeders trusted you with their identities? With everything being so hush-hush?"

Her mom frowned, shaking her head. "Let's talk about that another time. Right now we want to talk about you and your future."

"I'm really honored, we both are, to be included in the network," her dad said. "Your people have always been kind."

It sounded so weird, so foreign, for her dad to address her that way. 'Your people.' Like she was something so completely different. She glanced at their family pictures on the wall. She wasn't her daddy's little girl. Not really. She hadn't expected something as harmless as his statement to bring tears to her eyes.

"Will you guys take in more kids? When I'm gone? If I go?"

"No," her mom said. "Well, there's a lot we're not sure of yet. But you'll be our last female Seeder." She gave Mel a loving smile. "And we couldn't be prouder."

After a couple more questions, they dug in deeper, explaining the whole Seeder picture. While neither of her parents had personally been to the Green Lands, they conveyed the general landscape as they'd had it described—how breathtaking the scenery and ambient energy were.

The hardest part to imagine was the lack of modern technology, but it didn't seem like such a deal breaker when framed by the idea of a calmer, simpler way of life. No noisy traffic, not having to work constantly to be able to afford the newest cell phone or gaming system. Also shocking, was the lack of larger animals, which explained why everyone in the Green Lands was a vegetarian. Mel thought of a life without bacon and her mouth watered. Also not a deal breaker, but something she'd definitely miss if she went. The Green Lands were home to a wide variety of birds, snakes, small rodents, and bugs. The flora and fauna were diverse, a mix of an unlikely variety of life, some seemingly never having been identified in the human world.

Most appealing for Mel was the talk about how their communities were run. Every village had a focus on family and community. With families that large, they didn't have much choice.

People knew their neighbors well, and families were so much more intertwined than the regular American nuclear family. While she was usually the type to keep to a small group, she couldn't help but envision how friendly and open a place like that would be.

Not sure what all Devin had shared with her, or how much she'd retained, they went over details of culture and physiology. Mel squirmed in her seat when her mom briefly explained Seeder mating. She knew they were still talking about her behind her back, coordinating her training and protection detail, but at least they didn't know what had almost happened at the safe house.

And while it was uncomfortable, it was good to know they'd always intended to make her options clear. Devin had said her brothers wouldn't have normally come to the human world to tell her about Seeder mating, and she wondered if it was something they kept a secret until the girls returned, which would be a horrifying manipulation.

Once they finished laying it all out and she had plenty of answers, they asked if Mel had any more questions. She knew she'd have more, but she couldn't think of any at the moment.

"There's nothing else I should know?" she asked.

George looked to Pam, as if waiting for her to respond. She glanced back at him.

"I think that's pretty much it for now. We'll let Ben know you're ready to get back to work," her mom said.

Her dad sent off a text and his phone buzzed with the reply. "He'll probably be about a half hour or so. We'll give you some time to think?"

They all stood and exchanged long, tight hugs.

Mel was grateful for some time to mull things over. Despite the monumental decision before her, Mel found her mind focused on Devin. She knew it wasn't fair that she'd snapped at him when leaving the safe house. And that she hadn't said more than a handful of words to him over the last couple days. It wasn't his fault. She wondered … if that night, those things, had happened when she'd still had her charm on, or before her change had started… But it didn't matter. That wasn't the way it had happened. And she wouldn't have been ready for that step, anyway.

She lay down on the couch, tucking her hands under her head. She'd been lied to, and controlled, her entire life. Resentment mingled with guilt. She was still in the dark about so many things, and had now taken on the active role of being the liar, to the rest of the world. She'd moved from one prison to another.

Tears filled her eyes. She had really fallen for Devin. Whole-heartedly. She asked herself at first if it was just the heat of the moment, that she'd told him she loved him. But nothing was the same without him there, without his smile and reassurances. Without his dorky quips.

She frowned and wiped at her tears. Finding out that one last detail, that night—one more restriction, one more thing she couldn't control—that was what had thrown her over the edge. Knowing she wanted to be with Devin, it felt like she was cornered into giving up her human life. He'd said as much, that they couldn't be together if she chose to stay. And it had sunk in a little more that last night. It wasn't that they *couldn't* be together, it was that they *wouldn't*. He could physically survive here like their dads had, but just like he'd said—he had come for his own family. Asking him to abandon his way of life would be as cruel as the impossible decision she was being forced to make. She wanted to ask him to choose her, to reconsider staying in the human world. But it didn't feel right. She couldn't fault him for knowing and embracing what he was, *who* he was.

But who was Mel? Who was Saff? Devin was a Seeder because that's what he had sprouted as, and that's what he'd been raised as. Was Mel a human, because she'd been raised that way? Or was she a Seeder, because that's how she came into the world? The blessing, and curse, was that she even had a choice in the matter. She knew that she should be grateful to be able to choose her future. But it certainly didn't feel like much of a blessing at the moment.

Mel pulled out her phone and typed a message: <I'm sorry.> Devin didn't deserve her anger; he hadn't earned it. Mel stared at the phone's screen, her finger hovering over the send button. Instead, she deleted it. This was too much. She needed more time to mull it over. And this wasn't a conversation to have over text.

Ben arrived shortly thereafter, ready for more strenuous training. What he had put her through the night before had just been a warm-up for the beating she would take that night. Her energy was completely expended between exercises to try and lengthen the amount of time she could keep her blades out, and new fighting techniques.

Learning to channel her energy in hand-to-hand combat was on a whole new level, though. If she could move her focus to the right muscles, bones, and skin, letting the energy settle in, she could swing faster, punch harder, and stand up to more severe blows. He unapologetically beat the crap out of her. She took it, for the most part, without complaint.

Mel had just enough energy remaining to heal the cuts she was left with. She barely managed a shower and then promptly passed out, sleeping like a rock.

Chapter 20

LUCKILY, THE NEXT DAY AT school was a little less stressful. Devin texted to say he wouldn't kiss Mel at all, unless she initiated it, that he didn't want her to feel uncomfortable. He assured her he was there for her in any way she needed, and understood she wanted her space. She was grateful for his understanding, giving him a brief hug and holding hands where appropriate.

Zach walked her home after school and they settled down in the family room to do homework. She came back from a bathroom break and he again hid his phone suspiciously.

Knowing this was the kind of thing she should probably report to Devin or Ben, she decided to nip it in the bud instead. They didn't think Zach could be trusted, but she knew she was safe with him.

"What's that about?" she demanded.

He furrowed his brow. "What?"

"You. Your laptop, and phone." She frowned. "Since when do you keep secrets from me?" She knew she was being a hypocrite, but still...

He shook his head. "Don't worry about it."

She crossed her arms, studying his face. "Please?" she pleaded. "Just tell me? I don't care what it is." She couldn't handle more secrets, least of all from him.

He sighed, pulling out his phone and holding it up for her to see. She took it from his hand and sat down next to him, looking it over. The screen displayed search results.

"Tabatha?" Her eyes grew wide, looking up at him. "What's this about?"

He shrugged. "It was just too weird, the way she left." He paused, looking down at his hands. "I just thought ... if I could find her, and get more answers..." He looked back up, pursing his lips. "I didn't want you to know I was looking. I know how much her leaving hurt you. And ... I've checked a lot of places. Even obituaries... It's like she vanished into thin air. And ... I didn't want to tell you until I actually figured out what was going on."

Mel bit her lip and started to cry. She knew Tabatha's sudden departure had bothered him, too. But she hadn't realized he'd been obsessing this way. She wanted to comfort him, assuring him that Tabatha was fine. But she couldn't.

He cocked his head to the side, frowning. "This is why I didn't tell you." He gently took his phone back.

She wiped away her tears. "No. I'm fine. I promise."

They sat in silence for a minute.

"Did you want to look over any more notes?" he offered.

"I'm really wiped out. Can we take a break and just chill for a minute?" she asked.

Mel scooted a little closer and leaned against him, resting her head on his shoulder.

He leaned his head against hers. "What's wrong?"

"Can we not talk? I just need this." The sheer magnitude of her daily existence was wearing her thin. She struggled to keep her composure; luckily, he couldn't see her face.

"Yeah, Mel, of course." He wrapped an arm around her.

After a few minutes, he spoke up. "You know, I noticed you've been tense the last couple of days. It's okay if you don't want to talk about it, but just know that you can." He then suggested, "Would a shoulder massage help?"

"Oh, gosh, I would be an idiot to turn that down." She got off of the couch and sat in front of him. Mel had been so comfortable with Zach for years, that something like a simple shoulder massage wasn't loaded. It had taken her a while to realize that it might not be appropriate anymore, after she started dating Devin. But he had been understanding of their friendship, especially since Zach had backed down after Mel chose Devin. She frowned—Devin was being really patient while she was sorting through all of this. She still wasn't sure she could meet his expectations.

Zach's hands worked magic on all of her knots and tight muscles. "Seriously, what *have* you been up to?" He moved his hands from her neck and shoulders down to her upper arms and rubbed them reassuringly.

She flinched and recoiled at the pain in her right arm.

"Sorry, you alright?"

Before she could stop him, he lifted her sleeve to reveal a giant bruise from Ben's training the night before. She'd only had enough energy to heal injuries that broke the skin, or were visible when fully-clothed. The bruise had somewhat faded already, but didn't automatically heal as quickly as her cuts had when she was blooming.

"You're kidding me!" he exploded. "What the hell happened?"

Pulling her sleeve back down, she turned to him. "You're seriously overreacting. I got it in gym class."

Zach scowled. "Why would you lie to me? That jerk's not worth it!"

She furrowed her brow in confusion. "What are you talking about?"

"I saw the way you reacted the other day, when Devin touched you. It's insulting that you chose a jerk like that over someone that genuinely cares for you."

"Don't you dare!" she snapped back. "You don't even know the half of it. Devin would *never* hurt me."

Ben appeared in the doorway. "Go home, Zach."

"Stay out of it, Ben," Mel ordered.

Zach looked between them. "If it's not your boyfriend, was it this psycho?"

"Don't!" Mel barked at Ben, who was clearly about to lose his temper. "Let's go for a walk, Zach." Mel got off the floor and walked up to Ben, who was blocking the doorway.

"I don't think that's the best idea," Ben advised forcefully.

"Get out of my way or I'll find a way to make you regret it," she threatened.

Ben didn't budge.

Knowing Zach couldn't see from behind her, she intentionally shifted energy to her eyes, briefly flashing them neon green. "Move."

Ben glared, whispering, "That's a stupid way to make a point right here and now." After another moment of their stare-down, he stepped aside.

Zach followed her as she charged out the front door and down the street.

"Seriously, Mel, what's going on? This is not normal behavior for you."

She kept silent as her frustration festered; she had to put all of her effort into centering her energy.

"Have I ever lied to you?" she asked.

"I guess I don't really know, do I?"

She couldn't assert herself as being honest now… She actually *was* lying to him, at minimum a lie of omission. "Can we just rewind things? I don't want to lose you, and I don't want to waste any time fighting. If I tell you I'm fine, can you please just believe me?"

He pressed his lips together. "I don't know what you want me to say. I don't know if I can just drop it."

"If you can't drop it, then... I don't know. You're making things so much harder." She choked down her energy to bury it, but she couldn't keep from tearing up.

He sighed and pulled her into a tight hug. "I just want you to be okay," he whispered.

She nodded and then gently pulled away from his hug. "I..." It was ridiculous that she couldn't even say that, well ... she couldn't even say that there were things she couldn't say. She tried to think about it from a human perspective. What kind of normal drama could she make it sound like, but still convey the right feelings?

"Mel, I need you to know that I love you. Like, really love you." He searched her eyes for a reaction. "I know you haven't felt the same way about me, and you chose Devin. But my feelings haven't changed."

Her heart sank. "I thought we agreed to just be friends."

Zach shoved his hands into his pockets. "No. We never had that conversation. I just didn't push anything because I knew you were already with him." He frowned, staring into her eyes. "I really think we could be happy together. Things were less complicated and stressful for you before he came around, you can't deny that."

She closed her eyes and took a deep breath. "Zach, I love you, too. I don't *want* to live my life without you in it."

Cradling her head with his hands, he leaned in for a kiss. Mel's eyes shot open in surprise. She wasn't sure why, but she didn't stop him. He was sweet and tender. She found herself actively kissing back, being enveloped in the wealth of possibilities true friendship could offer. He'd never lied to her. Things were never complicated with him. There was something there that she hadn't ever allowed herself to feel about Zach before. She'd never needed to rush things with him, but everything felt so much more accelerated now. She might never get a chance to explore their possibilities if she continued her training.

And then thoughts of Devin consumed her mind.

She was about to pull back, but realized she hadn't been cautious enough to focus. She had to pull back emotionally for a moment while still kissing him, to concentrate on containing her energy before he could open his eyes and discover her secret. Once she felt her energy back in place, she stepped back.

"We can't be doing this," she said.

"Why not?"

She covered her face with her hands. "I ... am still with Devin."

"But are you going to stay with him?" His eyes burned incredulously.

"Zach, I ... have a thousand decisions to make. And I can't give you an answer right now." She shook her head. "You really shouldn't have kissed me."

His brow furrowed. "Maybe I shouldn't have. But I've waited *forever* for your parents to allow you to date. And then you don't even give me a chance. You date Blake, and Devin."

She was struggling to control her anger, and energy. "Maybe you would have had a chance, if you'd had the guts to ask me!"

He scowled. "I told you how I felt at the dance."

She frowned. He had. The night she started to bloom. The first night she finally gave Devin a chance. She looked down, hating every moment of this conversation.

He continued in her silence, "You can't tell me you didn't just feel something between us. Am I wrong?"

She hugged herself. "It's not fair to ask me that right now."

"That answers my question." He shrugged. "Ultimately, the choice is yours. But if he's hurting you, if he's not treating you right, I *won't* let him get away with that, no matter what your decision is."

"I told you, you don't have to worry about that."

He gently raised his eyebrows. "The problem is, I think I do. And you haven't given me anything to convince me otherwise. I'm serious. I'll go to the cops if I have to."

She shook her head, looking him in the eyes. "Thank you for caring. I mean it. No one in my life wants to hurt me. Not Devin, or Ben, or my parents. If I was being abused, I promise I would tell you, okay?"

"Fine." He scanned her face. "But I'll be watching. And … hoping you'll seriously give it some thought, the possibility of me and you."

Mel looked down the street to her house. Ben was, of course, watching them from the front porch. And to add to her luck, there was an extra set of eyes on them. Mr. Rasmussen, her biology teacher that lived a couple houses down, was out watering his front yard and glancing their direction from behind his chain-link fence.

"Can I bring your stuff to school in the morning?" she asked.

Zach looked over at Ben and nodded. "Sure. I don't have anything important due tomorrow."

"Okay. I'm going to go. Can we keep this between us for now, while I sort things out?"

"Yeah." He rubbed the back of his neck. "I think I'll spend lunch elsewhere, until you make a decision."

Even if Devin didn't know what just happened, things would never be the same in their little group now. She agreed it was a good idea.

As Mel returned to the house, she held up a hand to Ben. "I don't want to hear a thing."

"We need to get to work." He bypassed the obvious lecture she knew he wanted to give about wandering off unprotected.

"No, we don't. That's MY decision to make." She was fuming. "And what you just saw back there, that's *private*. So help me, if you breathe a word of it…" She knew it wasn't Ben's fault. She was just mad at the situation, mad at the world … or really, mad at the worlds—plural. Her eyes were glowing green, and she didn't care enough to stop it. Mel was at the end of her rope. Zach coming over was supposed to give her a comforting reprieve from the chaos in her life, not fan the flames.

Her voice trembled as her eyes moistened in frustration. "You have NO idea what this is like. If you back me into a corner, you *won't* get what you want!"

Ben didn't respond, instead letting her pass and go upstairs to her room. A whole evening, desperately needed for training, was about to be wasted.

Chapter 21

MEL LAY IN BED, SCROLLING through what must have been dozens, perhaps even hundreds of pictures on her phone. So many with Zach, or Zach and Tabatha. Tons now with Devin. Selfies with her parents on holidays. The saying 'best of both worlds' came to her mind, and 'have your cake and eat it, too.' Which ... really didn't make much sense, because why have cake if you can't eat it? But that was a tangent.

What did she want? Without the pressure, or the fear, or the unforgiving countdown. If she wasn't forced to make a choice, what path would she willingly take? If she had it her way, she would keep these cool new powers, and be with Devin, and not have to lose her mom and dad or Zach. But honestly, could a world with both Devin *and* Zach in it be what she wanted anymore? Would Zach be happy climbing back into the friend box? And would she want him to?

Whoever says it's a fantasy to be fought over by two guys, is an absolute idiot. She huffed. *Seriously though, can someone honestly even love two people? Friendship that blooms into love surely trumps passion, right?* But that wasn't fair to Devin. He wasn't just a handsome face with exceptional kissing skills. He'd dedicated his entire youth—more than any human really ever sacrifices for another—to coming here and helping his family *and* hers. And it was impossible to deny how much he cared for her.

When it came to love, she needed more information. What did the guys even have in mind? How serious was Devin, really? If she was willing to make a lifetime commitment to him, would he reciprocate? Was he just being a gentleman when he turned her down?

What was Zach's endgame? If she stayed here to be human, her lifelong expectations would still be in play. School, work, marriage, family—in whatever order they happened to occur. Did he want kids? Was he thinking that far ahead? What junior in high school is even considering that kind of commitment? Like Devin had mentioned, Mel wouldn't even be able to have human kids. She'd always imagined having a big family, though not as large as Seeders had…

And was she a fool to give up her powers, to turn down ever meeting her biological mother and other family, other people like her—knowing they also needed her powers—just for the faint possibility that a high school romance could work out? She scoffed at the questions running through her head. It wasn't just about who she would date or marry. It was about who she was choosing to become, the whole package.

Mel had less than three weeks to sort it out. The implications, the small details, the finality of it all was crushing her. She tossed her phone to the floor, put a pillow over her face, and screamed.

There was a knock at her door and it opened.

She removed the pillow from her face to see her mom standing there. Mel sat up in bed, hugging her pillow. "Sorry."

"You have a right to be frustrated, don't apologize." Her mom sat down next to Mel and smiled. "Your eyes are so stunning that way."

Mel had forgotten again. "Sorry." Regaining control, her eyes faded to their regular blue.

"Stop that. Never apologize for being who you are," her mom scolded. "It's time I gave you some advice."

Other than their conversation the day before, Mel's 'host parents' had stood back and let the Seeders take care of things. Her parents had said as much, that they knew it wasn't their place to demand or direct at this point; they trusted Mel was following the path prepared for her all along.

"I should have said something earlier. But I..." Her mom looked down. After a while she finally looked up and spoke again. "I understand your struggle more than you know. It's a hard decision. I know, because I had to make that judgment call myself at your age."

Mel's jaw dropped. "Wait, what do you mean?"

"I was a Seeder."

"What? No. But... you're human, you live here."

"Well, I'm human *now*. Because I stayed."

Mel blinked repeatedly in shock. She needed to know every detail of her mom's story and how she came to her decision.

Her mom took a deep breath. "Most Seeder girls only find out about their identities once the change has been completed. Generally, their parents give them the charm, and then when the biggest danger is over, they have to face the music and allow the brothers to step in and train. That's how it happened for me. That's how it happened for Murial."

Mel ached, hearing about both of her moms—sharing a story, divided by the worlds.

"The change happened smoothly for me. I was informed about who I was, what my heritage was. What the expectations of me were. I trained, maybe not with all of my heart in it, but I trained, did what I needed to do to stay hidden and safe. But when the time came ... I decided not to go."

"But why? Do you ever regret your choice?"

"When it comes down to it, I think I was just too scared. I didn't want to leave my family and friends; I didn't want to face the unknown. I worried I wouldn't be enough, that I wouldn't fit in, and get along with my family there, like I do here."

She paused, tucking a strand of Mel's hair behind her ear. "Do I regret my choice? That's hard to say. If I hadn't made that choice, I never would have met and married your father, and I wouldn't give him up for the world. And I wouldn't have been able to have you or Ben in my life, or any of the others we've fostered. Being human affords me peace; I don't have to worry about Ivies coming after me. Their focus is stopping Seeders from coming home. Once my time passed—so did the threat."

She sat pensively for a minute. "But I missed out on so much. I'll never be able to get over the shame of turning down my true nature, what I feel my destiny might have been. I gave up amazing power. Not that there's anything wrong with an ordinary life—you can be happy in either world, with or without the extra abilities. There are so many people I never got to meet. And…" Her voice pitched higher as tears filled her eyes. "I never got to meet my mother. I'll never stop imagining the pain my choices caused. She sent me out and trusted I would come back, that we would be reunited. And when I didn't come back … it wasn't because I couldn't. It's because I wouldn't."

Mel rarely ever saw her mom cry.

"Sweetie, now that I'm a mother, I can imagine how that would feel. I would never want to keep you from her. When we agreed to take you in, it was with a promise that we would be ready to let you go, when the time was right."

Mel wrapped her arms around her mom. After a minute, Mel dared to ask, "So, you think I should go?"

Her mom pulled back, wiping away tears. "I think you need to be careful and brave as you decide. You only have two or three weeks. Most girls might still have three months at this point in training—enough to learn, get there, and maybe turn around before rooting if they changed their mind. You don't have that luxury. And I think you need to devote every ounce of your energy to preparing to leave. It takes a second, when the time is right, to make a final decision. But if you don't do what you need to, right now, you'll only be robbing yourself of the ability to make that choice."

Mel nodded. She knew her mom was right. "I'll try harder. Can you tell me how it feels, when you take root in the human world?" It was nice to talk to someone that had been through all of this.

Her mom frowned. "Once your roots wrap around your ankles, you feel a heaviness in your energy, like gravity doubled. It takes about a month for your abilities to fade completely. You lose the ability to fly right away, but then transforming, extending blades, controlling the energy, and last of all, your eyes fade. The day I realized I couldn't do anything was a devastating day for me. That's when it really hit me that I had closed an important chapter in my life; I really doubted myself and my decision."

Mel sat in silence for a moment as her mom's haunting regrets hung in the air. "The Ivies really wouldn't care if they found out you were a Seeder, once you became human? Devin assured me you guys wouldn't get hurt, but I sometimes worry they would come after you guys, to get to me."

"We're fine." Her mom smiled. "It's rare for a human to get hurt in all of this. The Ivies think of humans like … I don't know, houseflies, and Seeders like mosquitos. One is annoying, practically unworthy of their attention; the other, they want to eradicate. We've got Ben, and we take all the precautions we can to keep ourselves safe. Don't worry about us."

"Okay." Mel nodded.

Her mom cocked her head to the side. "I noticed Zach's backpack is still in the family room. He went home without it?"

Mel pressed her lips together; she could almost still feel Zach's lips on hers. "I… I don't want to talk about all that. I'll clean it up before going to bed."

"Okay. But I'm always here for you if you want to talk." She gave Mel one last reassuring smile and wished her goodnight before heading out.

'I'm always here for you if you want to talk.' Mel wished that could be true, but it wasn't. If she went to the Green Lands, she couldn't just text her mom or sit down for a chat like this. And she didn't know if she'd ever have the same kind of relationship with Murial.

She took a deep breath, finding strength in her mom's advice. That she needed to prepare herself now, and the final decision could be made later.

Mel grabbed workout clothes from her dresser and changed. She went to Ben's room and knocked on the door. He looked surprised to see her when he opened it.

"Let's get to work," she said, making sure to add, "But I need to be able to heal my bruises, unless you want an investigation."

***

The next day, Ben agreed that Mel could take a couple hours after training to have Heather over for a movie. In the spirit of keeping up appearances, she would've called the whole posse together, but things were hardly in the right place with either Devin or Zach.

She'd left just enough time to shower and heal up before Heather came over. Mel silently chuckled as she finished getting dressed. Her life was the epitome of a dumpster fire right now. As if the whole Seeder thing wasn't enough, she apparently needed to add *every* aspect of her life to the crazy.

The doorbell rang and Mel bounded down the stairs to answer the door, grinning from ear to ear at Heather's bubbly smile.

"Come on in! I've got like a thousand kinds of chocolate and I intend to eat them all." Mel nodded in the direction of the family room and Heather giggled. "Sorry we always have to do things over here."

"No worries. I like your place."

They sat down and flipped through DVDs in awkward silence. Nothing jumped out at Mel, and Heather didn't seem invested in picking one either. This *was* the first time it was just the two of them hanging out.

"Sorry again about bailing on you for spring break. And thanks for coming over." Mel sat back on the couch. "I seriously needed some girl time."

Heather sat cross-legged on the other end of the couch, facing her. "It's okay. Boy troubles? What's up with you and Devin?"

Mel shook her head. She knew she wanted to talk, but wasn't really sure what all about. Looking at Heather's neck, she searched for a chain, just out of curiosity. She gave up, remembering Devin's description. It could be a toe-ring for all she knew, if Heather even was a Seeder. And she'd only be wearing it during her bloom, not before or after. But Heather could be anything.

"I don't know. Guys are just complicated, aren't they?"

Heather made a silly face and nodded. "They certainly can be."

"Are you dating anyone?"

Heather hummed playfully. "I've got one I like. But I don't want to jinx anything."

Mel chuckled. Heather hung around a lot of other people outside of their little group. She had enough energy to be a cheerleader, and enough heart to make everyone love her. Mel was honestly surprised she wasn't already taken. Being short and cute didn't hurt, either.

"Well, anyway…" Mel moved on, deciding she wasn't ready to spill her guts about anything. "Let's pick out a solid chick-flick we can watch without the guys."

"Yes!" Heather pumped her fist in the air.

Halfway through the movie, Ben made an appearance.

"Hey, girls." He smiled.

"Hi, Ben!" Heather greeted him in her usual cheerful voice.

Although Mel finally understood Ben's weirdness, it felt like overkill to have him pop in on just her and Heather, like her parents had for years when it was just her and Zach. But then again, he'd warned that Ivy females were rare in the human world, but not impossible.

Ben lingered in the doorway.

Mel waved him away with her hand. "Shoo! Girls' night!"

"Whatever." He rolled his eyes. "Goodnight, both of you."

It was getting late for a school night by the time the movie ended. Heather helped Mel clean up their disaster of candy wrappers and gave her a hug on the way out. This was what Mel had needed from Zach's visit. No guilt trips, no confusion. Heather wasn't Tabatha, but... She shook her head, wishing she could *really* confide everything to just one person. But she and Heather weren't on that level, even if she felt she could be trusted.

Chapter 22

DEVIN DESERVED TO KNOW THE truth about the kiss. They weren't officially broken up, after all. And Mel deserved to know where he wanted to be in her future. She texted to ask if they could train together the next night; they could chat then. He quickly responded, <We'll make it happen.>

They got in his car after school ended; it was quiet. They hadn't really even been trying to keep up appearances much at school.

"Ben said you want to focus solely on catching a breeze right now? Put fighting on the back burner?" he asked.

"Yeah, I think so. Where do you go for that?"

"Some of the basics we can do indoors. But the bulk of that training is best done outdoors, in the dark, away from prying eyes."

"Sure, let's do it." Knots were already forming in her stomach. "But can we talk first? Go on one of those nature walks you like?"

He agreed to take a little downtime and drove to a local park where they could stretch their legs and have privacy. The spring sunshine was invigorating, the fluffy clouds uplifting. The trickle of a nearby stream soothed her nerves. The walking path they were on was safe from unwanted attention.

She started, "I owe you a huge apology. I can only imagine what you think of me. I'm sorry I was such a jerk."

He kept silent but acknowledged with his expression how hurt he had been.

"I'm going through a lot, but that doesn't mean you deserve me taking it out on you."

He interrupted before she could continue, "Saff ... I ... or, Mel, whichever. It's not that I—"

"I know. You were a perfect gentleman." She shoved her hands in her pockets. "Honestly, you're kind of perfect in everything, and I take that for granted. I'm selfish."

"No," he interjected.

"Please, just let me get out what I need to say," she pleaded. "I need you to know where I'm at."

He motioned with a hand for her to proceed.

"I don't know if I'm ready to say it again, but I really did mean it when I said I loved you." Just saying it aloud again brought her butterflies. "My frustration after that night wasn't just about you turning me down. I mean, I think obviously a lot of it was my hurt pride. But I realized how much more that meant to me."

She frowned. "It was just one more thing that made me feel like I had no control over my life. That I have to make a huge and irreversible decision. I have to ask myself if I want to commit to that life. How do you know for certain that you're picking the right mate? Do we both want kids? In this world, you can have one at a time, pretty much whenever you're ready."

She threw her hands up in the air, exasperated. "In your world, we don't get to choose the timing. And if we do want kids, it's twenty-four at a time! And I wouldn't see you, or my daughters, for as long as I've been alive, and then I would be stuck there, forever, in a world at war.

"That's a lot of pressure, all decided in a moment of passion." She furrowed her brow. "Devin, I've never even dated anyone before you. I have a hard time just picking what to watch on movie night, for heaven's sake!"

He grinned at that; she was notoriously indecisive.

"And I don't know what you want out of life, what you want from me. It's not just fooling around and having fun in the human world. What if you fall for someone else while you're still here and I'm waiting for you back home? Or what if it's the other way around? I just… I needed to say I'm sorry. And I'm obviously considering all the factors involved, but I need to know what *you* want."

She paused for a moment.

"Can I call you Saff?" he asked.

She grinned, then it faded to a frown. "There's one more thing I need to tell you first. That is, assuming Ben didn't already tell you."

His face indicated he hadn't.

She closed her eyes, hating herself. "I don't want you to get mad, and I don't want you to hate me."

He grabbed her hand and gave it a squeeze. "Saff, I could never hate you."

"See." She took her hand back and shoved it into her pocket again. "This is you, being more amazing than I deserve." There wasn't an easy way to say it. "Zach kissed me." She looked for his reaction.

His lips pursed and nostrils flared, but he didn't completely lose it.

"And I think it's my fault—I said the wrong thing. And I kissed him back, and I'm not sure where I stand." She kept talking without hardly taking a breath. "He told me he loved me, and I told him I loved him. But it's not the way I love you. It's like, chemistry and friendship—you have more of one, he has more of the other. And I told him I didn't want to live my life without him, but, you know, I was thinking in a my-big-decision-ending-our-friendship kind of way, not in the standard human-pledging-loyalty kind of way. Either way, I said it, and he kissed me, and I'm more confused about what I want in life. And it's not fair to you, and I'm so, so, so, sorry."

He didn't respond, instead shoving his own hands into his pockets and reading her eyes. "You need to give me some time to think about it. Let's keep walking."

After what felt like an eternity, he began to talk. "I need to be practical, but I also need to be honest. Mel, I still love you. But the truth is, I can't get distracted by *your* feelings."

He frowned, his dark brown eyes showing his struggle. "That might sound like I don't care, but the fact is, I didn't come here to fall in love. I care about our world. I care about our people. Our survival and happiness. I care about my sisters, and my family. And I wouldn't trade any of that, or my powers, for you. And I know you wouldn't ask me to. And I'm not asking me to do that, either."

She swallowed the lump in her throat as he continued.

"If you choose to stay here and forfeit your heritage," he raised an eyebrow, "I hope you do it because you are *absolutely* sure you want the entire book, not just the next chapter that may or may not work out like you want."

His gentle eyes were piercing, pleading. "I want you to return home, not just because I love you, but because I know your family loves you, and *all* of our people will welcome you home with open arms. You were meant to be there—you would absolutely love it. You could be so happy, Mel."

She had to give it to him; he was even more mature than she had given him credit for. He was more than a flirt that could make her swoon. He had his priorities sorted out more than she had ever come close to with her own.

He glanced at her neck, then slowly reached over and pulled the long chain out from under her shirt. The charm faced in, like he had originally told her to wear it. He grinned and gently slipped it back in place. "You know this doesn't help you anymore, right?"

She blushed. "Yeah, I know."

He nodded. "About Zach... I'm not mad at you. You deserve to figure out what will make you happy." He rolled his eyes. "Doesn't exactly make me like the prick any more than I used to."

She wanted to say something in Zach's defense, but she knew Devin had a right to his feelings.

"If you want to know the truth, what I want, what would be my ideal... I would pick you every day of the week. I've met plenty of girls in both worlds, and you're the only one I'm crazy about. Despite everything I've said, I would be absolutely devastated if you didn't come back."

His eyes glistened with emotion.

"I could see us loving every day together. I really could see us having a family, taking on challenges together, just like we're taking on challenges together right now, Saff. I understand most human teenagers aren't even close to thinking about this kind of thing. But ... you're not human. You're different."

He stopped walking and grabbed her hands. "Now you know, but I'm only one piece in your puzzle. You have a lot of other pieces to put in place." He looked her in the eyes. "You need to focus, and be free to explore, Saff. I'm here for you every day, until either one of us leaves. I'm here if you need to vent, or need a hug. And as much as I want to sweep you off of your feet this very moment and remind you how much I love every part of you..." He frowned and swallowed. "I'd also be willing to step back, and just do the job I came here to do. First and foremost, I'm one of your protectors. If you need to, spend some time with Zach."

He paused. "To be clear, I'm not saying I'm okay with him launching himself at you the way he did. And he can't distract you, either. And I think I really need to stress—we still have no way of knowing he's human like you're assuming." He lifted his eyebrows. "That's exactly what Blake tried to do, right? Kissing you while you're dating someone else? Pretty Ivy behavior."

"It's not the same thing." She wanted to explain how it all stemmed from Zach trying to protect her. It was nothing like Blake attempting to kiss her while twisting her arm. She decided it wasn't worth her time trying to hash it out. She knew how it compared and that was enough.

He sighed. "The leeches don't have to kill you. Remember that all they need to do is ensure you don't make it home. Not that you can't have human friends that would genuinely miss you... Either way, if you need to sort out your feelings, then," he paused again, like it took everything he had to complete his sentence, "then sort through your feelings with him. I'm assuming we're on the same page, that ... if you're going home, you're obviously going to have to give him up. And if you stay ... you and I could only be together for so long. Just... I don't know what I'm trying to say. I don't want you to choose me as a default. I want you to choose me because you love me, as much as I love you."

She nodded. "I don't know what I'm going to do with all of that, but I'll really give it some thought." She pursed her lips. "I'm starting to question whether or not I believe in karma. Because I've never done enough to earn someone like you in my life."

He blushed.

"Can I ask you one more thing?" she said.

"I think I have one more answer in me."

"Can I have a hug?"

He grinned. "I have an infinite supply, just for you."

She fell into his arms, breathing deeply. When she started to pull away, she couldn't help herself—she leaned forward and kissed him ever so sweetly. Soft, gentle, slow. Every memory of her feelings for him came flooding in. Their last night of passion, spending a week together in seclusion, their secret relationship, their first kiss, even the first time they sat next to each other, and she knew he wanted to hold her hand. More than that were the sacrifices, the jokes, the meaningful conversations, the way they were able to work through problems together. She quietly moaned and took a deep breath.

She loved him—she knew that. Zach was a different kind of love. But Devin... She knew who she wanted to be with, with every fiber of her being. He pulled her in tighter, echoing the magnetism she felt within their souls. She wondered if their supernatural energies had anything to do with their chemistry, and if it was fair. Even if it *was* a factor, she couldn't fault the advantage more than she could his handsome eyes or dimples.

As she released him and gazed at his face, his eyes darted around. Luckily, they were still alone. She realized she hadn't been careful about her changes. He focused back on her, locking eyes.

She wanted to tell him that she *did* love him. But she'd decided—her choices needed to be separate. She wasn't going home for him. And she wasn't choosing him just because she chose the Green Lands. She was teetering on the edge of decision, but fear held her back.

Time. More time.

Luckily, he didn't demand an answer. He smiled lovingly and asked, "Should we get back to flying practice?"

She wondered if his question held more weight to it than it sounded. "Yeah." She thought for a moment. "If I go home, to your home..."

"Our home?" he corrected with hopeful eyes.

"Back *there*... What am I supposed to do with my life? Other than exist ... with energy?"

He smiled. "I guess we need to go over the brochure a little better, huh? But you, I could see you being a mentor. That's what I want to be, when I go back. Teaching the younger boys how to blend in over here, that kind of stuff."

He gently lifted her chin. "You care. You worry about your parents, and Zach, and hurting their feelings. And you're stressed and confused. When you get back, you'll have mentors to help you master your abilities, but they'll also help you find your way. I can't imagine anyone better suited to that kind of work than you, when the time comes." He rocked his head back and forth. "I mean, there's art classes, too." He grinned.

She pulled him in for another hug. "Thank you."

Chapter 23

TO MAKE GOOD USE OF their time before dark, Devin and Mel went back to her house to practice in the garage, as they usually did for training now.

Mel went over the techniques that Ben had recently taught her. Devin was able to give her extra tips on how to focus her energy to achieve what she wanted; he was a better teacher on the energy side of things, compared to Ben's focus and specialty on form.

As they took a short break, Devin's phone chimed. He read the message and couldn't contain his excitement. "Change of plans!"

They hopped in the car and started driving.

"I really want to focus on catching a breeze, what's so important?" she asked.

He still had a grin on his face. "We're going to practice. But we've got a bit of a drive to go to a location further out. We're meeting up with some people."

"Really?" Her excitement was growing to match his. "Who am I going to meet? Someone we don't have to keep our distance from?"

"We can make some exceptions when Seeders are leaving, as long as we're careful. Saff—Thod's eleventh daughter is taking off tonight." He reached over and squeezed her hand.

"Wait, Thod? My dad, right? Will he be there?"

"No, sorry. He only accompanies the last one back. Which is going to be you, so that's a special honor. But as long as we're discreet and aren't followed, you can see how it's done, and meet your sister, and your brother that's escorting her."

She beamed. "Oh my gosh, that's… How long till we get there?"

***

Mel and Devin drove far out of town. As the sun dipped below the horizon, the evergreens became taller, thicker. Leaving paved roads, they drove deeper into the woods, the car jostling them on the bumpy path. They slowed and creeped to a stop. There was already another car parked in the area. They hopped out and Devin guided Mel to a clearing on foot.

Under the glow of a full moon and stars, it was a breathtaking scene to behold. The clearing ended in a cliff. Looking beyond the cliff and past the sea of trees, the faintest glow of their hometown glimmered on the horizon.

They approached a group of three others, including Ben, excitedly chatting.

"Bonnie?" Mel said.

"Hey! Oh my gosh!" Bonnie ran up and hugged Mel as Devin left to go talk to the others. "As if I am not already nervous and excited enough, I'm so excited I get to meet you this way!"

Mel knew Bonnie mostly through her older sister. Bonnie was only a sophomore, but Devin had explained that it was planned that way to space everyone out, just like they made Ben a senior and Mel was a junior. Having massive attrition in just one grade in a given town would raise more red flags than was necessary.

"So … you're Thod's daughter? What about your brother and sister?" Mel asked.

"Boring humans." Bonnie laughed. "Well, I mean, typical families, right? But everything got so exciting when I found out and started training. We only just got to tell my brother and sister last night. Can't trust them as far as we can throw them to keep a secret. Well, they understand how serious it is, so they won't blab, but still. Didn't want to risk anything until I was gone."

"I guess we haven't really talked a lot about my exit. I imagined your family would be here to see you off," Mel said.

Bonnie looked hesitant to answer. "We decided to say our goodbyes at home. If it was only my parents seeing me off, we could trust them with the location." She wore a warm smile. "But they told me I had a sister that could use some support."

Mel glanced at Devin, who was talking to Ben and another guy she only recognized as a new kid in school that year.

"For me?" Mel was touched Bonnie would give up a special moment with her host parents for her. "Aren't you nervous? That's a huge decision!"

Bonnie's smile widened. "You could travel the whole human world and it would never compare to this adventure. It's what we're meant to do, Mel."

A calmness swelled in Mel's heart. She looked Bonnie over. "No bags. I guess I hadn't thought about that. And what's your cover story?"

"I tucked away some photos in my pockets. I left my charm for my sister as a gift. Everything else … it's not that big of a deal in the grand scheme of things." She leaned in and whispered, "I burned my school books last night just for fun."

She chuckled and continued, "It's kind of a rite of passage, if you want to do it. Get out of those annoying human public schools and transfer to one in the Green Lands. And my cover story is my dad got a job offer in Chicago. He has to start right away and we're moving. All of our parents know when they take us in that they may have to uproot themselves. It'll be an adventure for my siblings here, anyway."

Mel turned her attention to the other guy who was now walking toward her with open arms.

"Melody! or Saffrona? Not sure what to call you." He gave her a big hug. "Back home, they call me Kyle."

"Either works. You're one of my brothers?"

He beamed with pride. "One of Thod's best."

"So, what's *your* cover story for leaving?" Mel asked. She realized he might not actually be leaving for good. Some brothers escorted sisters home and returned. But this was during the middle of the week and he definitely couldn't be back by the start of school the next morning.

He responded in a rather convincing Slavic accent, "My host parents dropped me off at the airport earlier today. Unfortunately, I'm having to cut my foreign exchange year short to return home, because of a death in the family." He went back to speaking normally. "You kinda feel bad for making people worry about you, but they'll get over it."

Mel's mouth hung open. "So, your host family never knew what you were?"

"No, definitely not. A lot of us guys, and I'm assuming the Ivies, too, are with hosts in the dark. Real foster parents and the like."

Ben reminded them that they had to keep their reunion short. They needed to see Bonnie off, and Mel needed to get back to training.

"Okay!" Bonnie squealed with excitement, her eyes shifting from light brown to neon green. She turned back to Mel one last time. "I'll see you on the other side. Oh yeah, I think I'll be going by my other name over there. Call me Rose when you see me next!"

Rose and Kyle moved further out and talked in preparation. Ben walked over and put his arm around Mel. "This is going to be you soon."

They watched the brother-and-sister duo talking and gesturing, doing a preflight check.

"Make sure to pay attention to everything they do, especially Rose," Ben told Mel.

"So, we literally jump off of a cliff?" Mel said with a gulp, realizing how badly it could go if she didn't master the right skills in time.

Devin answered, "Take-offs in the Green Lands are ten times easier, with the energy of the realm. And especially when you're so new at catching a breeze, having a running start in a location like this can make all the difference to get you going."

Her fears were trying to pry into her moment of happiness and wonder. "You say we 'catch a breeze.' What if the air is still? What if I don't learn in time?"

"You'll get it, Mel," Ben said. "We're going to make sure of it."

"And we don't actually need a gust of air," Devin said. "While it's helpful, we can fly without it. When you get back home, you'll be able to commune more with the energy in nature, not only what you have in your body. This is just the start of it. You can control your own breeze—your body working in tandem with nature."

His explanation was so poetic. Lifting her hand, she focused on the air around them. She tuned in and sensed the rhythmic motions surrounding her, the push and pull of tidal forces, the unheard song formed by the whisper of wind grazing leaves. Mel grinned, watching her new brother and sister intently.

Seeder girls always had a personal escort to get home. The escort would guide them, coach them if they were struggling on their journey, and help by opening the rift between the worlds. It would be the trip of a lifetime. Long and strenuous, but worth every ounce of energy, and every moment of preparation, that it consumed.

Rose transformed next to her brother. Her hair shifted from dark brown to a glowing yellow. Blades protruded from her arms. Legs covered in roots peeked out from her shorts. Mel noticed the roots extended to Rose's ankles, just barely starting to wrap around, but still having some time before they completed the final stage of rooting.

Rose faced her palms away from her body and they glowed. She sprinted and leapt from the cliff without hesitation. Her body took a small dip in the flight path and then soared higher. Her posture was somewhat precarious; it took a while to stop wobbling, to embrace the wind rather than trying to fight it.

Kyle walked up to the cliff and jumped forward, doing a somersault in the air and fully transforming, picking up speed quickly to coast by Rose's side. They aimed for the clouds and disappeared from sight.

Mel stood with her mouth open, dumbfounded at what she'd just witnessed. Devin looked at her and grinned. Ben gave her a side hug and announced it was time for him to go.

"I've got to take the car back to Bonnie's family. You two need to get to work."

Mel turned to Devin. "How am I supposed to learn to do that in enough time? I saw her ankles, she's about to take root any day!"

"It's a lot of hard work and focus, I won't lie about that. But don't freak out. Rose could have returned at least a couple weeks ago; she practiced enough. She stayed longer to spend more time with people here. It's not impossible to learn by your deadline, not with how much raw energy and talent we've seen in you." Devin grinned again. "Plus, this is the cliff your mom first caught a breeze from. It's in your blood."

She smiled. Sometimes it was confusing, which 'mom' or 'dad' they were talking about. This time she knew—Murial once took her leap of faith from here. There was a rightness to this place.

An engine started in the distance and the crunch of wheels on gravel faded. Now it was just Mel, Devin, and the crickets in the woods. The breathtaking view in such a secluded space would make this a perfect getaway for lovers. But romance was the farthest thing from Mel's mind. She knew how much she needed to focus. It would take everything she had to try and replicate what she'd just witnessed, in the two to three weeks she had left.

"What's first?" she asked her trainer.

Chapter 24

THEY COULD ONLY COVER SO much of their training at the cliffs. Different aspects could be better taught in other locations—more space to run, softer places to land.

Since they were already there, and energy was his forte, Devin ran Mel through meditation exercises focused on blade extension and simultaneously moving energy to all parts of her body, strongest in the hands and core. It was an insane amount of multitasking—a lot of things to focus on, and balance. She could concentrate and flare her blades to their full extent, but would struggle to keep them there when she shifted focus to moving energy to all parts of her body.

After a couple hours in body-centered exercises, Devin let her take a break by working more on her relationship to the wind. She shifted the energy to her hand, raising it in the air. Mel could sense the smallest of movements, the currents that flowed around her. Waving her hand, she perceived the disruption she was capable of making as her gesture cut through the sea of oxygen, causing waves that dulled to ripples before continuing on their path.

There was something so profoundly rich about this experience. Something that had been awoken in her.

***

The gravel crunched under their tires late that night, hushing as they reached paved roads.

"I had no idea what all we're capable of. How big this all really is," Mel said in awe. "I wish we would've started earlier on flying."

He smirked. "You have to walk before you can run, and you have to glow before you can fly. One step at a time."

"How am I supposed to keep up appearances at school? I don't mean relationships or controlling emotions anymore. School eats up so much of my time. I'd rather be out here focusing on this. I really want to give this a chance."

Devin took a deep breath. "That's actually something we were going to talk about tonight. You know better than anyone—we're rushed. Thod and your parents agreed you don't need to do homework anymore. But we can't have teachers getting suspicious about your grades plummeting. We don't normally have to go this far, but we're going to have your work taken care of for you."

"What?" Mel could hardly believe what she heard. "I've never cheated in my life! Well, there was that one time in first grade I helped a friend on a spelling test. But we got caught, and Mrs. Goff tore up our tests." She shook her head. "I promised myself I'd never cheat again."

"I know, and that's a great thing about you—you have integrity and a good work ethic." He added with a smile, "You're a good girl, right?"

She considered the course of action that had been decided on. Focusing on her priorities, cheating on homework seemed pretty trivial. She accepted it with a heavy heart. "I get it."

"We're only doing it because we feel it's necessary. It's risky even giving an excuse, like you started experiencing migraines or something like that. While we can use those kinds of covers to our advantage, we want to avoid suspicion at all costs. Every incident out of place adds to the list of an Ivy on the hunt."

"And still no news about Blake or Ken, about other Ivies identifying me? Or … that one guy? I don't feel like I've had any extra eyes on me since I returned."

Devin shook his head. "No, there hasn't been any chatter. We're not sure how many Ivies are positioned in our neighborhoods and school. For all we know, they only had those two, plus a general—which we know for sure they always have, and we need to stay vigilant on that account. Most communities aren't as concentrated, so when our dads teamed up, it went against the norm. As long as they haven't figured that out, they may not have dedicated as many soldiers as they normally would for this large of a group of Seeders."

"But we really have no way of knowing? It could just be a general left, or half a dozen Ivies? What about back-ups, replacements?" she asked.

"Mid-year is highly suspicious. It's not impossible; even humans move mid-school-year sometimes, but it's less noticeable to move troops in the summer, like me showing up at the beginning of the year." He added, "We've got good intel to monitor that kind of thing."

Mel thought about it, trying to remember any instances where there may have been the tiniest hint of an Ivy, of something off. "I recall … overhearing you talking to your 'uncle' a while back, in his office. He's obviously not a brother, but I get the impression he knows what's going on…"

He flashed her a stern look. "You know I can't give you a 'yes' or 'no' about anyone." He reached over and squeezed her hand. "Whether he's blissfully unaware of what's going on around him, or he's deeply entrenched in our lives, just know the Vice Principal is a good guy, alright?"

"Okay. I guess you can at least give me *one* person to feel good about. I'm assuming you would organize things so you knew for sure none of us were hosted by an Ivy," she conceded.

They pulled up to Mel's house and parked. "Do we know what my story will be? My parents and I haven't really talked about it... Will they need to move?"

Devin turned in his seat to face her. "There's a list of options. Your parents, Thod included, will narrow it down. But you normally get some say in it. Obviously, we try to avoid anything too tragic. Throwing a fake funeral is not only expensive, it's hard on everyone."

"Yeah ... well, if I jump off that cliff and I'm not ready, at least they won't need to fake one of those."

Devin frowned at the grim statement. "You'll make it."

They got out of the car back at her house and she gave him a hug. "You're not just a great boyfriend. You're a great teacher, and friend, too."

He tucked her hair behind her ears. "And you are not just a great girlfriend."

***

After going inside, Mel slowly climbed the stairs to the second floor, using the railing to pull her up. Her feet were heavy from exhaustion. But more than that, every step was intentionally taken, deep in thought.

Everyone else had turned in for the night. She changed into pajamas, then sat on her bed and focused on seeing her roots. They bulged out like thick veins and made their way down, twisting around her legs—only when she transformed, of course. She'd been disgusted with them at first; they reminded her of the Swamp Thing. But they came to be a unique part about her she didn't mind. Like fingerprints, no two Seeders had the same root growth pattern. She looked down, feeling them extending to her knee now. Her legs were like a calendar—each small extension was one more moment counting down to the inevitable rooting.

Devin had to explain it to her a couple times back at the safe house. The complexities of their maturation process and limitation in their powers were pretty intense. All Seeder boys rooted around the time of their sprouting. Devin said their roots didn't run as deep, and that's why they could come and go more often, and even reside permanently in the human world, without harm and without losing their powers. Mel had come to understand that 'rooting' was really just another way of describing their connection, and even dependence, on the energy found in the Green Lands. The females were more connected—that explained the difference in energy they could harness, but also the physical limitations and requirements they had to live by.

Mel ran a finger across her lower roots. The growth was slow, but constant. Their path down to her ankles *literally* represented her ticking clock. Her physiology and permanent binding to whichever world she was in at the time, depended entirely on these things. Once they reached her ankles and wrapped around, forming a link on each one, the process would be complete.

Still staring at her roots, Mel mused on the events of the day. Something about that night had cleared her head. It wasn't just about comparing pros and cons. It wasn't what she wanted versus what others wanted, or about what she had perceived as being taken from her. She started to see this opportunity in a new light. A giant step in fulfilling her potential.

Mel thought about her mom's words, her regrets. She pondered on Devin's insistence that he wouldn't ask her to give up anything for him—it was a grand gesture considering his declaration of love.

She needed to stop fighting her decision. She needed to pick her path and face it without wavering.

Looking around her room, Mel saw things through a different lens. They were just that: things. Her painting supplies—if her biological mom liked to paint, she could get a new set there. Trinkets, clothes, even her oldest stuffed animals—replaceable, and the memories attached to them could stay with her.

What future was she really going to miss out on here? Art was a hobby. Travel was a fun goal. But she hadn't narrowed down what she would study in college, she still had a half dozen options she was considering. Mel shook her head with a slight smile. Her parents may have kept her true nature a secret, but they'd prepared her for this. They'd always told her to take time off after high school to consider her options. They'd known this day would come, and she loved them that much more for it. And the Green Lands, everything there was so … simple, basic, compared to the modern world she'd grown up in. But simple didn't mean inferior. She now understood what Devin meant by there being a pull to the Green Lands. She'd felt that by the cliff.

Mel considered what pictures she would take, starting a to-do list for her remaining time. She'd need to print some photos, like Bonnie had done … as she wouldn't be taking her cell phone where they were all currently stored. Devin had explained that electricity didn't work the same there—modern human electronics were useless. Mel asked herself what she would wear, and if she should pack things up to make it easier for her parents to donate. Would she take time to revel in a rite of passage like burning her school books, too? She still had a little while for those minor details. She could think about them while zoning out in classes.

But she'd made the most important decision. Mel was going home.

She took a deep, calming breath and closed her eyes, imagining what it would look like from the clouds. The weight of the decision melted away. This was the most at peace she'd been since the day of her attack.

The chime of her phone pulled her down from the clouds.

A text from Zach.

"Crap," she whispered.

***

Mel was itching for classes to pass by on Friday; each brought her closer to the weekend with free time to train. So naturally, each class felt hours longer than the one before.

Fourth period came with a surprise. A new lab partner was paired up with Mel. A new student, having transferred in the middle of the year. A boy. She focused more on controlling her energy as her mind ran through every scenario. Could he be a new Ivy, if her cover was compromised? Could he be another brother in their Seeder network, set up as extra protection?

Or is he just a normal human and you're completely losing it?

The Seeders were convinced Blake and Ken got lucky, that they hadn't actually known Mel's true identity before the attack. And it made sense. She'd been lit up like a Christmas tree, out in the open on the day of her botched bloom. Anyone, green folk or human, would have known something was up just by walking past the gym at the right moment that day.

Not so lucky for the Seeders, was the fact that at least one Ivy remained—and knew Seeders were around.

Ken and Blake's bodies were gone. And they'd been pierced by Seeder darts. No news reports ever spoke about them, no rumors circulated at school, and Seeder attempts to look into their cover stories for having gone missing turned up nothing—the lies about Blake and Ken's disappearances were just as reliable as any Seeder or Ivy fake identity or cover.

Mr. Rasmussen asked Mel to hang back after class. He waited until all the other students had filed out of the room, casting a glance at the cut-out window in the door.

"Ms. Walters. I wanted to chat. Is everything okay?"

"Yeah, of course," she lied. Things were less stressful now that she'd made her choice, but there was still a heck of a lot going on. *Especially* with a new concern popping up in his class in the form of her lab partner.

"It just seems like your mind has been wandering. You used to always be so active in class."

She kicked herself for not doing a better job at keeping up the facade. *Just a couple more weeks.* "No, sorry. Just family stuff."

"I always care about my students, especially the bright ones that show a love for learning. Is there anything I can help with? I'm here if you need someone to talk to."

"No. I'm fine, thanks. I'll swing by the guidance counselor if things don't settle down."

"Sounds good. Just remember the offer stands. I'd hate for your final grade to suffer because of a bump in the road."

The classroom door swung open. Tom stood at the door.

"Oh, hi, Melody," he addressed her once he noticed there was a student in the room. He turned to Mr. Rasmussen. "I was walking by when I remembered our need to talk about that suspension. Could you swing by my office at the end of the day?"

"No problem."

Tom nodded. "You've got a crowd lining up out there—make sure you give Ms. Walters a note if she's going to be late for her next class."

"Of course. We were just going to discuss our newest transfer. We were finishing up."

Tom raised an eyebrow. "Newest transfer?"

Mr. Rasmussen smiled. "New lab partner."

"Ah, gotcha." Tom nodded. "I think that would be great for them both. Anyway, sorry to interrupt you. I'll see you later." Tom threw Mel a smile and left the room.

Mr. Rasmussen turned his attention back to Mel. "Rick just transferred from Lakeside. I think you'd make a good partner to help him get caught up. He could really use a friend, transferring this late in the school year. That won't be a problem, will it?"

A month ago, this would have seemed like a regular conversation. 'How are you doing?' 'Get to know the new kid that showed up out of nowhere in the middle of the school year.' But now, everything was suspicious.

Mel focused on keeping her energy in check. Her emotions flowed over her heart, but under the surface enough so her body language didn't give her away, either. She realized this was the kind of training her brothers went through for years, but she was getting an immersive crash course, on-the-job training, in the middle of fighting to stay undetected.

"Yeah, sure. Why not?" she offered.

Mel grabbed her backpack and left the classroom. Mr. Rasmussen opened his door for students to find their seats. She pulled out her phone and texted Devin.

<Office. Now.>

Chapter 25

DEVIN ARRIVED AT THE OFFICE only moments after Mel.

"I need to lie down for a minute in the sick room," she said. "The Vice Principal called you down here? You in trouble?"

He picked up the hint with a nod. Mel patted herself on the back. She was getting used to this working-undercover business. Knowing Mr. Simons was at worst benign, she hoped he could pull some strings and help.

Mel headed to the nurse's station and Devin pulled out his phone.

She put on her best act of a stomachache to garner pity and gain entrance to go lie down. Fortune shined on them; there was no one else in the sick room right then.

"Do you think you need to call home? Or do you want to wait awhile and see how you feel?" the nurse asked.

"I don't want to bug my parents. Can I just lie down for a little while?"

The nurse finished checking her temperature. "Sure. If it gets worse, let me know. There's a trash can right here next to the bed if you need it."

The phone on the wall rang, and the nurse answered. "Sure, I'll be right there."

After hanging up, she turned to her patient. "I'm just going to be a few doors over. I'll be back in a while to check on you."

As soon as she left the room, Devin slipped in and rushed to Mel's side.

"What's up? Are you actually sick?"

"I'm fine," she said.

He let out a sigh. "A bit of an elaborate plan for a make-out rendezvous in the middle of the day, don't you think?" He smirked.

She scolded him with her eyes. "I'm worried. I figured it's best to pass on this information in person, not in text, right?"

He motioned for her to continue.

"Mr. Rasmussen... He was being weird. He seemed pretty concerned about how I'm doing. Could he be an Ivy?"

Devin's face gave nothing away.

She continued, "Or, if he was worried, could he be..." She asked with her eyebrows, not daring to finish her question. Could he be her dad, or Devin's dad? Just checking on her, knowing she was going through a hard time?

It was Devin's turn to give the disapproving expression. "You know I can't tell you either way. We're not playing a guessing game. But it's good to hear observations I can pass on. He lives on your street, right? Was there anything else?"

"Yeah, I pass his house every day when I walk to school. And he just partnered me up with a guy that recently transferred," she added.

"The new kid didn't attack you in the middle of class, right?" he said matter-of-factly. "We're aware of any new transfers."

"So ... maybe I overreacted."

"No, it's good. This is the kind of observation that helps keep you safe. But maybe next time don't be quite as cryptic, just give me a smidge more to know you're not in imminent danger?"

Her face scrunched in embarrassment. "Sorry ... yeah..." She didn't want to sound crazy or waste any more time, but figured she might as well just throw it all out there. "One more thing." She lowered her voice. "Since there are two Seeders teamed up in our town, could there also be more than one Ivy general?"

Devin tilted his head ever so slightly. This time he gave away more. He looked curious. "Anything's possible."

"It's probably nothing... No, it's stupid."

"Mel, spit it out. We don't have a lot of time."

"Tom?" She waited a second. "I know. You can't say anything. He came by when Mr. Rasmussen was talking with me. It probably meant nothing. He thought it was good for me to help the new transfer. And then I thought about how he asked me weird questions after Blake first attacked me, and then he asked about you and Ben when he caught me looking in the gym after spring break. But no ... he couldn't be. I can't imagine an Ivy getting so close with my parents. I'm just being paranoid now. But ... then again ... Blake and Ken..." She rubbed her temples. "Gosh, I'm sorry. I'm losing it. Everyone seems suspicious. I was even starting to think my P.E. teacher could be one of them. I can't wait until I can put this all behind me."

She figured she might as well round off her explanation of suspicions. "Mr. Cress, my gym teacher. He was there and noticed how sick I was before the attack. He didn't insist I come down here to the sick room, so maybe he was keeping an eye on me. And ... I saw him jogging down our street the other day. Does he even live close to me?"

Devin shrugged. "We'll look into all of them, okay? I promise, we won't let you down."

She'd almost felt the tiniest bit calmer a couple hours ago, working on her mental to-do list for leaving her human life behind. Now her heart wouldn't stop racing. Maybe the Ivies had moved on. If they knew who she was, why wouldn't they have come by her house to finish her off already? What was their plan?

"How do they even find us? My parents told me there's only a few million green folk back in the Green Lands. What's the likelihood they'd focus resources in the right places to find us? Or care enough to send more backup?"

Devin frowned. "I can't give you all the answers you want."

Mel huffed. The secrets were getting old.

"It's not what you think." He looked her squarely in the eyes. "We genuinely don't know some of those things. How they find us— sometimes ending up in the same places as we are in the human world. We don't know how all of their powers work." He shrugged. "Or even how all of *ours* work." He frowned again. "Love, I don't know. I wish I did."

Her heart sank further, grasping at straws. "You've never met one other than Blake, right? It sounds like interactions between our people are rare. Maybe I'm not worth the bother?"

He held her hand. "No. I've never knowingly met one other than Blake. But you've seen their handiwork. We keep ourselves safe by staying within our borders and staying hidden when here. They could happily stay in their own kingdom. Not taking this threat seriously only risks your life."

She felt a headache coming on.

Devin must have sensed it, squeezing her hand. "I would kill for you and I would die for you. You know that, right?"

Mel swallowed hard. She knew that—he was a soldier, one of her assigned protectors. She wished he didn't have to be either of those things.

He flashed a comforting smile. "And so would Ben, and all of our brothers and dads. I understand that the vast majority of human teens aren't really up to snuff on this kind of thing. But they don't grow up the way we do." His voice was soft, his face relaxed. "I know we dropped the ball. Epically. Unforgivably. Idiotically. That was once. We won't make that mistake again. Please try to trust the plan." He lifted her hand, giving it a gentle kiss. "I would have killed for you before I even knew you, before I loved you. If you can't trust our dads, please try to trust me."

She loved that he knew how to wash away her worries. How he could make sense in this chaos. "I'll do my best." She gazed into his eyes. "I really do lo—"

Their time was up; the nurse walked back in. "Excuse me, do you need some help?" she asked Devin.

He was still crouched down next to where Mel was sitting. "No, I just saw Mel come in here and wanted to make sure she was okay."

The nurse frowned. "This isn't a social club. Get back to class. Make sure to grab a tardy slip from the office."

"Yes, ma'am, sorry." He gave Mel a reassuring smile as she lay down.

***

They met at their lockers after school. "So, did you get a tardy, or did you get a pass from the Vice Principal?" she asked.

Devin raised his eyebrows. "I don't believe my attendance record is any of your concern."

Mel leaned in and whispered, "Just wanted to see if I was right about strings being pulled by a certain someone with power."

He whispered back, "I'm insulted you think my uncle would give me preferential treatment. Surely, that's what you're implying?" He straightened up and asked at a normal volume, "By the way, who do you want to hang out with tonight?"

She stood up straight, rolling her eyes. "Fine."

His warning, the one that ended the conversation, was his way of asking if she wanted to train with him that night, or if she would be punished with Ben. Not that Ben was bad, but she and Devin were on better terms now, and she'd rather spend the time with him.

And he'd won their secretive battle of wills and wits. She wanted to find out if Mr. Simons was in the know; a helpful human, or perhaps even one of their dads. But she knew better. She needed to stop testing Devin. Though she *was* a little turned on by the thrill of the chase, and his competence as a covert operative was undeniably sexy.

They left directly from school for their nightly training.

"A warehouse? We have a whole warehouse?" Mel had assumed they would be doing more flight training outside.

"Our dads have had a long time to accumulate wealth here, it's not like they squander money on vacations," Devin explained before giving her the grand tour.

The warehouse was closed tight. Doors locked; windows covered. They would have total privacy with lots of space. There wasn't much to see in there, only the necessities.

"As you progress, we'll obviously need to work outside at night. But this is perfect when the sun is up, especially for flight basics."

They did a quick review of what they had gone over the night before. She still struggled the most with keeping her blades out, especially when focusing on other things she needed to do concurrently.

"Think of it like good posture," Devin coached, "the kind no one has anymore. If your shoulders are up and back, your neck and the rest of your body are in the right places and work better. Imagine your blades like that. Lock them in place."

She visualized it the way he explained, then smiled when it appeared to do the trick. They did more practice 'communing with the wind' as he called it. A warehouse wasn't the draftiest of places, but they had fans they would use at different speeds. Even then, she would need to learn to manipulate the air without a breeze.

The latter half of the night, they moved over to a stack of squishy foam mats. She realized things were getting serious when he mentioned next up was learning to hover.

"I don't expect you to fly around in here. We'll start with the fans. You'll focus with everything we've been doing, and you'll learn to balance yourself and get a small lift."

That was a huge leap from everything she had learned so far. They used different settings on the fans and changed up the direction of the air flow. For hours, she worked to balance the variables required for flight—mental concentration, proper posture, and centering energy in her core while carefully spreading enough out to the rest of her body. She felt defeated when she barely got the teeniest, tiniest lift at the end of the night, despite Devin's praises.

Mel lay face down on the padded mat.

"Do you have any more in you tonight?" he asked.

She moaned.

"I can't tell if that was a 'heck yes' moan, or a 'screw you' moan," he teased.

She rolled her head to the side. "I'm calling it."

She wanted to get home and shower. Her distracted mind was probably hampering her efforts, anyway.

Her phone chimed after she scraped up the wherewithal to stand. It was Zach. <Still on for midnight?>

She was grateful none of their recent practices had involved bruises. Zach wouldn't be fretting about her well-being that night.

She turned to Devin. "You promise, no one's noticed *anything* suspicious? No more Ivy movement out there?"

He gave her a reassuring smile. "I promise you. We're being extra careful."

Chapter 26

ZACH HAD BEEN TEXTING MEL about wanting to spend time with her. She had been too tied up with her secrets to carve out time or attention for him like she'd hoped to. But when it came down to it, she'd made her decision, and he deserved to know where she stood. She agreed to meet him down the street from her house at midnight.

The only sound in the house was a box fan her dad always had on at night for white noise. Mel gave herself plenty of time to inch her way through the house, to sneak out undetected. Slipping out through the small garage door was her best bet to avoid the motion-sensor lights at the front and back doors. She power-walked to the edge of the street, glancing over her shoulder regularly. A figure approached from the shadows—Zach was on time. The irony wasn't lost on her that every part of her life had now become a clandestine affair; full of secret meetings, code words, fake identities.

She launched herself into his arms in a bear hug. It felt amazing. She lingered there, not wanting the moment to end. Mel knew that once she pulled away, things were going to change, and there would be no undoing it.

"Hey, what's with all the mystery?" Zach asked.

"Things are just crazy, and busy."

"Okay... You're still acting weird. Are you alright?"

"You know, all things considered, I'm doing well."

He lifted his eyebrows; his curiosity was apparent under the faint glow of a nearby streetlamp. "All things considered?"

"This may sound weird, but can you tell me about your childhood before we met?" she asked, thinking this was the only way she might be able to suss out, for absolute certain, if he was somehow an Ivy. Of course, if he had convinced her of his ignorance thus far, he probably wouldn't skip a beat in continuing to keep his identity a secret.

"Umm..." He continued to look confused. "Well, what do you want to know? You know I was born in Dallas and moved here the summer before we met in school. That's ... all..."

She sighed. What did she really hope to learn from questioning him about his past?

"Is this about the other day? Do you need more time? Or..." He squinted as if trying to read her mind.

"Devin and I ... are... Things are complicated right now..."

He bit his lower lip. "'Complicated' isn't exactly synonymous with 'broken up.'"

"I need you to understand that he's not the reason for my decision. Neither are you." She realized she wasn't making sense. "Dating isn't my main focus right now..."

He was visibly disappointed, but not devastated—it wasn't an outright rejection.

Zach shook his head. "Okay, Mel. I understand. You're still my best friend. And I've waited this long; I can wait until you sort out whatever it is you're dealing with."

Her heart sank. Time—he didn't realize how finite hers was.

She'd been fighting a battle in her heart, ever since she'd found out she might need to leave. And she couldn't keep it inside anymore. Zach had been hurt by Tabatha leaving, too. It would be that much worse, knowing now how he felt about her, to just leave him without more of an explanation. She was certain he could be trusted.

"I need to tell you something, and doing so puts lives at risk, especially mine—which I know sounds like overkill, but hear me out." She had been working on how to word it just right all afternoon.

He looked understandably concerned by her ominous pronouncement.

"I'm not from here." She looked to see if there was a reaction. Nothing that gave him away yet.

"And I'm going to be leaving." She waited to see what he would do. If he were an Ivy, surely vague hints such as this would be evidence enough to elicit a response.

"You're not really making any sense. From where? Going where?" he asked.

"I need you to promise to not freak out. Look into my eyes."

He cocked his head slightly. "Okay..."

She pushed energy to her eyes, gazing into his while hers changed.

His jaw dropped. "What's going on? How are you doing that?"

She suppressed the change, reverting to normal.

"I'm not from here."

He scoffed. "Are you trying to tell me you're an alien?"

She grinned at his guess. "No. Not quite that crazy... At least, I don't think so."

She cupped her hands, moving in closer, practically pressing herself against him to use their bodies as a shield. She looked down, and he followed her gaze. A small ball of light rested in her palms. She reabsorbed it. "It's not just a magic trick." She moved back a pace.

"But how do you do it?" he whispered. "Where are you from? How long have you known?"

"Even if I had the time, I couldn't explain everything to you." She frowned. "I'm moving away in less than two weeks; I … might not ever see you again."

"Why? Why can't you stay? I can keep a secret!" Zach protested.

Mel started to get more emotional than she'd expected to. She'd worked it all out; she'd practiced her lines to avoid this.

"I believe you; I just don't have a choice." She knew that wasn't true, but it was an extremely watered-down version of the truth. She didn't have a choice in the *timing* of it…

He tilted his head, looking past her. "We have trouble."

She whipped around, ready to do whatever she needed to. It was Ben. Of course, it was Ben. It was *always* Ben.

She rattled off a warning. "I told you lives were in danger. Yours could be, mine absolutely is. You can't say anything, you have to pretend like you've never seen anything, or heard anything. Like nothing has changed. I'm serious, Zach."

He was breathing heavier and turned his gaze back to Ben, who was quickly closing in on them.

She looked back. "Ben won't hurt me. He's not the problem. Promise me, you know nothing."

"Yeah, yeah, of course." He nodded.

"Get back to the house, Mel!" Ben ordered from a few feet away, as loudly and forcefully as possible without being too loud for that time of night.

She gave Zach another quick squeeze. "You need to go."

He looked distressed, as if not wanting to let her leave, afraid for her after her ominous warning.

"Go. I'll be fine."

He started backing away down the street, keeping his eyes on them.

Ben scowled at Zach, then turned to follow Mel as she ran past him back to the house.

Ben caught up to her, entering through the front door right behind her.

"YOU ARE SO SELFISH!" he belted once the door was shut.

Mel wasn't sure if he was mad just because she'd snuck out, or if he had actually seen or heard anything.

"YOU KNOW WHAT? I AM!" she screamed back. "Sometimes we *get* to be selfish."

He glared. "I'm at least glad to know the new security cameras work."

She swallowed hard, feeling beyond stupid. They obviously would have added more security measures, she just hadn't noticed them.

Pam and George rushed out of their room at the commotion. "What's going on?!" George demanded.

Ben was seething mad. "Zach. She revealed herself to Zach."

Pam and George looked at her disapprovingly.

She defended her choice, throwing her hands in the air. "Why does it matter? If he was an Ivy, we'd know now. You're welcome. Then you could kill him and stop worrying about it. Just another mark on your tally board. But he's NOT one of them."

Still clearly livid, but no longer shouting, Ben let Mel get under his skin. "You have absolutely no way of knowing for certain what he is. You're a horrible judge of character. You're a moron! You even think our dad is one of them."

Her eyebrows raised at the slip and he pursed his lips, obviously realizing he'd said too much.

She looked from Ben to her parents. Their eyes were wide. They shook their heads ever so slightly, remaining tight-lipped.

"You know what? I don't even care right now. You think I'm selfish. But I think Zach deserves closure about my leaving, just as much as my parents do. Even Bonnie got to tell her brother and sister."

Ben gave her a death glare. "Do you know what happens when a Seeder family gets compromised? Or were you and Devin too busy groping each other to discuss the risks?"

Mel clenched her teeth.

George spoke up. "That's enough, Ben!"

Ben turned his anger on George. "It's not even *close* to enough!" He glanced back at Mel before dropping his gaze with a guilty frown. "*We* all let you down, not realizing you hadn't been wearing your jade." Ben looked back up, meeting Mel's gaze. "But what you just did. That was *all* you."

Mel averted her eyes in shame.

"A few years ago, an entire family from a neighboring village was wiped out. *Every* daughter. The dad and *every* son sent to this world. Maybe you're too selfish to care, because you're the last daughter from our family left here. But Dad and I are still here, too. And maybe I thought you'd give a damn about Devin's safety, and that of his family."

"I'm sorry," Mel whispered with tears in her eyes.

Ben glanced at the ceiling, shaking his head. "We do the best we can with what we have. But when things go wrong for us, it can go from bad to unbelievably worse in a heartbeat." He turned his gaze back to Mel, his eyes scanning her face. "Or would you have preferred Dad to raise twelve daughters all alone, secluded their entire youth up in the mountains somewhere, to keep you safe? This isn't a game."

She frowned. "I know it's not a game."

Ben narrowed his eyes. "Go to bed. You have a whole day of training ahead of you." He stomped up the stairs.

Mel followed after him to her own room, unable to even look at her parents as she passed them. While she normally would have stayed up all night festering over what Ben had said, her mental, emotional, and physical capacities had met their limits. She was out cold the moment her head hit the pillow.

Chapter 27

MEL WOKE TO A DOZEN texts from Zach. She kicked herself for not texting him before falling asleep—reminding him to keep his cool, and reassuring him she was fine. And of course, he was freaking out.

<Are you ok?>

<Mel?>

<I'm worried about you.>

<Please answer me.>

<Are you ok?>

<I promise I won't say anything. Please just respond.>

She sent off a reply. <I'm fine. Sorry. Went straight to bed.>

He immediately responded. <You scared the daylights out of me! Can we meet more to talk about this?>

<No. Don't text. Business as usual.> She couldn't risk her phone, or his, falling into the wrong hands. Written communication always had to be extremely limited and coded amongst the Seeder network in the human world.

Mel finally rolled out of bed at 10 a.m. Only her mom was still at home, doing breakfast dishes. Sitting down at the table, Mel looked at her mom sheepishly, waiting for her to speak first.

Her mom met her gaze and continued cleaning, eventually breaking the silence. "Ben's right. You can't be doing this."

Mel switched to staring at the table. "I don't mean to keep screwing things up. But I felt like it was a calculated risk worth taking."

"Maybe your calculations were off." This was not Pam's kind, nurturing voice. She was ticked. "You could have told him your cover story the night before you left. He'd have more closure than anyone else will, with you disappearing suddenly." She huffed. "You didn't have to give away the farm. He didn't have to learn about your true nature."

Pam and Ben had both made some extremely valid points. And Mel realized that. "But…" She still tried to defend her decision. "I *know* Zach is good. And I remember how hard it was for Zach and I when Tabatha left. I didn't want him to go through that again. It's not fair to him."

Pam sat down with her at the table. "You, of all people, know that life isn't fair. You didn't sign up for all of this. We don't always get what we want. Zach will learn that lesson himself, one way or another." Pam stood up again. "You know who *did* sign up for this? All those boys working so hard to keep you safe, giving you a chance at finding your way home. Is it fair to them?" She walked away. "I'll be in my sewing room."

Mel sat in silence, stewing in the shame of her constant mistakes. She was pulled from her solitude by the front door opening. Walking up to Ben, who'd just come in, she looked down at the floor. "I can be ready to start in five minutes."

He walked past her. "Good for you, you're not my problem right now."

She looked up as he rounded the corner to go upstairs. "Devin said you were taking the first half of today."

He gave no reply as he continued to his room. Her phone chimed. It was Devin.

<Be ready in half an hour.>

Mel sighed, shoving her phone back in her pocket. *Time for damage control.*

Walking into her mom's sewing room, Mel sat quietly on a spare rolling chair. Pam glanced over out of the corner of her eye, sorting through an old shortbread tin filled with miscellaneous bits and bobs.

"If I'm going to leave, I don't want to waste any of the time I have left fighting with you and Dad."

Pam sighed, turning to give Mel her attention. "If? I thought you'd decided."

Mel bit her lip. "I did. I just… You said Ivies don't bother humans, right? Maybe it's safer if I stay? For me? For everyone? Give up being a Seeder?" It hurt, just saying that out loud.

Pam shook her head with a frown. "If they know you're a Seeder, they're not going to wait and ask if your rooting has taken place, just to leave you alone. Your dad and I are relatively safe because they know I'm too old to be a Seeder female in the human world. Despite their lack of apparent ethics, I think Ivies want to avoid problems with humans as much as they can. This whole war, being played out in the shadows of the human world, is only possible because of the cover humans afford green folk. Ivies seem to want to avoid public discovery as much as Seeders do."

Mel looked down, fidgeting with her hands. "I can't win. I'm sorry. And I'm sorry Ben was a jerk to Dad last night."

Pam's sniffling caused Mel to look up.

"Ben wasn't wrong to be mad. We could have done things differently. Your dad and I will never be able to forgive ourselves for that."

Mel's eyes teared up. "But I do."

Pam gave her an appreciative smile. "I agree that we should put these arguments behind us. How about you keep being the amazing student I know you are? Instead of math, get some straight A's in catching breezes."

Mel grinned. "I'll see what I can do."

***

"You look well rested," Devin said as Mel got in the car.

She actually was, for a change, but the small talk felt almost condescending, despite his friendly voice. "You don't have to patronize me. I'm sorry." She thought about it. "I'm sorry about *some* things. Not everything." No one could convince her that Zach wasn't safe. But she could admit to herself that the way she'd revealed herself to him hadn't been the smartest thing she'd ever done.

Her phone chimed.

Devin glanced over. "Zach?"

"Yeah, he's texting me every half hour to make sure I'm still alive. It's going to be a long weekend."

"Maybe we should put it on silent," Devin suggested.

Halfway to the warehouse she asked, "Is Ben not working with me because he's pissed?"

Devin didn't answer.

She wasn't surprised. "Now I know what it feels like to be a pariah."

He spoke calmly. "Mel. I could go off on you. Trust me. I wanted to, when I found out. But I'm guessing you've already had that. You need to be more careful in your choices. Even in the Green Lands we know what Pandora's box is. You can't *fix* everything with an apology, and you can't just *unsay* something."

He sighed. "I told myself I wouldn't lecture you. Let's just focus on the work at hand. We don't even know if we have two more weekends. Let's make the most of this one."

After another five minutes of silence, he chuckled and rubbed his forehead. "Honestly, maybe we should be thanking you. Everything has gone so smoothly for our families up until this point. What's the purpose of all our training if we can't use it, right? You're keeping us on our toes."

Mel pursed her lips, shaking her head. He was always generous with her.

"I get that you guys don't trust my judgment. But I'm telling you, he's a good guy. Just like you. I know it."

Devin smirked. "While I appreciate the vote of confidence, you hated Ben and liked Blake…"

She wrinkled her nose. "Maybe I don't have the best track record… But," she raised a finger, "back then I didn't understand what was going on. I do now, and I'm still saying Zach's a good guy."

He sighed again. "I get it. He's your friend. You like him."

She frowned. "You guys don't understand why I told him. But you didn't see his face after he admitted to looking for Tabatha's obituary."

Devin furrowed his brow. "What?"

"He really misses her. I couldn't tell him what happened to her. But he confessed he's been looking into her disappearance."

Devin scratched his head. "Well, that's good to know. It didn't occur to you that an Ivy would be serious about tracing a returned Seeder's cover story?"

She scowled, annoyed she'd said anything. "It's not like that. We were both really close to her."

"Really?" He raised his eyebrows. "Equally close? Did he kiss her, too?"

"Never mind." Mel crossed her arms. "Just … you guys need to do a better job with your cover stories if you don't want people digging."

He shook his head. "Yeah, we'll see what we can do. I mentioned your dad killed a couple Ivies last year, right? It's not like anything that's happened with you, but we got kind of spooked. There were other circumstances; it wasn't great. She left earlier than she had to. I'll admit, it was rushed."

They pulled up to the warehouse. "Text him that you won't be responding for a few hours. We don't want him filling out a missing person's report."

***

They worked for two hours before breaking for a bite to eat.

"We're going on a field trip," he announced, grabbing his car keys. "Follow me."

Devin wouldn't say where they were going. It had to be important if they were taking time away from training.

Mel was confused when they finally pulled into a half-full parking lot on the other side of town, facing a brick building. "A library?"

"Wait here," he instructed.

After five minutes, he came back out. He was visibly unhappy, but he didn't take his mood out on her when he got back to the car.

"You get one chance, Mel. I mean it. And I want you to remember, with absolute clarity, what your priorities are, and what the effects of your choices are."

He spoke slowly, enunciating each word. "I want you to walk in there with one motto in mind, okay? 'Bare minimum.' You started this; you make this go away." He searched her face. "Room 12A. You have one hour, not a minute more."

Mel was still unclear what he was expecting her to do as she opened the car door. She stopped for a moment when he added, "And this never happened, do you understand?"

She nodded.

The silence in the library was punctuated by the soft beep of a barcode scanner, a printer busy at work in the back room, and the occasional whisper between patrons. Mel asked a librarian where she would find room 12A and made her way to it without much trouble.

There was a hallway with several small rooms, private rooms with narrow windows in the doors. They could be used for quiet studying or meetings of perhaps four people each, max. She opened the door to see Zach. He sprang from his chair and pulled her into a hug.

"Are you really okay?" he asked.

"Yes, I told you. I'm fine."

They sat down, facing each other with the small table between them.

"Yeah, well, you'll have to forgive me for worrying after the bombshell you dropped last night."

She fidgeted with her hands and scrunched her face. "Sorry, that could have gone smoother."

He sighed. "You weren't kidding about this being life and death, were you?"

She shook her head. "Wish I was."

"That boyfriend of yours is a piece of work. This would be the first time I've been threatened with being murdered in my sleep. And trust me, he was convincing."

She pressed her fingers to her lips.

"Let's start with this. Just to get it out of the way. How much is *my* life in danger? And my family?"

She lowered her hands. "He would do it." She repeated Devin's advice to herself. 'Bare minimum.' But she felt the emphasis was necessary for Zach to realize the severity of the situation. They needed to rein it in before it got away from them. "And he would get away with it."

Zach looked uncomfortably surprised by her casual confirmation.

"But only if you did something to betray me. That would be the *only* reason he or anyone else would go after you. Same with your family."

He nodded. "That is ... good to know... Just so we're absolutely clear, what constitutes betraying you?"

She frowned. "I'm sorry, I never should have said anything. Ignorance is bliss, right?" She traced patterns with her finger on the table. "I guess I would say there are two ways you could betray me and it wouldn't end well. The first is to attack me."

His face contorted at the incredulous suggestion.

"I know, you would never hurt me. Zach, I get it. We're just laying it all out on the table, right?"

"Right. No hurting you. Twisting your arm or leaving you bruised isn't on my agenda."

That felt like a cheap shot. But ... fair enough, considering he always came to her aid. It had to be insulting to have his integrity questioned like that.

"Okay. The second way you can betray me is to let anyone know about me. My world. My people. And I know you can keep a secret, but it's not just that. There are..." She paused to be careful and concise, asking herself, *Does he need to know this? Will this put someone else at risk?* "There are people that want to hurt me. Think of it like the witness protection program. Yeah, that's a good comparison. They don't know who I am. But they want to."

She pondered, asking herself if she should tell him they had already tried. No, that would only make him more worried. He seemed to understand how serious this was now.

"Any behavior out of the norm could tip them off. Looking around anxiously, asking me a question about all of this. We really have to pretend like everything is normal. I've only known about this a couple of weeks. Hopefully, I've concealed it well enough that you didn't notice a change?"

He bobbed his head, wrinkling his nose.

She lifted her eyebrows. "Okay, other than the bruise and my fight with Devin. Nothing else too weird?"

"Yeah. I guess you were normal-ish."

She rolled her eyes. "Thanks. Glad to hear I'm doing so well. I'm giving myself a pass because we're so close that you might notice more than the thugs out there."

"Alright. I think we're clear. I have a blip in my memory from last night, I refrain from trying to hurt you, and I don't have to look over my shoulder every waking moment? Or I guess even when I'm not awake, judging by what lover boy said."

Mel tried to keep a straight face. "That pretty much sums it up. See? Easy peasy."

He frowned. "And what about you? Why do people want to hurt you? How can I help keep you safe?"

She blushed. Always wanting to be the knight in shining armor. "Other than keeping my secret, there's nothing you can do. It's being handled. They want to hurt me because I'm different. They are … specific people, with specific reasons."

"Wow, could you be any more vague?" he mocked.

She frowned. "The only reason I even told you was for your benefit, I didn't want…" She stopped herself. Would mentioning Tabatha's ghosting be giving too much information? "I didn't want you to worry about me when I suddenly disappear. Because I will. And I want you to know it doesn't have anything to do with you. And that I'll be safer, and happy. And I'm sorry, because I know it's bad timing, now that I know how you feel about me, about … us."

He looked down at the table. "Why do you have to leave so soon? And if it's so important to leave quickly, why are you waiting?"

Her heart sank, thinking of their many years together, all of them filled with great memories. "Remember what you saw last night? I'm physically not normal. It's related to that. That's all you have to know. I don't get to choose the timing. No one does." She reached over, grabbing his hand, getting his full attention. "If I could delay it, I would risk hiding here longer. Things … could have been different. I… I can't give you the chance you want. I'm sorry." She bit her lip. "You'll always be my best friend. I'm sorry."

They sat for a moment in silence. What more needed to be said? That was the bare minimum, right? She looked at the time on her phone—they still had half an hour left. They both stared at the desk between them. He, probably evaluating what he could ask. She, considering what else she could get away with telling him.

He braved the waters first, looking at their hands. "How many others are there involved in all of this? I'm guessing ... Ben, Devin, your parents?"

"My parents are normal. They're not my birth parents. Like you, they just want to protect me. I can't say anything about anyone else. Just know that Ben and Devin are good guys."

"How did this all start? How did you get wrapped up in all of this?" he continued, laying out his curiosities.

"It's just a ... my people versus their people thing. I didn't do anything. I'm just lucky enough to be on the good side. Where I'm from, where I'm going back to, our people have been at war for a long time. I was sent here for my safety ... and I'll be safe again when I leave. It's complicated."

"And you're one hundred percent sure there's no other way to make this go away?" His eyes were sad. "You can't just leave for a little while and come back? We can't see each other ever again? Just losing another friend like Tabatha? Poof!"

She hoped her eyes hadn't given away anything when he mentioned Tabatha's name. "If I don't leave soon, I will ... miss out on very important parts of my future. I'm not able to go and just come back when I want."

She had thoroughly probed every possible loophole with Devin long ago. Why couldn't she just make the journey, form her roots, catch a breeze the next spring, and spend as much time in the human world as she wanted for the next decade, until she permanently rooted to the Green Lands? Completely logical, right? Nature was too cruel for that.

There was a reason she would only be able to visit once a year for a week in the spring, at least until she was old enough to have a clutch. If Seeder girls rooted in the Green Lands instead of the human world, they literally started dying when they came back for a visit. More than a week and necrosis set in. They rotted from the roots up with the lack of ambient energy. It would be painful, and there was no cure. There were a lot of lose-lose details in this package.

Was it fair to give him a speck of hope? Or risky? He deserved some honesty, and she wanted it personally, anyway. "There may be a chance—and I want to stress the word 'may'—that I can come back for a week each year to visit. But that's all. Don't ask how, don't ask when. But maybe we can set up something."

He perked up at the news. "And there's no possible way for me to visit you? Wherever you're going?"

Her heart ached as she shook her head. That was a resounding 'no.' Even if, somehow, miraculously, they found some kind of way to get him through a rift … Zach would die. Seeder lands were still haunted by the poison that had forced them to send her to the human world in the first place.

She looked at her phone more frequently, monitoring the time. They had five minutes left, and she wasn't sure if Devin would come in to fetch her, or if he'd wait in the car. She didn't want to risk him coming in at the end.

"Can I give you a hug?" she asked, and he obliged. It gutted her, knowing they weren't going to have many more of these. There was so much more she wanted to say, to do. Instead, she leaned back from their hug, gave him a kiss on the cheek, and fashioned the least-sad smile she could muster.

Mel wanted to say more, but apparently, she wasn't very good at goodbyes. She didn't know if they would have another time to be so candid, but the sentimentality of the circumstance was getting to her. She wanted to dart out of there before she started to get choked up. Mel gave him one more quick hug. "See you at school on Monday. Business as usual." She left with two minutes to spare.

Devin was waiting in his car, listening to music on the radio. She wasn't sure if he'd been waiting there the whole time or if he'd left and come back, happening to get the same parking spot. She hopped in the car and buckled her seatbelt.

He handed her a smoothie; evidently, he *had* left. "Peace offering."

She smiled as the engine turned and they reversed, heading to the warehouse to get back to the perpetual grind of training. She took a sip of the orange-raspberry smoothie and glanced at Devin, grateful he'd given her the opportunity to work things out with Zach.

Devin didn't take his eyes off of the road. "If anyone asks, how did our afternoon workout go?"

She took a cleansing breath. "I'm exhausted from nonstop work, not even a single break."

"And you don't think we should have any problems?" he asked.

"We're set. Not a single lion, tiger, or bare ... minimum."

"Good."

It's not like the car was bugged, but ... plausible deniability.

Chapter 28

THE ENTIRETY OF MEL'S WEEKEND was consumed by training with Devin. They returned well past midnight both Saturday and Sunday. Her parents' lives were on hold for her; they focused on grabbing any moment where she could take a breather to reminisce over photo albums. They even cancelled Sunday dinner with Tom, which she felt was a bold move, something out of the ordinary that could give them away. She kind of wanted to say goodbye to him, granted … he wouldn't know it was a goodbye. But she would still see him at school, and that would have to be enough.

Luckily, Zach got the hint and only texted her a couple times a day to see how she was doing instead of twenty times.

That is, until Monday. He flooded her with texts Monday morning. He wasn't going to let her go that easily. Zach latched on to the little things that she had or had not said.

<This isn't your war to fight.>

<What happens if you stay?>

<Is not leaving an option?>

<I'm sure we can find another way.>

<It's not just me that will miss you.>

After the first one, all she replied was, <Business.>

After the second and third, she replied, <I don't know what you're talking about.>

She ignored him after the fourth.

After the fifth, she responded, <Lunch, doors by the tracks. STOP.>

She did her best to not throw him dirty looks that morning. And she didn't dare tell Devin their secret meeting hadn't gone off without a hitch after all.

Zach was waiting for her by the doors at the start of lunch. The gym hallway that led to the tracks was often pretty empty, which she definitely had the misfortune of knowing firsthand.

She ushered him out the door. "We can't talk about this. I told you. Especially in writing."

He pleaded, "Just give me some time to figure it out. I don't want to lose you. Even if it's just as a friend!"

She raised her voice, "You need to let it go."

"Everything okay here?"

They turned to look. Mr. Cress, her P.E. teacher, was walking past. "Shouldn't you two be in lunch or class? Care to explain?"

Mel tried her best, not sure if he had heard their conversation. "We just needed some fresh air; we'll head back to the lunchroom."

She and Zach put on the most genuine smiles they could manage and went back inside. She looked over her shoulder to see if Mr. Cress was observing them through the window, but she couldn't see him. Zach was practically knocked off of his feet as Mel shoved him to the side, into the closed gym door. She wasn't pulling any punches—she used her energy to boost that push. Mel had never expected to use her energy against Zach, and she hadn't fully intended to, but he was taking things too far.

She quietly nudged him through the door as he rubbed his shoulder in shock.

Pointing to the center of the room, she whispered in a threatening tone, "I was almost murdered, right there! If you want that to happen again, keep asking questions. If you want to be my friend, you'll accept that I have nothing else I can give you."

She promptly left the room, looking around the hall to make sure they weren't being followed. It took all she had to keep her energy locked away as she marched to the lunchroom. She regained her composure, opening the door to the bustling heart of the school full of ignorant human teenagers munching on highly questionable pizza and gossiping about normal things she no longer had time for.

She sat down next to Devin with a fake smile. "Chatting with Mr. Cress," she explained. It wasn't a lie. They'd spoken briefly, and it might or might not be important. But it gave her an excuse for being late. She gave Devin a kiss on the cheek and munched on a couple of his fries.

She glanced at the lunchroom door a couple times, fighting back tears, trying to keep up her facade. It wasn't like Zach would be walking through them. He hadn't been eating with them, anyway. But this time, it wasn't because he'd kissed her and was hiding from Devin. *What did I just do?* He'd been taking things too far, but she knew that she had just crossed a line, too.

Zach didn't text her even once after that.

He didn't try to keep up pretenses, either. No locker drop-by, no hug, no anything. She hadn't even left, and their friendship was over. In her heart, she knew it.

***

The countdown to takeoff was merciless. That weekend, what might be their last full weekend by the looks of it, Ben finally agreed to instruct Mel again. His techniques helped round off everything Devin had been training her in. During daylight, they practiced in the warehouse. She was hovering successfully with different wind speeds and directions. At night, they drove to an old, abandoned speedway where she could get a running start to practice taking off.

Her first time at the old speedway, Ben explained the proper technique and pointed out a short ramp to help her get some lift. Mel stared at the ramp, rehearsing every instruction she'd received on catching a breeze. She focused the energy in her core and sprinted to the ramp. Right before running out of space at the end of it, she pushed energy to the muscles in her legs, kicking off and up. Before gravity called her back down, she rushed a portion of energy to her hands, balancing herself out. Almost simultaneously, with head-to-toe Seeder energy keeping her up, Mel focused on the wind. The breeze was barely there. Delicately reaching a smidge more into her core, she stretched extra energy to her hands and they glowed. Communing with the surrounding air, her hands stayed flat but tugged at the air and she rose higher.

Mel was flying. She was *actually* flying. Soaring to a few yards above the asphalt, she carefully turned her hands and body to veer to the left, hoping for a safe landing on the overgrown grass. The resistance of the surrounding air was like gently pushing against a trampoline; it had a little give. Aiming for the grass, Mel's eyes widened in preparation. She recalled Ben's advice about moving energy to her arms and legs last-minute to strengthen those muscles and bones so she wouldn't break anything on a rough landing. Unlike the soft pad keeping her safe in the warehouse, the ground outside was not so forgiving.

That first flight did not end gracefully. Nor did the first few after it. More than once, she had to pick a chunk of gravel out of an arm or leg before healing after a crash landing. But Ben was there to correct and cheer her through it.

In the end, the landing wouldn't be a concern. Once they crossed the Green Lands threshold, the energy would help balance her, and Thod could help guide her down. But if she couldn't nail a decent takeoff and sustain a breeze, she didn't have any hope. Not even two guides could carry her—Seeders weren't built to transport anyone but themselves. The act of taking seedling daughters between realms was only feasible on their first day, right after sprouting, because of how lightweight they were. Anything bigger or heavier, and it was too draining to make it.

It was decided that Saturday would be the day. They *might* be able to push it until Sunday, *maaaybe* Monday. But it was better to be safe, rather than sorry, when it came to unpredictable biology, and, heaven forbid, inclement weather that would make things more challenging.

Mel worried about Zach's radio silence. She messaged him a couple times to ask how he was doing. He ignored her at school and via text. Her heart ached; so many years together, so many memories. Aside from her parents, she'd miss him the most. And her honesty had ruined everything between them. Honesty, and maybe a little temper.

Risking the potential red flags, Devin, along with Mel's family, made a last-resort grab at any time they could, to finish preparing her. A doctor's note was forged, excusing Mel from gym class, and instead of having to sit out in class and watch, they made it possible for her to leave school early, since gym was her last class of the day. That kind of exception, she assumed, could only be thanks to Devin's ties in the office. They wouldn't risk getting Devin or Ben out of class early, but she had the keys to her mom's car and the warehouse. She could get started on her own.

Friday arrived—still nothing from Zach. Mel typed up a dozen texts to ask him to come over one last time, only to erase each one. She couldn't risk screwing everything up now, just because he was throwing away their friendship. Or could she? How much risk did it really hold, when she knew he was human?

Each class she attended held special meaning. It was weird, studying the faces of those around her and knowing she might never see these people again. She actually liked school, but she was also excited to take courses in the Green Lands—lessons on culture, powers, history, all of it. She spent the freed-up gym hour organizing her room and pictures, setting out clothes, trying to keep it together.

Taking a quiet moment to think, she lay on her bed, staring at her ceiling and running through her checklist. It was still so crazy to imagine she was moving to another realm. Somewhere on the same planet so wholly different. The glow-in-the-dark stars on her ceiling made her smile. She could only really take with her what could fit in her pocket. Maybe she could take this part of the world, this part of her first home, with her. She stood up on her bed, grasping for a couple stars. Pulling them off, she squished them together with the mounting putty on the backs. She blew out a long breath, setting the stars on top of her small stack of pictures to take when she left.

"How are you doing?" her mom asked, popping her head into Mel's room.

Mel took a deep breath. "I think … that I don't even know how I feel." She shrugged.

Her mom leaned against the doorway. "Sometimes, there's no right or wrong answer."

Mel nodded pensively. "Yeah."

"Meals tomorrow, what do you want? Anything's on the table."

Mel smiled and thought about her list. "Surprise for breakfast, steak for lunch?"

"You got it! I'll need to do some shopping. Want to come with?"

"Could you actually drop me off at Dad's work? I'd love to spend a little time there."

Her mom nodded with a smile. "That's a great idea." She reached into her purse. "But first, a little something special. Doesn't quite make up for everything, but…" She handed Mel a chocolate bar. "From the World Market. Made in Costa Rica."

Mel beamed, giving her mom a giant hug. "You really do speak my language."

Fifteen minutes later, Mel arrived at her dad's chiropractic office.

"Hey, you!" the receptionist greeted her.

"Hi. Is he working with a client?"

"Yep, two more today. Want to use one of the massage chairs in the back room?"

The idea sounded like heaven after all the hard work she'd put in. It was a training-free night, a time to rest and recuperate. Ben and Devin felt confident that she was up to snuff on her breeze-catching ability. "Yes, please!"

The woman guided Mel to a small back room and turned on a massage chair for her. Every muscle sighed in appreciation.

After a little while, her dad joined her. "Hey, stranger! I didn't expect to see you here." He shut the door behind him.

Her face lit up and she leapt out of the chair to give him a hug. "Just missed you."

They sat down on an adjustment table side by side.

"Hmm. Missing me? You're not even gone yet." He winked.

Mel frowned. "I know."

He took off his glasses, wiping them clean with the bottom of his shirt. "Well, I guess we're not on the same page, then. Because your mom and I are already making plans for all the fun things we'll do when you make your first trip back. It gives us something to look forward to, and we'll have a laundry list of all the things we'll want to hear about with your education and experiences." He replaced his glasses, giving her a smile.

She sighed, grateful they were both being so understanding about her choice to leave, or at least acting like it. "Are you guys being honest with me? Would you tell me if I was making the wrong choice?"

He put a hand on her knee. "Only *you* know the right choice. And yes, we're being honest with you."

Something had been nagging Mel since her talk with her mom weeks ago, when she'd found out her mom had passed on the Seeder life. "What are the conditions you had to agree to when you took me in? Is making sure I go back one of your responsibilities?" She looked down at her hands. "Devin and Ben say most girls choose to return and I wondered, you know…"

"Ah, I see. The conditions were to raise you safe, and give you a happy, normal life. I suppose we didn't hit the mark on some things." He frowned. "But no, it's not like we're censoring or lying about anything to coax you into going home. Your other dad knew our story before allowing us to take you in. He didn't ask us to hide anything." He shifted to face her more head-on. "When you're over there, your Seeder family will be there to help you, but they're different, and in their world, you're an adult already. You'll be expected to make your own decisions. I'm sorry we didn't do better at preparing you for that."

Mel hugged her dad. "I vote we agree to not apologize anymore. Me, for leaving and being a pain. You guys, for being a smidge imperfect."

He grinned. "A smidge, huh? I guess I'll take it."

There was a soft knock on the door.

"Come on in."

The receptionist opened it slightly. "Sorry. Just checking if it's okay that I take off?"

"Yep. Thanks for your hard work."

She smiled. "It was good to see you again, Mel. See you Monday, Dr. Walters."

Mel and her dad stayed silent for a while until they were sure she had left the building.

"So … she doesn't know yet?" The guilt stabbed at Mel.

He took a deep breath. "That she's about to be out of a job? Not yet. Not until you're gone."

They'd decided it would be best to have George move his chiropractic practice across the state. Mid-school-year exits were always the worst to cover without a tragic ending. The Walters opted to move; they'd always known it was a possibility and had saved for it. Mel would 'transfer schools' and be with her dad while her mom stayed behind and packed up, meeting them later and allowing Ben to finish out his year at the same school.

Thinking of the receptionist, Mel frowned again. "That's not really fair to her, is it?"

He nodded thoughtfully. "Sometimes, you have to choose yourself. You can't make everyone happy." He nudged her arm. "Plus, I've got a friend across town needing a new receptionist. It'll be less of a drive for her. She'll be taken care of."

Mel took a deep breath and let it out. *Sometimes you have to choose yourself.*

Smiling, Mel looked at her dad. "This would have been a lot easier of a decision to make if you guys were horrible parents."

He grinned. "Ditto, kiddo." He slid closer, giving her a side hug. "Well, I imagine your mom is waiting for us and we have things to do, don't we? Want me to crack a few bones first?"

Mel almost laughed. He hated people calling chiropractors 'bone-crackers,' but he used it jokingly with Mel and her mom in private. She glanced down at the padded adjustment table they were sitting on. "Let's do it. I want to be in tip-top shape for tomorrow."

After a quick adjustment, Mel and her dad headed home and took family pictures with her mom in front of a green screen, including a few outfit changes. As was common for Seeders, they would edit them and post them on social media after a daughter left. The frequency of posts would trickle off until 'she' would post that she was going to take a social media break.

And then she'd never come back from that break.

Mel set the table for their last family dinner. "Why only three plates? Is Ben not eating with us?"

"You'll see." Her mom hinted at a surprise.

***

Devin showed up to take Mel away on a last date. It would be only Ben and her parents eating at home. Mel hesitated at first, but her parents reminded her they'd spend all morning and afternoon together the next day before she left. Devin's hopeful smile won her over in the end, knowing she might not see him for a couple years as he continued to watch over his remaining sisters.

She was all smiles in the car. They'd snuck a few kisses over the last week and a half, but not much had been said about their relationship. They knew they were on the same page from the time she'd made her decision to leave, and officially let Zach know.

Devin held her hand as he drove to a secret location. It was at least a half-hour drive and her stomach was protesting. But he insisted he wanted to get out of the city. Have it be private, secluded, special. They pulled into some camping grounds, not officially open for the season yet, but affording a beautiful view of nature. He grabbed a blanket from the car and laid it down in a clearing, along with some takeout boxes.

"Chinese, bold choice for a picnic." She nodded.

"I figured it would travel well, and I know it's one of your favorites."

She loved that he remembered little details like that.

They sat, chatting and enjoying their food, reminiscing, and talking about what it would be like for her when she arrived in the Green Lands.

"I'm sorry we never got around to having a full-day human adventure." He frowned.

Mel shrugged. "Yeah, I guess it just wasn't meant to be." Visiting Zach, giving Devin a better human experience—these could all be done on future visits. But with such limitations on her time when she'd come back to visit her parents, she couldn't be certain what that would really look like down the road.

"How about this? I'll make time while I'm still stuck here to take an entire day and go do any one human experience you think I should try; I'll do it in your honor."

She looked down at their dinner with a smile. "Mmm. Great Wall of China."

He poked her in the ribs, making her squirm. "Maybe something just a little closer?"

"Okay, fine. Have you been to a theme park?"

He shook his head.

"Then that's it. I declare you must ride at least one roller coaster and eat lots of cotton candy. Oooh, and an elephant ear."

He raised an eyebrow. "The ear of one of those giant animals?"

She smiled, remembering they didn't have anything nearly that large in the Green Lands. "It's the name of a dessert."

He nodded with a smile of his own.

"Take one of your sisters. Heck, take Ben along. Heaven knows he needs to learn to relax now and then."

Devin laughed. "Deal. And in return, I promise to show you all of my favorite places when I get back home."

She held out her hand and they shook on it. She looked forward to finally seeing the Green Lands for herself. And the thought of exploring them with Devin by her side, filled her heart.

"Fortune cookie time," she announced while handing him one. "You first."

He cracked it open. "It reads: 'You are the luckiest guy in the world and should kiss the girl next to you.'" He grinned and looked up at her.

She giggled. "I mean, you've got to listen to what the cookie says." She leaned over and kissed him. She then took it from his hands and read the real message. "Seek out the things you most want in life."

"I'm good." He winked.

"Well, I'm offended. You lied about what it said," she kidded.

"I'm sorry." He pouted dramatically. "Do you think you could forgive me? We could kiss and make up?"

She let out a melodramatic sigh. "I mean, I guess so."

Devin grabbed her hands, inching closer. He kissed the backs of her hands, the palms of her hands, her forehead and cheeks. He nuzzled her neck and whispered, "I love you." And then he moved in for the real deal. It was good they were in an uninhabited area. The glow between the two of them might have been brighter than a bonfire. Luckily, Seeder energy couldn't actually burn.

As they caught their breath and watched the light fade, they stared into each other's eyes. "I love you, too," Mel confessed. "I always will."

Devin sat for a moment, running his fingers up and down her calves. "How are they looking?"

She revealed her Seeder legs. There was barely enough of a gap in the roots wrapped around her ankles to place a pointer finger where it would finally close, sealing her fate. She prodded at the ends that were the bane of her existence. "What if we surgically implant something between them, so they can't join? No rooting in either world. Free as a bird to go between both? Problem solved! Voila!"

He shook his head. "But honestly, no cold feet, no last-minute doubts?"

She shook her head as well, a little unconvincingly. "No, I really don't. I just wish it hadn't ended this way with Zach. If I hadn't screwed that up, I wouldn't leave with any regrets."

"You did your best. That's all any of us can do."

"Yeah, I guess so." She frowned.

Thinking of something she'd been considering, Mel took a deep breath. "Do you know what I think?"

He raised his eyebrows. "I suppose I don't."

She narrowed her eyes. "I think you've known for a long time that Zach is human."

He cocked his head to the side. "Why's that?"

She smiled. "Because you left me alone with him for an hour in the library. After Ben's tirade, that was pretty ballsy."

Devin smiled as well. "It's true I got an earful from Ben after what you did. That's why we kept your visit a secret." He pursed his lips. "How would you feel if I told you I'd bugged that room?"

Her smile dropped. "I'd be pretty upset..."

He looked her squarely in the eye. "Well, I didn't. Though I thought about *telling* Zach I did. But that would have been a hollow threat. And if you needed a goodbye with him, I figured it might as well be a sincere one. I wanted you to both be able to speak your mind."

She nodded. "Thank you."

He wore a faint smile. "There's a balance somewhere in there. Safety and happiness. If I'm being completely honest ... I did have one of our family members walk past and glance through the little window in the door a few times. Just to make sure he wasn't hurting you."

Mel sighed.

Devin reached forward to hold her hand. "You can't fault me for being protective when I'm *literally* one of your assigned protectors. And it's not like you've had all that much training for an attack. This isn't just me being some jealous boyfriend."

She had to concede the point. She'd thought it was a little reckless, no matter how much she appreciated being given the opportunity to chat with Zach. "But didn't he prove himself by sticking up for me when Blake was all over me in the hallway?"

Devin shrugged. "He could be a better actor than Blake. It wouldn't take much—we didn't suspect Ken. Or it could have been part of Zach and Blake's plan all along, to pull any suspicion away from Zach."

She raised her eyebrows in challenge. "Okay. What else do you have against him that makes you suspect he's an Ivy?"

"He pointed out your budding, when your arms were itching."

She'd given that some thought, but who *wouldn't* take note of their friend scratching their arms for the entirety of a conversation? "Yeah, well he's pointed out spinach in my teeth before, too. And I don't think he was somehow implying I was part plant by mentioning it."

Devin chuckled. "Add that to him looking into Tabatha's disappearance."

"We agree to disagree on the importance of that one." She lifted her eyebrows in challenge once more. "Anything else? How about the big thing in his favor? I've known him since the *fourth* grade."

Devin shrugged. "Why should that matter?"

"Because that's a lot of years in the human world when they know they can't even spot us blooming until we're teenagers?"

He shook his head. "That doesn't matter. Seeders send boys over that young, why shouldn't Ivies?"

Mel furrowed her brow. "Really?"

He nodded. "Deep covers. Every Seeder family sends one. As young as possible to make the journey and be embedded into daily life in their respective community."

Mel gulped, hating herself for having done something else she couldn't take back—sending a letter to Zach.

That was the one thing she couldn't resist doing—making one last effort with him. They'd been friends for too many years to allow their friendship to just slip away at the end so unceremoniously.

If she was right about the timing and he followed the instructions on the envelope, he'd open it after she was already gone. She wasn't going to screw things up, not again. She hadn't divulged the exact date or time of her departure (though she'd already told him an approximate deadline previously); she hadn't given anything else away. Just a heartfelt goodbye.

That was the compromise she'd settled on instead of texting to ask for a visit. The day before, she'd slipped it in the mailbox as the mailman approached, taking a deep breath, and slowly letting it go. She'd patted herself on the back, thinking how that chapter was being closed. The last box on her to-do list had been checked.

"Anyway." She wanted to change the subject, realizing she couldn't do anything about it now. And all of Devin's objections were still just conjecture. "My fortune. I'm assuming this is the most important piece of advice I will ever read in all of my existence."

She snapped the cookie in half and pulled out the little piece of paper. "'You will soon find something you have lost.' Well, that was anticlimactic. It couldn't say 'spread your wings and fly' or something like that? Anything about my future? I vote we swap."

He nudged her arm. "I vote we share mine. Our futures, our fortunes. I like the idea."

She stole a smooch. "I like that, too."

After the sun set, they lay down on the blanket, staring at the sky as the stars began to appear, cuddled up next to each other.

"Twenty-four hours," Devin announced with a melancholy voice.

"Do the Green Lands share the same stars?" she asked wistfully.

"I think so."

"Will you think of me each time you see the stars?"

"Every night, Saff."

She sat up and rolled over, pinning him down. "I have something I plan to take with me to remember you by." She pulled out the charm that had been hanging around her neck. "This is where it belongs, sun-side facing in."

They shared a warm smile.

"But I never really gave you anything special in return. As a thank you for the gift. For everything you've done to keep me safe," she said.

"I love the painting you made me. I—"

"No. I mean *really* special."

He tilted his head to the side.

She rolled off of him and sat cross-legged. "Come here."

He sat in front of her, also crossing his legs.

"There are rules that come with this gift," she said.

"Okay…" He smiled.

"We stay sitting just like this," she explained.

"I can handle that."

She leaned in. He followed her lead, meeting her lips. It was soft, slow, intentional. The energy flowed from her heart to her lips, imparting Devin with something special, something that was often given as a token when Seeder women were seeing off the men they loved. A human teenager might still be a bit young to know what they wanted. But they weren't human. She knew she had met her match, her mate.

They went back to cuddling and gazing at the stars.

"Is there only one match for a Seeder? Like soulmates?" Mel asked.

He kissed her on the forehead. "You know about the mating for life thing. So, yeah, after you … get married—'cause that's extremely important to Seeders, even if it's not for all humans—then I guess you're soulmates."

She nuzzled closer. "I mean before that. Could you be equally as happy with option A as option B? Or is there some kind of energy thing that makes you destined to pick just one person in particular?" With so much still left to learn, she wanted to know how much free will she really had in the matter. She didn't just want her physiology telling her Devin was the right one for her.

Devin tickled her arm, barely grazing his fingertips across her skin. "No. It doesn't work that way. Seeders date and choose just like humans do." He whispered in her ear, "But I know you're the one for me. If you'll have me. You know … someday, after we're both home."

Mel smiled wide. "I love you."

Not much later, she was falling asleep on Devin's shoulder when he decided to call it a night. He took her to the car and packed up their picnic.

"I suppose keeping you out all night before the big day is not the best way to get either of your dads' blessings," he whispered, grabbing her hand as she nodded off against the car window while he drove them back to the city.

Chapter 29

THIS WAS THE LAST DAY Mel claimed permanent residency in the human world. Waking up, it felt like a day of celebration, like Christmas, or a birthday, but somehow more somber. It was a day of dichotomies.

Mel's parents surprised her with chocolate chip pancakes, bacon, and eggs for breakfast. There was an unspoken pact to stay positive. Mel smiled while watching them cook together in the kitchen. Her mind wandered to her Seeder parents, and how they would finally be reunited and get opportunities like this again. She surveyed the dining room and kitchen. This was the home she'd grown up in, the one she would be leaving for good. Like the chocolate chips that morning, it was all a little bittersweet.

As they sat down and ate together, Mel couldn't help but smile. All of the practice, hard work, and stress had been worth it. No one dared say anything, not wanting to jinx it, but she'd made it to the end of her time there—still safe. The Ivies hadn't come for her. A small knot in her stomach reminded her that she couldn't pat herself on the back yet. Not until her feet left the ground that night.

After breakfast, she considered texting some of her more casual friends. She couldn't say goodbye, but perhaps something like she hoped they were having a good weekend. But at that point, it was better to stay silent or they might wonder why she didn't give them her cover story then, before disappearing into thin air. She was more the type to keep to her small, closer group of friends anyway. She thought of Heather. Maybe she and Zach ... probably not. But it would be nice—hopefully they would still hang out and it could help with Mel's absence.

***

In the early evening, Mel was pacing unrelentingly across the living room, checking the bay window every minute or two.

"Cool it, Mel. You're going to wear a hole in the carpet," Ben teased. "Pam and George will have to replace it to sell the place."

Knowing they were going to have to part ways for some time to keep up their ruse, Pam and George went out for a date night, allowing Mel to meet her dad, Thod, at the house in private. They planned to rendezvous at her departure point. They would say their final goodbyes there.

They had ordered pizza as Mel had requested for her 'final meal.' Just the thought of calling it that made her nauseous. She picked off a couple pieces of pepperoni, but that was all.

Ben and Devin sat on the settee, refusing to spoil the surprise. She was a jumble of excitement and nerves. Based on Ben's previous outburst, she'd narrowed her guesses down to Mr. Rasmussen, the teacher that lived on their street; Mr. Colburn—Tom; or Mr. Cress, her P.E. teacher. Ben had said Thod was someone she'd suspected of being 'one of them,' which she assumed meant an Ivy, but they'd been talking about Zach, so it could have meant she had pegged him as a human? But it wasn't like she went around labelling humans; they were kind of the default assumption. 'Human until proven Ivy.' The only time she recalled sharing suspicions about an Ivy general was that day in the nurse's office.

The fact that Thod texted to say he was running late just added to the torture. But the man had a lot to do; he had nearly twenty years invested in the human world. Money in bank accounts, a house to sort out, a job to resign from, and a convincing cover to enact for his personal disappearance. He wasn't just leaving the human world willy-nilly. Thod's cover story had to be as convincing as Mel's, if not more, to ensure no disruption to the Seeder network left behind.

Ben would stay through the summer. As part of their agreement to help Devin's dad with his last two girls, Ben would help train and hopefully escort one back before school started up again in the fall. He was set to graduate in just a couple months anyway and was limited on how much help he could give in a high school he would no longer be welcomed at.

Every time Mel saw movement of someone driving or walking by, she would jump to the window. She was ecstatic when a figure actually approached their house, finally. She squinted to see his face. Not Tom. It would have been a perfect fit; he'd always felt like an uncle. She felt bad for being disappointed to see Mr. Rasmussen walking up. They'd never had any real rapport between them, though he did show, at least a couple times this school year, that he cared about her well-being. And he probably intentionally kept his distance from all of his daughters. It made sense. They would have time to really get to know each other and grow their relationship.

Ben stood up next to Mel, looking out the window as she prepared to go to the door, able to finally greet him as her birth father, the orchestrator of her journey here.

"Take her to the family room," Ben ordered. "He shouldn't be here."

"What? Who is it?" Devin asked, while grabbing Mel's hand and pulling her past the front door.

"Just stay quiet. If we're compromised, they may still not know about you."

After Devin whisked Mel into the family room, they remained quiet, listening carefully. "What's going on?" she whispered. "Is Thod not Rasmussen?"

Devin shook his head, his eyes growing wide. Mel recognized the fear in his expression, and Ben's concern. There was a zero percent chance he was coming over as a neighbor needing a cup of sugar. Mr. Rasmussen had no reason to be there that night.

The door creaked open. "Mr. Rasmussen, I'm afraid you've caught me home alone. Were you looking for my foster parents?" Ben's voice was cool as a cucumber.

"Ben, right?" the older gentleman asked.

"Yes, sir."

"Might I come in for a moment, give your foster parents a call? They were expecting me but must have forgotten."

That was a load of bull.

"Sorry, they're really strict about—"

Ben stopped talking, his voice muffled as they heard shuffling in the hallway. The door slammed closed.

Devin peeked around the corner and swore under his breath. "He can't take a general alone," he whispered. "Let's have you go out the back while we take care of him."

Mel swallowed hard. She didn't want to just run like a coward. But it was time she followed orders.

She snuck down the hall to the kitchen. Twisting the handle, she glanced back. Devin, Ben, and Rasmussen had taken the fight into the living room; she couldn't see them.

Hesitating, she opened the door, ready to do as Devin had asked.

Ivy vines wrapped around her arm, yanking her into the back yard.

"Devin!" she screamed.

A hand covered her mouth while more vines began to wrap around her other arm. Before the sharp leaves could puncture her free arm, immobilizing her blade, she forced her energy into it.

Her Seeder blade sliced clean through the vine wrapped around her forearm. The portion of the vine around her upper arm remained. She tried to yank her wrapped arm away, gasping in pain as the embedded leaves tore through flesh.

Mel pushed more energy to that arm, strengthening her elbow and damaged flesh. With all her strength, she jammed her elbow into the ribs of the Ivy holding her hostage. Knocking him off balance, they landed on the grass.

Just one more quick tug freed her arm. She rolled over, using her free blade to hack the vine off of her other arm. With two hands free and new vines emerging, she tussled to keep the Ivy from wrapping her again.

She clenched her jaw, staring down into her attacker's eyes—just another teenage guy, one she didn't recognize.

Their bodies lurched to the side and Mel tumbled off of him. She looked up to see Devin extending a hand. The Ivy was unresponsive after the swift kick to the head Devin had given him.

"C'mon. Let's get you inside while I help Ben," Devin said.

She took his hand, leaping up. They ran inside together.

Devin pointed to the family room. "Stay here, hide, and be silent."

Mel glanced toward the backyard as she followed orders. "There's another one!"

"Stay," Devin repeated as he turned to the back door again.

The Ivy beat him to the door, entering and extending vines. Devin jumped into the air, kicking the Ivy's chest with both feet. The Ivy was hurled backward into a large glass window. The glass shattered and he landed in the backyard.

Devin used his blades to balance himself and land upright.

He ran back to the family room. "Get back. You're supposed to be hiding." He handed her his cell. "In contacts, under Emergency Two. Call my dad."

Mel took the phone from him, nodding. Glancing over Devin's shoulder, she spotted the Ivy who'd crashed through the window. Bloody, he climbed back inside.

Mel didn't want Devin and Ben both risking their lives for her while she cowered in the background. But she knew she wouldn't be much help, either. Her fighting lessons had only covered defensive strategies. They'd been forced to spend more time on flight training.

She extended her hand to Devin, offering a portion of her energy. "Behind you. Let me help."

He shook his head. "No, you *need* that tonight. Make the call and get back!"

Her stomach knotted as she stepped back and eyed the phone. Her hands shook as she clicked the on button.

Only to find a password screen.

She flinched with each *thud*, *slash*, and *crash*. Plenty of noise coming from the living room meant Ben and Rasmussen were still alive and at it. Another loud smash of glass in the kitchen made her jump.

Mel peeked around the corner.

It was Ken, one of her original attackers.

And the one Devin had kicked in the head was on the approach from the backyard.

She couldn't just stand there. A highly trained general was bad enough, but now her protectors were outnumbered.

Mel wrung her hands. Seeder or Ivy, these boys had trained for *years*. She only had a couple weeks under her belt.

There's one thing I can do.

"Devin!" she called out, drawing his attention, and Ken's.

"She's down the hallway," Ken announced to the other Ivy.

"Dammit, Saff!" Devin slashed through a vine wrapping around his wrist, shoving Ken back and lunging to intercept the other Ivy on his way to the family room.

She held out her hand, cradling a ball of light. "Take it!"

"I said no!"

No one else was getting hurt on her account. She couldn't lose Ben or Devin, and she couldn't just wait for their dads.

Even if she didn't have enough energy to make it to the Green Lands before rooting, as long as they all made it out of this, she could live with her fate.

"It's *my* choice!"

They locked eyes.

Devin understood what that meant.

He stretched out a hand, accepting the energy. Balling his other fist, he flicked it at the closest Ivy.

Three large darts sunk into the Ivy's chest with instant success. He keeled over. Ken looked down on his fallen comrade, his face turning a fierce shade of red.

Mel's heart was racing. This time, she was seeing the action up close, and she was *fully* aware of her surroundings.

"That's enough. Get back!" Devin ordered before tackling Ken.

About to follow his orders, she froze in place. Another kid was approaching from the backyard.

That makes five of them.

And right behind him ... was Tom. They both held their human form.

That is, until the teenager extended his vines at the open door.

Tom yanked him back. Baring his Seeder blades, he slit the boy's throat.

Mel's eyes grew wide. Devin wasn't wrong to admire her dad. He had some serious brute strength.

Tom's eyes now glowed green, meeting her gaze for just a moment. "Get back!"

"Ben's got a general in the living room!" Devin called out. "This one's mine."

Mel was slowly stepping back to follow Tom's orders, but instead, leapt back into the family room as Ben and Rasmussen rushed past, taking the fight to the kitchen.

The doorbell rang.

SERIOUSLY?! If that was a Jehovah's Witness, they were going to be sorely disappointed, because *no one* was going to open that door.

Mel peeked out to look at the closed front door and then turned her head to witness the brawl raging in the kitchen and dining room.

Rasmussen and Tom dripped with disdain and loathing once they each recognized the other for what they were. Rasmussen threw Ben against the wall with a huge *thud*, opting to focus on the leader instead.

Ben blinked, disoriented and twice as bloody as Devin, who ran to his side. Mel craned her neck to see Ken lying on the floor behind the two leaders, Devin having taken care of him.

Her stomach churned at the sight of all the blood.

"What are *you* doing here?!" Devin sized up the newest addition to the fight as the front door opened.

"Where's Mel?!" The panicked voice belonged to Zach.

She stepped through the doorway to see Zach standing still, his wide eyes darting around in horror at the blood-smeared walls and corpse legs sticking out from the kitchen.

"Don't hurt him!" Mel screamed.

Devin looked at her in disbelief. She was drawing a line in the sand.

"He's not here to fight!" she yelled.

Zach was holding an envelope—no vines poking out anywhere.

Devin eyed Zach, then yelled for Mel to get back again as he helped Ben up.

Tom hacked at each vine thrown his way by the Ivy General. Devin and Ben approached from either side of Tom, each grabbing a vine and tugging it back. Tom shoved Rasmussen against the wall, moving one of his blades up to his throat.

The boys took their blades and slit deep into Rasmussen's wrists. He grunted as his extended vines went limp, disconnected. No replacement vines made an appearance.

"Take her. We can handle this!" Devin told Tom as they held Rasmussen against the wall.

Tom surveyed the room and ordered his troops, "Get what you can. Don't take too long."

He charged down the hallway, grabbing Mel's wrist, heading right toward Zach.

Zach had his hands up in surrender, eyes wide and yelling, "I'm just normal!"

Tom grabbed Zach by the shirt and tugged him along, fully transforming into his human form seamlessly before exiting the door and heading to his car parked on the street. He looked Zach over. "Front seat." He turned to Mel. "Back seat. Now."

Mel stopped. "Ben didn't look so great. I can help." She looked into Tom's eyes, pleading.

He looked down, stern. "You think I didn't see that? Backup is on the way. We need to not make a scene. Get in the car."

Mel swallowed a lump in her throat. "Okay."

She and Zach scurried to their assigned places as Tom took the driver's seat and nudged the car into drive.

They left the bloodbath, not peeling out—but casually, quietly, unassumingly going along their way.

Chapter 30

JUST BEFORE LEAVING HER NEIGHBORHOOD, Mel spotted Vice Principal Simons driving by, heading toward her house. He and Tom gave each other a nod.

"Devin's dad, right? Kind of obvious," Mel said.

Tom shook his head. "Maybe obvious if you know what Devin really is."

She glanced at Zach; he was pale with shock. "Zach, I'd like to introduce you to my biological dad."

"Principal Colburn?!" Zach's whole face was lined with surprise.

Tom kept his attention on the road while wiping blood off of his face. "I've had my eye on you. My daughter's insistence that you deserve to live is somewhat compelling."

She knew the situation was still grave, but she couldn't fight a small smile. Tom spoke like a true father. *Her* true father. One of them.

Mel looked down at her arm. A vine still dangled from it, the leaves embedded in her skin. She winced, carefully tugging each leaf free.

"Yes, sir, I … um…" Zach stuttered at yet another mention of his demise.

"Tom, I swear it was just bad timing. He was coming by to see me about the letter in his hand." She tossed the vine remnant on the car floor with a look of disgust.

"Saffrona." Tom shook his head in exasperation.

She frowned. She genuinely hadn't thought a tiny letter would have hurt. "I'm sorry, I know. I suck at this." Either way, the damage was done … and in a way … she didn't hate that Zach could now be part of the most important moment of her life.

"Sir, I promise I've never meant to hurt anyone, least of all Mel. And I'll keep your secret, and do anything you want." Zach bargained for his life, adding that he hadn't told anyone anything, hadn't let anything slip. He'd just barely read the letter and drove right over.

Tom waited to reply. "I'm under the impression you understand how serious this is to us. And that you know you're being watched. You'll need to be convincing that you know nothing about my people, and about what you just saw."

Zach nodded vigorously.

"You'll report to Ben when I'm gone—he'll let you know our expectations. For now, you can prepare to make both of our disappearances convincing; you can be a witness to our cover stories."

"Yes, sir."

An enormous weight lifted from Mel's shoulders. But something was tapping her in the back of her mind. "How did they find out … Dad?"

"Obviously, Ken made it out, so they've had you and Ben pegged for a long time. For all I know, Rasmussen heard or saw the wrong thing that pointed him to tonight." He ran his fingers through his hair. "I had a lot to take care of. I might have let something slip."

She felt a smidgen better; but they didn't really know the truth of it all.

Tom shook his head in frustration. "It doesn't make sense. If they knew … why would they wait? Nuren, right? That's what they said? You're absolutely sure?"

That stupid name. "Yes, that's what I heard." She wished she remembered more. But even if she had, it wasn't like Blake had monologued about some terrible plan.

Tom sighed. "The network will keep an eye open. If royalty is closely involved, that must have something to do with their tactics."

Zach kept quiet, his eyes darting constantly between Tom and Mel as if trying to make out what they were talking about.

Mel's mind wandered back to the home she'd grown up in, worrying about Ben and Devin. She allowed a sigh of relief to escape now that Devin's dad was there for backup. She thought back to all of her attackers and frowned. "I warned Devin about Mr. Rasmussen."

"I know," Tom said with regret in his voice. "And I'm sorry. Human laws, public school politics—it's messy. And…" He huffed. "Simon and I hatched this plan to team up before we'd ever even met your mothers. We can get fake identities, but we still had to work our way up the system to place ourselves in a position that high up at your school. Fat lot of good that did us in spotting their covers." He gripped the steering wheel tighter. "Someday, I hope you'll understand what we tried to do, and how we had to do it. At least you'll make it back home safe."

Mel's heart sank as the reality set in. She hadn't conserved her energy the way she'd needed for her trip. And time was in short supply.

"I … helped in the fight," she confessed, knowing they might be wasting their time driving out to the cliff.

Tom blew out a puff of air. "How much?"

She swallowed hard. "Just some hand-to-hand stuff and one round of darts." She intentionally didn't mention *who* she'd helped, not wanting to get Devin in trouble.

"We'll see."

Mel frowned. She could feel the energy that had drained from her. Zach glanced her direction, as if asking for an explanation. She couldn't give it to him. She couldn't explain to him that her decision would be final that night, and it might not be what she'd originally planned on.

"Mel, you're bleeding," Zach said, mirroring Mel's frown.

She surveyed her right arm. It was already healing a smidge where she'd just plucked out the Ivy leaves. Glancing at her left arm, she recognized the source of Zach's concern. She still had chunks of skin dangling from when she'd first yanked to free herself from the vines. Her upper sleeve and part of her chest were soaked with blood, but upon closer inspection, the actual bleeding had stopped. "If I heal myself, does it use up my energy?"

"Don't do it," Tom blurted. "Unless it's life or death, at this point." He looked back at her in the rearview mirror.

"It's not pretty, but I'm not bleeding anymore..."

He nodded. "Good. We can check it out when we get there." Tom craned his neck around, ensuring they still weren't being followed. "Your body will naturally heal some on its own. You can't really control that. But the energy you channel to your hands is expended once it leaves your hands. Even if it's back into your own body. It changes. It's not infinite."

Mel nodded. She'd probably learned that at some point and forgotten. One month was *definitely* not enough time to learn and retain it all. She wanted to draw a breath of relief at having escaped the attack, but Ben and Devin were still back there. "Are you sure they'll be okay?"

"How about you try trusting me for once?" Tom asked.

She pressed her lips together, nodding.

***

Tom kept scanning the area to make sure they weren't being followed. Taking a brief detour, he drove them to a warehouse Mel hadn't seen before. After parking the car, they got out and switched vehicles before proceeding on their way.

"Are we still going to be able to make it to the cliff my parents are meeting us at?" Mel asked.

Tom glanced at a message on his phone. "Yes. Not a lot of cliffs in the area. And it's still the best option. We really don't need to add more humans to this mess by having any see you jump off of a building."

"You're what?!" Zach's eyes shot to Mel for an explanation.

She grinned. "Oh. That. Yeah … I can fly now."

He pursed his lips, nodding. "Why not, right?"

Not much later, their car crept to a stop. George's car was already there.

"Stay," Tom ordered. He popped the trunk and got out. After closing it, he opened Mel's door and gave her a bottle of water. Crouching down, he looked at her injuries with a frown. She wasn't all that thirsty, but she knew it helped speed up recuperation, so she cracked the seal and began to drink.

Tom grabbed a first aid kit from the trunk, wrapping gauze around her injuries. "We'll see how these look in a few minutes." He glanced down. "Let's see your ankles."

Mel felt self-conscious, with Zach peering over to look. Of course, he'd just seen the others in full-on Seeder transformations, though their roots had been hidden.

She focused and revealed them. Tom looked to see how close they were to finishing the change. She was crushed, seeing his reaction. They were cutting things close, maybe too close.

He shook his head. "We should have done this yesterday. But we still have time." His eyes focused on hers. "If you have enough energy in you. It's not an easy journey."

She drank more water, not sure what to say. There wasn't a precise answer. This wasn't Trigonometry. Even if she could catch a breeze, which she felt she definitely had enough still left in her to do, just making their way to the rifting space was supposed to be grueling.

Tom studied her face. "Both Ben and Devin say you're pretty impressive in the energy department. Can you channel it to your hand so I can see? It'll give me a better idea of where we're at."

She curled her hand into a cupping shape, pushing more energy down. She smirked a little, looking over her shoulder to see Zach in awe, witnessing this particular ability for the second time.

Turning back to face Tom, she was surprised to see him wearing a wide smile.

"That's good. That's actually ... great." He raised his eyebrows. "Your mother didn't have that much power when we met, and she was rooted."

Mel pressed her lips together, tears filling her eyes. Her mom, Murial. She desperately wanted to meet this woman. And ... this was giving her hope that she could. "You think I can still do it?"

He nodded. "Finish the water. Take a breather while we wait for the guys to finish up." He tucked a wisp of hair behind her ear. "In the end, it's your choice. And you're the one that needs to listen to your body. But ... if you have it in you ... it would mean the world to your mother and I, having you back home."

She nodded. Clashing with the sweeping relief was the pang of guilt. Zach had just heard that—this was *her* choice.

"Speaking of parents," Tom said. "How about a hug and then we go meet up with Pam and George? They've got to be worried."

She smiled and stood up, giving Tom a tight squeeze. Her mind replayed her mental checklist of trying to figure out who her biological dad was. Tom had seemed like an easy answer, spending lots of time with different families in the school district. Though an Ivy on the hunt could've easily done that too, or just a lonely human principal...

Tom bent down before shutting Mel's car door. "Come on, Zach. You've already seen enough at this point, you might as well join us."

***

Passing the trees into the clearing at the top of the cliff, Mel was instantly on edge. Next to her human parents was another teenage boy, one she didn't recognize.

Tom leaned over. "Your brother."

Her nerves calmed. "I thought it was just Ben left."

Tom grinned. "You think I wouldn't send a son to get backup after one of my girls was attacked? And that I wouldn't do my best to look after Pam and George?"

Her heart melted. Though she kind of wished this new brother was back at her parents' house, helping Ben and Devin, Mel was grateful her parents had been kept safe.

"We were starting to wonder..." Pam began; her eyes widened as they approached. "Good heavens, what happened?! Is everyone okay?"

Mel ran up and hugged both her and George.

"A couple troublemakers," Tom said. "We've got our people finishing things. But I'm sorry to say your house will need a good deal of cleaning."

"Right," Pam acknowledged in a daze, fixated on the blood that covered his arms and shirt.

Mel pictured the bodies now overlapping on the kitchen floor. That was *not* what they'd bargained for when they'd offered their house for a meet and greet.

She gave her new brother a hug and thanked him. He smiled and briefly introduced himself.

Mel then pulled Zach to the side. "I don't even know what to say at this point."

He furrowed his brow. "You ... um... He said you get to choose?"

She frowned. "It's more complicated than I explained. But ... yeah."

"Is it because of *him*?"

She knew he meant Devin. "No." She pressed her lips together. "I tried to tell you ... but it didn't come out right. Both choices had sacrifices. I'm sorry." Her heart ached, knowing Zach wasn't getting a fair chance. If she'd never met Devin, if she'd just been a regular human, they could have had something. But that wasn't who she was—she was invested in the next phase of her life.

He looked at the letter still clutched in his hand. His head bobbed in thought. "You said you can't give me what I want. But what I want ... is for you to be happy. Otherwise ... what kind of friend am I?"

She hugged him to within an inch of his life. "I promise, next spring, I'm going to come visit you, and Devin and my parents, for an entire week. Pencil me in!"

He nodded in agreement and looked her in the eyes. "You're *sure* this is what you want? Whatever you're leaving for?"

"I'm sure of it." She kissed him on the cheek, grabbing his hand and holding it while they waited for the rest of their party to arrive.

Chapter 31

AFTER TALKING MORE PRIVATELY WITH Pam and George, Tom—or Thod ... Mr. Colburn ... her dad—came over to Mel.

"I was kind of hoping it was you." She smiled.

"I'm glad you get to be the one I go back with." His smile softened his intimidating features. "It's been a long time coming. I'm really proud of you. Do you feel ready?"

"I don't know. I think so." She was bouncing with nerves. "Tom, I mean ... Dad?" She looked over at George. "I don't really know what to call you..."

"As long as it's not Mr. or Principal Colburn, I'll be happy." He reassuringly rested his hand on her shoulder.

Mel went back and forth between holding Zach's hand, and fidgeting with her own hands while pacing. The five of them stood around, chatting.

"We can wait a little longer, but we don't have all night," Tom said.

"I can't leave without saying goodbye. They're coming, right? You're sure they're alright?"

"They can handle themselves." Tom tried to calm her down. "But we need to get you out of here sooner than later. Your rooting is close."

Mel swallowed hard. Each moment that passed was one of agony.

She gave a sigh of relief once Pam and Tom finally got a text from Ben that they were on their way.

The stars and moon were out, and the only thing holding Mel back from the biggest leap in her life was waiting for the crunch of gravel under approaching tires. They heard the expected noise in the distance. Tom was cautious, just in case they may have been duped or followed. Mel was practically breaking Zach's hand, with energy magnifying her anxious squeezing.

But it was going to be okay. Devin emerged from the trees, a sight for sore eyes. His eyes lingered on Mel holding Zach's hand as he approached. She released it and ran to give Devin a hug. Zach stood there, rubbing his aching hand.

She quickly stepped back, panicking. "Where's Ben? Is he okay?"

Two recognizable voices came through the trees, even laughing. Ben was quite a sight to behold, his light tan t-shirt darkened with blood. Walking next to him was a blonde.

Mel turned her focus back to Devin with a smirk. "Heather? Your sister?"

He grinned. "Yeah."

Ben approached Tom, giving him a manly hug. Heather shyly greeted Tom with a handshake.

Devin held Mel's hand and had her hang back as the others chatted. He looked into her eyes, worried.

"It's okay," she reassured him. "He thinks I can still make it. And I do, too."

His eyes stayed fixed on hers. He cautiously nodded. "Okay." He scooped her up into his arms, squeezing tight, her feet no longer touching the ground. "I couldn't lose you. I don't want to ever lose you."

She soaked in the warmth of his embrace. "I couldn't lose you, either."

Devin put Mel back down on the ground and wrapped his arm around her shoulder, turning to join their audience.

Ben grinned with a glance at Zach, who was still clearly in shock from the events of the evening. "Seriously? Who invited a human to the show?"

Mel threw daggers with her eyes and Ben raised his eyebrows playfully. "They'll let any ol' riffraff in around here." He laughed, Devin joining him.

Mel rolled her eyes.

Pam responded to a look Tom was giving her. "Speaking of, Zach, why don't you come join George and I for an all-human chat and let them get caught up."

After they stepped away, the Seeders could talk more freely. Mel was grateful to *finally* be let into the inner circle. Minutes away from leaving this world, they no longer needed to keep secrets from her.

Her new brother left to patrol the area while the others had their debriefing.

"You're sure it's taken care of?" Tom asked the boys.

"Yes, sir. We've already got our people on clean-up." Devin reported. "We had a few more show up after you left."

Tom furrowed his brow. "Few?"

Devin glanced at Mel before turning his focus back to Tom. "Five more."

Tom looked to be as shocked as Mel. "That's … a lot. I don't get it." He shook his head. "Anything useful?"

Ben spoke up. "We got the impression Blake didn't make it. The leech wouldn't give us much. I'm pretty sure Rasmussen *wasn't* Nuren, but he did make some vague threats once we brought Nuren up. We'll keep our eyes peeled." A mischievous grin overtook Ben's face. "Rasmussen really didn't have nice things to say about you, Principal Colburn. But you'll be pleased to know he 'handed in his resignation' before we left."

Tom smiled. "And no cops?"

Devin shook his head. "That hedge did us some good, covering up the backyard, and we reached out to our human connection in case any disturbance reports came in."

Tom surveyed the group. "You've done a great job." His phone rang and he excused himself.

Mel looked over the guys, checking out their injuries. They had both taken a beating, but Ben barely had an inch of him not covered in blood. "How much of that is yours?"

He shrugged. "I'll be fine." He glanced down at Heather. "Heather wants to specialize in healing after she comes home."

Heather met his eyes. "Heather can speak for herself."

Ben grinned.

Heather turned her focus to Mel. "But I do. I'm excited to learn all the different techniques."

Mel studied Ben and Devin again; they still had a lot of injuries. Though it was astonishing they made it out at all, with that many Ivies showing up.

Heather must have understood her concern. "I'll finish them up. I just needed to make sure the two of you didn't need my help before your journey."

"You're not returning tonight, too?"

Heather shook her head. "I don't know how to catch a breeze yet. This is still all pretty new to me."

The girls unwrapped Mel's injuries at Heather's urging. A lot of it had already started to heal itself without extra effort—they figured they could make it work. Heather focused her attention on Mel's upper arm. Mel winced as she poked and nudged ripped skin together, giving it a healing touch.

"Just make sure you're not doing too much," Ben coached. "If you get too dizzy, take a break." He slipped his arm around Heather's waist.

Mel glanced between the two of them with a smirk. "So … Heather… You told me you liked hanging out at my house. I guess I see why."

Heather continued to focus on Mel's arm, grinning wide. "A person's allowed to have more than one motive for being somewhere."

Devin chimed in. "The irony of these two dating, after all the grief he gave us!"

"It's new." Ben glared at Devin. "And *we* know what it means to take things slow and be *discreet*."

Devin pursed his lips, raising his eyebrows, and looked at Mel as she stifled a laugh.

Tom returned as Heather finished healing the worst of Mel's injuries. "Alright, that was Simon." He glanced at Mel and Heather. "Simon is actually his first name back home." He cleared his throat. Anyway, we discussed a lot, but he's going to have to mull over some things and make the final call." He focused his eyes on Heather again. "*When* you return, and if you and your host family should leave the area now, are things you're going to need to have a conversation about. I'm sorry it might not go the way you planned."

Heather frowned and nodded.

A wave of guilt washed over Mel. "I'm sorry."

Heather gave her a smile. "Both of my human parents are nurses. They're really supportive of what I want to do. We'll… We'll sort it out."

Mel nodded, still feeling immensely guilty. If Heather had just finished her bloom, a normal bloom, she still had months left. Mel would've given anything for that extra time with her parents. And she'd potentially just robbed Heather of that.

Tom turned to Devin and Ben. "As for you two, you're staying for now. Unlike what I had to do last year … well… Ten bodies have to go missing. It's up to Simon who stays and who gets sent home, and when. For all I know, the two of you will be back tomorrow. That's all his call." The boys both nodded.

Tom recommended Mel say her last goodbyes with her parents and Zach as they finished up their briefing, leaving his last orders with the boys.

Heather gave Mel a quick hug. "I'm excited to be neighbors. Those boys or not, I still want to be your friend."

The Walters cried, not wanting to end their hugs. Pam slipped Mel a piece of paper with their new address and contact information for next spring. They would leave their plans open. Mel tucked it safely into her pocket alongside her photographs.

She wiped a couple tears from her eyes. "I'll make you guys proud."

George put his arm around Pam, rubbing her arm. "We're already proud of you, sweetheart."

Zach obviously tried his best to be brave and friendly, but the reality of losing her forever was sinking in. Heartbreak mingled with shock from the night's events showed through sad eyes and a forced smile.

After all Zach had just witnessed, Mel was confident she could soothe him a bit. "You can stop looking for Tabatha." She gave him a half-smile.

He looked down, slowly nodding in realization. "One of your kind, too?"

She leaned over to make eye contact. "Turns out she's my sister."

He smiled and shook his head. "I really never stood a chance, did I? I can't compete with both her *and* Devin."

She frowned. "Please don't look at it that way." She thought of her dad's words. *Sometimes you have to choose yourself.* "I'm not choosing between people. I couldn't. It's not between you and Tabatha or Devin. Or between my sets of parents. The only person I'm choosing is me, okay?" She considered how she'd decided to start going by Saff permanently after returning to the Green Lands. "I'm choosing who *I* want to be."

He pulled her into one last hug. "I think I get it. And I'm here to support you. I'm glad you'll have a friend waiting for you on that side. Tell her hi for me."

Mel leaned back, smiling. She hadn't planned for him to be there for her final goodbye, but she realized she had one more thing she wanted to do. Reaching into her pocket, Mel felt for two glow-in-the-dark stars, smooshed together with mounting putty. She blushed, showing them to Zach. "Maybe it's silly. I only took two down so the sticky stuff wouldn't mess up anything in my pocket." She bit her lip. "But these are from my first home. And, um, you'll always be a part of that." She pulled them apart, offering one.

Zach took it with a grin.

"Just know you have a friend thinking of you." She smiled as she carefully put one back in her pocket, the sticky side facing the back of a photograph.

They were interrupted as the Seeder group approached. Tom spoke with her parents and Ben took Mel to the side. She looked back to see Devin and Zach awkwardly shake hands. Heather watched on with a smile.

"Thank you so much for being there for me. And sorry for being such a pain," Mel apologized to her battered brother. "I'll find a way to make it up to you when you get home."

He smiled warmly. "Just do me a favor and try to follow some rules for a change."

She twisted her face in guilt as she opened her arms. He looked down at the fresh blood all over his clothes.

"I don't even care right now," she said.

He opened his arms and she nestled into his embrace. They may have been the same age, but she'd always see Ben as a big brother.

He spoke softly into her ear, "You know, Mel. I have a lot of sisters, so I can't pick a favorite. But I can comfortably say you were the biggest thorn in my side."

She backed up and punched him in the arm.

"But..." he added with a chuckle, "you're the only one I ever had to share a bathroom with, so that gives you a special place in my heart." He winked and she gave him a reluctant smile. "You'll do great." His eyes wandered past her.

Looking over her shoulder, she saw Devin and Zach watching them.

"Devin and I will take care of each other. We'll be back before you know it." Ben let out a loud sigh. "And your little friend, we'll watch out for him, too, as long as he knows how to keep his mouth shut."

Ben gave her one last quick hug and left her side, allowing Devin to approach.

Devin took her by the hands. "Have I told you recently how much I love you, and how much I'll miss you?"

She bit her quivering lip and nodded.

He gave a soft smile. "Hey now, you're going to be too busy getting to know everyone back home, and absolutely falling in love with everything there, to waste any time worrying about us on this side of things."

Mel wanted more than anything for Simon to send Devin home right away. But that wasn't fair of her to wish that. He'd made it clear he wanted to be there for his sisters. And creating convincing covers couldn't be that easy.

Her trembling voice betrayed her as she tried to hide her feelings. "It'll be great. Stay safe. And tell that last sister to hurry home?" She added with a small chuckle, "I'd tell you to rip off the proverbial bandage and get it over with, maybe lose her jade charm … if I didn't know firsthand how traumatizing that is. Is she somewhere in her blooming already?"

Devin shook his head with a frown. "Not yet. We never know the timing of these things. But girls generally bloom around the time their moms did. So, hopefully not too long now."

She nodded, finding hope that it would be sooner rather than later.

Devin swallowed, looking into her eyes. "Like your dad said… I might be back tomorrow. Or it could be a couple years. It's not fair for me to ask you to wait for me."

"But I'm going to, anyway."

"Then I'm the luckiest guy in either world." He smiled. "I'm not going to ask if you're ready. You are." He peered into her eyes and then pulled her in tight, whispering, "I'm so excited for you. Tell everyone hi for me." Devin released her from his grip and glanced over his shoulder. Their time was up; everyone was ready and waiting. "The stars. Every night, right?"

She nodded and he gave her one last, tender kiss.

They turned to rejoin the rest of the group. Rustling came from the trees to Mel's right. She gasped, gripping Devin's hand tighter and freezing in place.

Five more teenage boys stalked into the clearing, spreading out and forming a line between the farewell group and the parking area.

Seriously? Her heart raced—they were now cut off.

Devin squeezed her hand, whispering into her ear. "It's okay. All family."

Her eyes darted between the guys, doing a double-take, recognizing one. Kyle, the brother whose cover had been burned as a foreign exchange student, had returned from the Green Lands. He stood there, grinning as he crossed his arms.

She looked back to Devin, reading his face. "But… You said… All of those are mine? You guys said only half of Seeder boys ever come over for protection detail over the years. Half stay to protect the border walls."

He smirked, putting his hands on her waist. "Four of those are yours. One is mine. I have more back at your house still cleaning things up, and watching over Heather's family, and my other sister. We didn't have to enroll them all in school to keep more eyes on you." He spoke softly, confidently. "I guess it goes to show our dads had a decent strategy, after all." He furrowed his brow, looking down. "And with all those eyes on the threat, this still happened. It proves we can't really underestimate the enemy, either."

"Hey." She caught his attention with a smile. "I can't even begin to say how touched I am. And I know this wasn't all just for me. But…" She swallowed, her heart swelling.

He looked her squarely in the eyes. "*Nothing* is more important to Seeders than family." Devin glanced around at their large audience, a smile growing on his face. He removed his hands from her waist, shoving them into his pockets. "And speaking of family. We have a half-dozen of your brothers, your best friend, and both of your dads watching us right now. Not to mention Pam. I think I'll take Thod's advice to 'keep my damn hands off his daughter' and, uh … let you leave with him now. The location's secured. You need to go home. Go start your new adventure."

She beamed, nodding and turning to Tom.

"It's time," Tom announced as she drew close.

Mel took a few deep breaths, walking up to her starting point. Closing her eyes, she focused every ounce of energy into the various techniques they'd been drilling into her. Her jitters were suppressed by the warmth of the energy actively flowing, covering her like a tight sleeve. She was a bit more nervous, having such a large audience for her first leap from a cliff, but their support balanced it all out.

Opening her neon green eyes, she knew this was the most ready she was ever going to be. Tom stood to her side, giving her a nod of encouragement. She looked over her shoulder one last time.

George held Pam in his arms. Zach stood still, looking mildly terrified with Ben and Devin planted on either side of him, their arms slung threateningly around his shoulders. She raised her eyebrows with a look of warning to remind them to play nice.

One deep breath later and she bent down to get a good stance for her running start off of the familiar cliff. Without hesitation, she sprinted, tuning out the world behind her to focus on her balance, her communion with the surrounding wind.

Squinting, as if reminding the elements that *she* was in control, Mel felt a gust of wind push her forward as she kicked off with one foot.

This was it. She was airborne.

She wobbled a little, like Bonnie had, correcting her balance to match the air around her. She shifted her energy around her body as needed to compensate for any changes in the wind. Mel didn't dare look back; she couldn't split her focus, couldn't jeopardize her trajectory. After flying for several yards and gradually rising, she caught sight of Tom passing her on her right. He nodded to indicate the direction they would go. She followed, and they climbed. There wasn't much cloud cover that night, but as they flew past the few wisps in the sky, the landscape below grew smaller, darker.

Time passed slowly, though she wasn't sure if it was from the strain of constant focus, or if they were actually flying for as many hours as it seemed. While her energy usually kept her body warm, the wind chill at this elevation licked unforgivingly cold against her face. It was especially frigid when they hit larger patches of clouds. She hardly noticed the flock of birds flying nearby, but she smiled once she recognized them.

Her tank was running close to empty, the sun starting to rise from the east behind them. Tom looked over and offered his hand. She happily grabbed it, grateful for the guidance and warmth. With his free hand, he gestured at the air before them. The sky rippled as a rift formed, only perceptible through their trained Seeder eyes.

Chapter 32

THOD LED MEL THROUGH THE rift he'd created. Once they passed through, she felt a surge of renewed energy. He released her hand, allowing her to rebalance herself. The air was warmer, easier to coast on. The energy of the Green Lands welcomed her upon her arrival. On this side of the rift, the sun was rising to their left and much further along in the sky.

Thod slowed his speed to match hers and raised his voice to give instructions on landing; she hadn't exactly mastered that part. As they coasted over hills and forests, not unlike those in the human world, she began to see signs of civilization—dirt roads, a variety of rustic buildings. She couldn't help but smile. It was real. It satisfied an intense curiosity that had pulled at her from the moment she'd learned her true identity. It filled a place in her heart she'd never realized was empty.

As they started to descend, she saw groups of people watching the sky. They pointed, looking on in anticipation. She wasn't sure if they knew who she was, or if they were perhaps hoping it was one of their own returning. Finally, after all the waiting, Thod gestured to a house—it was theirs. Behind the modest cottage, she could see what looked like a jungle of a garden, and another building on the same plot in the back. Near it was a clearing with a pile of straw, kept ready for new learners needing a softer place to land.

Thod went first, somersaulting in midair to slow his speed and find his footing, landing with both feet squarely on the ground to absorb his momentum. For the first time since her journey began, Mel felt a pang of nerves. She took a deep breath and aimed for the soft landing. Moving her focus from her arms to her feet, she tried to keep her balance and prepare for the impact. Faltering a little, she crashed into the pile at an angle. It was far from graceful, but she arrived home safely, without another scratch.

Having been hyper-focused on a safe landing, she hadn't noticed the crowd of people running to join them. Several young men and women her age approached Thod to welcome him home. First alarmed by his bloody appearance, they happily greeted him once he assured them all was well. Daughters, many of which had known him from his position in the human world, but never as their father, until after their departure. Sons, one of which she recognized from his time of deployment at her school. A couple of the guys hung back, having never met either their father or Mel, waiting for the crowd to clear to get an introduction. Three familiar faces ran to Mel first: Bonnie (now Rose), Tabatha (who was still keeping her human name for now), and Stacy (now going by Dahlia).

It was a warm homecoming, with tons of hugs and congratulations, squeals of excitement. Even if there were a lot of them, each Seeder to come home was cause for celebration.

Someone yelled from beyond the garden. A tall woman with shoulder-length auburn locks ran toward them, calling Thod's name. Matching the description Devin had given her, Mel recognized this woman—her mother, Murial. The kids made space as Murial approached, her eyes growing wide at the dried blood Thod and Mel were covered in.

Murial gasped. "Are you okay? Is everyone okay?"

Thod grabbed her hands. "Yes. We're all safe. Everyone." He pulled her in and squeezed like he'd never let go. She wept audibly, while a stream of silent tears cascaded down his face. Thod kissed Murial passionately, something he'd been unable to share with the love of his life for almost two decades. They might live longer than the average human, but every day apart was a battle. He held his wife's face, examining it.

Mel, who had decided it was time to go by Saff now, stood in place, shyly waiting for her turn to meet Murial. She clasped her hands in front of her mouth, smiling, touched by their love, their unity and sacrifice. She barely knew these people, but Saff knew she wanted that kind of love. Her excitement wavered for a moment as she reflected on Devin. She imagined this being their story, feeling a hint of homesickness. She knew each day without him would be one with worry, would be torture as she waited. Saff rubbed her charm and watched on.

Murial's eyes turned to her and she broke free from her husband. She moved past him, opening her arms to Saff. "Sweetheart. We're so happy to finally have you back!"

Saff ran into her arms; there was an instant feeling of familiarity. They had a lot of catching up to do; she wanted to learn so much about this woman. Murial stepped back, insisting on finishing up the healing Heather had started.

Excited whispering came from Thod's direction. A handful of kids Saff's age, neighbors, had joined the group after seeing Thod's return. She recognized some of them, and assumed the smaller woman trailing behind them was Sandra, Devin's mom. His family also wanted an update on their loved ones, the situation back in the human world.

Saff had a chance to meet everyone. Each hug helped replenish her energy, which had been exhausted by the journey. After a long reunion, many departed to continue their activities of the day. Her closest sisters led her to the kids' home in the backyard and showed her the space they'd prepared for her, leaving her to clean up. They scheduled a big family dinner that night to welcome her and Thod home.

She sat on her new bed, trying to take it all in. This was it, no going back. Saff looked at her roots. They had, at most, hours before her rooting would happen, and she would feel the irreversible tie to this new place.

Her true nature had been thrust upon her. Her future, however, had been a choice—and in that decision, she was confident.

Saff removed the paper Pam had given her with contact information from her pocket, along with the photos she had chosen. She glanced at them and set them on her wooden nightstand. She removed her chain, setting it aside as well. Remembering one of the photos had a bonus on the back, Saff carefully freed the glow-in-the-dark star. She smiled and stood on her new bed, sticking it up on her new ceiling.

A knock at the door claimed her attention.

"Yeah, come in." She got down from the bed.

Tabatha peeked in. "Hey … sis. Just wanted to chat some more. Unless you'd rather get cleaned up first."

Saff looked down at all the dried blood on her clothes and sat on the bed. "It can wait."

Tabatha sat down next to her. "I missed you." She glanced at the pictures Saff had laid down. "Aw. I miss Zach, too." She smiled. "I think he had a bit of a crush on you."

Saff blushed, looking down into her lap. "Well … Yeah. Guess he did. But that wouldn't have really worked out, right?"

Tabatha nodded with a frown.

"But I think he'll be okay. He knows about us. He was at the cliff when I left. He says hi."

Tabatha beamed. "That's awesome." Her eyes wandered to Saff's shirt again. "Sounds like you have one heck of a story to share."

"You could *definitely* say that."

"Well … I really should let you get cleaned up and settled in." Tabatha stood, reaching into a dresser drawer. "I helped pick out a few outfits for you." She set some clothes on the bed. "Oh, yeah. Let me show you how the lightkeeper works. This was my favorite thing when I first got here." She reached past Saff, picking up what looked to be a paperweight.

Saff was mesmerized once Tabatha explained how it worked. The bottom was dark, a thin disk of jade. The upper portion was a dome of clear quartz. "Give it a try," Tabatha encouraged.

Saff held it in her hand. Following her sister's instructions, she put a finger to the top of the quartz and transferred the smallest amount of energy into it. She covered the dome with her hand and the energy spread evenly throughout it, creating a soft glow. "A lamp." Saff grinned. Something as simple as learning to use a Seeder lamp was exciting, and this was just the beginning.

"And then touch the base to draw it into the stone. It keeps it there when you're not using it," Tabatha said. "Maybe every month or so, it might dim and you just zap it back to full strength."

Tabatha gave her one more smile before leaving. "I'm sorry I didn't get to give you more of a goodbye. I'll have to tell you all about that chaos. But I'm glad you're here now. You always felt like a sister. I'm excited to show you everything."

With a smile on her face, Saff headed for the solar-heated shower to clean up. She took her time getting there, and back to her room, admiring their humble abode. The house was beautiful—all raw, unpainted wood. Hand-crafted rugs and furniture using natural fibers. Stone tile and metal for fixtures. Not a hint of plastic anywhere, other than the piece of home now stuck to the ceiling of her room. A piece of her *old* home.

After the grueling events of that day and night, all her body and mind wanted was a good rest. But she wouldn't get a nap. There was too much to learn, too many people to meet, too few hours to see it all. Saff got a tour of the property and surrounding areas. She particularly enjoyed getting to know Devin's mom a little better and giving her an update on how he was doing. Few knew the extent of Devin and Saff's relationship, or that Ben and Heather were an item back with the humans, but Rose gave her a reassuring wink as they left Devin's house.

A huge chapter of Saff's life had been closed. An adventure larger than she had ever imagined was now opening up to her.

After a long day of sights and learning about this foreign way of life, Saff was finally ready to drift into a deep sleep. Before she allowed her bed to claim her for the night, she sat on a chair in front of her new house, looking into the sky. She pensively rubbed her charm as the vibrant sunset gave way to darkness and brilliant stars. Nearby, eucalyptus trees rustled in a gentle breeze and filled the air with a refreshing scent.

She thought of what her human mom had said, how she'd described rooting in the human world. It wasn't like that here, at least not for Saff. It was like the comfort of a weighted blanket, a peace in her soul.

Keeping her from perfect joy was her guilt about the disaster left in her wake, knowing her parents and Zach would be having a hard time, and the fact that so many questions were left unanswered. Why had the Ivies handled things the way they did? And who was Nuren?

Saff studied the sun carved in her jade, thinking lovingly of Devin. Looking back up at the dazzling display in the heavens, she whispered, "Every night."

Did you enjoy Saff's story?

~Please consider leaving a review!~

On Amazon, Goodreads, and/or anywhere else this book can be found.

This goes a long way to support authors!

Don't forget to sign up for J. Houser's newsletter for publishing news, promotions, and bonus content!

JHouserWrites.com

Also, connect with the author here:

On Youtube, Facebook, Instagram, and Twitter under:

JHouserWrites

Order Book 2 Now!

J. HOUSER

2
SEEDER WARS
TRILOGY

TROUBLE IN THE GREEN LANDS

THE GAME IS CHANGING

It's been three years since Saff made the life-changing decision to embrace her Seeder nature and move to the Green Lands. She loves her job, her husband, her Seeder family, and everything about this enchanting new realm. Life couldn't be more perfect. Except for the disturbing new war tactics displayed by their enemies, the Ivies.

Rachel's senior year in high school is anything but typical. Discovering her true identity as a Seeder means learning new abilities, hiding from Ivy assassins, and preparing to leave the human world behind. But something's not right with her powers, causing crippling self-doubt and leading her to make unlikely allies. Rachel's ready to join the rebellion, helping to put an end to centuries of unrest amongst the green folk.

But people and promises are rarely as they seem in a war filled with secrets and misdirects.

Far from being on the same page, Rachel and her new mentor, Saff, realize they can only take the needed leap of faith by trusting each other. The ultimate goal for them both is to stay alive, find out who they can trust, and just maybe, if they can manage that, they can become part of the solution.

Prologue Excerpt from Book 2:
Trouble in the Green Lands

The Green Lands were divided into two peoples—the Seeders, and the Ivies. They once lived and associated amongst each other. Free to share the land, nurturing growth and community. But something changed over two centuries ago; a rising regime put an end to that. Where there was once community and cooperation, there was now conflict and contempt.

Seeder communities embraced the differences among their people. They found joy in simple comforts, honest work, and most of all—nurturing families and being wise stewards of nature. Their people were governed by elected officials, but you would hardly even know it. Each village would select leadership to coordinate with neighboring communities, but any sort of formalities and laws were minimal. A code of ethics was deeply engrained into Seeder society; it was rare to have a truly bad seed.

The Ivies turned to centralized leadership; they rallied around those who flattered them most. Pride swept through their kind like a whisper in the dark. A monarchy was established in the far mountains; the subjects withdrew from shared communities to start anew in their own kingdom. They were not without their own talents and skills, but their disdain for Seeders—and all that they stood for—grew. The Ivies claimed their lands were usurped, those very communities they had deserted in favor of relocation to start a new nation. Their leadership demanded the best and would settle for no less than respect. It needn't be earned when it could be taken.

J. Houser has spent most of her life in the Pacific Northwest of the United States. Her second language is Polish and she uses neither her A.A.S. in Culinary Arts nor her B.S. in University Studies. Instead, she takes snippets of dreams and a lot of 'what-ifs,' and is feverishly working toward her goal of being a multi-genre hybrid author. She's a firm lover of both Jane Austen and Stargate, and currently resides in Idaho with her lovable fur-child, Mia.